SHIVERS

SHIVERS

*When dreams and reality cross lines,
fantasy and reality meld and there is no safe place:
Shivers is a collection of short fiction
that will carry you into
the dark side of ordinary lives.*

SHIVERS

BY

KATHERINE IRVING

AMBER QUILL PRESS, LLC
http://www.amberquill.com

SHIVERS
AN AMBER QUILL PRESS BOOK

This book is a work of fiction. All names, characters, locations, and incidents are products of the author's imagination, or have been used fictitiously. Any resemblance to actual persons living or dead, locales, or events is entirely coincidental.

Amber Quill Press, LLC
P.O. Box 50251
Bellevue, Washington 98015

All rights reserved.
No portion of this book may be transmitted or reproduced in any form, or by any means, without permission in writing from the publisher, with the exception of brief excerpts used for the purposes of review.

Copyright © 2002 by Lori Philo
ISBN 1-59279-967-1
Cover Art © 2002 Trace Edward Zaber

Rating: R

Layout and Formatting provided by: ElementalAlchemy.com

PUBLISHED IN THE UNITED STATES OF AMERICA

*I want to thank my husband,
my eternal partner, for his patience as I exercised
and exorcized my imagination.*

*I would also like to thank Trace Edward Zaber,
editor extraordinaire.
After years of struggling to learn the craft,
acquiring a closet full of rejections and moving on
bad advise it was great to finally meet and
work with a professional.*

It was worth the wait.

WINTER SOULS

At night I call his name; exclamations of love resound over snow-blanketed hills.
Eric! I love you!
And he hears me. What joy watching him peer through the window glass, brown eyes knit in wonder, heart-shaped lips questioning, "Arianna?" Beautiful man shivers denial, guessing hibernal dark has robbed his sanity and at last he can call himself mad.

What damns one saves another.
Eric! My love!
It was midnight when I was born in a place not unlike this, untamed, unspoiled. Delivered into my grandmother's hands, I screamed my first breath while my mother exhaled her last. One born and one died in the dead of winter.

Gramma told me not to mourn my mother, as she was now free—her soul married to freezing winds. This contented her, and for that, I was happy. When seasons changed burnt colors to crisp white, Gramma's spirits soared, snowflake kisses resurrecting her smile. She lived for the reunion and withered as calendar quarters morphed, sprigs of green staining alabaster, reaching through the melt for...the sun forcing winter souls north to a place she longed to journey, but for reasons unknown to me at the time, could not.

I loved my Gramma. She died in spring.

When she passed, I searched for her, for my mother in the winter sky and found no one. Years I remained alone, waiting...for what? For

Love? Eric?

In our cabin he whittles, draws, writes—keeps his hands occupied hoping to tire the mind. That is why we could not exist together before; for Eric there is no peace in quiet, no pleasure in dark, no comfort in cold.

Paradoxical souls.

I am Winter Wind.

Eric, Summer Fire.

When I met him, my emotions overrode fact and I loved him. From the first moment until...

Iced nights destroyed him and he, me.

Eric! Merry, I dance about, kicking up puffs of snow. *Eric! I love you!*

And there he is. Nose centered in the window, he presses his hands in parenthesis around his face; coarse black beard bristles the glass, etching squiggles in the mist of his breath. The moon's glow reflects gold in his eyes and they search for me.

I am here! Eric!

His lips twitch and his eyes birth tears. He looks like a child. I know he misses me, regrets what he has done. If only he'd come outside, I could put his mourning to rest.

I owe him so much. He set me free from the damnable manacles of my body and ushered me into this that was my birthright.

Eric!

Sharp, precise, my cry cuts through the minutest chink and easily finds his ear. For a moment he stares, his beauty shining like the sun at night.

Alas, I cannot resist him there, so close, and I rush, smother the barrier between us and patter the glass with a thousand kisses. My affections liquefy, and like so many teardrops, fall.

He cries. Together we cry.

I love you, Eric!

He steps away now, back to the flaming hearth, and drops his head on the mantle.

How he misses me and I him. Once I was by his side, in our cabin. We were in love as no two people ever were before, nor will be again. Not a weak love that builds over time, simmering, teasing the boil. No! We met, looked into each other's eyes, and were instantly betrothed.

He built this cabin for us in these woods, deep within the thick, to sequester. For months he worked the wood—and as he constructed our home from the raw, so he made me—his touch bringing alive parts of my body that had thus far been a mystery. Beyond carpenter, Eric worked my flesh like a sculptor models clay, bringing beauty, rapture out of nothing.

Our lives were fantasy, days and nights spent in ecstasy.

But winter made him crazy; long nights drew over him like a black cloud. He pulled away from me, and I clung to him as if in holding his body close, I could ensure our promise. Perhaps I grabbed him too hard? Perhaps not hard enough?

Eric!

His hands became things of pain and I offered no resistance. I wanted him to have what he needed and bequeathed in every possible way; but the more I gave, the deeper his anger. He beat me. Threw me down. Kicked, over and over. For one crazed moment, I damned the winter for what it had done to him.

"I love you!"

He bade me speak no more of love. He hated me. When I refused, he grabbed my throat and squeezed, his touch setting fire to my neck. It hurt him to do that to me. Tears fell from his eyes. Hot, they splashed on my face. If only I could have wiped his cheeks dry, kissed away his sorrow. Even as his fingers buried into the flesh of my neck, I prayed he'd never let me go.

But he did. Eric released me, then fell in a heap and wept.

That was when I grew cold. A chilling wave worked throughout—to my bones. How I longed for Eric to stroke my flesh, stir up warmth, but he did not. Instead, he picked me up, carried me outside, and placed me in the snow; gentle, like a mother sets a sleeping child. Then, without a word, a kiss, or heartened glance, Eric walked away.

At first it was terror. Not of the dark. Not of the cold. The horror came in wondering if I would ever again feel his touch.

Eric! I love you!

My coffin was ice.

It was an unnecessary placement, for I am not dead. Oh it is true, my heart now frozen into a crystalline knot will never beat again. Even so, I am. My body passed, but my soul belongs to winter, my love to…

Eric!

Each time I call, I feel him getting…

I love you!

…Closer.

I love you!

There! The door opens and he rushes out. "Arianna!"

He throws open his arms, turns his eyes toward the heavens. "Ariiiiii! Arianna!"

I am under his feet. In front of him. Everywhere. Yet he refuses to see.

Eric!

He runs to the snowy mound, falls to his knees and digs. "Ari. Ari."

How cold he must be. Without gloves. Without shoes. Without coat or hat.

Tears sizzle in his beard. "Arianna!" Clawing, pulling, gnashing at my tomb. "Ariiii!" At last he finds the corpse; perfectly preserved, packaged in ice, its eyes open and fixed, its mouth a neat circle, flesh smooth gray, his fingerprints on the neck—black. Animalistic, he claws as if to free the thing and I feel anger tease.

Eric! I am here! I pummel him softly, tickle his ears, nip his eyes. Eric! But he brushes me away and continues to batter the corpse. Finally, he loosens one stiff hand, and in doing so, breaks off two fingers, one still wearing a silver band that matches his. "Arianna?" He shakes and pulls and my anger burgeons.

Eric? I am here!

He snuggles against the frozen thing, mewls over it.

Eric!

My power blurs around him, swirling cyclones of purest alabaster powder, and my breath shoots at him, a flurry of snowflakes.

Cautious, he turns to me. "Arianna?" It seems his eyes bore through me, and he burns, the heat of his body curling about him, a shimmering aura. "Ari! Ari!" He slaps at me and rolls atop the corpse, legs splayed around it, arms embracing it, hips grinding against it…

Eric!

…And I take him. He in my arms, we spin atop drifts, through forest trails, across brittle meadows, around upon iced rivers. It is a moment of fulfillment, completion.

Eric! I love you!

At last his fire cools and Eric turns his face up to me.

"Arianna?"

It is I.

He smiles and I kiss him. Tears freeze a path on his cheeks and I welcome him to a love that never ends.

WARM WET KISSES IN E-FLAT MINOR

JACK

The cell door opens, weathered hinges screeching like a cat in season. A dribbling yellow beam lights a path into the cell, beautiful, the first firelight I'd seen in days. Oh, what joy that small token offers. I could stare forever...

Then two dark figures move forward. The light breaks into minute slivers, mere flickers on the stone flooring and walls.

"Let go my coat!" The larger form pushes at the smaller, who falls down the crumbling steps, landing on his hands and knees with a breathless groan. "Make good use of what little time you have left, Swine. You'll be meeting your maker come the sun."

The huddled prisoner pleads, his hands clasped together as if in prayer. "Help me. I am innocent. Help me."

"Polished blade to your neck. That's all the help you'll get." The guard spits on his ward, then threatens to beat him for the sheer sport of it.

So much like my father. Not physically, for my father was handsome, while the man holding me captive is a behemoth with a belly as big as his chest as big as a barrel, hair like shrubbery, eyes, small dull stones set in leather, his face so scarred it remains beardless.

The resemblance is the quintessence, as if they were perfect creations of God. The way my father held his head, high and always looking over the top of his nose; shoulders stiff and pushed back; stomach taut, forcing his breath in short, quick puffs; hands and fingers in constant motion as if searching the air such as insects do with their antennae; he controlled his environment. Yes, the guard and my father and those of their ilk—men's men, superior. If asked, they will confirm as such.

Easy to hate them.

My father is—was—a beast; he and my mother mismatched. He a displaced Frenchman, boorish and brutal—mother an English maid, frail and ignorant but mannered. And what did they do but forge Jane and I—their freakish spawn—in unholy passion, drunk and lustful, so we were the anomalous product of absinthe intoxication.

Green Fairy. Ha! Emerald devil. Liquid demon.

"Sir, don't leave me. Please, listen—"

"Silence, Swine!"

Alas, the fellow, Swine, ends his request, crying into his hands while the guard grins victoriously. Three, maybe four teeth, large and animalistic, shine dully in the meager light. His laugh rattles above the howl of the hinges, the door closes, and we are left behind.

Three of us, and now the new, sad Swine, who seems destined to spend his final hours perched in a puddle of urine and tears.

Let him. It is of no concern to me. I am secured in my place, a nice dry corner of the cell, and my mates, Cullen and Marcus, remain curled together, both snoring. So what of the smells stinging the air, sour sweat, decay and human foul?

Nesting brings peace, and peace sleep, and sleep the blessing of dreams.

* * *

JANE

On clear and lovely nights such as this I try not to sleep. There is nothing more precious to me now than the world, quiet, cloaked in darkness, flaws hidden…perfect.

Besides, sleep has become a torment, my dreams persecutory. Nary a night passes where I do not find myself transported into secret places in my mind and there suffer.

And the worry.

Jack? Sweet Jack. How does he fare?

When I try to picture him, locked in a dreary dungeon, my imagination cannot begin to draw the portrait.

Horrible. How awful, it must be…like hell.

* * *

JACK

There are ways to survive in this humid Hades, and crying is not one of them.

Best to take to silence, force sleep.

Poor Swine, he begs in whispers, torturing himself. Obviously destined for the chopping block; crying will not alter fate.

I wish him a swift demise and say a quick thanks…for myself. After all, if these dull French knew of my past, of my crimes, of the depths of my evil, I, too, would be loosing my head.

But they do not, and I am not, and for that I am grateful.

"Sleep, sorrowful Swine, sleep," I tell him.

But he sobs with greater flurry. Alas, I turn away to enjoy what remains of the night.

Several feet above my head, barely visible but sorely appreciated, the moon smuggles in a few shimmering rays between a crumbling section of wall. Glorious sight—moonlight, rodents scurrying in and out of its path. How they manage to race high on the walls, I do not know.

Smart creatures, survivors, superior! Safe from the laws of man, the punishment of God and the torment of spirits.

With the pittering and squeaking of insomniac vermin, the soft snores of my mates and the murmurs of Swine, I watch moonbeams and wonder about Jane—if she misses me as much as I do her; if she continues to struggle with her personal demons.

* * *

JANE

Would that I could ride to the moon and slide down on the beam that would carry me to him.

To think that we, Jack and I, are at this very moment alive beneath the same moon is both a comfort and a torture, it being the physical entity that both connects and separates.

From my tiny window I am able to see the sky spread away…seemingly forever. It is a nice view, no cobbled streets, no rush and bustle of skirts and trousers, no dogs yipping, no carriages thundering hurriedly by, certainly not what we had left behind in London.

This is a pretty country, France, and I should like to remain.

But not like this. It is not home without Jack.

Nowhere is home without Jack.

Oh Jack! My poor, sweet, suffering Jack. I miss him, long to be with him, to hold him and have him beside me and…and…perhaps that is why God has separated us.

Together we create evil.

Together we…what we had done, the lives, the overwhelming guilt of the memories…

*   *   *

JACK

Memories kindle the fires of my soul. Without them I should not want to live. In this place, they are my only joy.

Swine nearby, however, interferes with my wakeful dreaming. He will not cease his crying, the noise insane. How am I to imagine myself at my old flat, violin in hand, silver goblet on the bed stand shimmering with the opalescent flirt of absinthe. How am I to…

"Quiet! Or I'll put an end to your tantrum in a right way!"

Ah, I should thank my cell-share, Cullen. Apparently, he has had enough of the sniveling. Good for him, Cullen, a man bent on the direct approach. Useful in this situation. Not always so, however. If Cullen had been less prone to blunt action he would not be in this prison with me. Burned his home—wife and daughter inside. One had torn his suit coat. Never told me which. His trial comes next week, and I have no doubt he'll be facing the blade soon after.

Cullen has little to loose, and I am certain he can hush a whimpering Swine. Apparently said victim-to-be has ascertained the same, as he has shut his mouth and fallen quietly onto his side, pulling his knees to his chest like a babe in the womb.

Ah, the womb.

God's knitting room; the dark place where He brings together human form from mere fluids.

That is where it all went wrong for Jane and I.

*   *   *

JANE

What a curse we have suffered together. Born as such—helpless infants without a chance to defend our case, to appeal, to secure release from our horrible physical sentences.

Since Jack has been imprisoned, the slow passage of time has set my mind free to think, my thoughts turning over and again to our making, to mother and father.

Had our parent's sins been so great that God had had to strike out at us while yet unborn?

*   *   *

JACK

As we formed in the womb, Jane and I were not alone, demons played with us, toyed with us, taunted. They tore us apart and reassembled and laughed at what they'd made. In a final insult, I and my sister were pushed into the world too early, too fast. Yet, against all that was against us, damned and doomed, we survived.

*   *   *

JANE

What are we? Neither male nor female, human nor animal; rather a marbled mix of all.

I suffer the worst of it, with a face like that of a monster, jaw warped—unable to suckle as a babe should—lips and nose coming together in a knot, then…later, teeth overlapping each other. Crooked face and twisted spine.

Overexertion causes great pain. Some days I take to bed and cry out to God to either heal me or take me home.

He has done neither.

I remain a malformed woman never to know the love of a man, feel the kick of an unborn child, experience true happiness.

And Jack. Poor Jack. Perfect creature in all ways visible. To look upon Jack is to view an angel on earth. Beautiful boy, small framed and well proportioned, with eyes the color of caramel, and hair, thick and curled, representative of the many colors of a wheat field at twilight—burnt orange, gold, rust and chocolate.

When I look upon my reflection, I often feel envious, Jack being dressed in all the beauty and I without a single pleasant feature.

Twins, yet poles apart, Jack and I were mother's pride and father's torment. He was repulsed by the sight of his children, called us blasphemes incarnate. Father said we were the Lord's punishment for his taking of our mother without marriage. At his more effervescent times, he told us we were liquid devils formed to flesh.

He referred to absinthe. I know this drink intimately. As does, Jack.

* * *

JACK

Without the bitter nirvana of absinthe and my violin I would have killed myself early on. But with the drink to open my mind and the blessing of genius fingers, I filled my soul, perfected my world.

Mother and Jane cried at my songs. Father hated both music and musician. When Jane and I turned thirteen, he left our home, forever. Pleasure to be rid of his wicked stare and grumblings.

In his stead, I became the man of the household, caring for my addicted, often hallucinatory mother and my shy, sad sister.

I used my gift to care for our bills, teaching music to the upper class. Not to boast, but to have me for a teacher was esteemed. There were—are—none better. Between lessons and tending to the household, I played for my kindred, chords and plucks, bringing peace to their miserable world.

How I loved to play for Jane.

Especially, Jane. Poor, ugly creature. Would that I could share with her my more comely features. Seemingly forged from rock, she's all misplaced straight lines and angles. And if her face isn't horrible enough, her expression is lifeless; her eyes dull gray, small and lusterless. I'd seen a toy once at a student's home, a stuffed bear with one ear missing and its button eyes sewn on crooked with mismatched thread. I felt sorry for the bear. Happy thing forced sad by sloppy handiwork.

Jane. Cannot smile. Walks hunched over as if to crawl within herself and hide. Keeps from people. Drags her feet around the house, walking from a room as if lost, her melancholy stumble drawing grooves on the plank floors.

Jane's footsteps—a crooked maze of time and sorrow.

Alone, at night, I cry for her.

Poor Jane.

Because she is such a monster and such an angel—a puzzled mess of beauty and ugly—I love her.

* * *

JANE

Ah, Jack. Because he is so beautiful inside and out, I love him.

He could have been so much more. With his innate talent, Jack should have played for kings and queens. And with his looks—lovely.

How he went daily and mingled among men and women, his deformity so severe, so horrendous, I do not know.

But he did. Without mourning.

At the end of the day he'd tell us where he'd been, the things he'd seen, and he'd play for us. And always there was the drink.

Mother sipped absinthe often, more so than not. Soon, Jack and I stopped trying to hide our love for the brutal, emerald drink and we three indulged together. Sinful? Certainly. Look at the name—sin buried within it. But it had a purpose, gave warmth to a family unit that had been served a cold blow.

Absinthe made our house feel like a castle, we the royal hosts.

And I—it carried me away to a place where my skin shone alabaster and my frame stood slender and upright. Dressed in a ball gown, fitted over soft curves and long legs, cleavage bubbling from the confines of hand-sewn lace, my face shining like the moon in a summer sky, heart-shaped mouth, cheeks like cherries, nose just so, and men—as handsome as Jack!—holding my hand as if I were glass and might break if handled too roughly. We danced and danced...

And Jack relaxed. He peeled off his gloves, dropped his neck scarf, loosed his shirt collar and—Lord, what beauty!

Sometimes he'd allow me to snuggle into him, lay my head on his shoulder and comb his glorious beard. So soft, the innocent feel of kitten fur.

Had God ever made a man as glorious as Jack?

* * *

JACK

We are malformed beings, freakish concoctions of absinthe and primal lust.

Absinthe.

The stuff makes me laugh and love, then hate and mutilate all in the same eve.

I think a better name would be "Insanity," or better, "The Resurrector," breathing life to emotions that have been long buried and counted for dead.

* * *

JANE

Absinthe killed mother. After a brutal fit of nightmares, her heart gave out. We found her in the morning, dead. At last, she was at peace.

After she passed on, Jack and I—just twenty—were left alone. Jack sold our house and we moved into a large flat in London. At first I missed the countryside and fresh air and the walks where I had been able to take fresh air uncovered. But after a while I secured a nice seat beside my bedroom window, and from my high and up position, watched the world below. It was nice. Peaceful.

Often, Jack taught lessons in the flat, and I listened to students try to play as he, each longing to rise above the master! Never had one come close. How they tried. And failed.

No one has ever been blessed with music like my Jack. His playing is a paradox; it is the divine beauty of an angel and the burning passion of Satan himself.

Several years passed like that and it was...

* * *

JACK

Life in London was fine, but if it not for Jane, I might have struck out, taken to America. New York or maybe Boston.

But there was no taking Jane abroad. It was all I could do to keep her happy and safe in the city.

She clung to the flat like a shadow. How unnerving to know she was always there. Whenever I entered or left, when I went to bed or arose, when I taught or read—she was there—always.

The walls of the apartment felt like tombstones standing all around me.

Determined to change that, one clear day, I begged her to walk with me. It was cool, the sky brilliant with sun and a gentle breeze lazing in from the south. Even so, she fussed and cried until I insisted. With as much of a pout as she could suffer, Jane fell to my request.

She donned one of mother's old hats with a huge brim and a gauzy bow that tied huge under her chin. Another scarf we tucked in the brim of the hat and let fall over her face. With skirt and blouse and collar and gloves and robe buttoned at the throat, she looked fine. As a matter of fact, with her standing still in front of me, a few feet off, I was almost fooled. She—my sad and ugly Jane—looked like any other woman, and I forgot that under the frills and lace was a scraggly, weary beast.

* * *

JANE

What a joy to walk with people and not feel like a monster.

Keeping close to Jack, I had my first long look at London.

Jack laughed along the way and said anyone seeing us would assume our closeness was us being newlyweds, and they would keep away, not wanting to disturb our joy.

I swear, my back straightened and my limp was less noticeable.

It began as a walk through heaven.

* * *

JACK

All went well, until we approached the edges of Whitechapel, the hell-bound population therein having spread out to enjoy the mild weather.

One of those being a woman, I later learned, was called Martha.

Aggressive, she approached, badgering for money. Jane hid behind me. I told the woman I had nothing to spare. She became enraged. With all the manners of a wasp, she buzzed around me, then fell upon Jane, pulled off the scarf, and screamed.

Strollers halted, everyone turned to us, and the woman bellowed again—the sound of a witch boiling in her own brew.

I can still see the sour spittle from howling Martha dotting the twisted creases of my sister's face.

"It's a monster! Good Lord in heaven, there's a monster on the streets!"

Jane crumbled in my arms, and I all but carried her home.

* * *

JANE

When I opened my eyes it was dark outside and the clock read eleven-twenty.

My head was a riot of pains, and my stomach heaved. I vomited and called for Jack.

How needy was I. After the woman had unveiled me in the park, Jack had rushed me home, where I'd cried in his arms like a heartbroken child.

He promised me nothing would come of it. The woman was no doubt a drunk, a prostitute, possibly insane. No one would listen or care.

"Drink. Calm down, Jane. It's all over now. You're safe."

And I drank absinthe in large gulps, and coughed and spat and drank some more. My face went numb. Never had I swallowed so much liquor. I remember Jack—smiling or growling—his face bunched—happy or angry—

Then…I don't know what…I awoke in my bed.

"Jack!"

The smell in my room was horrible. Vomit covered my pillows.

"Jack!"

I thought I might die for how my body felt. Tingly, almost burning. My eyes struggled to focus and my stomach would not settle. Momentarily, I wondered if my affliction had spread internal, as my tongue felt as if it had split, deformed and fuzzy.

"Jack!"

He did not answer. But I heard music.

It was the greatest challenge of my life to rise from bed and make my way down the hall.

The music assisted. It blew strong and relentless as if each note came with a hand pulling me, urging me to come.

Jack's bedroom door was opened. He was on his bed, one leg angled over the mattress, the other touching the floor. A cold breeze blew in from the opened window, and the curtains danced in long, soft, flowing sweeps. That same current beat on the candles, the tiny flames writhing as if they desired to fly away free.

I was entranced by the rush of cold air and the ballet of fire and lace, but was left breathless by the sight of my brother.

Shirtless, his chest rose and fell in deep, rapid swells. His hair was down and loose, curled over his shoulder in honey-colored drifts. A river of wet dribbled from his chin, down his chest, over his belly and into his navel, before disappearing into the waist of his pants.

Absinthe scented the air. Licorice and…something else…something like…

"Warm, wet kisses," Jack said.

"Jack?"

His face was excitement! Eyes wide and seeming to see something secret reserved only for him. His lips pulled open—smiling, I think—and I was drawn into his beard, unkempt, wild knots, like trees in a storm, branches blowing forward under a brutal wind, and was different in color. Darker. Not burnt wheat, rather mahogany.

And he played, his bow slicing over the strings as if he would sever them from the instrument. Back and forth, over and over, the bow rode, making music—powerful and sad and angry and dreamy. Emotions pulsing fiercely through the air.

Gooseflesh teased my flesh, my pores opening to the tune and begging for more.

"Warm, wet kisses."

Jack's fingers tightly gripped the bow, his knuckles bulging white, chin pressed hard into the cup, his shoulder bearing down under the weight of the attack.

I shivered and thought of my robe. How I wanted to wrap up in it, if only for something to cling to, but I could not move from that spot.

Trembling, I watched my brother, man-animal. playing in a controlled frenzy, his teeth shimmering with dew, eyes black and bold, his beard dripping onto the violin…red.

"Warm, wet kisses," he hissed. "Warm, wet kisses. Warm, wet kisses."

* * *

JACK

It was…blood bubbled from her opened throat…like little kisses…coming at me from some secret place within her body.

First a tiny knot of red, curling from top to bottom, then making a soft sound like a butterfly's whisper before spilling away to allow another and another and another.

Warm, wet kisses.

It's all I recall.

That and the absinthe and the music…and Jane, standing in my doorway, twisted creature dressed in white gown and vomit, quaking, eyes bubbling with fear and something truly ugly.

Perhaps, lust.

* * *

JANE

I do not know how long he played or how long I was held in sick fascination.

At first I tried to tell myself it was a dream, or worse, a hallucination played out due to absinthe poisoning. Lord knows I'd seen mother fall victim to visions.

But I knew it was real, and for some inexplicable reason, I knew…

Jack had done something. Be it a beginning or an ending, our lives would be forever changed.

Mine already was.

* * *

JACK

I would never again be the same man.

After that night...what I had done...I tried not to think about her...the blood...tried not to drink absinthe...but I did and I did and I could not...was...lost...

Until I met Polly.

She told me her hat was new and did a sloppy spin to show me round about. It was pretty, as was she.

The streets of Whitechapel were crowded and Polly was high as a bird, singing a sweet song. I promised her as much of my secret stock of the green fairy as she desired, and enough coin to purchase many new hats. She readily agreed. Without a home she was willing to share with me, we took to the streets, a back alley, where we shared sips of liquid dreams. Finally, Polly turned from me and hitched her skirts over her back, exposing her rounded end.

I was appalled. What was...I had never seen...

When she inquired what kept me from my business, I wrapped my hands around her throat and choked her. At first she was still, but soon she hit me and kicked.

I appreciated her vigor. She was stronger than mother—it'd taken little effort for me to stifle mother's life under the soft of her pillow—blessed peace to silence that woman's howling—

Watching Polly there, on her side, eyes bulging, mouth gaping, desire rushed over me like I had never felt before. I released her throat, and with one slice of my honed dagger, opened a path from ear to ear. Her skin lay parted like ripped lace. And the kisses fell. Crimson—not painted kisses, slimy oils on wrinkled flesh—rather pure and warm and bubbling.

Kisses. Soft sounds like angels flicking dewdrops from rose petals.

Kisses. Kisses. Warm, wet kisses.

*　　*　　*

JANE

I determined the red drops on the violin were blood, Jack's, droplets spattered from him biting his lip or tongue. A wound from the violent playing.

Never would I have guessed...

It was a week later, August the eighth, when Jack came home late at night, rushed to his room and immediately took up his violin. The music stormed through the walls, beat at me the same tune over and over. Every nerve in my body turned to fire. My hair seemed to come alive, tickling my scalp as if a million ants danced there. And my heart beat in my chest like a wicked drum, trying to match the pounding rhythm.

The violin wailed. It was the cry of an animal caught in a snare, the bawl of a hungry newborn, the rush of wind through spring leaves, the howl of torrential rain, the tortured song of the damned burning in hellfire.

I knew the tune well, had carried it in my throat for weeks. Horribly, wonderful song in Jack's favorite key, E-Flat Minor.

Once again, I went to his room and there was Jack on the bed, instrument buried in his shoulder, fingers crushed around the bow, his eyes wide and not blinking, thick beard dripping red, his lips twisted in a grimace as if he were in pain, his teeth pink.

I wanted to cry out to stop. The bow—it would surely burst into flames, or worse, Jack might explode.

But I held my tongue.

"Warm, wet kisses."

The next day news came of a girl murdered in Whitechapel.

"Warm, wet kisses." The words twirled maddeningly through my mind, intoxicating.

*   *   *

JACK

I can never explain the taste of absinthe filtered through the crimson spill in my beard, blood salting the green with copper and salts making it more bitter, yet more delicious, addictive.

If damnation has a taste, it is that.

When I took the first luxurious sip after returning from Polly, I saw Satan standing before me, holding my screaming soul in a clawed hand. He laughed and fire scorched my face.

I swallowed another mouthful of absinthe, swirled the bitter, licorice squall over my tongue, tasted the delicate flavor of blood, raised my instrument and played for him.

And Satan danced about the room, blowing flames at the walls, out the window, toward the ceiling, and all the while, my soul bellowed for release.

*   *   *

JANE

It was as if demons had become my roommates.

Jack was not one, but two or three people, and I never knew which to anticipate.

I asked if he knew anything of the happenings in Whitechapel. He only smiled, hugged me, gently drew his fingers over the curl of my spine and told me he loved me, and I should not be afraid.

But I knew in my heart, I knew.

The girl...the music...the red...

And he began to drink more and more.

And I, also.

Then there were letters to the police. Had Jack lost his sanity? He all but signed his name. Perhaps he wanted to be caught. Maybe...

Knowing not what action to take, I did nothing.

More women died.

* * *

JACK

With a twinkle in her eye, she told me I was handsome. Tall girl with blue eyes and yellow teeth. Her breath was foul but not as offensive as her dress. I thanked her for the kind appraisal, though, tipped my hat, offered my arm.

Oh, that place. Whitechapel. Full of the poor and the addicted. People stuffed into infested tenements, diseased children propped on skinny hips. I had fallen in love with the streets, wet, noisy, filled with smells that were both inhuman and exciting. Kind of like the perfume of this prison cell.

And the women, foul things, freakish, more so than I, for they had not been *born* wrong but had *made* themselves so.

What had started as an act of vengeance—a rebuke for a whore's teasing of my Jane—had become more. I had to take, open them up, see what was inside, steal the kisses, fill my beard with them, carry them home.

It was all I had.

Two that evening in late September. While I lay upon Elizabeth, I was almost caught. Before I made my way home, however, I met Kate. "Short for Catherine," she had told me. Quite drunk, just released from jail for that very offense, she was a fun girl and made me laugh. She'd be in for a beating when she got home. Her husband would be furious, she being so late. The prospect caused her to giggle and dance.

Silly. Silly Kate. So happy. But when I took her kisses—she staring up at me with hollow eyes—fury shook my limbs.

Damn these woman!

My moods volleyed like…

Women! Mother. Jane. Prostitutes.

And I, neither male nor female…that…that…born with such a cursed deformity…penis and vagina…my manhood constantly mocked by that…that thing. Without that obscene, womanly part…my…I could have functioned as…I would be a man. Just a man! A man!

Why? Oh why!

All the damnable women.

I tried to stay away…

Avoided Jane…

Vowed to keep from my absinthe…

But my promises meant little and my desire overwhelmed.

Ah! Mary Kelly—what a beauty. Figure like a cherub, soft and dimpled skin, sweet skin. I wanted to take some of it home…skin…within it, warm, wet kisses.

I was forgetting more and more about what I had done. Had become confused as to my motives.

And the afterglow dwindled…left me…

* * *

JANE

He was a wild man.

It was November eighth. Early morning, before sunrise. Jack yelling. He broke his violin. Smashed it against the wall, then stomped the pieces on the floor. All the while he cried, and over and over he said, "Warm, wet kisses."

Tortured soul!

Worse, we were not safe.

If they caught Jack…the papers were filled with the horrors of Jack The Ripper. My Jack.

Dear, beautiful Jack.

"Jack, we must leave this place. We must. I'm begging you. For me!"

* * *

JACK

I had to take Jane away before it was too late and they found me out.

And it would happen.

I could smell it. Them closing in.

It was her desire to visit France, and against my dislike for the place, we went.

As I had bowed to her wishes in respect to location, she, in turn, fell to mine and took a room in the convent until I could find proper lodging to ensure her privacy. The sisters there had accepted my generous gift and ushered Jane inside before she could change her mind.

Leaving her behind, walking the streets, and finally settling into a room in the hotel—being alone—it was one of the sweetest times of my life.

In celebration, I proffered a bottle of absinthe and prepared for a quiet evening.

One drink of the infernal green poison and I was mad! The absinthe of the French not being the same as I was accustomed. I am told I ran through the streets, assaulted a horse with a closed fist, then made a mess of a vegetable cart.

So I am locked in this hell-hole while Jane communes with the sisters.

Odd, they call themselves that. Sisters—wed to God. My sister—wed to—

*   *   *

JANE

The sisters here have told me much about Jesus, and it helps a bit to know He is with me in spite of…

Often I dream of Christ on the cross, thorns furrowed in his brow, blood dripping down his cheeks and…and I'm carried back to Jack.

Blood.

Warm, wet kisses.

I awake screaming.

*   *   *

JACK

Hell emerges from the cold rock. And it is deep green. Emerald-tinted flames ooze between cracked mortar and lap up the walls and over the floors like water sucking the edges of the beach.

Satan appears from amidst the fires, his mouth shooting sparks, his eyes dark green coals. With fists of knotted flames, he beats at me. It burns and I try to scream, but am mute.

Twirling in the blaze, like crazed ballerinas, are the women. Fire boils where they'd once had hair, and flames chug around blackened lips like tongues licking. With hands—charred lumps, fingers—bleached bones curling in and out, they beckon me.

Behind them is the demon of the drink—my tormentor from conception. He is tall and lithe, serpentine, with a scaled body painted opalescent green. He coils in and out of the shimmering swirls of fire and blows kisses to me, tiny emerald flames that suck my flesh like...

I awake, find my cell only damp rock, and swallow a scream.

* * *

JANE

Another night spent on Jack...thoughts of Jack...memories of Jack...

I must get some rest. Just a little while...

Turn nightmares to daydreams.

* * *

JACK

That terrifying vision comes upon me quite often.

I am hopeful that upon my release from this place and some rest it will leave me.

Ah! The moon has slipped away, bowing down to the sun. A few rays slip into this cell, more precious than gold.

Rodents no longer chase along the walls. They have retired to the floor to wriggle at my feet and nibble my trouser hem. Let them. Soon it will all be theirs. I'll no longer need this suit of clothes or burlap sack. Would that I could give them up now, but in these dwindling moments of confinement, I shall retain them, the last of my creature comforts.

I'm told that I'll be set free today, some time in the afternoon.

My solicitor has taken to me and agreed to post my fine. Upon my release, I shall return his favor by teaching music to his children and wife. It is my intention to pay back his kindness in full, take on more clients, save money and...

America.

* * *

JANE

The new day brings new hope.

I long to see my brother again. It is my heart's desire to tell him about this salvation of which I have learned and accepted. After all these years, I can offer to Jack that one thing that has always been out of his reach.

Peace. Blessed peace. Peace eternal.

* * *

JACK

Before I embark on my voyage to a new world and a new life, I'll say good-bye to Jane and give her the gift of the one thing for which she has always longed.

My kiss.

* * *

JANE

Salvation.
We can…

* * *

JACK

Let hell have her, and in time, I'll follow. What other course? We are two souls born of a poisonous womb, destined to subsist in the foul and burning belly of the devil, forever.

I long for a drink.
I yearn to play.
And…

INHUMAN CONDITION

The elderly man stood inside the store entrance, his hand extended to Minnie Mooney in welcome. "Well, it looks like someone is without a smile! Not to worry, young lady, I've got one to share."

"Keep your nasty hands to yourself. And while you're at it, clean your glasses. I've got corns older than you. Dirty old coot." Voice like broken glass, words razor-edged, nothing could shred more efficiently or with more pain than Minnie and her saber tongue. The old man's smile fell to pieces.

Quick, I reached out to him and cried, "I'm sorry!"

Too little, too late. The apology was lost in the shuffle of Minnie's noisy heels and all I was able to do was ruffle the cuff of his pants. If he noticed me, he didn't show it. Poor old guy.

With a piggish snort, Minnie rushed to the service counter, dragging me with her, the hard soles of her shoes grinding through me with each step. As always, her movements were vicious. Everything Minnie did was executed with malice. She even slept angry. Thankfully, I was not privy to her dreams. I shiver to imagine!

"Filthy old coot." She wore her vile temper like armor, words the weapon of choice, and although the store door greeter was well out of earshot, Minnie continued to thrash him. "Hands and mouth running for first place in the *Pervert of the Day* race. I ought to go back there and teach him some manners…"

I stared up at her. Ugly thing. Tiny eyes—bullets. Nostrils like screaming mouths. Pale skin wrinkled in ugly downward twists, pulling her taut lips into a harsh curve. Painfully thin. A walking skeleton covered in weathered leather.

Yes, I hated her. Who didn't? If only I could do something; throw myself into her path, trip her, knock her to the floor—down to my turf. How I yearned to.

But I couldn't, could I? What can a shadow do? Slip and slide about the body, entrapped, doomed to human whims and motions, peace coming only with the setting sun. Sometimes I dreamed of separation, of freedom. If only.

Suddenly, I was ripped from the floor and shoved against the vinyl wall of the service counter. Having been a smear against the dirty white on countless occasions, I knew this place well.

"May I help you, ma'am?"

Minnie lifted her skinny arm and hoisted me from the service-counter wall. Toppling over the edge of the counter, I was able to put a face to the delicious voice. Shivers went throughout as I gazed upon a stunning girl; skin the color of milk chocolate, eyes like little worlds glowing in the heavens, an enchanting smile cutting a heart-shaped pink. "Beautiful" didn't justify the sight. She was a living angel. Disregarding her plastic name-tag—Wanda—I named her myself.

"Angel!" I cried.

"Give me my money back." Minnie's voice drowned me out. She giggled as was her way, a sound like an angry animal's growl married to a baby's hungry cry, then dropped the can onto the counter. Whack! An exclamation point. "Give me my money back." Minnie snorted, stood straight, crossing her arms over a boyish bosom. Before I was pulled off the counter, I threw Angel a smile. If she saw it, I did not know, for once again, I found myself staring at the shoe-smudged tile floor.

"A refund, ma'am?"

Minnie leaned in close, drawing me over the counter's edge. "Do you need a hearing aid?" I slipped around the can of nuts and stalled at an awkward angle that put me face-to-face with her. Minnie ignored me as I gnashed out, biting and spitting; she was occupied, drawing a bead on Angel with her wicked gray eyes.

"Oh! Uh, ma'am, do you have a receipt?"

"What do I need a receipt for? This can has your name on it. Can't you read?" Minnie tapped out the letters of the store's name one at a time. "Your name. Your nuts. They're stale. I want my money back."

"Without a receipt we can't give a cash refund. However, I can replace the product."

"Don't give me a song and dance. I want my money." Minnie licked her lips. "Dumb-as-dirt little darkie."

"What?"

The shock in Angel's voice hurt me, but energized Minnie, who moved in for the kill. I was torn, sad yet grateful, because in narrowing the gap, Minnie carried me with her. I rode past the nuts and up Angel's long body before finally settling upon her luscious face.

"Oh, so you *do* need a hearing aid. I repeat. Give me my money back, you dumb-as-dirt little darkie."

"Oh!" Angel slapped the beauty of her mouth with both hands, and in doing so…she…she…she touched me. It was extraordinary! I'd never felt anything like it. I—I—I fell in love.

"You get someone up here with a brain to take care of this problem. I don't have all day to translate from *English* to *Idiot*."

Angel's eyes blurred. Gently, I brushed her wrinkled brow, her cheeks. Hot tears burned me, but I didn't care. "No, Angel, please don't cry."

"What did you say?" Minnie asked.

Angel shook her head. "I—I—I— Nothing. I—" She pressed a phone to her ear, edged the mouthpiece into her cheek.

"Shhh, Angel. Shhhh." What a pleasure to comfort her, to stroke and snuggle her sweet skin, to ride the curve of her lips. "Shhh." And those lips parted, allowing her pink tongue to slip through, then tenderly lick, coating them with angelic dew.

"I—I need a manager to service." Angel's chin dimpled, trembled, and once again, her tongue dabbed.

Unable to control myself, I spread over her, whispered, "Angel, I love you," and kissed her.

"Oh!" Angel's eyes grew wide. "Oh my!" Dropping the phone, she rushed away.

"Noooooo!" I screamed before splattering onto clear laminate.

Minnie's steel eyes glowed. Painted cheeks burned crimson. Puffed proud like a bantam rooster, she stepped away from the counter and yanked me to the floor, where I scuttled around her ankles, struggling to break away. I bit and poked and pushed against the cruel beast, but remained stuck.

"I hate you, Minnie Mooney!"

My cry was smothered by her alarm-clock voice. "I demand service. I want my money back."

"I'll give you service." I grabbed her calf and pinched.

"Hey!" Minnie shuffled her feet, thereby kicking me across the floor, under the greeting card display, back up the side of the counter, and over the edge.

"Mrs. Mooney. You've made another one of my employees cry."

A familiar voice. Turning as much as I was able, I saw that someone had taken my Angel's place. The service manager, a bright woman—young with ancient eyes, wearing a name tag that read, Ramona. Over her blue button-down smock hung a rope of keys, which she fingered with the authority of a prison keep. I liked Ramona. She was no stranger to me, as we three had all been together in that exact position before.

"I'm not here to make friends," Minnie snarled.

"That's obvious," Ramona said, her smile a stunning mix of Mona Lisa and scorpion.

"Time is money. While you're talking, you're stealing. These nuts are stale."

"Looks like you've eaten more than half? Did it take you all that time to decide you didn't like them?"

"I don't owe you an explanation." Minnie set both hands on the counter, her fingertips pattering like tribal drums. Diamonds and gold sparkled on a canvas of liver spots and bulging veins.

"I can give you another can of nuts, Mrs. Mooney."

"You must have fat in your ears. I said I want my money back."

"No refunds without—"

"I've got better things to do than argue with a fat-head. Give me a new can of nuts. A fresh can."

Motionless, eyes fixed, the manager persevered with a stonewall smile.

"There better be a can of nuts coming."

A hand reached over Minnie's back and a can of store-brand mixed nuts landed on top of me. Thwack! Minnie grabbed the can and I fell off the counter—but not before I saw the manger's lips twitch in an upward curve. "*Your* nuts," she said.

"What did you say?"

"*Your* nuts."

"You think you're funny?"

"Yes, Mrs. Mooney, I do."

"I'll show you funny. We'll see who laughs last."

Minnie spun on her heels, propelled me forward and back, and headed for the door.

I grabbed the tiles, swept the floor, and cried out—"Angel! Angel!"

The doors slid open and the sun shrunk me to a tiny knot. Minnie kicked me all the way to the car.

"Damn fat-head. I'll show her funny. Funny she wants, funny she'll get."

*   *   *

"I want the number of your corporate office." Seated on the couch, phone cocked on her shoulder, mixed nuts by her side, phone book on her lap, Minnie fondled a pencil, bruising it with a pinch as she spoke. "Uh huh. And could you spell that for me, please?" Her voice dripped honey.

Unable to escape, I did my best to move away, but was forced to remain sprawled in a puddle on her feet. The afternoon sun usually allowed an unwinding stretch, but I couldn't enjoy it. Too consumed with thoughts of Angel. What an uncomfortable situation, to be fixed to one and love another. Desire blocked by circumstance—I'd always assumed that to be a human condition, yet there I was suffering.

I looked up at Minnie. Barbaric eyes. Snarling lips. Iced heart. What was Minnie's condition? We had been together since the beginning, six decades and counting, and the change in her was incredible. Once she'd been a vibrant, giggling, free-spirited girl, quick to smile and full of piss and vinegar (her mother's favorite analogy). Yes, those were fine days, times when being a part of Minnie Mooney was a blessing. To ride along with her, hold her at night, share her joy in swings and jump ropes and tea parties—so long ago it seemed more like fantasy than memory.

What had happened to Minnie's desires? Where once she'd dreamed of marriage, birthing children, and planting flowers in a picketed garden, she now had all the vibrancy of those flaking brown husks that crumble off the salted peanuts she chews all day. I wondered if perhaps her emotions lived in me, having dropped off day after day, and year after year, until all that remained was the miserable Minnie I hated.

"I want to make a formal complaint and I'll follow it up in writing." Minnie tapped the book and grinned. "Oh, yes, she was the most rude little thing. Why, I've never heard such talk coming from such a pretty little girl." Minnie's pencil scratched. Her eyes glistened. A trickle of spittle dampened her lips. "Well, thank you. You have been so kind." The phone beeped and she tossed it onto the couch. "Chalk one up for me! No. Make that two. One fat-head manager and her crybaby darkie."

How easily Minnie took joy in wounding. What a soulless beast. And I felt accountable. To remain with her as a silent witness and refuse intervention put me under the light of guilt. But I was not like Minnie Mooney! To reinforce this assertion was the indisputable fact that no more than two hours previous, I had fallen in love. That evidence alone set me apart from her.

I jolted upright. "Apart?"

Minnie dropped the phone and whipped around, pulling me with her. "What?"

The answer was clear! "Apart!"

"Who said that?" Minnie twirled—the most graceful moves I'd seen her execute in nearly half a century. Around and around we spun.

"Yes, Minnie! I will go on without you!" Over the furniture, up the walls, I danced.

"Hey! How? Who's there?" Minnie stumbled, grabbed at the air, and all the while I whirled in a circle about her.

Merriment forced my laughter. My voice had never been so strong.

"Who?" Her hands slipped through me as I rose up over her. "Who—who's there?"

"It's me." Energized, bold in the waning sun, I came for her.

Anger filled her eyes where there should have been fear. "You!" She growled a guttural sound like a cat hacking on hair. "It's you. All this time—these years—I thought I was—it's you!"

And I fell upon her, filled her until she gurgled and slumped to the floor. Exhausted, I lay beside her. Hours passed and I remained, steadily growing, slowly pulling away, watching my outline reshape. Beautiful. I didn't look like Minnie Mooney at all.

Soon, the sun pulled in its insidious glowing arms and disappeared behind the horizon. The light in the house extinguished and it was dark. Without one look back, I arose from the floor and slipped under the door and enjoyed my first feel of complete freedom.

Fool that I had waited so long. Fool!

And everywhere were shadow kin affixed to trees, flowers, rocks, and reeds; hiding in culverts, scurrying about the lights on the highways, and none of them taking heed of my cries of freedom, none of them wanting the power, none of them to ever be more than servants to the tangible.

Ignorant. Cowards. Lost.

But not I. The desire to stroke cocoa skin, to caress sweet locks the color of night, kept me moving forward. By dawn I was curled up on the rubber mat behind the service desk.

There, I waited. Throughout the morning, several employees claimed their spot beside me, none my Angel. Time passed and my anxiety increased. There was no way I desired to spend a night in that place with the shadows lurking nearby. Seemed they thought me distasteful. And I thought them litter and told them so.

Afternoon came and went and the early blur of twilight approached. My impatience burgeoned, and just when I thought I couldn't bear another second, Angel came. She strode behind the desk, her smile so bright I thought I'd shatter. Ahhh. Human perfection. How I longed to hug her feet, sidle her legs, stream over her body, and revisit the soft of her lips. But I could not. Not yet.

Angel had a shadow of her own.

Shuddering, the little gray patch screamed, "You!" Apparently, I'd left a lasting impression. "Get away f—f—from her, f—f—from me." Stubborn thing wrapped tight around her feet.

No matter. I extended as much as I was able, and stalked.

Unaware, Angel worked, her shadow moving around her, sometimes chasing over her body, running through her hair, all the while fixed on me, sure to keep me in the periphery. Damnable splotch. Useless dust wipe offered her nothing, drooled over her like a stain, spoiled her.

But I held my ground. Waited. Cool and controlled. And was rewarded when finally, bending to retrieve her pen from the floor, Angel brought her shadow to me. While the weak thing quivered on the floor, I attacked, stomping upon him, ripping him to minute bits. The last I saw of the insignificant blemish was a ragged sliver of gray struggling to crawl under a box labeled "Lost and Found."

Good riddance.

I claimed my prize—my Angel. She gathered her pen, stood, brushed a stray lock of hair behind her ear, and I fell upon her. "Angel, I love you." Kissing her over and over. "Angel. Angel. Angel."

"Are you insane? Get your hands off me!"

What was this? Appeared we were not alone. Beside us was a short boy wearing red cheeks and a look of surprise. "W—what. What are you talking about? I only came to get the stapler."

Angel took a step toward him and I rode upon her shoulder like a badge of honor. Her cocoa eyes creased beautifully. "I don't know why you did that. But don't you ever touch me like that again. I'll report you to management."

The boys' cheeks burned red. I thought I saw a curl of steam twirl from his ears. "I swear I didn't. I wasn't even near you. I just took the stapler. That's all, I swear. Really..." The apologies trailed away with his form until the embarrassed lad disappeared around a rack of pantyhose.

Brave girl, my Angel. I kissed her, she shivered and spun around. "Who's there?"

MOTHERS, SONS AND MONSTERS

From the instant Captain Rasmussen had assigned her the job, Wanda Breedlove had felt it, a scorching stab in her guts, like someone had turned a gas flame to low burn in her belly. She imagined blue with white-tipped fire melting her insides.

Call it instinct. A premonition. Or seeing through denial at last.

It couldn't be happening. No way. But every pencil stroke brought truth to life before her eyes. The curve of his jaw. His hair, each shaded strand slightly curled and thick, lightly brushing the top of the ears that were set low, slightly under the cheekbones.

"A—And h—heee—" Hillary cried, tried to wipe her tears, and bumped her head with the stabilizing board holding her IV lines. It was the third time the girl had forgotten she was hooked up to pumps. Such an unnatural condition. Wires, tubing, beeps and whirs.

"Shhhh. You're hurting yourself, Hillary. Please, try to be still." Wanda patted the girl's foot through the sheet. Little.

But Wanda had seen smaller feet, those of her baby boy's. Born ten weeks early, he'd been tiny, nothing more than a skeleton covered in wrinkled skin. Legs the size of her ring finger. Cotton pads taped over his eyes. Needles in his belly. Leads adhered to his chest. Wanda had stood in front of Ryan's incubator fourteen hours a day, leaving only when the nursing staff shuffled her off to a cot they'd set up in the employee lounge.

For months she'd watched and waited alone.

Ryan's daddy had taken one look at his premature son, fallen back a step and yelled, "For the love of God, that isn't a baby…it's a science experiment!" He had run from the intensive care nursery straight to the nearest bar. Two hours later, he'd crashed his car into a phone pole.

While Ryan had fought for life in his humming, beeping, temperature-controlled bubble, his daddy had cooled in the morgue downstairs.

Hospitals. Horrible places. Wanda hated them, had spent too much time in them, had vowed never to enter one again.

But there she was, in critical care, and although merely doing her job on visitor status, anxious to leave.

"Hillary? I've got enough for now. You rest and I'll come back later today or tomorrow." Wanda pushed her pencil behind her ear and set her artist's kit and pad on the bed. "Shhh." She stepped close and smoothed back Hillary's hair.

A crusted mat of blood, hair and skin crunched under her fingertips and Wanda grimaced. Poor girl. Took a beating that would have killed most. Apparently Hillary had a thick skull. No joke. She'd obviously come from strong stock; solid features over a heavy skull. Nordic beauty. Fortunate. The doctor's were optimistic she'd heal—on the outside, at least. Who knew what wounds lay open, festering in her mind. Raped, beaten and left for dead; sixteen-year-old whose only care yesterday had been which jeans made her look like a pop star. Today, trying to survive a vicious attack.

Suddenly, Hillary gripped Wanda's wrist with such strength that Wanda gasped. "No. Please, Mrs. Breedlove. I want to finish. Before I…before…" Hillary's eyes locked on Wanda's. "Do you think I'll ever forget this? Can I? Will I?" Her chin quivered.

"I don't know." Wanda fought tears, didn't want to cry in front of the girl. After all, it was hypocritical sorrow. "I think…in time you will heal and the memory will fade. Give yourself time."

Wrong answer. Hillary pushed her head into the pillow and sobbed.

"It'll be okay. Shhh." Wanda straightened the sheet around the girl's form, sidestepped the IV pump and picked up her pad and kit.

"Don't go!"

"I can come back tomorrow. You rest up and we'll try again."

"No. I have to finish. Please."

Wanda sighed. She didn't look at Hillary, couldn't bear to see her pleading eyes. "All right. A few more minutes. We'll see how it goes. If it gets too much for you, I'm leaving. For your own good."

Wanda settled into the chair—straight-backed, orange vinyl seat, hard and cold like the rest of the furniture. Blasted hospitals. Sketching composites for victims and witnesses at the station was far easier. Wanda's element. Busy. People going in all directions. Noisy. Phones ringing. File drawers sliding open and closed. Laughter, angry shouts and whispers. The atmosphere was alive.

Hospitals felt like death, smelled sterile and stale, and were unnaturally quiet. Especially in Hillary's room. It was as if all the staff had taken a vow of silence, as if a raised voice or a clipboard clanking on the counter or a squeaky shoe in the hallway would shatter the girl.

It only helped to amplify Hillary's sorrow—sniffles and whimpers and moans sounding like a storm.

"...His nose. It was..." Hillary thumbed through a book of facial features with her good hand. "Kind of like...no, smaller...mmm...like this one." She pushed the book at Wanda and tapped out a nose with her finger. "Kind of like this, only not so long. Same shape but shorter."

"I've got your nose."
"You give me that back, Mommy!"
"I can't. See. It's here in my hand."
"That's just your thumb!"
"You're pretty smart for such a little boy."
"I know."

"Can you do that?"

"Uh huh. I think so." Wanda put her pencil to the pad and sketched the nose as Hillary had requested. Usually the sound of the lead brushing lines onto paper soothed. As the nose took shape, however, Wanda heard fingernails scraping on a chalkboard.

"How's this?" Wanda's hands shook as she held up the pad.

"Still too long."

"Okay." Wanda erased the nose and sketched one a little shorter. "Better?"

"Good. That's it."

"You want a break yet?"

"No." Hillary was already pushing through the book. Eyes of various shapes, sizes and widths flipped page after page. "These are the ones. And they were brown. Dark. So...dark..."

Wanda pulled the book from Hillary's hand, looked at the eyes and took up her pad.

"*Peek-a-boo, I see you.*"

"*Mommy!*"

"*Peek-a-boo! I see you, my beautiful brown-eyed boy.*"

"*You too, mommy.*"

A nurse came in, read the monitors, wiped up Hillary's tears with a damp cloth, smiled at Wanda as if she were royalty, then silently slipped out.

They all expected a miracle, Wanda to sketch the murderer and him in custody within an hour. Monster in his cage. Society safe. Big sigh of relief.

Wanda returned the smile, then went back to work, finished the eyes, added lashes—long and thick and sketched in the eyebrows. High and circular.

"Like this?" She turned the pad to Hillary, who gasped and closed her eyes. "Yes. Yes. Yes."

"Hillary?"

The girl kept her eyes closed and spoke, her voice soft and controlled as if she was reading from a book. "His mouth was full, thick lips, but not fat. And it turned up at the left...like...his smile went sideways. Crooked."

"*Backward Elvis. You've got a sly little smile, young man. That grin's gonna knock the ladies dead.*"

"*Aw, mom. I don't like girls. I like you.*"

"Hillary?"

She didn't look.

"I'm just about done. You want to tell me if the mouth is—"

Eyes opened and closed. No more than a blink. "Yes. It's him. It is. You did it, Mrs. Breedlove. Thank you. Thank you." Tears squeezed from Hillary's closed lids, rolled over purple cheeks—the deep color of summer plums—before wetting swollen and cracked lips.

Wanda wished the girl would stop crying. It looked like it hurt.

"Now I am really going to go. This is enough for the detectives to go on. You did a good job. You're a strong girl."

"Thank you for helping me."

Wanda stood by the bed and rubbed Hillary's hand.

Thanks to her, the police were at turning point in the investigation. A six-month rape and murder spree—seven girls dead, their naked bodies dropped on the side of the main highway like garbage—could be drawing to a close.

They had a witness. And a face.

Soon Hillary fell asleep, her sobs dying out, replaced by deep breathing. Sole survivor lost in dreams.

Wanda watched Hillary's chest. Up and down. Up and down. Slow. Regular.

The light from the drawn blinds shone in shimmering slivers, throwing tiger stripes on the walls, floor and bed.

Wanda had finished the sketch quickly. Why not? It was a face she'd sketched hundreds, maybe thousands, of times.

They wouldn't be expecting her back at the station until shift change at six-thirty.

At that moment, Ryan was probably on his way home from his classes at the community college. Good boy. He'd decided to stay in town for the first two years of school to save money. Wanda had been relieved, not so much for the money, but for the fact that when her son left home he'd be taking a part of her with him, a part she didn't know it she could live without.

Just the two of them all those years. They were a team. More than mother and son.

She couldn't live without him

Emotions, like an electric shock, surged from Wanda's chest and rippled throughout her body.

Hillary whimpered.

Wanda looked at the girl with a mixture of pity and loathing.

Images flashed in her mind. A pillow over Hillary's face. Hands pressing it over the girl's nose and mouth. Held there until...

Ryan in the sandbox building cylindrical castles, riding his first big-boy bike, holding out a handful of fresh-picked daffodils on Mother's Day.

Hillary in pain. Not only a solution to a problem, but a merciful end to her suffering.

The piles of bones behind the garage when Ryan was eight. Small animals. Dismembered. Some bound with wire.

Hillary's face swollen, disfigured, inhuman.

The magazines hidden under Ryan's bed. He'd been twelve. Black-market smut. Girls being tortured. Scenes of rape.

"No," Hillary murmured.

Ryan had sat down to dinner last week, his face raked with scratches—the day of murder number seven. "Basketball game," he'd told her. "Jump ball gone bad."

Hillary kicked her foot. Fitful sleep. The muscles on her face quivering as the flesh reacted contrary to the body's desire to rest.

Ryan and his fascination with handcuffs. Had an extensive collection. Wanda had added a pair to it, Christmas present two years ago.

Wanda set her hand on the pillow under Hillary's good arm, then slowly pulled it away. Her fingers twitched. What a dainty hand.

Michael Moyer had called Ryan a pansy, told him he threw like a girl.

Before Ryan had been able to split the boy's head with a baseball bat, Wanda had tackled her son, wrestled him to the ground and taken it away. One week later, Michael had fallen out of a tree, broken his neck. Ryan had witnessed, but been unable to help his friend.

Hillary slept.

Saltwater filled Wanda's mouth and she was reminded of her pregnancy. So sick. Vomiting all the way to the end always with a prelude of saltwater. This was no time to puke.

Keep it together. Focus. The face had been drawn. Proof. Ryan was a sadist and murderer. Her son. Her baby. Worse, this girl could take him away.

As soon as Captain Rasmussen had told her about the victim in the hospital and ordered her to do the sketch, Wanda had known the killer might be Ryan. She'd drawn according to Hillary's request to either affirm or dissolve her fears. What Wanda hadn't known was what she would do if the sketch had proved her gut feelings true.

Now she did.

Wanda swallowed, bent over Hillary, ran her fingers down the girl's chin—the only spot on her face without a bruise. "I'm sorry." Slowly she raised the pillow and lowered it over the girl's face. "I'm so sorry."

Hillary gurgled. Her body hitched on the bed. Her head and legs and arms jerked as if she were being pummeled by invisible ghosts.

Wanda held the pillow secure.

The girl flounced. Her IV line trembled. The board strapped to her arm smacked the bed. The sheets freed from the corners, exposing a pea-green, plastic-covered mattress. Clear tape covered a jagged rip on the side.

Monitors beeped, and still Hillary fought. Incredibly strong.

How long before a nurse rushed in to check?

The girl squeezed Wanda's arm. The door swooshed open and Wanda pulled away the pillow.

"What's happening?" the nurse asked as she rushed the bed.

Wanda couldn't answer. What *was* happening? All she could do was stare and tremble. She felt like she might urinate. Right there. All over herself and the floor.

"Hillary?" The nurse was by the bed, trying to get Hillary to stop thrashing. She pushed a button and yelled. "Seizure! Code three. Damn!"

Wanda groaned and stepped back from the bed. Alive. Still alive. And Hillary whipped her head from side to side, her eyes wide open, gasping, tongue lolling from her mouth.

A chorus of soft-soled shoes whooshed into the room and arms from unseen bodies pushed Wanda aside. Forceful. Shoved her out of the way.

A wall of backs dressed in blue and white geometric shapes, smiley faces, and teddy bears encircled the bed, blocking Hillary from sight.

The artist's kit, sketchbook, two pencils and an eraser scattered onto the floor.

Outlined in buffed linoleum, Ryan's face stared up.

Wanda lunged to retrieve it, but a hand landed on her shoulder and pushed her into the corridor.

As she peered through the small square window in the door, another hand with French manicured nails, ring finger dressed in a diamond solitaire, yanked the curtain closed around Hillary's bed—green, orange and brown vertical waves like an ocean gone astray. Shadows rippled behind it, hunchbacked monsters trying to keep the girl alive.

"What is it? What's happening?"

Wanda spun and focused on a large woman with familiar eyes—Hillary's. A pale man had his hands on the woman's shoulder.

All gone wrong. Wanda licked her lips and forced speech. "She...she..."

A young man pushed a cart between them, opened the door, rammed the cart through, and closed the door so fast that he might have been an illusion.

"Mr. And Mrs. Klein?"

As one, the couple turned to a floor nurse, a plain woman with eyes like valium and a voice to match.

"Our daughter...what's happening? What's going on in there? I want to see my baby?"

Audible sedative poured from two perfect pink lips. "Not now. Why don't you come with me? We'll go and sit in the waiting room."

And the nurse whisked them away. Hillary's parents. One smooth sweep of her arm and they were gone.

Wanda stood in the hallway and waited. For what? Hillary to tell the nurses that Wanda had tried to smother her? For one of the nurses to grab up Ryan's face and yell, "Here's the bastard! We've got him, right here!"

Would cops—people she knew by name, had shared lunch with and exchanged Christmas cards—come to arrest her? Would she room with her son in the holding cell?

Sweat stung her underarms, her eyes came in and out of focus, and Wanda wished herself dead.

Time passed as if God had snatched up Father Time and tossed him into a vat of molasses.

The clock might have stopped ticking, but Wanda's mind sped in circles.

Ryan taking his first steps.

Hillary kicking like she was on fire.

Miss Tippy, Ryan's kitten, floating in the toilet. Poor little thing had fallen in and drowned.

Hillary, thanking Wanda for her help.

Wanda trying to kill her—*You're welcome.*

Ryan with a booger on his finger, screaming for help, fearing he'd ripped free a piece of his nose.

"Wanda?"

Thursday nights. Homemade pizza. Ryan taking over the kitchen to prepare and Wanda left with the beautiful mess.

"Huh?" She looked into the face of Captain Rasmussen. Best known for being able to direct his cops and investigate crimes without ever having to leave his office, apparently he'd decided to break tradition.

He smelled like coffee and breath mints. Repulsive. "What's going on in there?"

"I don't know," Wanda cried.

Rasmussen wrapped his arm around her shoulder. "Look, I'm sure she'll be just fine. The doctor told me she was doing better than he'd expected. He said…"

The door to the room opened and a stream of hospital employees flowed into the hallway—silent, but for one nurse sniffling on tears.

"Is she okay?" Rasmussen let loose of Wanda and she distanced herself. Took several steps away. "Is she…the…is she all right?"

"She's gone."

Black squiggles wriggled in front of Wanda's eyes and she took several deep breaths. Gone? Dead? Dead!

"Wanda?" Again Rasmussen had his unwelcome arm around her. "Tell me you got the composite. Tell me, you did."

"I…I…" She wept.

"Ma'am?" Another nurse. So many faces. This one was young and sad and apologetic. "Your things." She handed Wanda the artist's kit, a pencil and the sketchbook.

Wanda took the kit, shoved it under her arm, reached for the pencil and slipped it inside, then tried to take the sketchbook. Her hand shook and the pad fell.

"Hey!" Rasmussen snatched it out of the air. "Did you get it, Wanda? Is this…?" He gasped.

Tears ran down Wanda's cheeks. "He…he…he's…"

"My God, it's ruined!" Rasmussen turned the sketch to Wanda.

The hair was intact, but the rest of the features were a smear—eyes, nose and mouth blending into each other. Waffle prints from nursing shoes decorated the page. It was ripped in a triangular tear, chin to ear.

Wanda took the pad. Her stomach jumped and she almost laughed.

"Can you redo it?"

She pulled up her eyes and looked at Rasmussen.

"Was it a good sketch? Did she say it was? Was it our boy? Can you redo it?"

"Y—Yes. I can." Carrying the pad, Wanda took a seat at the nursing station. No one asked her to move. After turning to a fresh page, she began to sketch.

Rasmussen's voice boomed in the background. "This SOB better hope it's not me who gets him. He won't ever see the inside of courtroom."

She drew the eyes, small and close-set. One slightly drooped.

"We've got dibs on who's gonna throw the first punch."

Rounded jaw with a large mouth. Thin-lipped, downward smile.

"Monster like that doesn't deserve to live."

A patch of freckles on the bridge of his nose.

Wanda felt giddy, had never drawn with such ease. Ryan was safe. She couldn't wait to go home, hug him, feel his heartbeat against her own…

"Captain? Sir? I know who he is."

Silence dropped on the nurse's station.

All eyes turned to a small girl, unkempt hair, glasses, skinny, bland. Her name-tag touted her to be Vicki, Nurse's Aide. She was blubbering, as if heartbroken and eager to share her pain with the world. "I saw the picture on the floor. I...I stomped it. Kicked it and ruined it. I couldn't let..." She licked her snotty lips. "He's a nice guy. We shared a class together, last semester. Humanities. H—He...he talked to me sometimes. Real nice. I can't believe it."

Rasmussen fell on her like a vulture on a dead yak. "You know this guy?"

"Yes." She bawled, mewling the sound of an animal caught in a snare. "Yes, I do. It looks...looked just like him. Perfect picture. He's so cute. And nice."

"What's his name?" Rasmussen puffed his barrel chest.

She blinked and sniffled and rubbed the back of her hand across her face. "He's so nice."

Rasmussen's cheeks burned crimson and his hands curled into fists. "Do you know his name?"

"I mean it, though, he's so nice to me, I can't believe..." Looking around the nurse's station, Vicki took time to hold the stare of everyone for a second or two. She bore the face of a toddler who'd broken mommy's favorite lamp and didn't know whether to confess or fib. Finally, she sighed and dropped her chin. "Ryan."

"Ryan? That all? Just Ryan?" Rasmussen was chugging like a freight train.

"Ryan Breedlove."

Rasmussen looked at Wanda—and she at him.

Putting her hand in the middle of the new sketch, she drew her fingers into a fist, tearing the page free and crumbling it into a knot.

"Wanda?"

THE ARACHNASSASSIN

The rhythmic whimpers of mourning men and women became as the voices of spirits, as if the members of his tribe had passed and cried to him from the world beyond. In place of the pained wails came a clamor like quick wind ripping through a skinny, tree-lined path—thick and mixed with rustling leaves and the complaints of bending timber.

With the roar of the contained storm, began the vision.

At first it was black and gray edges encircling a blast of white—bright, intense as a lightening strike. Sharp. Blinding. And it hurt. He wanted to close his eyes, block it out. Little good that would do; his lids were clamped tight.

Why he always struggled against the coming of the vision, he did not know. He'd invited it, drank the venom to bring it, knew the physical and emotional responses. Still, when it came—the rush—the agony of the shift between here and the place between, always made him long to return.

Then it changed. In a snap. Black, gray, and vicious white...to smooth, cool blue.

Better.

One at a time he felt his muscles relax and seemingly melt away until he was weightless and out of his body and in the sky flying effortlessly. Not as a bird soars, working, flapping its wings, rather with the ease of a leaf floating on the surface of running water, rising and falling with the swells, and swirling circles in gentle currents.

Above the trees and over the great river—the giver of life—he drifted. Freedom. It was the part he loved most; the time before the answers, the time of simply being one with the totem, riding her powers to a world only he could enter.

But the answer came quick; his pleasure cut short. The totem was anxious. Pictures of faces and places flashed before his eyes. He looped around and around the images and burned them to memory as he slipped closer to earth.

The totem showed him four, and with the four, she spoke. The language was one he'd never heard and therefore did not understand, but he worked his lips over and over until the sound he made matched hers.

She was pleased, as was he. The place she showed was near—two, three days run.

Before the vision released him, as the images blurred back to gray and black and blistering white, he squeezed a smile, eager to share his news.

It appeared *they* would be coming to him.

* * *

Rubbing the sleep out of his eyes, Joel stumbled to the door, fumbled with the bolt lock, and twisted the grimy doorknob. "Coming."

A sharp clack sounded as the locking device popped. He was about to pull open the door when something tickled the back of his head. He released the knob, snapped up his hands, and swatted the air. They sliced a clean path, hitting nothing. "Gawd," he mumbled, envisioning that whatever had been teasing his hair had fallen and was now scurrying at his feet. He wiggled his toes in the soiled carpet and snorted disgust.

Nasty place. Everything felt dirty, gritty, slimy as if the entire population of Manuas, Brazil, was on permanent siesta, no one pushing a broom, slinging a mop, lifting a hand to the filth. What a primitive, prideless people.

He worked his fingers into his scalp, searching. No bugs nesting. What he found instead was his hair mashed up on the back of his head, sweated into the shape of a duck's ass. Old fart's hair—pillow imprints on the backs of fuzzy gray heads. At a boyishly handsome, toned and tanned, thirty-two, Joel wouldn't be caught dead wearing an old man hairstyle.

He smoothed it down and there was another knock on the door, reminding him why he'd risen from bed.

Someone had stopped by?

Joel blinked. Still night. Pale moonlight drooled through the window, turning the dingy sheets butter yellow. White stucco walls had grayed while the corners of the room were dressed in dark shadows. The bedspread, a threadbare splash of red, yellow and purple flowers and palm fronds, covered the dresser like tropical vomit. He'd immediately pulled the vile thing off the bed and thrown it aside. Joel knew what hotels did to save money. Skimp a bit on the laundry; wash the sheets and reuse the covers. So what if a busload of tourists had slept on it, partied on it, and done who-knows-what-else on it?

He shivered and tried to read the time from his travel alarm. It glowed like a red-faced demon and he couldn't focus.

Another knock.

"All right." As Joel reached for the knob, his bowels rumbled. Where was the bathroom? To the right. Slow, his memory crawled out of a fog. Yes, he'd already spent several hours in that cramped damp space.

And more blanks filled in, like turning the pages of a picture book, the story unfolding, image upon image. After he'd checked into the hotel, he'd suffered an hour's long, stinging bout of diarrhea that had left him exhausted, but unable to sleep. Finally, he'd chewed a roll of antacids, swallowed two sleeping pills, and prayed his colon wouldn't act without consent.

His bowels quivered, then stilled. Never again. No more business trips outside the good old US of A. If he couldn't be guaranteed a suite in a five-star hotel in a city where English was the primary language, Joel Ryan wasn't going. Simple. He hadn't burned away six years at Harvard, then secured a spot as consulting attorney for Magnum Exports (a position superior to vice president, if you asked him) to spend time in a place he considered one sneeze away from hell.

Brazil. How uncivilized.

A knock on the door.

Joel stared at the knob, thought of Los Angeles, and decided that he'd give up everything: the seven-figure salary, company car, and million-dollar house—complete with indoor swimming pool, tennis courts, and climate-controlled library—to be with his new wife, Melody. Joel missed her as much as he hated where he was. A day spent thumbing through furniture catalogs or choosing colors for the guest bathroom would have been a kinder adventure than the one he'd so far endured. When he got home, he'd shower until the water went cold, then slip between satin sheets, hold her perfumed body and—

Another knock. Persistent.

Joel sighed and opened the door. A tarnished, brass number three glistened in the hall's lamplight, and a hand of thick air grabbed his nose.

"Yeah?" He squinted at the visitor, his vision swimming behind a sedated, murky veil. "Who..."

Two light feet tapped on the worn carpet inside the entranceway and a dainty hand slapped the door closed.

"What?" Joel swayed backward and curled his toes into the carpet. It was enough to keep him upright while he focused.

Before him stood a small man. If determination of gender had been based on stature alone, the visitor could have been mistaken for a woman. When he spoke, however, the bass voice clinched the decision. "*Tomkal winton.*" All man.

In the moonlight, his skin glowed with a misting of sweat. Round cheeks, the color of molasses, rode on top of a solid square jaw. Medium length hair, black—almost blue—perfectly straight and baby fine, covered his head. Damp, deep black eyes peered, shining like little lamps.

"W—who are—?"

Before Joel could finish, a creature the size of a man's muscled fist leapt from the visitor's hand and landed on Joel's shoulder, covering it. A garbled moan burbled deep within his throat as he stared down at a tarantula. Eight long, thick legs, covered in mousy fur and striped with glowing orange hairs, secured a hold, then moved gracefully up to his neck.

Joel jerked his body from side to side, but the tarantula would not be thrown off. And Joel made no move to swat the creature or smash it with his hand. He wasn't that kind of guy. Cerebral, a real renaissance man, he honored the needs of nature, allowing all creatures big and small their assigned place in the life cycle. At least that's what he told his friends. The truth was, little critters with segmented bodies and multiple legs turned his manhood to pudding. While other boys ripped the wings off flies and trapped glow bugs and spiders, young Joel had slipped away to the sanctity of his room to enjoy the sanitary hobbies of stamp collecting and reading.

Fear made him the prefect victim. Defenseless, he watched as the tarantula's twin curled fangs spread open, then plunged, cutting perfect parallel punctures in his flesh.

The effects of the bite were instant. Joel fell to his knees. Throat muscles constricted. Breathing halted. Nervous system paralyzed, heart stalled in mid-beat, Joel toppled, his stiff body bent in the shape of a "V"—dead before he hit the floor.

Dank carpet fibers absorbed the post mortem froth that bubbled from his mouth.

*   *   *

As the visitor moved forward and extended his arm, the tarantula shifted. "*Mantad goyo im.*" (Praise you, blessed totem.) The tarantula crawled onto the man's hand. "*Mantad goyo im.*" Both spider and hand disappeared into the soft folds of the man's baggy overcoat.

"Joel Ryan. Magnum Exports. Ambassador Hotel number three," he said to the corpse. "*Tomkal winton.*" (You murder our children.)

He was Akan, Man of the Totem, Hunter of Man. Swallowing a sob, he turned away. Airy steps took him to the hotel door. He opened it, stepped out, closed it behind him. After his eyes adjusted to the dull globe lighting the hallway, Akan walked carefully from door to door, studying each as he passed.

"Timothy Winter. Magnum Exports. Ambassador Hotel number nine."

He stopped in front of the number-nine door, brushed his fingertips over the greenish brass marker, and listened. Vacant. He'd return to the false forest outside the hotel—a tiny patch of palms and flowering shrubs—rest and wait.

The tarantula in his pocket squirmed, and even as tears dripped down his cheeks, Akan whispered words of comfort. He didn't enjoy the assignment, but the people of his tribe and the beasts of the forest— their combined lives—depended on him to execute a task that was loathsome to his spirit. For them, he would continue.

He'd done it before, several seasons back, before he'd become a husband. Two white men, their bodies and limbs concealed in tan cloth, had carried odd black weapons—big, shiny, cumbersome and humming like the quiet snore of a newborn. Excited, the duo had circled the perimeter of the encampment, chattering to each other, systematically aiming the weapons at the individual people of the tribe. Even at night. Red stars blinked on the weapons and tiny twin suns glowed, illuminating paths through the dark. Feeble hunters, the two men hadn't tried to cover their invasion. For three days and two nights this went on, the men coming closer and closer, always the weapons perched on their shoulders, shining, blinking, humming, until finally Akan knew it was time to seek guidance from the totem.

He'd prepared the venom potion, drank, entered the vision and received the answer.

There had been a collective gasp when he'd revived and retold the judgment. Violence was reserved for game—birds and wild boar. It was not tribal custom to take life for reasons beyond food. Without protest, however, Akan accepted the new responsibility and, along with his honored title "*Won Montad*"—Man of the Totem—he was called, "*Nomdat Ir Won Kim*"—Hunter of Man. The children had practiced saying the title, over and over again, their dark eyes peeking at Akan, then quickly looking away lest they were caught staring. Honored, Akan held their small awed voices in his ear as he slipped into the forest that night and fulfilled the order of the vision.

Immediately after, the tribe had relocated. Twice in his young life, Akan had helped pack and move, each time to avoid being discovered by the white man.

Sadness settled in his belly. He knew that, with the activity increasing, more men and machines creeping into the rainforest, they'd have to uproot and settle again.

How many times? Why couldn't his people be left alone?

Akan envisioned home, the way it had been before the most recent mining expedition, before Magnum Exports had fouled the water. Open hovels with thatched roofs against a green and brown landscape, children running free at play, young women nursing babies, elders preparing food, men assembled for a hunt or retelling stories of centuries past.

He recalled the last time he'd held his newborn daughter, her tiny, withered body trembling in his hands. She so small and innocent, for days suffering the effects of the poison until she'd at last gave her final breath. He'd laid her to rest beside a tiny mound, the grave of his two-year-old son.

After he'd buried his children, his wife, Uru, had wandered into the forest, never to return. Many women had turned to a similar escape, the guilt...the guilt...

If only they hadn't fed the children the fish.

It'd been the celebration of the second moon, the tribe's most sacred night. All families gathered around a pit fire, men dressed in grass skirts, woman wearing headdresses of feathers and flowers and adorning their bodies with greenery, bringing the beauty of the forest into the camp. First the elder men danced and chanted, retelling the birth of the tribe and the union of tarantula and man as co-protectors.

As the chanting increased pitch, the young men joined in singing promises to the forest of their eternal service. The women and children circled the dancers, humming and swaying to the beat. Praises were sung to the trees, to the land, to the water, to the totem. And after the dance came the banquet. Roasted wild boar and fruit. Tribal rules forbade children and nursing women to eat the meat as it sometimes carried a stomach sickness that was serious for little ones. Instead, they ate fish. After the feast, the mothers grew sick and the children sicker. Two children died during the night. The next morning, able men and women carried the ill to the river, hoping to wash off the wicked disease. Dead fish bobbed atop the water. The greenery around the water's edge had turned brown. And the air was still and silent—as if the forest has inhaled a deep sigh and would not release it. It was then they understood that the sickness was in the water—in the fish—the same fish they'd fed the children to protect them.

Over the next few days, the entire population of children died. Twenty-two tiny graves encircled the encampment.

Akan shook his head and forced his thoughts to his mission. Slender fingers trailed over his pocket and he spoke to the tarantula, his voice projecting the respect due to the tribal totem. "*Montad goyo im.*" (Praise you, blessed totem.)

*   *   *

"I'll...we'll be over later. Right now, I've got to pick up some things at the store. Jackie forgot to pack my razor. Flippin' idiot! Good thing she's got those double-D hooters."

Tim laughed into his cellular phone while he threw a handful of dirty clothes into the corner of his room. He loved talking about his wife to Eddy, knowing how his boss felt about her.

"Boobs or brains? Can't have it both ways." A pair of black socks drifted to the pile. "If I thought she was smart enough, I'd say she left my razor out on purpose—just to be a pain in the ass. I wouldn't let her come with me. Told her babes with blond hair were a hot commodity and I couldn't risk bringing her along. She's pretty mad. Said she'd wear a hat. A hat! Gotta love her, huh?"

Oh yeah. Tim *knew* Eddy was picturing *loving* Jackie. Ha! Gave Tim leverage. Proved which man was smarter. Eddy had enough money to build himself a fleet of Jackie's, but he didn't. Apparently, the fat old cowboy would rather fantasize over someone else's property. No matter. Someday Tim would bring Eddy's dreams alive, give Jackie to him. A present. And good riddance! Plastic Fantastic

Jackie had all the personality, imagination and flexibility of a Barbie doll and justifiably so, as her prominent body parts had come at a high price from California's best surgeons. Tim liked to mention that when she got fussy. Funny stuff!

"Well, that's enough about the old ball and chain, huh? I...Joel and I'll be over later. After I get back from the store, I thought I'd shower up, then maybe he and I could grab some lunch. I was thinking we could stop by about four o'clock or so. As soon as I'm done with you, I'm going to check out the local color, if you know what I mean?"

A brown girl dressed in a sleeveless blue shift and black sandals stepped out of the bathroom. Long black hair fell to her buttocks and swept her back as she moved. She was beautiful in a plain way, young in an illegal way.

Tim eyed her greedily. Expert sheet dancer, knew how to move and didn't need instructions. Perhaps he could get her back to the States, put her up somewhere, keep her for a side dish. Who knew—if the little girl treated him right, maybe he'd even ditch Jackie sooner and have this tropical sweetie as his main course.

Curling his fingers up and out, Tim beckoned her. "Actually, I already took a dip in the local pool last night. I met this—"

A soft tap sounded on the door.

"What?" Tim turned to the noise. "Oh! Hey Eddy, someone's at my door. I hope it's not Joel come to whine about how he misses his wife. Crybaby!"

Another tap, this one louder, more insistent.

The girl ignored both the knock and Tim's outstretched hand. She retrieved her bag, opened it, and counted a fistful of colorful bills.

"Aw! I really gotta go. See ya later, Eddy." Tim snapped the phone closed, threw it onto the bed, and kicked a wadded pair of boxers into the pile. He went to the door, throwing a wink at the girl on the way. "No need to count it, honey. It's all there. You deserve it. No one's asking for a refund."

Tap. Tap.

Tim peered through the peephole. Whoever was on the other side was small. All he could see was the top of a head covered in a cap of sleek black hair.

"Who the hell?" The interruption spoiled his plans. He would have liked to talk the girl into a quick game of hide-the-pony before spending the rest of the day with drab-as-a-slab Joel. Pushing his eye close, trying to catch a glimpse of the person under the hair, was no use. Very short. Maybe another girl? "Mmmmmmm." An immediate picture of brown twins bouncing in his bed sprang to mind. Without inquiry, Tim unlocked the door and pulled it open.

The fantasy vision shattered. In its place was a very real man. Girl-sized, dark-skinned, and dressed in a baggy brown coat that fitted him like a tent. Without a word, he stepped into the hotel room.

Tim scowled. "What can I do ya for, my little friend?"

If the man understood sarcasm, he didn't show it. Spinning on his heels, he faced Tim and spoke. "*Tomkal winton.*"

The man's behemoth voice revived Tim's humor. Big grin rippling on his face, he drew an invisible line in the air, connecting the girl to the visitor. "You two know each other?"

The uninvited guest glared at the girl (his first show of emotion) and an embarrassed flush rouged her honey-colored cheeks. Dropping her eyes to the floor, she clutched her purse to her small bosom and rushed out. As she left, the visitor's lips curled down (his second show of emotion) and he turned back to Tim. "*Tomkal winton.*"

"Hey now, don't be mad with her. She's been well paid. Even if you have to split it, I'm sure you'll both be very happy." Tim laughed with a little less joy than he would have liked. An invisible weight pressured against him, billowed around him, and was slowly closing him in. Too bad he hadn't pulled back the curtains, opened the windows. Sunlight and air—even the thick air of Manuas would have been welcome.

For the first time in a long time, Tim felt discomfort in his surroundings. Unusual? Unheard of. Timothy Winter was *the man,* the guy called in to solve problems that couldn't be fixed using black-and-white policy and procedure. Street smart, with a genius I.Q., he'd risen from an entry-level position in Inventory Control to V. P. of Magnum Exports in under a year, kicking stunned men off the rungs of the corporate ladder without a glance back. Nothing...no one riled Timothy Winter.

"You gonna tell me who you—"

The visitor slipped his hand into and out of his pocket while he spun and kicked the door closed. Direct hit. Eight legs gripped Tim's sideburns as the tarantula straddled his face.

* * *

Pascual grabbed up a fistful of papers. "I will fix these schedule. My men are ready tomorrow." He wore his usual expression—pinched, black marble eyes with three thick brown wrinkles dissecting his forehead so it looked like chunky pieces of mud pie.

"Thanks, 'Scual. Tim and Joel should be stopping by pretty soon and I want everything to be signed and sealed so we can start excavation ASAP. Oh...that means *imediamente*."

Pascual tipped his head and his scowl deepened. "I know well A-S-A-P." He spat out the "P" as if it was bitter in his mouth.

"Yeah 'Scaul, I bet you do. Sorry about that, man. But while I'm dolling out lessons, let me remind you to lighten up. That face of yours! You're gonna worry yourself into an early grave." Eddy slapped Pascual on the shoulder, then settled his Stetson over his brow and sat back in a lawn chair, ready to add to his deep tan while studying a stack of contracts.

Contracts. Wonderful things. Took messy and made it neat. Even Pascual was on contract. He'd penned his name on papers designating him an employee for "Services as Required" at Magnum Exports. That made him available to everything from serving food, hiring laborers to work the rainforests, translating, putting up a buffer between Eddy and his crew and the occasional rowdies in Manuas, and supplying Eddy with a room in his home.

"Early grave is what I avoid for you and me." Pascual turned on his heel and walked to the house in military fashion. Eddy laughed softly, thanking his lucky stars that he had the man on his side.

In Pascual's case, loyalty had been bought at first, then grown into something real. Working together over the past four years, Eddy had eased into a comfortable position within Pascual's family—a sweet combination between the eccentric uncle and Santa Claus. Every trip, the boys got their Hot Wheels cars and the little girl something Barbie and the baby, Eduardo, anything Lakers. Eddy loved them and they loved him—a contract of heart and soul.

Too bad Eddy couldn't develop similar relationships with his underlings at Magnum Exports.

He'd tried hard with Joel Ryan. Poor kid had the personality of a two-by-four, but Eddy appreciated his anal honesty and prayed he'd never leave. Eddy had tried to loosen him up, invited him to parties, and had suggested that Joel might enjoy dressing in the company's "California Cowboy" style—jeans, boots, button shirt, and bolo, and of course, the Stetson. But Joel would have nothing of it. He was Harvard, gosh darn it.

Then there was Tim Winter. False-faced piece of crap. Looked like an idiot in a cowboy hat. Smart and motivated and just arrogant enough to think he could rise above them all. Had his eye on Eddy's chair! Eddy had tried to warn Tim against such desires by retelling a *bible-story-a-la-Eddy* about Lucifer and God. "You know, Tim, Lucifer thought he could be as good as God, actually thought he had more on the ball than God—He who had created him and given him a nice piece of real estate in heaven! Arrogant little angel, Lucifer wanted more, wanted to be the top gun, had his heart set on God's big spread. Now God's no dim bulb, Tim. He knew what Lucifer was up to, and he not only threw the SOB out of heaven—Lucifer and a bunch of whimpering demons—but damned them all to eternity in the lake of fire. Too bad Lucifer couldn't just leave a good thing alone, huh?"

Tim had howled like a jackal at the obvious analogy, and it was then that Eddy knew he'd soon be playing God with Tim's job. That crap-eating grin of his would be the first thing to go. The second thing would be Jackie.

Jackie and Eddy. Eddy and Jackie. Sounded good. So much for the secret rendezvous, however. Pascual had set the whole thing up. He'd even sent his wife and kids out of town for the week so the house would be empty most of the time. While Eddy had Tim running errands, he and Jackie could spend time together, alone. She'd teased Eddy, hinted about a little surprise she had for him, something small and lacy and red. When she'd called to tell him that Tim was making her stay home, she was crying like her date for the prom had canceled, dropped her for another girl. It'd taken Eddy nearly half an hour to calm her down, promising everything would be all right.

And it wasn't a lie. It'd just be a matter of time and a few loose ends...

"Eddy!"

Eddy turned to the voice. It'd come from Sam Bird—his face a riot of emotions.

"What've you got there?" Eddy peeked out from under the brim of his hat, one eyebrow raised.

Chugging like an old locomotive, Sam braked in front of him. "Found this in the car." Chug. Chug. Cheeks red. Nostrils flaring. "On the front seat." Eyes wide. Chug. Chug. "It's got our company name written on it."

Eddy suppressed a grin and feigned concern. "What is it?"

"I don't have a clue." Chug. Chug. One final puff of air. "No name. No return address."

Medium-sized cardboard container. Flimsy. It reminded Eddy of the boxes back home that came stuffed with a dozen glazed. "I'm hoping for donuts, Sam. Open it."

Sam looked at Eddy as if he'd sprouted a curly tail and wings and was getting ready to take flight. "If you think for a minute that I'm going to open this, you're nuts. I've had enough of the threats, the dirty looks, being spit on and cursed at in words I don't even understand to last me a lifetime without opening a surprise package from some whacko activist."

"Whackos? I don't think so, Sam. If you're gonna be in this business, you have to learn this place. Look beyond the tourist traps and the whitewashed hotels and you'll see a poor people. The ones who don't curse you, threaten you or run screaming from you, will be all over you with open hands and empty pockets. They're not crazy, just trying to survive."

Something Eddy knew well. His parents had been two walking-talking pieces of crap. His mother had split for Hollywood when he was five, hell-bent on becoming the next Goldie Hawn. Last Christmas, after three decades of invisibility, she'd rolled up to Eddy's door dressed like a gutter-crawling hooker and had tried to make nice with her long-lost and very rich son. He'd said, "no thanks," shut the door in her face, watched through the window as her rusted-out convertible smoked a gray path away, then opened up a brand new bottle of JD. Eddy threw the cap away before he took the first sip. He wouldn't need it. The celebration would last to the bottom.

His father had spent a great deal of time staring at the bottom of a bottle. Drank his way from job to job, bed to bed, dragging Eddy along like an old suitcase. One Halloween eve when Eddy was nine, his old man had downed a fifth of gin, then put on a ski mask and crawled behind the wheel of a friend's car going out for tricks-and-treats as a cat burglar. "Meow!" he'd screeched into the night as he drove away. One block later, he jumped the curb and took out three kids dressed as angels and their expectant mother. Four counts vehicular homicide equaled twenty to life. One week later, he'd choked to death on a pack of cigarettes someone had shoved down his throat.

It was the best day of Eddy's life. The State sent him to live with Gram—God's greatest creation on earth. How his father had had the privilege of being raised by such a woman and turned out as he had only made Eddy hate him more.

Gram taught him everything, but most of all, how to treat people, especially women. She likened it to blackberry picking. A woman was a tender berry and a man needed a gentle hand or he would bruise the fruit, spoil it. It wasn't long before Eddy could pick a bucket of berries—enough for two pies—and still have clean hands.

He imagined Tim in a berry patch, grabbing fistfuls of fruit, juice running down his fingers and arms, stuffing his pie-hole, red drooling down his chin...

"Eddy?"

Sam was eyeing him funnily and Eddy blushed. He hoped the hat hid his color and whipped out a big smile. "The rainforest has made me a rich man. It's like a treasure hunt out there and I'm a pirate. I've got it all, Sam my man. Travel, people who look up to me, a ranch on the California coast. And this place..." Eddy fanned out his hands, wagging the contracts in the air. "This is where it all began." He put the papers into his lap. "You can have your Silicon Valley, your chips and bytes. This is where I want to be. All those boardrooms and big-assed secretaries and three-hour lunches have put a yellow stripe down your back."

"Is that so? Let's see who's yellow." A sarcastic grin cut a sideways line through a matching set of sunburned cheeks. Sam tossed the box.

Eddy deflected the carton and it dropped onto the grass, settled on its side, then shook.

"It's alive!" they screamed in unison—Sam's voice terrified, Eddy's childishly enthusiastic.

"Throw it over the—" Before Eddy could finish, Sam grabbed the box and spiraled it over the twelve-foot-high security fence.

"Good throw, Sam."

"Yeah. Good thing for you. Why don't you beef up the security around here? A fence and a bilingual Indian don't exactly spell 'safe' in my book."

" 'Scaul's good people and all the security we need. When I found him, he was living on the edge of the forest with a rundown farm, a dirty wife, and three under-fed kids. He's one wealthy, thankful, and loyal man. I'm his money tree. We won't let anyone close enough to knock me down. We're perfectly safe with him."

"Activists...crazies everywhere. Never know what to expect." Sam shivered.

"You ever been poor, Sam? I mean dirty, grubby poor?"

Sam shook his head.

"Then you'll never really understand." Eddy dipped his eyes down to the contracts in his lap. His tanned belly had turned a deeper shade of brown, his hairy navel a white eye in a mountain of fat. A crying eye. Sweat trickled down his bulging stomach like teardrops. Looking at his belly, Eddy's thoughts bounced between missing Jackie and the sad fact that he needed a diet. She deserved it.

"You're pretty casual about all this, Eddy."

"Look, this is the real world. If you want to make money, suck up your gut and deal with it for a few weeks. These people are all talk. Passive complainers. Every once in a while someone throws themselves down in front of one of the excavators. Big deal. It's not like they've come at us with guns or anything." Eddy scratched his double chin.

"Well, I'm telling you, this is my first and last trip. From now on, whatever you need from me, you can get from me back home."

"Wussy."

"I've been called worse."

"Edward Baker."

Sam inhaled quickly, making a girlish, high-pitched whine. Eddy snapped his head around to the voice. Who could have moved so close without being heard? Quite a trick in the short-trimmed, crisp grass. Eddy had joked about it in the past, called the lawn one step above walking on cut glass.

But it hadn't provided the usual crunchy alarm. A small man with indigenous features stood several feet away. His feet were bare and the grass didn't seem to affect him at all. "Edward Baker."

"Who are you?" Eyes on the visitor, Eddy aimed his voice at the house. "Pascual?"

"Edward Baker."

The man was tight with his words. Eddy swallowed a mouthful of sour. "Pascual? You sleeping on the job? We got company!"

The lack of an answer struck a nerve, as if Eddy was a sea captain who'd just spotted a skulking ship on the horizon, a skull and crossbones flag flapping from the mast. "You a friend of Pascual's?"

"Edward Baker." The little man had his hands down to his sides, fingers dangling from the cuff of an oversized coat. Small head, huge eyes, enormous presence.

Eddy stacked the papers in a neat pile and stood. His belly shook and a brown wave of flab pushed over the elastic waistband of his shorts. "You're looking at him."

"*Tomkal winton.*"

Eddy lowered his chin. Not only did the voice inspire respect, but he was intrigued. Although, the unnamed man bore the distinct physical characteristics of the locals, his language was new. A challenge. He hoped the visitor spoke English. "Look, I don't want trouble. I'm a businessman. That's all."

The man took a step closer. "*Tomkal winton.*" His round eyes joined his voice in authority.

Sam reached for the phone on the lawn table. The visitor snapped his hand in the air—*Stop*—while maintaining eye contact with Eddy.

Sam let his arm drop.

Anger bit Eddy on the back of the neck. How vulnerable was he, standing outdoors dressed in shorts, sweat, and Stetson? He pictured his shotgun propped against the wall beside his bed, loaded with two rounds of OO buck, enough power to make a puzzle of a man's guts. Fool.

Eddy let his shoulders slack and spoke, his voice low and controlled. "Look, I'm not gonna take all the trees. I've already donated a sizable portion of the land for conservation purposes. I'm not a bad guy. I know the rainforest holds many interests for many people. The bottom line is this—I bought it and I need to clear it. Not all of it, but most of it. If you want to sit down, we can talk about it…civil."

The visitor answered. "Joel Ryan. Magnum Exports. Ambassador Hotel number three. Timothy Winter. Magnum Exports. Ambassador Hotel number nine." He spoke with the same declarative emotion of a morgue attendant reading toe tags.

A compelling mental picture flashed before Eddy's eyes; white sheets draped over corpses, the cold dead bodies of his associates, Joel and Tim. What saddened him more than that was adding Pascual's name to the list. Thank God the wife and kids were out of town. Thank God he didn't have Jackie holed up inside the house waiting for him.

Eddy's stomach suddenly felt like a hot rock. "What is it you want?"

"*Tomkal…*"

Sam jumped two steps forward, lips twitching, sweat slick on his nose. "You know what? I've had enough of this place. If you'll both excuse me, I'll be taking myself back to the States…posthaste."

"Samuel Bird." The intruder held Eddy in his stare.

"Yes. Sir." Sam snapped a nod, jerked another step. "That's me. Pleased to meet you and goodbye. This man here—" Sam pointed a trembling finger at Eddy while he took one shaky step toward the house. "He's the money-man. He'll take care of you."

As Sam walked past, the visitor moved quickly and smoothly. A tarantula landed on Sam's back in the flat spot between the shoulder blades.

Before Eddy could react, Sam landed face down on the lawn, making a sound like bagged garbage falling on a bed of gravel.

The tarantula crawled up and over the dead man's shoulder, down his arm, across his hand, and onto the grass.

"*Tomkal winton.* Edward Baker."

And the tarantula headed toward Eddy.

Sweat swirled over his barrel belly and wet the front of his shorts. A few stomach hairs caught and tugged, stinging like bug bites, but Eddy didn't move to adjust the waistband. Instead, he put up his hands.

What he had witnessed could not be. Eddy had exported tarantulas in the past, knew a lot about them. Tarantulas were not deadly predators. Big? Yes. Hairy? Yes. Most. Intimidating? Definitely. Deadly? No way. Their bites were a nuisance, painful. The urticating hairs were bothersome. He'd inhaled some of the expelled, tarantula body hairs when he'd first become interested in them. After that incident, he'd spent two solid weeks fighting the irritation in his nose and throat and had learned to handle the creatures with greater respect.

The tarantula continued its approach. The visitor waited silently.

Eddy dug deep, trying to uproot buried information. The tarantula creeping toward him reminded him of the Lasiodora parhybana, but the legs were longer, the cephalothorax larger, and the abdomen more oval. There could be only one explanation. The creature that'd killed Sam within seconds of a bite was an undiscovered species. And beyond the fact that it was deadly, the blasted spider allowed itself to be handled as if man and arachnid worked as a team. Unthinkable!

The spider's body made a shadow in the grass. Thick and limber, eight legs pumped, and the sketch of its outline smeared.

"This spider of yours. Quiet interesting. If you want to talk a minute, I bet we could come to a profitable understanding."

Eddy took a step backward.

"I don't know how you and your family are set up, but I can promise you a rich future."

The tarantula approached. Grass crunched.

Adrenaline surged, stimulating nerves that Eddy didn't know he had. Pinpricks tickled a path from behind his ears and down his sides. The bottoms of his feet itched. He swore he could feel the hairs in his nose wriggling.

The spider was inches away. Eddy's heart beat war drums in his ears.

He retreated another step, felt the aluminum edge of the chair scrape his thigh. "If you would just listen. For a minute."

The tarantula's shadow covered his toes. It pulled up one leg and set it down on Eddy's foot.

Heavy thing! Eddy's family jewels crawled up into his belly and he teetered backward, fell over the lawn chair, and landed on the grass. His hat slipped off. Eddy felt powerless without it and looked up, hoping the man would see the surrender in his eyes.

The visitor stared, tears streaming down his cheeks, his sorrow obvious. Still, he made no move to help and gave no indication he would.

The spider climbed up Eddy's legs and over the rise of his stomach. Then, they were face-to-face.

As the tarantula's fangs spread, Eddy felt a deep sadness cuddle his heart. It all seemed unfair somehow. He imagined Gram perched on a cloud, shaking her finger, scolding him for allowing himself be cornered, and knew she had a right. He'd tell her so when he saw her again. And although a reunion with Gram would be nice, Eddy wasn't ready to go. What about Jackie?

Jackie and Eddy. Eddy and Jackie. Sounded so good.

Eddy looked into the two perfect ebony balls that were the tarantulas blind eyes and put his dream there, in the reflection...Jackie moving gracefully over the dance floor, Eddy's arm around her shoulder, his hand resting in the small of her back. A song was playing, a tune he'd seen her moving her lips to while the top dawgs of Magnum had gathered at his beach house for a weekend fiesta. Jackie had been sitting by the pool, margarita in hand, bikini holding her body like Eddy wanted to, singing under her breath to a song by Dwight Yoakam. Eddy liked Dwight. Great musician, genius wordsmith, voice like melted butter, born to wear a cowboy hat.

It was a pretty tune. Slow. "...I'm a thousand miles from nowhere...Time don't matter to me...I'm a thousand miles from nowhere..."

And they danced. Jackie was a blackberry, dressed in white silk.

*   *   *

The vision had shown him four and there had been five.

Akan and the totem had failed.

He'd been home a week and had felt the tension within the tribe steadily mutate from shock to anxiety to angry fear.

How could they have failed? Had Akan done something wrong? If they couldn't rely on Akan and the powers of the totem, could they survive? Would the next disease take them all?

While sharing food in a midday communal, Tipi kept her hand over her belly, fingers gently stroking the early swell of pregnancy, her hand never straying as if she could keep her unborn child safe simply by holding. Tipi did not look at Akan, but the others did.

Akan felt their eyes upon him. They wanted a guarantee. Cowards, no one would speak out loud what he already knew. They wanted him to ensure that Tipi's baby—all the coming babies—would be born into a world of safety. The tribe wanted to know that they would never have to suffer as they had months ago.

Akan ate, drank, and tried to ignore the stares. He could not. Could one overlook a spear thrust in his chest? Could one overlook fire chewing away the flesh? Could one overlook the attack of a hundred rabid animals?

No. And that was how he felt. Under siege by the people he had risked his life to save.

After a while, Tipi began to sob, cuddled her belly with both hands, stood unsteadily, and ran, disappearing into the folds of her hammock.

Still, no one spoke. But the eyes, the feelings behind them...

Wanting. They wanted more and more and more.

They looked to Akan for salvation!

So be it. He'd give it to them.

Akan spat out a mouthful of fish and went to the totem. She sat on a thatch mat and was beautiful. After returning, the tarantula had gorged, then, in a three-day half-sleep, she'd molted. Yesterday, she'd fed again. Her body was thicker, stronger, and her movements quick and confident. She was energized.

Akan placed a red berry in front of her, stroked a trail over the hairs of her body, and whispered a chant under his breath. After she punctured the berry and released the venom, Akan mashed the fruit into a mixture of cassava, pepper, palm root, and rainwater.

With the cup held up to his mouth, he trailed his eyes over the line of his people. A few cast stares at the ground. The rest, however, waited, seemingly unconcerned with the danger and pain of entering a vision. For the first time in his life, Akan felt contempt simmer in his soul, anger for his own.

He drank.

His screams of agony blistered his eardrums, multiplied, then coupled with the roar of the internal wind. The vision came with a rage, tearing through the black, gray, and white. He never saw the blue. Instead, images came like punches, beating his face and head. Over and over they smacked, and he saw and memorized. Two called as one. Two called as one. Distant and coming. Two called as one.

And his eyes snapped open to a collective gasp.

Akan had brought the storm back with him. Fierce wind tore through the encampment, lifting palm fronds from poles and throwing them into the jungle like spears. Men and women screamed and grabbed each other, a few tumbling and rolling over the ground. Baskets of cassava tipped, the brown vegetables bounding over the dirt, knocking into ankles, pounding toes and feet. A few of the wounds brought blood. And there were more screams, and several men ran into the tree line for cover. Arms wrapped around her body, one old woman rolled like a crooked log and butted up against the edges of the fire. Hair sizzled and smoke curled around her head before she pulled up onto her hands and knees and crawled away, mewling like a dying boar.

A tiny white cyclone twirled around Akan, sucking up dirt and bits of ember and thrusting the debris through the air, stinging the huddled crowd like insects.

As he sat on the ground in the middle of the chaos, Akan felt something scratch his leg. It was the totem. She had walked beside him and had two legs resting on his thigh.

Akan looked from her, to his terrified people, then back to the tarantula.

"*Montad goyo im.*" (Praise you, blessed totem.)

He watched the storm and laughed.

Two called as one. Distant but coming.

Salvation?

He would not wait.

*   *   *

"You want to tag along with me when I go out to see Eddy Baker next weekend? It'd be good experience to see how I work the contract with him. And if the education isn't enough, you'll get a first-hand look into the little commune he's building on his ranch. It'll be a fun trip, Mikey. A father and his son visiting the folks of Looneyville." Mike Fink Senior snorted a laugh and whacked the ball from the tee with a smooth, practiced stroke.

He had an appointment with Eddy to work out the contractual agreements to buy and reopen Magnum Exports. Fink had wanted to get everything in black and white sooner, but Eddy wasn't cooperating. He'd wanted time to settle in his new wife, Jackie, and a handful of Brazilian exports, some widow and her four kids.

"Looneyville? Isn't that a little harsh, Dad?'

"No, Mikey, it isn't. The man survives an attack by some venomous spider that leaves him dead on one side so he'll be moving around on two wheels for the rest of his life. And instead of vengeance, he builds himself a little fortress, fills it with misfits, and plans to live happily ever after." He laughed without joy. "More than that, I really do think this whole thing's messed up his head. I don't care what the doctors say. I can't get a straight story out of him. Keeps babbling about Arachnassassins and blackberries and Dwight Yoakam. He oughta be in an institution. No! That's wrong. He oughta be wheeling himself over the border to hunt down the thing that put him in that chair. That's what a sane man would do."

"Nice shot, Dad. Looks like a straight line to the green." Mike Fink Junior took a step forward and patted his father's shoulder. "I wonder if you've thought there might be a reason why Eddy doesn't want to go back there. Maybe he's not crazy, but smart. I wonder if you might be jumping into this adventure thinking too much about the money. I mean, with Eddy wanting to sell the whole thing so cheap, maybe you should think a little more about why a man would bail on a multimillion-dollar business. Personally, I think we should go into something else."

Mike Fink Senior putted the ball into the neat round hole. "That's a birdie for me."

"I'm still up by two." Mike Fink Jr. grinned broadly at his father.

A cool day in Southern California, brisk wind whipped the flags. They were almost finished with the first round of golf. Senior Fink was a good player. His son was better. It was the one thing in which the younger Fink excelled. Senior Fink grinned. He had a feeling his son was being easy on him. Never had they been a mere two strokes separated. "I'm going for it."

They loaded into the golf cart and zoomed to the next tee. "Can't you do anything easy, Dad? Rainforests? It's all too controversial. Not even politically correct. Stay away from this. Clearing the land, the trees. The ecosystem depends on—"

Mike Fink Senior laughed out loud, stopped the cart, pulled out a driver, and walked to set his tee. "Ecosystems? You're not paying attention, Mikey. It's not the trees or the land. It's the spider. Do you know what scientists might be able to do with this neurotoxin? Would you still say no if you knew you could cure disease? If you could help people live normal lives?" Smack. A slice. One hundred yards into the sand. "Damn! All the excitement is ruining my game."

Mike Junior sighed. "Nothing ruins your game, Dad. And that stuff about disease, that's not fair."

Senior Fink turned to his son, knowing he was thinking of his mother. When they'd left her that morning she'd been moaning, waiting for her morning dose of medication to kick in. "First—you are correct, nothing ruins my game. Second—you're wrong. It is fair. If finding that spider can help just one person, we owe it to them to find it."

"Come on, Dad. We're not just talking about a spider. It's a killing machine. More than that, someone—a real live human—had to be behind it all. You think that little spider sat and drew out a plan of attack, then executed this mission alone? Someone out there hates—"

Mike Fink Senior cut his son short. "All part of the game. It's what I do best. I've already made up mind. We're going for it. We'll find that creature, and when we do—" He scowled and glared, his gloved hand over his eyes like a shield. "Hey! Hey there you! What's wrong with you? Get out of the way!"

A small man, dressed in a baggy coat approached. The breeze ruffled the coat so it billowed around him like a parachute. Fine black hair danced on his shoulders. Eyes like marbles shone brightly in a backdrop of golden brown skin.

"Who is it, Dad?"

"Some foreigner. They come here and think they can go anywhere they want! I'll make a formal complaint when we get back to the clubhouse. He's trespassing on private land!" Mike Senior stuffed the driver back into the bag. "Send him on his way, Mikey. It'll be good practice."

Mike Junior walked across the green.

As his son moved away, Mike Senior watched the little man's lips curl into a snarl while he slipped his brown hand into his coat pocket.

In that instant, fear like nothing Mike Fink Senior had ever known—deeper than when they'd diagnosed his wife with Parkinson's, deeper than when he'd woke in the emergency room after surviving a head-on collision, deeper than he thought humanly possible—bit his heart.

He screamed, "Mikey!" and ran toward his son.

Mike Junior turned, his eyes pinched and sad. A tarantula sat on his shoulder, fangs slipping into the flesh of his neck.

NOWHERE TO HIDE

His first memory was Peek-A-Boo; Daddy hunkered on the floor beside him, then suddenly disappeared behind hairy fingers.

Curious Baby waited. After a moment, he looked for Daddy, bobbed to the side to see behind the hands.

"Nope. I'm not there."

Daddy's voice without his face?

Stretch up high, then peek over the top of the hands.

"Wrong again."

Daddy?

Maybe Daddy wasn't behind the hands at all. Perhaps...in back of Baby.

"Uh uh. I'm not there."

Then it was true, Daddy had disappeared. Poor Daddy. Poor Baby, he wanted to cry. His lips puckered and he sniffled.

"Such a Crybaby!"

What!? Where!? Did the hands eat Daddy? Reaching out, Baby grabbed one finger and pulled and...

Daddy's face came at him—huge, all teeth and eyes. "Peek-A-Boo!"

Eyes!

And Baby screamed.

Eyes!

After a while, Mama told Daddy, "Stop, you're scaring him."

But Daddy didn't stop. Not until Baby screamed so hard he could no longer see…not Daddy…not the fingers…not the eyes that saw Baby no matter what.

"Peek-A-Boo!"

Eyes behind. Eyes in front. Eyes that see no matter what.

Nowhere to hide.

*   *   *

They were scuffling around in the hallway.

Hushed whispers came from under the door.

"How long do you think he'll stay in there?"

Exhaling deeply, He wormed deeper under…farther away.

Cruel eyes. Wicked eyes. They have all got Daddy's eyes.

Nowhere to hide.

*   *   *

Little Boy found Daddy's soft pocket—the one he hid in his pants. PAYDAYS, Daddy patted it, called it fat and smiled. While Daddy was in the shower, Little Boy took out the soft pocket. What was inside that made Daddy so happy?

Pretty papers, greeny, wrinkled and soft.

Little Boy ripped them into different shapes and made Daddy a big stack.

Daddy walloped Little Boy, but good.

"I knew you were out here doing something evil!"

Eyes far. Eyes near. Eyes that see what most only hear.

Nowhere to hide.

*   *   *

He couldn't…wouldn't go out there.

Someone giggled and He swallowed sour spit.

"Shhhh."

Damnable eyes. Unholy eyes. Eyes like demons. All their eyes.

Nowhere to hide.

*   *   *

It was nice under the bed. Buried away at night, Boy found peace. Best when he pulled down the comforter so it brushed the floor and acted like a blockade.

If Daddy caught him there, he got whooped.

"Wussy Boy, acting like a little baby."

Eyes up. Eyes down. Eyes on the rooftops. Eyes on the ground.

Nowhere to hide.

*   *   *

The sounds from beyond the door escalated.

He pictured them huddled together, peering at the wood.
"What's He doing in there?"
"Shhhh. For Pete's sake, He'll hear you."
"What…"
Something brushed against the door and it was quiet.
But He knew they were still there.
Eyes scorched Him.
Drawing his knees to his chest, He whimpered.
"We'll give a few more minutes, then we…"
Probing eyes. Knowing eyes. Shrewd, lewd, stabbing eyes.
Nowhere to hide.

* * *

When Daddy got his JUST DESERTS, they moved to the country and Boy's new room opened on to a patio. Beyond that was a meadow, horses, a small barn and a tool shed.

Under the bed was no longer a good thing. From there, Boy saw night critters lurking around.

Several sets of yellow eyes shone from the black beneath the tool shed.

Boy screamed and screamed.

Daddy blistered his bottom.

"I'll give you something to cry about."

Eyes in. Eyes out. Eyes everywhere. Eyes all about.

Nowhere to hide.

* * *

His throat burned. So dry.
What He wouldn't give for a sip of water.
When He licked His lips they came away dusty.
Beyond the door, feet rustled.
How they wanted…
He blinked back a tear.
"Excuse me. Get out of the way, please. I'm going in."
Sneaking eyes. Spying eyes. Closer…closer…closer the eyes.
Nowhere to hide.

* * *

The garden shed trembled like a black shadow under arms of fire—gold, red, yellow and hot white curling up and over the plywood roof. Thick black smoke carrying the scent of burning rubber bore a column through the pale blue sky.

Ducked behind the hedgerow, hand wrapped around a smile, Boy

watched fire chew away the wood.
All eyes dead under the shed.
Nowhere to hide.

* * *

Someone knocked on the door.
His heart raced and He felt his guts turn to pudding.
He couldn't face the eyes.
The explosion...they all wanted Him...
The door opened.
"Sir?"
Invasive eyes. Insidious eyes. Coming. Coming. Enter the eyes.
Nowhere to hide.

* * *

After countless nights without sleep, Boy crept across the meadow and into the barn. There was a haystack, deep and heavy. He slipped into it, snuggled and buried until darkness immersed him.

He tried to arise before Daddy, and usually did.
When Daddy found him, it hurt.
"I'm getting sick and tired of having to beat you, Boy."
Eyes in the night. Eyes in the sky. Always...never closing eyes.
Nowhere to hide.

* * *

By now, every news team would be broadcasting the explosion.
When He'd watched the preliminary reel, He'd seen a wall of debris that had moments before been homes, businesses, the major part of a Midwest state, rush the camera, then...fuzz.

All eyes had opened with a start and immediately turned to Him.
"Help!"
Eager eyes. Angry eyes. "Only You can save us" eyes.
Nowhere to hide.

* * *

Something dug into the haystack. It sneezed and woke Boy. When he rolled over, Boy found twin emerald eyes staring at him, inches from his face. Black cat. It drew its claws and hissed.

Boy choked the thing to death and carried it and laid its carcass beside the road.

Day after day, the school bus carried Boy by the body. It took forever for the cat to decay. Even after it was gone, bagged up by State Probationers, he saw it.

As the bus rolled by, Boy felt the eyes and....

"Hissssssssss."

Unlike the eyes under the shed, these eyes survived—remained undead.

Nowhere to hide.

* * *

Two suicide bombers with enough explosives to flatten the nuclear plant had walked right through the front gates.

A whole state leveled?

Millions dead?

Winds carrying radiation over miles and miles?

"What will we do?"

Millions of eyes. Billions of eyes. Innumerable, immeasurable, impossible eyes.

Nowhere to hide.

* * *

His wife was a good woman. They'd planned on a great future together. She wanted to have a ton of kids and they'd all stand behind Him while He set the world on fire.

Sometimes at night, He'd watch her sleeping, eyes bobbing beneath her lids like little beetles under a rug.

Often He slept in a small spot in the closet in the den.

Like Daddy, she'd find Him there. Instead of beating Him, she cried.

"Why are you doing this to me?"

Sad eyes. Sorry eyes. Weepy, sleepy, freaky eyes.

Nowhere to hide.

* * *

The door opened with a hush.

Someone coughed and the door closed. Click.

He pulled his knees to His chest so it was hard to breathe.

"Sir? Are you here? I can't see…"

Eyes…

Nowhere to hide.

"Sir? I…"

He scrambled out from under the rug and crawled on his hands and knees to the dark place behind the desk.

"Sir! It'll be okay. I've already called for the doctor."

Punch the button. Punch the button. Punch the button.

"Oh my God! Sir? No! Don't!"

He pushed the button, entered the secondary request code—P-E-E-

P-E-R-S—then smiled.

"No…you…we'll all be…Mr. Preees-iii-deeent!" The aide fell to his knees and blinked loose a tear.

Young eyes. Sincere eyes. Hot and wide with fear eyes.

"Mr. President. What have you done? Why? We'll all be…"

Scorch the eyes. Fry the eyes. Burn and forever close the eyes.

"All eyes dead under the shed," Mr. President said. "Nowhere to hide."

WALK WITH ME

Rain fell hard. Wind whipped the air like a slave master. Because the weather was horrible, it wasn't odd that a man would be dressed in a long coat. That would be acceptable—expected. What was not normal was the presence of the man.

"He must be soaked through. Wet to the bone." With her hip rested against the counter, cup of coffee steaming in her hand, Claire stared at him, a blurred shape through the kitchen window.

The man stood on the tree-lined embankment in the deadly drizzle as if there was no storm. Heavy droplets pelted his face and head. Flattened hair, spread on his skull like an ink stain. Liquid beads collected on his eyelashes, then splashed onto his face when he blinked. Rain fell like tears onto his cheeks.

And he stared at her.

Claire cuddled the coffee.

Walk with me.

He held up his hand waist high, rolling his fingers in and out. A slow, rhythmic, beckoning.

Walk with me.

Claire shook her head and splashed coffee onto her fingers. "Ouch!"

"Now what's the matter?" Curtis' voice carried downstairs from the loft.

Claire was already running her hand under a stream of cold water. "I spilled my coffee. Burned my hand."

"Klutz."

"Well, *thank-you*, Mr. Compassion." After she patted her hand dry, she retrieved her cup.

"Do I need to call 911?"

"Knock it off, Curtis."

"Want me to run out and get you a tippy-cup?"

"Go away."

"Ah! To go away. You'd like that, wouldn't you?"

Claire dropped her head. "More than you know."

"I heard that."

"Good." Claire waited for a comment, but heard only the pattering of the computer keyboard. Curtis surfing the internet. Sounded like plastic rain.

Rain. She returned to the window. The man stood in the downpour and stared.

Walk with me.

His hands called to her. Long fingers curled and uncurled like tongues lapping rainwater. Mesmerizing. And his eyes—like planets, dark and faraway, emotionless yet passionate. Lifeless, they boiled with energy. Cold, they steamed with invisible heat. A figment of her imagination, or the incarnation of her fantasies? Either way, the man sparked heat within. Not a comforting warmth, like snuggling close to a quiet fire, rather a stinging excitement matching the thrill of a first kiss.

Claire shivered and watched him.

The rain increased, as did the wind. Water slapped his skin. Droplets shattered, multiplied and splattered again. Claire could almost hear the individual beads pound his face, head, and long brown coat.

Walk with me.

Weather battered and he persevered. The man stood his ground, lips pressed in a dry smile, fingers performing a water ballet.

Walk with me.

"What are you looking at?"

Claire jumped, splashing lukewarm coffee onto her sweater. More coffee spilled to the floor as she spun to face Curtis. "What's wrong with you? Sneaking up on me like that?" She swatted at the stain on the sweater, then pulled it away from her skin.

"What sneaking up? You haven't been listening to me at all, have you?"

"No. And you know why? Because I never know if you're talking to me or your screen."

"A-ha. Good answer. Never thought of it that way. 'Tis true that I enjoy being with my computer more than I enjoy being with you. And do *you* know why?"

Claire didn't answer.

Curtis grinned. "Every touch of the keyboard ensures a response. A lot more fun than what my touch brings about with you."

"Take a walk."

"A walk?" He laughed. "Out there? Yuck! Nothing to look at but trees. Miles and miles of wood. How I hate wood. This house is made of wood. *Coffin*s...are made of wood."

"Shut up."

"That's the difference between you and me. You love wood, don't you, Claire? You feel all safe and secure in this highly mortgaged coffin we used to call a home?"

"Shut up!" Claire brushed by him and entered the bathroom. After she slipped off the sweater, she threw it into the sink, turned on warm water, and scrubbed the stain. Over the burble of water splashing, she heard Curtis rustling around in the refrigerator.

"Looks like *I* need to get groceries. Remember when *you* used to go to the store, Claire? You used to get groceries and shop and everything else normal woman do?" The refrigerator door slammed. The clank of condiment bottles and jars rang out like shrill exclamation points. Footsteps sounded as Curtis took the stairs two at a time, retrieved his keys, then bound back down. The front door opened and closed.

"Jerk." Claire dropped her sweater into the sink and left it to soak. Dressed in bra and jeans she returned to the kitchen window. Drizzled landscape, slippery green trees outlined in a charcoal sketch of clouds. Pastel roses arched over, as if in prayer. Gray puddles spotted the muddy drive. The man was gone.

Claire sighed and went to the loft to fetch a clean sweater. She missed him.

Had she lost her mind? It was possible. Why not? She'd lost everything else. Laid off from work, she'd started a home-based business that had drained their saving's account, then failed. Gone was her self-respect, and what esteem she'd retained, Curtis had stripped away. Claire's world had become a melded mess of days and nights spent in a self-made cocoon. The longer she stayed at home, the more fearful she became of the outside world.

Curtis hated the changes in her. It was obvious. Their evenings together consisted of cool conversation over dinner, followed by a few hours of witless insults over the drone of television sitcoms and the nervous peck of the keyboard.

Curtis escaped to the Internet.

Claire had her man. He'd been gracing the bank outside the window more and more frequently the past few months, as if cued to her loneliness. The first time she'd seen him, she'd screamed, called the police, reporting a stalker. They'd found nothing. Curtis had mocked her. But the next day the man returned. Staring. Eyes burrowing. Hands calling. It was then Claire knew he was something greater than a Peeping Tom or a pervert on the prowl. The man was there for her...for Claire, unrelenting in his request. *Walk with me.* If only she could. *Walk with me.*

"I can't go out there. I can't."

Her voice echoed back, "I can't."

* * *

Curtis slipped into bed, smelling of soap and toothpaste. A wisp of damp hair ruffled over Claire's shoulder before he rolled away from her.

She forced a calm into her voice. "Get out of my bed."

Curtis snickered.

"I said, get out of my bed."

He flopped onto his back and nestled his hands behind his head. "I won't."

"You've been gone since noon. It's three in the morning. You come home, take a shower to wash off the smell of sex, then expect to crawl into my bed?"

"*My* bed, Claire."

"Get out!"

"I pay the bills. It's my bed. You get out."

"Who do you think you are? This is just as much my—"

Curtis swung his legs over the edge of the bed and stood. "You better watch yourself. Maybe you forget *who's* supporting *who* around here."

"This isn't a business arrangement! This is a marriage." Claire jumped from the bed to face him. "Everything for you is a big tradeoff. You pay. You play. You don't want a wife. You want a servant, someone to service your needs!"

"Do you *know* someone like that? I'd like to meet her."

"You make me sick." Claire rushed to the dresser and pulled on a sweatshirt over her nightie. After she slipped into a pair of jeans, she fell onto her hands and knees in search of socks.

"You going somewhere?"

The edge in his voice turned her bowels to pudding. "I can't stand you. Can't stand to be in the same room with you. The same house." Socks in hand, Claire kicked her boots down the stairs.

"Oh! This I gotta see."

Claire was on the edge of the steps when Curtis called to her. "If you're really going, you'll need these." She turned and the car keys hit her in the face, slicing a line down her cheek. "You remember how to drive, Claire?"

A growl started in her throat, lifted her off her feet, and she charged, wrapping her hands around his throat. They struggled for a minute that played out like hours, bare feet performing a war dance on hardwood floors. All the while Claire focused on her husband's eyes, bulged and distressed. It pleased her and she was about to tighten her grip when his look changed, showing fear. Curtis stumbled, windmilled his arms. Claire let go.

The sound of his body tumbling down the stairs was louder than she could have imagined. He landed at the bottom with a resounding crack. Then it was quiet. From where she stood, he looked comfortable, as if he'd chosen that particular spot to rest.

"Curtis?" Bare feet padded down the stairs with caution, testing each step. "Curtis?" He did not stir.

Finally Claire was beside him, heartbeat in her ears, bile swirling over her tongue. With quivering fingers, she brushed his hair. "Curtis?"

His head rolled to face her, then he opened his eyes wide and snarled. "I'll get you." A feral growl followed the threat.

She screamed and tripped over her feet.

Slowly, he tried to stand. "You stupid"—he grabbed the stair rail—"crazy"—lifted his body from the floor—"bitch!"—then screamed and dropped. "My leg! My God. You broke my freaking leg!"

Claire took a step back.

"You idiot. My leg! I can't believe you did this." He curled his body around the leg and kept screaming at Claire. "What are you doing standing there? Help me! Call an ambulance! Do something!"

Finally, Claire ran to the phone. One sharp beep for the number nine. Another beep sounded for the number one.

Walk with me.

Her finger hovered over the buttons and she looked up to the bank outside the window. Hands called to her like waves on the ocean.

"What are you doing? Hurry! I'm hurt!"

Walk with me.
Claire stared, wished the man inside.
Walk with me.
He wanted her. His persistence was a promise.
Walk with me.
"Claire! For the love of God, help me!"
Walk with me.
Claire dropped the phone, moved to the back door, turned the knob, and opened it.
"Damn you. Help me!"
Walk with me.
Carried on a stinging breeze, rain peppered her face. Claire put one foot outside and stopped.
Walk with me.
His eyes locked on hers and she moved forward. The mud was thick and she fell.
Curtis yelped for her. "Claire!"
She stood and walked to the embankment. It was steep, drooling and slick.
Walk with me.
Dropping to her knees, Claire crawled. Halfway up, she slipped and was about to slide back down when the man grabbed her by the wrist and pulled her up beside him.
"For God's sake, Claire!"
Claire looked up at the man; the moon lit his eyes and her fears melted away.
She was ten feet from her house, farther than she'd been for more than a year and she was not afraid. Mud covered her body, but she stood proud as if dressed in furs. Tears streamed down her face and she was happy.
"Claire, help me!"
Her husband's cries pattered her ears, and she felt nothing for him. Her focus was on the man.
Walk with me.
With a giggle, she answered. "I will."
And the man smiled for the first time—the radiant pledge of a new day. After he softly drew his hand over her cheek, he began to unbutton his coat. Slowly, one at a time, he worked his way down. Watching his fingers move, Claire felt faint with excitement, a virgin's anticipation bubbling in her gut. As he slipped the last button through the hole, the

coat flaps opened slightly, allowing a flash of bright light to leak out.

She gasped and teetered.

"Claire! Help me! Please!"

The man wrapped his fingers around the material and pulled, opening the coat wide to a world where Claire would never have to be afraid again. Silvery-white, glittery dust swirled over her feet. Shimmering particles showered over her like evanescent fire, transforming her to beautiful. She reached into the mist and stardust warmed her fingers.

"Claire?"

She looked over her shoulder and found Curtis lying in the doorway, his eyes an odd jumble of angry and sad. Grinning, she turned away and stepped one foot into the man's secret universe. A gust blew over her, tugging her hair away from her face, drying her tears, rippling the fabric of her sweatshirt. It was a feeling she had never felt before or could have imagined. Freedom. And love. And safety. The man was the answer to her prayers, the metaphysical realization of paradise. Claire inhaled a deep breath and slipped into the coat, disappearing into a glimmering cloud.

"Claire!"

*   *   *

Starbursts flashed on the man's coat and his eyes burned like bright white flames. He lifted his arms and light streamed from his sleeves in phosphorescent columns. He threw back his head and a loud retort pierced the night air, cracking the quiet like a rifle shot.

The rain stopped.

"Claire?" Curtis crawled over the threshold.

The man closed the coat, turned, and walked into the woods. Trees lit up around him like lamps. Swirling trails of glistening lights cut a path for his feet.

"Don't go." Curtis cuddled himself and watched the man walk away.

Soon, dense trees blocked his sight until all he could see were a few flickering dots, dipping and twirling amongst the branches like fireflies.

The wind whistled past his ears and Curtis thought he heard laughter.

"Claire?"

BEDBUGS

Corey didn't like him in her bedroom. Partial to solitude and perfection, cleanliness and order, his presence added clutter, made the room look dirty.

Her bookshelves were stocked according to size to keep a smooth line. (Books that didn't fit the plan had a place in the closet behind closed doors.) The white stucco walls were bare to avoid contrast with the minute floral print of the blue and beige sofa and overstuffed chair. Two blue throw rugs sat in front of each to keep the carpet from being soiled. Television, stereo, and movie player were stacked on a three-tiered wooden shelf, each one partnered with its respective remote control. All stood dust free.

She didn't like the way he whistled under his breath. The tune of "The Itsy Bitsy Spider" came from somewhere deep in his throat. It wasn't true whistling; rather an unnatural noise, an irritating sound produced as he forced air over his tongue and through his clenched teeth while he hummed.

...*went up the spout again*...

Agitated, she pecked the keyboard and wished him gone. How could she work with that man buzzing around, invading her space, bruising her ears with his eerie song? As soon as he'd stepped inside, her imagination had stepped out. The blank screen staring back at Corey remained as such. There'd be no award-winning short story that afternoon. With a cluck of her tongue, she peered around the monitor and watched him.

...The Itsy Bitsy Spider...

She didn't like the way he moved. He seemed to glide, to flutter on his tiny feet as he made his way around her small apartment. Beaten brown loafers carried him with the grace of a ballerina and the accuracy of a master thief. Soundless, he left nothing behind him, not even a footprint in the carpet.

...climbed up the waterspout...

He whistled his way around the bed and passed in front of the archway that separated the bedroom, kitchen, and bathroom from the living area.

...down came the rain...

She didn't like his face. His head was perversely round and sunk deep into the hollow of his shoulders, as if it had been set there with great force. His skin was flawless, without wrinkle or blemish. Eyes—shining black marbles sat close on either side of his tiny knob of a nose, bestowing a constant expression of wonder.

...and washed the spider...

Then he was in the hall, slowly making his way to the kitchen.

...out came the sun...

The words of the nursery rhyme buzzed through her mind—a patch of angry mosquitoes—as she watched the exterminator move.

She didn't like his body. His legs wobbled in his uniform slacks. Gaunt, anorexic, his limbs were a complete contradiction to his bulbous belly and barrel chest.

Corey snorted, snatched her eyes away, and strummed the keys as if in the process of tickling the letters, two or three might combine themselves together and give up a word, a sentence—anything.

Still nothing. She couldn't write. Her creative process was as tasteless and dry as the Thanksgiving turkey she expected to find at her father's house the next day. Dreaded celebration. Another forced family gathering, old wounds reopened and new injuries created. Mother's ashes on the kitchen counter, impossible to avoid. Last Christmas, Corey had wondered aloud at the feasibility of cremating a body bloated with cheap wine; then she'd lifted the urn, run it under her nose, and pronounced the bouquet "bitter and nauseating." Her father had cried and she'd almost regretted it enough to apologize.

The rest of the crew was freakish on the best of days. Aunt Rita, a psychic reader with a clientele of housewives and teenage girls looking for love. Her son, Frank, mama's boy with a face like a taco gone wrong. Uncle Norm. When was the last time he'd spoken? Silent and still, he added as much to life to a room as a doorstop.

And they'd all be together around the tiny kitchen table, dusty turkey, slippery yams, Rita's cigarette smoke, Frank's acne...

What a waste. How she wished she could avoid it and spend the day in the comfort of her own company. The thought of personal contact, senseless chatter...

A metallic clanking sound begged attention. The Bugman was in the kitchen, knocking the spray canister against his leg while he squirted his chemical into the utility closet.

...went up the...

She didn't like the color of his skin. White. Unnatural. The color of old bones, or the chilled skin of a cadaver.

She didn't like his hands. His skin was dry and taut on his bones, like twigs covered in a fleshless hull.

How long did it take to spray an apartment? It seemed he'd been there for hours. Worse, he was enjoying it. Humming and slinking about as if he knew his presence was an irritant and took pleasure in expanding the torture.

Miserable creature. She didn't like him. Nothing about him. Corey didn't like him at all.

As that thought fluttered through her mind, he looked up. His shining brown eyes punched her, and Corey lost her breath.

Halting his song, he smiled. Blanch lips, the color of modeling clay, cracked back over two rows of small teeth. Discolored. Yellow. They looked like dried-out bits of corn. Kernels of corn set in paste.

Corey didn't return the smile. Instead, she whipped her head away and stared out the window. The song began again.

The Itsy Bitsy Spider went up the waterspout...

Palm fronds battled the wind.

...down came the rain...

Gray clouds, outlined in black, promised to soak the earth.

...and washed the spider out.

It was still early, only four o'clock, but she knew she'd seen the last of the sun.

Out came the sun and dried up...

"Done."

*...all the rain...*Corey continued the song in the privacy of her mind.

"Done."

...and the Itsy Bitsy Spider...

"I'm done."

Corey gasped, shook, and looked up. He was beside her. They were shoulder to shoulder.

Anxiety morphed anger. "W—what?"

Quick, damp puffs, his breath warmed her hair while a candied perfume lingered in the air around him. "All done here."

His eyes locked onto hers and Corey's bowels danced. Something scalding and sour jumped from her stomach, burning the back of her tongue. Reflexively, she pulled back her hand, ready to swing out, wanting to swat him, squash him...but stopped.

Instead, she lowered her arms, pushed away from the monitor, and stood. A self-proclaimed expert at exits, she'd dispel him with quick sarcasm. "Oh? You're...you are..." No biting words? "You're..."

"Done."

"Done?"

"Yup. Done. Done what I came for."

"Oh, well, all right." Instinct told her to be quiet and allow him his leave, but her nervous tongue wagged. "Big waste of time, you know." She took a step back. "Like I told you before, I've never seen a single bug here. And I am really clean. As you can see, there isn't anything around here to attract a bug. Nothing." Another step. "Nope. Never a single bug. Not one."

His eyes twinkled underneath the brim of his cap—a flash of lightening behind a cloud. "People don't see what they don't want to see. People don't like bugs, so they don't see bugs. Don't like it, don't see it." His voice was enthusiastic and he trembled. "Don't like to think about the fly puking on a coffee spoon, or on the sandwich before they eat it. Can't stomach the thought of the cockroach crapping on their floors and on their counters and in their clothes. Don't see people looking too hard for the worm stuck to the bottom of the lettuce leaf, or the broccoli head, before they shove it into their mouth. No one looks at the dust on the walls left behind by the moth. And they don't give much thought about the diseased needle plunged into their arm by the mosquito, the same needle that they used to suck the blood from a dog...or a rat..."

Corey grimaced.

The Bugman giggled. "Don't take time to think about the spider that lives in the walls. Spinning its web just inches from their heads, sucking the life out of a living dinner while they dream in their beds." His expression turned wistful. "They're everywhere."

After he blinked several times, the Bugman grinned, turned his back to Corey, and sashayed to the door. When he'd opened it, he twisted around his head to face her, the quick motion producing an eerie sound like rice cereal popping in cold milk. He shimmied his shoulders and something crackled. "Sleep tight."

Corey shivered, the tiny tickling of a thousand ants trailing up her spine.

"Don't let the bedbugs bite."

His words whistled through the air and landed on her ears with a sting.

* * *

The knock startled her. Corey blinked, then scowled. How long had she been standing there staring at the closed door?

Another knock. She took a step and faltered. Her knees were stiff and achy. Scowling, rubbing her legs, Corey hobbled to the door and, without inquiry, pulled it open.

A voice rushed through the crevice, heavy with the smell of hops and barley. "Hey. Sorry to disturb you, but I wanted to tell you that you might want to park in the street for a couple of days. We're having the roof re-tarred and it might get on your car. You know, if you keep parking next to the building like you do."

Corey glared at the apartment manager with the same enthusiasm she'd offer a stain in her underwear. He'd a habit of walking the halls. She'd heard him shuffle to her door and stop many times. There he'd stand, she supposed to catch an audible glimpse of her private world. And when they met face-to-face in the hallway or on the sidewalk, she'd always cold-shoulder him on his way. His invasive stares made her skin crawl.

If he was aware or bothered by her distaste, he didn't show it. "Thought you'd want to know. The way you're always washing it and stuff. Hate to get it all tar." He stood silent as if awaiting an answer.

When Corey offered nothing, he turned to go.

"Wait!"

The manager turned back, his smile showing off a nice set of teeth, an immaculate contrast to his whiskered face and sweat-stained T-shirt. "Yeah?"

"Uh...thanks."

"No problem." Again he waited, boyish smile, eager eyes.

Corey stared silently until finally he shrugged and moved to leave.

"Wait!"

With the same obvious expectation, he drew around, grinned, and sucked in his gut. "Yeah? Can I do something for you?"

"The Bugman...the exterminator...is he on a schedule? I want to know when he's coming back."

Instant frown. The manager's lips mashed into the bottom of his nose. "Bugman?"

"Yes. Bugman. He was here today. Spraying."

"We don't have no Bugman."

"He was just here. I assumed that he worked for—" Fear strolled in and took a slow bite out of her tongue.

"No way. He don't work for me. You got a problem with bugs, you take care of it." The manager rubbed a newborn beard and snorted under his breath.

"He was—today! He sprayed."

"Must be a mistake. I don't know nothing about no Bugman. You sure you didn't call him yourself?" His bloated face and five o'clock shadow swallowed up his accusatory eyes as he nodded his fat head toward her in question.

"I didn't hire him! Why would I be asking you about it if I hired him? I don't have bugs!"

"Well, I'm sorry about...about whatever." Two steps back. "I'm glad you don't got..." Another. "I'm glad you don't got bugs." When the heel of his foot caught on the neighbor's welcome mat, the manger stumbled, turned, and hurried down the hall.

Corey stared at his back. "Pervert." She stepped inside, slammed the door closed, and leaned against it.

Sleep tight. Don't let the bedbugs bite.

So tired. It'd been a long and frustrating day. Stupid manager. Too busy undressing people with his eyes to keep tract of what's going on in his building. Blasted Bugman. Nasty little freak.

Sleep tight. The living room was dressed in shadows. Later than she'd thought. Time for bed? *Don't let the bedbugs bite.*

Corey turned her head, looked into the bedroom. *Sleep tight.* Slow feet carried her over the floor. *Don't let the bedbugs bite.* Heavy lids blurred her vision and she teetered.

Sleep tight. Don't let the bedbugs bite.

She stared at the bed, ran her fingers over the blue and white patchwork quilt. It would be so nice to lay down, to curl up, cuddle, to wrap up like a caterpillar in a...safe and warm...snug as a bug in a rug.

Sleep tight. Don't let the bedbugs bite.

She smiled and pulled back the covers. Freshly laundered sheets rippled, setting free the smell of manufactured spring. "Mmmm."

Sleep tight. Don't let the bedbugs bite.

The words blew through her mind like a swarm of locusts, so it was all she could hear, all she could see, all she knew.

* * *

Pain plucked her from sleep. A vicious stab in her throat, it felt like a hot iron, a flaming icicle had sunk through her flesh and buried in her esophagus. Immediately after the pain, came a wave of numb. Legs, arms, head, and chest all tingled for a moment, then went to sleep. Collective calm overcame her muscles.

Fear ravished her mind.

She couldn't move. Corey felt the weight of the quilt, the touch of the sheets on bare legs, her warm breath drifting over her lips, but she was immobilized. Her throat felt scorched as if she'd swallowed fire and it'd stuck halfway down. Struggling, making the sound of a death rattle, she was finally able to swallow a wad of stale spit. It did nothing to soothe the burn.

In her mind's eye she flexed her throat muscles and extinguished the fire. In her mind's eye she inhaled a lungful of air and screamed. In her mind's eye she kicked off the blankets and ran from the room.

In her bed, however, in the black of night, she lay still, frozen.

Questions choked her while terror tripped up and down her spine. What was happening? A stroke? Seizure?

Help me! Could she think a plea loud enough to summon help? *Help me! I can't move!*

And something moved. The covers.

The quilt and sheets slipped off her shoulders. Slow and methodical, the material pulled over her chest, belly, then hips. Fabric caught and nudged the elastic band of her panties—gentle like a lover teasing in the dark. Then a quick tug loosened the sheet and it slid down her thighs, knees, calves, and feet. Goosebumps danced on her flesh. How she wanted to pull up the covers, wrap them around her head, hide.

Exposed. Defenseless. She waited.

Weight bobbled on the mattress as if someone—something—had crawled onto the foot of the bed. Casually, it crept upward, brushing against her—tickling her ankles.

A moan choked in her throat and a single tear strolled a hot path over her temple and into her hair.

The mattress sagged and the bed frame groaned.

Cool and coarse, something rubbed against her bare calves.

The mattress shifted. Bedsprings rippled under her back and the thing slid up the length of the bed, graceful labor bringing it closer to her face, her eyes.

Corey fought the paralysis. If only she could move to defend, or at least make a sound. But her muscles remained unresponsive, and all she could force was a sad mewl.

If the intruder in her bed had noticed the noise, sensed her fear, it wasn't deterred. Rather, it continued to inch upward, slow and steady, the mattress shifting from side to side. Bristled appendages sidled her legs, brushed her hips. Something hard prickled the damp flesh on her arms.

Was it human? She prayed so, but knew it was not. The weight. The feel. Whatever had invited itself to her bed was monstrous. Corey whimpered, exercised her throat, begged a scream. Still nothing more than a wounded sob. But if no one could hear her cries, surely they could hear her heartbeat...loud...pounding in her ears...so loud it hurt. If she'd had the means she would have ripped open her chest and tore out the beating muscle simply to end the racket.

Help me!

The bed frame squealed. The intruder continued up.

Voices laughed in the street below, sounding like the slow dribble of partiers that took to the streets after last call. Corey fought to turn her head, throw her voice out the window to let them know she needed, "H—H—H—H—" Vocal cords twittered, but her plea remained secret. Another bout of laughter—a girl screaming playfully. So close. People...if only...

Help! Help me! Please! Help!

Then she smelled it, a sickening sweet aroma—a familiar odor that revived her memory. Tears pooled under her eyes, then spilled. Something caressed her cheek. Alive, quivering, inhuman, it lapped her tears.

Another creak and it was beside her. Corey felt a weight rise from the bed and settle above. She stared up, focused, and saw it.

Eight gangly legs, covered with sharp barbs, sprouted from a plump circular body. On one of the hooked black spikes hung a tattered piece of patchwork quilt. A small round head rested on top of the thing's massive chest. Eternally black, two eyes glared at her with joy. In the cool moonlight, its body and face shone like an oil slick. The mouth opened in a quivering smile. It was stuffed with small teeth. Sharp. Yellow. Kernels of corn set in paste.

Her bladder released. Corey ignored it. But she could not ignore the beast as he bent over her with his cotton-candy breath. She could not ignore him biting down. She could not ignore the feel of his teeth ripping her flesh, locking onto her shoulder bones.

Corey gurgled on tears.

Then she was moved. Secure in the creature's jaw, her body turned. Corey watched the cracked pattern of the ceiling tiles rotate. The overhead light came into sight, the opaque glass covering the bulb littered with the dusty corpses of a dozen insects, their gray powdery husks muting the glow.

The light drifted out of sight and Corey saw the window, remembered the people out there and tried to call out again. "H—H—H—"

The moon shone bright and full and looked like it was smiling. Then suddenly it swirled into a cyclone of light and Corey heard a sharp thud. A million little flashes exploded before her eyes and a snap like bones smacking together filled her ears.

On the floor. When her vision recovered, she saw her bare feet wag in front of her, then slip out of sight. Her body turned sideways and she faced the dark space under the bed.

The creature dragged her there, past the rusted bed frame, under the springs clotted with dust balls and yellowed wads of fiberfill, and to the wall, where several inches above the baseboard, was a hole.

The spider pushed through it, knocking the opening wider, then carried Corey through it, to the space within the wall. It was illuminated with a ghostly light that leaked in from minute cracks in the wallboard. The glowing slivers looked like alien rays piercing the dark. Nestled within the silvery shadows lay the web.

The monster unlocked his jaw. Corey dropped from his mouth, fell face down, then rolled once until the glistening strings caught her. Suspended in the gooey hammock, she opened her eyes wide, adjusted to the light, and spotted a gray mass inches from her face. It was large, humanoid, and from between the clingy threads, frozen in a claw-like pose, a boy's hand reached forward. Outlined with the spider's threads, a dark brown eye stared back.

A scream scrambled up and down her vocal cords before frittering out.

And once again, Corey was moved. Her body was lifted, then

turned around and around. She felt something warm and wet cling to her skin and knew she was being mummified, envisioned her body being swallowed up in a silken wrap—like the boy's.

Around and around she spun, each revolution bringing her back to face the eye. Feet, calves, and legs were meticulously wrapped, she always finding the eye, it always there and staring back, wide-awake at sleep.

Turn after turn the eye remained her focal point, until suddenly, the cocoon holding the boy jiggled.

Gluey fibers wrapped around her belly, she twirled back and the quivering cocoon ripped, a black gash separating it in two.

She spun, returned, and the sack fell open as a wiggling black leg popped through.

Her arms fell into place and sticky strings covered her chest and shoulders. She found the boy's cocoon in time to see a spider the size of a kitten emerge. Then another. And another. And another. And another.

She spun, and a dozen newly hatched spiders swarmed over the boy.

She spun.

On wobbling legs, they spread over him, then in a single seemingly choreographed motion, they latched onto the fibers and sunk their fangs deep.

She spun.

A slurping, greedy noise filled the airspace.

Corey moaned, her voice lifting over the sound of the feast.

And the spinning continued. Around and around, Corey always finding the boy's eye, taking comfort in his eye, needing to look at his eye, having to keep her attention off the little beasts devouring the corpse.

After she spun a final spin, covered to her neck in gluey fibers, Corey was dropped and settled beside him.

So close. So close she could feel...heat. And more. His eye. Dark, staring eye. A single tear formed...and fell.

* * *

"Alive!"

Something tugged, had a hold of her arm. Bursts of light came and went.

"She's in there tight. Lucky she didn't smother."

"Alive! He's alive!"

"Grab her feet and I'll unroll her."

Roughly, her body jounced and twirled and she focused on the light. A dusty globe dotted with dead bugs. Her bedroom light?

"He's alive!"

Faces peered down at her, making a broken circle.

"Yeah! Whatever. Knock off the yelling. The whole building's coming awake." The apartment manager rubbed his beard and shook his head. "Man, she's always been a nut, but I've never seen her this bugged out."

Needles shot into her veins as hands pulled off the last knot of her bed sheet.

"No! Let me go!" She swung out, but someone grabbed her wrist.

"Just get her out of here, will ya? My tenants got enough problems without her freaking them out."

"There, there, Little Miss Muffett, you don't want to hurt anyone, now, do you?"

The voice was irritating, made her scared, and Corey tried to fight again, but a warm wave shuttled through her body and she couldn't move. Her body relaxed and she sighed.

"That's better, now, isn't it?"

Corey wobbled her head to find the owner of the voice. It'd come from a small man dressed in the colors of the Fourth Of July. Blue slacks, red shirt, white patches on his chubby chest. His fingers were kneading IV tubing, and he was smiling down at her, humming.

The Itsy Bitsy Spider went up the...

His lips pulled up in a smile to show his teeth. Small. Yellow. Kernels of corn set in paste.

Down came the rain and...

She screamed the sound of a train wreck, steel wheels screeching to a halt on rusted rails.

FREEZE FRAME

Lilly had her hand in her pocket. Arthritic fingers held the picture tight as she made her way down the hall. Floors buffed to a high shine. Air scented in institutional antibacterial lemon. Sound absorbent ceiling panels did little to disguise the soft echoes of patients and nurses, the patter of footsteps, or squeak and rattle of the medicine cart. A constant jumble of sounds; there was never absolute quiet.

"Lilly?"

She turned to her name, but did not answer.

"You going in to dinner?"

She looked from the floor nurse to the dining area, then back. "No."

"Aw, come on. Open-faced roast beef sandwiches today. I saw a nice green salad and fruit cup, too. I know you like fruit cup. If you go in and join the others, I'll see what I can do about getting you an extra. How about that?"

That would be a nice treat. Lilly almost smiled. She liked Holly. The young girl was a good nurse and treated her patients with a respect and decency that most of the veteran nurses had abandoned years ago.

Again, Lilly looked toward the dining area. After a moment, she shook her head and ran her free hand through her frazzled gray hair. "No. I don't want to go in there." She added to her pout and pulled up her eyes to Holly. "Can I take it in my room? I am really hungry. I can't eat…they all…I just can't go in there."

Holly stuffed a pen behind her ear and wrapped her arm around Lilly. "You know you can't eat in your room every day. If you ever want to get out of here, you have to be able to associate with other people. You can't keep hiding in your room. You've come so far, Lilly. Aren't you about ready to take another step?"

"I..."

"Whacko!"

Stuck together in Holly's hug, both women turned to the voice. Sadie walked toward them, two fingers held up in a peace sign. "Hey! You must be the whacko old lady I heard about. Lost your whole family?" A piercing cackle sputtered from between a sideways smile.

Lilly pulled away from the nurse and shivered. Sadie's reputation preceded her. Manic-depressive, borderline paranoid, Sadie had been a resident of Hillside, a privately owned mental hospital, on and off her entire life. The last stay was pronounced by the court after she'd tried to kill a delivery man. Apparently, he'd handed her a package, then asked for a signature. It'd been a bad day for Sadie and his intrusion into her "safe place" had pushed her over the edge. She'd grabbed the pen and driven it into his chest. The pen had lodged near his heart before finally breaking in half. Good thing for him. Stopped the blood flow. The doctor's had been able to save his life.

"I didn't loose them." Lilly ducked her head and hid as much of her face as was possible in the collar of her sweater. Severe depression and withdrawal. She knew her diagnosis was evident in her appearance, speech, eyes—her entire being.

"A liar and a turtle." Sadie took a quick step toward Lilly.

With the speed of a trained professional, Holly intercepted, throwing out her arm and catching Sadie across the chest. The nurse's cool blue eyes carried a warning that she also put into words. "If you can't behave, Sadie, I'll see to it you spend a few days back in B Ward. How about that? You want to go back there? I'd think you'd like the extra freedom here. More privacy. Better food. It'd be a shame to have to go back so soon."

"Oh no! I'm not going back there. You see the loonies that live there? Buncha nuts!" Her volatile temperament shifted, Sadie's smile turned down and she looked at Libby as if genuinely concerned. "Hey, sorry, old woman. Heard the rumors, is all. Heard you lost your family."

Lilly took a step backward. "My family went away. They went away and left me behind." Lilly snuck her hand back into her pocket and found the picture. Tenderly, she brushed the surface with her fingertips. It felt warm. Soothing and sad.

"Yeah? Lucky you. If you spent any time with *my* family, you'd wish they'd do the same." Sadie's emotional thermostat convulsed and she laughed. A round of eerie giggles bounced off the walls.

Holly tried to change the subject. "Sadie, you had your dinner yet?"

"No. I was going there when I saw this one." She pointed at Lilly. "Thought I'd introduce myself."

"Lilly?" Holly's voice was gentle. Lilly wanted to ignore it, but couldn't. She turned to the nurse. "Sadie was going in to dinner. You want to go with her? She's a little noisy, but it's mostly talk. She really is a nice lady."

Lilly peeked over the nurse's shoulder. Sadie watched her with the eyes of a hawk and suddenly, Lilly felt like a mouse, a tiny rodent in a field under the shadow of a deadly predator.

Sadie opened her mouth and twisted it to form the word "Whacko," while she drew curly-cues in the air by her head with her finger.

Lilly made her decision. "No. I'm not hungry."

Holly sighed. "You need to eat and Sadie would be company."

Sadie pushed up her nose like a pig snout. "Yeah! Come on. I'll be good company. You can tell me why you're here. Maybe we can figure where your family went."

"Sadie!" Hands on hips, Holly scolded her patient. "I swear, if moods were colors, you'd be a rainbow."

A single tear fell onto Lilly's cheek as she turned and walked away.

"Lilly? I'll bring you in something later. I'll—"

Lilly was already in her room. She didn't like to shut the door on Holly, but she had to get away from Sadie and her chatoyant personality.

Safely inside, Lilly relaxed a little, and moved to the window. She looked down at the grassy lawn and found Mr. Chapel. The old man was seated on a bench, hands rubbing up and down his legs. Up. Down. Up. Down. Obsessive compulsive, he couldn't keep his hands still. Up. Down. Up. Down. His children paid for his stay—a private room. They didn't visit him anymore. Hands on legs. Up. Down. Up. Down. His irritating behavior separated him from the rest of the patients, so he sat outside whenever possible. Up. Down. Up. Down. When he came in, he played with the light switches. On. Off. On. Off. They'd disabled the switch in his room, but he fondled it anyway.

Lilly watched him. Up. Down. Up. Down. Mindless, she ran her hands over her legs. After a moment, she shook her head and blinked. He was contagious. She stepped away from the window and Mr.

Chapel, lay on the bed, and took the picture out of her sweater pocket. Immediately, tears came to her eyes.

Freeze Frame. Her granddaughter, Caitlin, was on her knees in a chair next to the kitchen table. A birthday cake was lit up in front of her. Six candles burned. Next to her stood Lilly's daughter, Melody, mouth spread in a wide smile. By Melody's side was Kevin, Lilly's son-in-law. The young couple in the picture had their eyes cast down, watching their daughter.

Make a wish, Granny!
Caitlin, you're the birthday girl, you make a wish.
You too, Granny. We'll both make a wish.
Make a wish, honey. Make a wish and blow!
I wish...
Don't say it out loud. It won't come true.

Lilly relived the birthday party every day, all day. Where the voices left off, there was the picture.

She sniffled, wiped her hand over her nose, and stared. The photograph throbbed in her hand.

Freeze Frame. The three people she loved more than life itself only a fingerprint away. Guilt overwhelmed, but the picture, the moment caught forever in time...

"You all right in here?"

Holly pushed open the door and walked to the bed. In her hand she held a fruit cup and a spoon.

Lilly tried to slip the picture back into her sweater, but Holly saw it. "That the picture?"

"Yes."

"Can I see it?"

Lilly quivered. She didn't like to share the picture. Even though she cared for Holly—loved her—Lilly was hesitant.

"You don't have to."

Relieved, Lilly smiled weakly. She looked at Holly for a moment, stared into her eyes, then in a remarkable show of trust, turned it so the nurse could see.

"Your family?"
"Yes."
"Beautiful. Happy."
"It's her birthday."
"The little girl?"
"Yes. Caitlin."

"She looks very happy. She's really going for those candles."

Enough. Lilly turned the picture away. "Yes."

"And she's six?"

Even though Lilly was aware Holly knew the answers to the questions, she responded. "She's six. Six years old."

"That's a great age. I have a niece who's ten. Another good age."

Lilly's lips pulled down. Her chin dimpled, then trembled.

Holly continued. "And that's your daughter?"

"Melody. She just got her hair cut that day. I think she favors me with her new haircut."

"Well, I never saw her with longer hair, but from what I could see in the picture, I would agree. She does favor you."

"Kevin liked it longer, but he told her she'd be pretty bald. He's a nice boy."

"He looks nice. He has a kind smile. They make a nice couple."

"Yes."

"That is a great picture. Everyone's so happy. Cheerful. I see why you like it so much."

A tear dripped from Lilly's eye.

"Lilly? I don't know what happened to your family. It's a horrible unanswered question and I'm sorry. But don't you think it would be a good idea to put the picture away for a little while? Wouldn't you like to see what it would be like to take a step forward and let the past be in its proper place?"

Lilly shook. Dew dampened her lips. The picture disappeared into her sweater pocket. "No. No. No." Lilly left her hand there and held the photo close.

"Don't you think that whatever happened, wherever they are, they would want you to go on with your life and be happy with the memories you have? It's obvious that you loved them and they loved you. They wouldn't want you to be so sad for so long. It's been almost a year now."

Lilly crumbled into a ball and rocked back and forth, the stiff mattress making a sound like dry leaves crumbling. "It's all my fault!"

"Can't be your fault. Come on, Lilly. Stop this!"

"I wish. I wish. I wish. I wish." She rocked and cried.

"You can't wish them back."

"I wish. I wish. I wish."

Make a wish, Granny!

With the flash of the camera...Freeze Frame.

"I wished them into the picture! It's a magic camera! God, forgive me! I wished them into the picture!"

"Lilly! Snap out of it! I won't listen to any more of this." The nurse hugged Lilly.

"She's a real whacko!"

Sadie stood in the doorway. A gravy stain had blossomed on her shirt. "Loo-ooo-ny tune! I know a nut case when I see one."

Holly jumped from the bed. "Sadie, you're a human ping-pong ball. Get out of here." She grabbed Sadie by the shoulder and led the woman away.

* * *

Night in the hospital was an eerie time. Artificial quiet. Drugged silence. A dim yellow beam colored the hallways, the light bouncing off the blue and white polished tiles and reflecting dully in stainless steel doorknobs. Patients lay in their beds like stacks of cordwood, lumps under crisp sheets. Most of them looked forward to the night and the dreams that came with it. For a few, however, no amount of medication could silence the mind enough for peaceful sleep.

Pure insanity was a blessing. The truly insane didn't know they were crazy. To teeter on the brink was terror. To be able to imagine insanity, feel it, taste it, and know it wasn't to be, kindled the deepest fear. Lilly's fear.

She sat in the chair beside her bed and watched the moon slowly make a path across the sky, all the while wishing for madness to take her away. The guilt of the photo combined with the desire to be with her family was too painful. Lunacy would be a sweeter ride.

She took the picture out of her pocket and looked down.

Freeze Frame.

Lilly pressured her fingers against the photograph. Barely perceptible, she could feel pulsations. With her eyes closed, she listened and heard each individual heartbeat.

"What you got there, Lilly?"

Startled, she dropped the picture onto her lap. Sadie. Her shadow drooled over the floor like an oil spill.

"N—nothing."

"The picture? Your family?"

"Nothing!"

"Let me see it."

"Go away."

"You got the guiltiest conscience I ever met."

"Get out. Get out of my room!"

"Make me."

Sadie approached one step. "Let me see the picture, then I'll go."

"No."

"I'm not leaving until I see it."

"No."

Sadie flew at Lilly with amazing speed. A powerful combination of anti-depressants and tranquilizers should have slowed her down, however, her feet seemed to glide on air. With a snap, she snatched the picture from Lilly's lap.

Sadie held the photo close to her eyes as she spun away. "Cute. Cute. Cute."

"Give me back my family!" Lilly stood, then settled on her haunches like a lioness ready to pounce.

Sadie wagged the photograph in the air and danced.

"I got the who-ole wor-rld in my hands. I got Lilly's little wor-rld in my hands. I got the who-ole—"

"Give me that…or…I'll…I'll…"

"You'll what?" Sadie was energized. Merriment lit her eyes.

Lilly lunged, caught Sadie by the arm, spun her around, and punched her.

"Ow!" Sadie stopped dancing and turned to face Lilly. Childlike sadness tugged a scowl. "Hey. I'm just playing." Sadie dropped her arm and cautioned a look. "Here." She held out the picture while rubbing her sore arm. Lilly gripped the corner, but Sadie jerked it back.

"Psych!"

Lilly growled, tackled Sadie, and snatched the picture. Sadie screamed. The photo ripped in two.

Cease-fire. Both women stood tense. The photograph hung in Lilly's hand. Fluid dripped from her fingers. Multicolored. Red. Blue. Purple. Green. Yellow. Brown. Black. A slick psychedelic puddle grew on the floor at her feet.

Two sets of eyes looked down, then simultaneously, back up to Lilly's hand and the damaged photo. It throbbed visibly. Pulses of color squirted from the tear.

Another round of screams, louder.

Lilly pressed her fingers around the photograph. A kaleidoscopic stream bubbled through.

Sadie's face crumbled. "It's alive." Her tone was soft. "There's people in the picture." Louder. "There's people in the picture!" The volume of her voice increased. "There's people in the picture." Her exclamation seemed to shake the heavy panes of shatterproof window glass. "It's alive! There's people in the picture! There's people in the picture!"

Lilly moaned and applied pressure to the tear. Fluid throbbed from the cut, burbled over her hands, and splattered the front of her nightgown.

"There's people in the picture. There's people in the picture! God save me! It's alive!"

Two nursing assistants rushed the room. One big. One small. Both wore frowns. "How did you get in here?" They charged Sadie.

"It's alive!"

"Calm down now, Sadie. You relax."

"There's people in the picture! There's people in the picture!"

Four arms wrapped around Sadie and dragged her from the room.

As soon as they were gone, Lilly pulled up the picture, holding her fingers over the tear. Color spurted.

Freeze Frame. Caitlin was on her knees in a chair next to the kitchen table. Her purple dress had faded to pink. A birthday cake sat before her, chocolate frosting the color of clay. Six candles burned butter-yellow flames.

Lilly cuddled the picture and cried. Colored fluid sputtered.

"What happened in here?"

She cried and did not turn to Holly's voice.

"What did Sadie do?" Holly walked toward Lilly and slipped. "What the..." She windmilled her arms, then balanced and pointed to the mess on the floor. "What is this?"

Lilly didn't answer. She clutched the picture in her wrinkled hands and snuggled it close to her heart.

Holly's soft-soled shoes squished in the spill. "What happened?"

"They're dying. They're dying."

"Who?"

"Help them. Please, help them." Lilly held out the picture.

The flow had eased to a light drip.

Freeze Frame. Caitlin's dress had faded to tan. Melody's brown hair, gray. Kevin's blue eyes, blurred, the color of wallboard. The chocolate frosted cake looked like a lump of sand.

"Oh my..." Holly covered her mouth with one hand and took the picture in the other.

"Help them. Please, you have to help them. Bleeding. Bleeding to death."

Freeze Frame. Caitlin's dress was dingy white, the outline fuzzy. Melody had rippled into a dirty smear. Kevin had disintegrated into a fine charcoal mist.

Bright liquid beads dropped onto the bed.

Freeze Frame. The bodies in the picture had clouded into ashen mounds.

A solitary drop of purple, marbled with yellow and green, clung to the corner of the tear.

Freeze Frame. They were gone.

"Ohhhh! No! No!"

The droplet broke free.

Holly dropped the photo. It landed in the damp colorful swirl that'd formed on the blue blanket.

Lilly fell over it, curled into a ball, and rocked. "They're dead! They're dead! They're dead! Sadie killed my family. Murderer. Murderer."

* * *

Lilly stood outside the fenced yard, purse over her shoulder, camera in hand. Eyes squinted against the sun, she peered through the loose links. The hospital sat in the far corner of the property like a brown smudge in an otherwise colorful landscape.

Every day for the past three months she'd gone there.

She'd been free for nearly a year. Hypersensitive personality. Inexplicable chemical reactions. The great diagnosticians had puked their opinions. With pompous psychiatric confidence, they'd dismissed what had happened as a freak incident. Even Holly had ascribed to the theories. After several months bouncing between wards, insisting her family had been murdered while being entrapped within a photograph taken by a magical camera, Lilly had finally performed for them. In order to secure her release, she'd falsely accepted their explanations. Deemed cured from both delusions and depression, she'd been released.

"Depression my behind. Illusions be damned. I know what's what. She killed my family." It felt good to speak the truth out loud. "Sadie killed my family."

Lilly looked at her watch. Three o'clock. Recreation would soon commence.

The side doors of the building opened and a handful of patients from A Ward stepped into the sun. Mr. Chapel went directly to the bench, sat, and stroked his legs. Two female patients walked hand in hand to the flower garden. Several nurses gathered in a group to smoke and exchange the latest hospital gossip.

Lilly exhaled sadly. Today would not be the day. Sadly, she opened her purse, ready to drop the camera inside.

"Wacko!"

Lilly snapped her head up, followed the voice, and found her. Sadie. She stood next to Mr. Chapel, her lips pulled into a sharp smile so she looked like a snapping turtle.

Up. Down. Up. Down. Mr. Chapel's hands worked over his slacks.

"You're a nut case, old man. A real loony. I don't know what you're doing, but if you don't stop soon you'll rub your legs right off. Yep. You crazy wacko, you'll rub yourself away."

Up. Down. Up. Down. He didn't respond. Up. Down. Up. Down.

Sadie had set the stage perfectly. Lilly fingered the camera and made a sympathetic wish. *Poor old man. All alone and weary. I wish he'd be still.*

The camera clicked. After a metallic whine and a snap, a photograph popped from the machine. "You'll be happier this way, Mr. Chapel." Lilly grabbed the picture, slipped it into her sweater pocket, and immediately brought the camera back up and aimed.

Sadie hopped up and down in place, her finger pointed to the empty bench. "He...he...he disappeared!"

Through the view window, Lilly watched and smiled.

"Son-of-a-gun! The man disappeared! Oh help me! Oh my...oh help!"

Lilly steadied the camera. "Sadie, you crazy, nasty woman, you killed my family." She made a wish, pushed a button, and Sadie disappeared. Gears rolled. A picture slid out. Lilly snatched it, dropped it into her pocket, turned, and walked away.

Screams came from the fenced yard. Incredible noises.

Lilly held her purse in one hand, camera in the other. An arthritic finger itched on the red button. According to the numerical readout, she had seventeen pictures left.

LOVE AFTER DEATH

Put aside, if you will, any preconceived notions you may have regarding haunts and the afterlife. Until you've been there, I assure you, it's all moot theory.

Now, being human, as I'm sure you are and as I once was, I realize you are set in your ways and probably not easily swayed. It is necessary, however, to continue this story with the clearest of body, mind, and soul.

Body? Indeed!

Goodness me! Dear reader, it is also necessary that you find patience with me, as I have a tendency to unleash my humor randomly and without provocation.

Ah! Comedy! How useful to conceal the darkest of deeds and the most heinous of crimes. Not only has my comedic attitude been a blessing in masking my somewhat macabre activities, but I can also attribute finding the love of my…death…to this newfound mentality.

Oh blessed are we to be together, the bunch of jolly old souls that we are today!

Excuse me? Who am I? How did we all come to be?

Many questions. Please, sit and let me tell you. It is a story that pours easily from my lips. Oh! And do let the candles burn. This is not a tale to be told in the uncharted passages of the dark.

My name is Winston, Winston Pearl. I was born, raised, and met my death in this very house. As a man, I occupied these rooms for fifty-two years. In death, my residence totals another forty. So, all in all, I have lived here, in one form or the other, for nearly a century.

What? Leave here?

Never! The mere thought of passage from this existence to the bright scalding light beyond scares me to death!

Alas! Please excuse me! I swear, I'll try to keep more to the story and less to the jest if I'm able. Both fun and laughter are new to me and I find myself quite attracted to both. After enduring the varied dreadful pains required to reach this plane of existence, I've found that a chuckle here or a giggle there is good medicine for the soul.

Anyhow, back to the facts. I wasn't always this content, mind you. When I first made my entrance into this world beyond I was desperately lonely. A Spartan and solitary man in my past life, I had never suffered as I did in my new fatal beginning. And even as meaningless and hollow as it had been, I missed being alive!

Cursed was the day I died! Cursed was the day my soul passed from my tortured body, destined to eternally linger and wander the haunting halls of this house, my home.

Why, it was nearly two months before any living soul made the discovery of my death! As it happened, a lowly bill collector came to visit one dreary day and noticed my home in disrepair, apparently vacated. He assumed that I had spirited away without bringing current my debts and immediately sent for the sheriff, whereby my house was seized by strangers!

Now. Stop here. Take a moment to imagine my despair. Poor me! The forgotten ghost! After having watched my physical body succumb to the nasty stages of decay and witnessing wretched vermin gnaw the meat from my bones, I was then forced to stand defenseless whilst strangers bagged my remains in disgust. I was heartbroken to observe that I had been reduced to nothing more than a sack of musty rubble. Those horrid creatures—both man and mouse!—wasted no time in stripping my home of all that had made it mine, pleasure in the job obvious in their eyes!

Dejected, shocked, filled with sorrow, I remained in painful solitude, a sad, sad soul.

Oh! The horror! Death was dastardly!

Appalling in thought?

Horrendous in the physical realization!

There are so many facets of death of which I'm sure you aren't even aware. We feel! Oh yes! Can you comprehend the biting irony? After enduring an entire life with all the God-given feelings that made living life hell, I found myself plagued with those same emotions in death!

Suffer?

This is not an appropriate word to describe the agony. I, the same fellow who previously denounced the afterlife, determined that body and soul ceased to exist as one, now stood in grave error. It wasn't so! I suffered terribly. It appeared that my death would be no more rewarding than my life. Depression invaded my soul like an incurable disease.

It was at the time when I thought I could no longer bear the heavy burden of my despair that everything changed. A young family moved into my home. And although at first I felt invaded upon, I admit my spirit rejoiced in the shocking transformation.

They appeared to be a genteel family. Two parents and two children. The elders seemed like good, kind folk, and the youngest of their offspring—a boy—was well mannered for his age, which I guessed to be about three. All this aside, however, the most fantastic addition, my saving grace, was the eldest child.

The daughter.

Exquisitely beautiful in a round and healthy way, she grasped at womanhood with the most perfect vigor. I guessed her to be sixteen. And as she toured my home, touching everything with youthful curiosity and excitement, she gave the old rooms new meaning.

New life!

I was rejuvenated. At long last, the afterlife supplied a taste of happiness!

Her name was Rebecca.

Ah, that name! As lovely as the girl, it suited her spirit like a well-worn glove.

I fell immediately in love with her...

Love...

In love with her...

With her.

And now I must take momentary pause. This frivolous emotion was new to me. In my past life, I had completely rejected the notion of love and romance. As far as I was concerned, all that rubbish was for the ignorant and weak of personality. Like humor, I had no need for the distraction.

In my new spiritual residence, however, in the dark yet wondrous plateau beyond, I found that I had motive and means to draw upon this extraordinary emotion.

Hopelessly in love, I yearned for my little Rebecca in a way I thought myself incapable.

If I could have, I would have died for her. If I had been able, I would have...

And yet again, I wander in my words, stray from my tale, lead away on tangents. Regrets to you. My story progresses.

The family settled in, each taking to his own routine.

From my ever-present voyeuristic perch, I watched, amused, contented for the most part, until I realized that a bird's-eye view was unsatisfactory, the separation too great. More, my attentions had mutinied, their sole intent focused only on Rebecca. I realized she had become more than a preoccupation.

She had become an obsession.

Obsession.

A devouring, driving desire.

Desire.

She was the liquid to quench my thirst when all was parched, stale and dry in my wretched soul. Yes, I admit my insatiable need to be with, to feel, and to touch, my Rebecca completely took control of my already jumbled mind. I knew I would not rest in these halls until I had made some effort, taken action to make her notice me.

Well, action I did take!

And notice me?

She did!

It happened one evening after I had tucked behind her reflection in the vanity looking glass. From this vantage point, I was able to watch as she drew her brush ever so softly, sensuously, through her long auburn hair. Ah! That hair! The colors. Delicious. Beyond fall, to the winter sunset. Warm sun slipping behind frosted mountains, leaving trials of gold on the snow. With each pull of the brush, she stroked not only her silken strands, but my heart strings.

All at once, I lost control. The sensations...the vision of...I reached out my phantom fingers through the looking glass and I tried to...

What a horrific mistake!

The glass shattered!

How?

I didn't know! I don't know.

Truly! How was I to predict the outcome to my simple and sincere show of affection?

And Rebecca?

Well, as she sat there bathed in innocence, she witnessed her image diffract into a million spidery cracks.

Splinters, glistening shards of glass, tinkered at her feet.

Decorations for delicate toes.

Like dangerous diamonds sprinkled, a dusting of...

Oh! Oh! Excuse me!

The image. I was simply picturing...excuse me. Where was I?

Oh! Yes! The mirror. In response to this phenomenon, Rebecca opened her sweet pink lips and loosed a most hideous scream.

Oh my! How that tiny girl screamed.

The last thing I remember was watching her run from the bedroom, auburn locks trailing behind, remarkably reminiscent of a royal cap caught in the flirting fingers of a sudden breeze.

It was with that snippet of bittersweet imagery etched in my mind that I took my leave.

I felt it best to go away, then, for a little while.

I was mortified, baffled with my newfound capabilities, and I felt a solicitous week of soul searching, spiritual mending, would do me good. As you have probably guessed from my aforementioned lack of willpower, however, I was sooner to leave self-proclaimed exile than anticipated. My feelings for Rebecca bested my good sense.

So once more, I sought her presence. And again, I found her in her room.

This evening she was seated on her bed, lost in concentration, deep into something held tightly in her hand.

What was it?

Why! A letter! Words of love scribed to MY...to MY...

How did I feel?

Dare you ask? I was outraged!

The wanton look in her eyes! The despicable, traitorous little... Disloyalty! In my home! In m—my presence!

My anger was justified. I snatched the letter from her dainty white hand, crunched it into an edible wad, and popped it into my mouth.

What to do, then?

Why, what else? Swallow! I swallowed the letter whole!

Viola! The problem seemed to be solved.

Alas! I was dead wrong. Rebecca screamed another ghastly howl, then ran straightforward to the safety of her mother's arms.

Now this abrupt end to my second grand appearance should have upset me. I should have felt a little remorse.

But I did not. Instead, I felt quite wonderful! Indeed!

And my joy burgeoned in days to come.

Not only had I forced the attention of my love, but my activities caused much talk within the household. The more little Rebecca insisted her room was haunted, the more her father proclaimed her an overanxious girl in need of extra concentration spent on schoolwork and less time spent primping for the town ruffians. Mummy and the boy, however, talked about me as if I was real. In their eyes, I was a harrowing entity. The nervous trio of believers respected me and my powers more than I could have imagined!

Proud! Proud! Proud!

I was so very proud of myself. And wouldn't you be?

Of course! And I grew prouder each day, listening to them talk amongst themselves in hushed whispers. The child staring wide-eyed at his mother and Rebecca blushing, her delicate hands clutched to a blossoming bosom.

My delight overflowed. And—listen to this—when I laughed, the youngster would turn in my direction! At those moments, when I vocalized my emotions, it appeared the little dickens could hear me!

Poor boy!

Alas, how he suffered under my assault—The Mischievous and Merciless Winston Pearl! I played many dreadful tricks on the little man, all of which sent him directly to his mummy, or to Rebecca, for comfort.

Jealous I was. How I wish she could have cuddled me as she did her younger brother.

So you can see that, even though I had ample distraction with my pranks and hoaxes, everything I did brought me back to Rebecca.

Thoughts. Feelings. Heart and soul.

Deeper and deeper I fell.

More and more I became consumed with a grim hunger.

Stop?

I could not! How I tried!

I swear to you, on my death, I did. I tried.

Love, lust, passion? I was but a novice armed to the teeth with indeterminate powers, trapped in the playing board of a treacherous game of which I knew not the rules. Everything I had become, all that I was in this afterlife, was in contrast to what I had been before.

I had been a bland man. An accountant. Boring. Bachelor. Cold.

Certainly not the affable sort to whom you listen. So, this new high-spiritedness delighted me beyond narration. I felt free! And although I know this is incorrect, I felt alive!

Love had ignited a fire, resurrected my dead heart, and fueled my poltergeist activities. I was becoming incorrigible with my lust for merriment, and it occurred to me that it was time to supplement my existence before my celebrations forced me to loose all control.

I decided my beloved should join me.

The construction of a workable plan consumed my thoughts for every waking moment. I had to have Rebecca, but I needed to be certain her demise was as pleasant as possible for her, thereby insuring her spirit to be as content as mine.

How?

I concluded to take her whilst she slept.

Could I, a frolicking spirit, somehow take her life and whisk her soul into my lusting arms as she lay lost in the dreams of the innocent?

This I did not know.

With no one to guide me, and without proper instructions, I set about to test my plan on my own. It seemed appropriate to attempt this feat with the little dickens first. If my theory worked with him, then I would take my Rebecca precisely the same way.

Here is what I did.

Late one evening, after the family was asleep, I entered the little one's room. Sparing the details, let me just say I was quick, and soon the rascal's spirit, all confusion and wonder, was nestled against mine.

Inquisitively, he looked from me, to his lifeless body, and back again. He repeated this action several times. Then, in his naiveté, he commanded himself to wake up. I laughed and ruffled his feathery hair.

I must declare, by this time I had developed a fondness for the tyke and I was pleased to have him by my side. Momentarily, however, fondness was unrequited.

He tried to dash away from me, and I had to spiritually grab him and make him stay. Sparing no words, I simply told him that he was dead. As his hand tightened anxiously in mine, I quickly assured him I was also quite dead and perfectly happy to be so.

Thankfully, he calmed, and I was able to tell him of all the many and wonderful things available to him in the afterlife. Alas, youth is so easily persuaded that soon he was appeased and again snuggled by my side.

Joy! Joy! Joy!

I can't explain the thrill of having a companion after all that time!

So before you accuse or condemn me, please remember my joy! Also, consider the feelings of the newborn ghost, as he was happy, too!

As if he was my own son, I scooped up the baby spirit and together we set forth on a tour of the house. Lovely trip, and all was well until we entered his parent's room. As soon as he saw his mummy, he began to wail.

This was something I had not envisaged.

I also had not anticipated the mother hearing her son's cries from beyond.

Goodness! What a mess I had made! Why, if the little specter was going to cry every time he laid eyes on his mum, then my plan would never work. Quickly, I embraced the small spirit and implored upon him this question. "If your mummy was with you here, now, would you be quite content?"

He sniffed ghost snot up his nose and nodded.

So be it. I had no other choice.

Really! I didn't!

Well, scoff me if you must, but I would like to continue.

By now, the mother had made her way down the hall, quick feet fast approaching her son's room. I rushed forward, hefted the rug, and snagged one foot. Praise be to my expeditious interception, she lost her balance and sailed straight away tumbling down the stairs. As luck would have it, her neck snapped, and by the time she stilled at the bottom, she was more than ready to join my clan.

I can see the distaste in your eyes and I implore upon you to continue. Before you waste your sorrow and tears on the woeful mistress, continue.

There was a hidden side to the gentle loving mummy. Ugly. A side I was most shocked to encounter. When the madam's spirit finally gave up the ghost, she was not as ready to accept death as death was ready to accept her. I tried desperately to explain that I had been dead for quite some time and was dealing with it rather well. I also made her aware of the fact that her young son had been dead for a short time, and as of yet, seemed to be handling the situation with ease.

Mummy was not at all pleased with my explanations. She began to hover—not the gentle floating to which I had become accustomed—No!—she hovered maniacally about our heads and the accident site. Then, unbelievably, she began to howl and curse.

Unnerved, the boy spirit shed phantom tears and cried out in his new afterlife voice. "Mummy's a demon. Only demons curse!"

Petrified, he threw his soul against mine for protection.

Had I created a demon?

Her language was admittedly beyond reproach.

Were we destined to spend eternity with a cursed spirit?

I, for one, knew that I could not take it.

Alas, luck favored me once more and I did not have to endure the torture of demon mum for long. During her zealous rampage, she disrupted several pieces of furniture and knocked over a vase and a framed painting. Sleep arrested, the father bound from his room to check on the sudden noise. As fate would have it for him, the poor fellow stepped to the banister at the exact moment the agitated mum hoisted a kerosene lantern. Father received the lantern full in the face. The globe broke and kerosene spilled.

Rebecca awoke.

Rushing from her room, she brushed against her father, the flame from her sputtering candle igniting the man like a torch. He fought the fire, beating his chest and head until he finally toppled over the edge of the banister. Engulfed in flames, he fell to his death.

Newly orphaned, Rebecca stared in terror.

Bad for her...horrible for me!

My plan had taken a lethal turn!

The small spirit, all snivels and quivers, clung to me. Mummy quieted a little after she joined her husband's newly released spirit. Rebecca, however, was still out of my reach!

What a dilemma!

Never being quick with decisions, I had to think fast.

What could be done to salvage the situation?

Hurriedly, I gathered the spirits together. I explained the problem at hand and sincerely tried to make the afterlife seem like a blessing. While I held their attention, I professed my love for Rebecca and my future plans.

Much to my surprise, they were receptive and acquiesced to assist.

So it went!

It was easy!

As I looked on, the new spirits each went to their perspective bodies, anchored a solid grip, then through great concentration, mastered them back to lifelike positions.

Through Rebecca's eyes, it appeared that her dead mother, father, and brother—who snuck soundlessly from the bedroom beside her—had come alive, each approaching her with outstretched arms.

Charred flesh fell from ghost-white bones as her father stumbled forward. Mummy bound up the stairs, head bouncing from left to right. And of course, the little dickens traveled toward her in his wonderful new shade of blue.

The shock was too much. Her heart failed on the spot.

Rebecca's spirit bolted free. I grabbed her and held her till she calmed.

It was then, she became mine forever.

Forever. Forever and ever and ever.

Forever…

A 'B' MOVIE AFTERNOON

"Who's that tall drink of water?" Teresa pointed her finger toward the pool.

"W—what's that?" Sounded like Nicole had been snoozing. Her voice cracked. She peeked up under her hand.

"Who's that guy? Over there. He's staring at us. Me, to be exact."

"Gawd, Teresa. Yuck. That's Loni. The groundskeeper. He's—"

"He's cute."

"Don't even think about it. He's not for you."

Teresa sat up on her elbow and squinted a smile, hoping to hit Loni with it.

Wasted flirt. There was a strong competition under way between brilliant rays of sun and searing glare of pool's reflection. Both produced a blinding light. Both heated up the concrete deck to a dangerous degree. Both were invisible and brutal. So far, it was a dead heat. It wasn't a fit day for man or beast. Looked like Loni had escaped.

"Darn it." Teresa rustled around in her sister's purse, pulled out a key ring, and unstuck her thighs from the sweat-soaked seat, making a sound like a baby sucking from a bottle. She stood over Nicole, throwing a long shadow over her face. It accented a scowl. How many times had she seen that face. Poor Nicole. Always the lady. Never had any fun. "I'm gonna go check your mail."

"Leave him alone, Teresa."

"Leave *me* alone."

"He's a weirdo."

"You're a prude."

"Hey! I said—"

"Don't wanna hear it, little sister." Teresa palmed the keys and walked past the pool house to a row of aluminum mailboxes. Keeping one eye on the task at hand and one eye open for any sight of Loni, she fumbled with the tiny lock. With a muffled click, the door popped open and a coupon flyer fluttered out. "Whoa!" Teresa grabbed at the colored piece of paper, snatched it out of the air, and simultaneously dropped her keys.

"Come here, you." As she bent to retrieve them, a tanned hand reached over hers.

"Got it." Loni stepped in close, held out the keys, and said, "Here," his smile splashing over smooth white teeth like a waterfall.

Teresa dove in. "Oh." Feeling heat wash over her cheeks, she tipped her head and averted her eyes in a schoolgirl tease. "Thanks." Her hands played with the air for a moment until he finally dropped the keys into her palm.

"You're most wel—"

"Teresa." Nicole pushed between them and took a stance like a prison guard over her sister. If her eyes could have spoken, they'd have told Loni to go drown himself.

He grinned and nodded. "Well, hi, Nicole. I guess you know this lovely little lady. Aren't you gonna introduce us?"

"This is my sister. Teresa. She's only visiting for the weekend. Her boyfriend's in the Navy."

"Lucky guy." Crystalline smile flashing brightly, Loni stepped around Nicole and brushed against Teresa.

"They're engaged, Loni."

"That so." He fumbled with his mailbox key, then looked up to Teresa. "I'm usually pretty good with my hands. Can't seem to get this key to work today."

Splash! Teresa jumped in. "There's a trick to it. You just need to wiggle it. Wiggle it around a little."

"Wiggle it?" Shimmering green eyes, nescient pools, peeped from a bronzed face.

"Yeah. Once you get it in, you just wiggle it a little. Let me show you." Teresa trailed her fingers over his, took the key, slipped it into the slot, and as she had prescribed, wiggled it around. The door swung open.

"There you go."

"Oh! You are good. Thanks." Loni lowered his head and looked inside, his cheek running over Teresa's stomach. "Nothing here, though."

Nicole nudged her sister until she moved. "No mail for you. Too bad, so sad, Loni. Looks like no one likes you. Come on, Teresa."

Before Teresa stumbled away, Loni threw her a wet wink.

Squish!

Under protest, Teresa walked with Nicole back to their poolside chairs.

"He's too cute."

"I told you, he's a jerk."

"What do you know?"

"There's always a stream of girls going up to his apartment. He lurks around the apartment buildings…this pool. He's supposed to be working, mowing the lawn, trimming the hedges—something. I've never seen him do anything. He gets a tan, eyes up girls, and smiles. That's what he's good at. I don't like him. He's…he's…diluted."

"What the heck does that mean? Diluted?"

"He's transparent. He's got no substance. There's something about him that's not quite right. He's slick. Slippery. Wishy-washy."

"You need to put on a hat, little sister. Sun's frying your brain. Turning you into a thesaurus."

"He's…"

"Delicious. I could pour him in a glass and drink him up."

"Teresa!"

"He kind of looks like Brad Pitt."

"That's great. He looks like Brad Pitt, so let's jump on him. I've got monopoly money that looks like real money. Let's go to the mall later and spend it."

"Are you sure we're sisters? I mean, when I talk and you talk it sounds like two people who don't even know each other, nonetheless share the same gene pool."

"Teresa, he's bad. I don't know what else I can say. Just stay away from him. You do still have a boyfriend, don't you? Weren't we just talking about him and—"

"You sound like Mom."

"Now that hurt."

"You do, Nic. Did you forget that I'm the big sister here? I'm supposed to be giving *you* lectures."

"Sorry."

"Uh huh. Remember, I'm older and wiser."

"What you are is full of crap...and pink. You ready to go inside?"

"I'm going to sit here a while longer. It's nice."

"It's blistering hot! And I said, you're getting pink."

"I'll put on more sunscreen."

"Too late, you're already burning. Let's call it a day."

"Take a snooze. Can't you just relax and enjoy the sun? I can take care of myself."

"No you can't."

"Can to."

Nicole laughed. "You sit here, then. I'm going to pick up a movie and some groceries." She packed up her purse and towel, then threw a bottle of sunscreen at her sister. "Use this."

"Nag." Teresa caught the bottle, popped the top, and squirted lotion onto her arms. Aloe and coconut scented the air.

"You want anything special? From the store?"

"No. Uh uh. Whatever you get is fine. You buy the food and I'll cook it."

"Deal. See ya later."

"Later."

"Stay away from that drip."

"Yep. Whatever you say, little sister." Teresa watched Nicole walk away and laughed softly. "Worrywart." Settling back, she closed her eyes.

* * *

"Hey there, sleepy girl."

Teresa's eyelids snapped open with the jolt of a spring lock. Immediately she squinted against the blazing sun. She saw a blurry round outline and a smooth smile gushing from a pair of perfect, plump lips. Teresa blinked. Above the lips were two aqueous green eyes. The face swam in and out of focus like a gently rippling reflection on a quiet pond.

"Oh!"

"Oh, to you! Hey? Where's your sister?"

"She's...she is...went to the store. She went to pick up some—"

Loni cut the sentence short. "So you're all alone?"

Teresa looked around the pool deck. "Yeah. It looks that way. I—"

Again, he forced her sentence to a premature end. "It looks like you've had enough." Long tanned fingers pushed down her bikini strap to expose a fine white stripe outlined in red. "Give me a straw. You're done."

"What?"

"You're done."

Puzzled at the odd word choice, Teresa looked down at her shoulder. "Y—yes. It looks like I've got a burn."

"It's not too bad yet. Needs care. I've got something that'll put out that fire. Cool you right down. Come on." He extended his hand.

Without hesitation, Teresa slipped the strap into place, dipped her hand into the curve of his fingers, and stood.

Gurgle, gurgle, glug.

"Allow me, *mon petit*, sweet treat." Loni scooped up Teresa's towel, her shorts, and the bottle of lotion.

Hand in hand, they walked to the building and up the stairs.

*   *   **

"Teresa!" Nicole stood beside the empty deck chair. "Teresa!"

"She's at my place."

Nicole spun on her heels and bumped into Loni, almost knocking him into the water. For a moment, he lost his wise-guy expression, his eyes growing wide and his lips crinkling into a crooked "O" as if he'd seen a monster. His arms cartwheeled while he grabbed at air, but he continued to lean over the edge. Finally, he grabbed Nicole and pulled himself level.

"You almost pushed me in!"

She didn't have to ask if he was upset; his cheeks flamed red and his nose crinkled up, crowding his eyes so they pinched together like a wild cat. Nicole expected him to extract twenty claws and rake her face. "S—sorry."

"I can't—" He stopped quickly, took a breath, unwrinkled his face and began again. "I don't care for the chlorine boost in the water here. Good for bacteria. Bad for my…skin." Loni threw a wary glance at the pool, then brought his stare back up to Nicole. "No harm done." He laughed. It was a shallow attempt to cover anger. Barely submersed, irritation roiled under the surface ready to emerge with a savage splash.

Nicole took a step back.

Loni tried to douse the harsh sound of his voice and cool down the flare-up with a cheery giggle and lippy smile. "Like I said, she's at my place. I took her up there for a little drink."

"She needs to…it's time to…" Another small step back.

"Aw, don't be that way. She said you'd be mad. Why don't you come on and get her." Nicole glared. His outline seemed to blur.

Features oozed out of place, then congealed back to their original form. She shook her head. The heat? The reflection of the pool? The anger—both hers and his? She blamed the phenomenon on a cocktail of emotions.

"No. I don't think so. We've got plans."

"Come on." Without another word, as if he'd said all that needed to be said, Loni turned and walked away.

She watched him go. He moved with the grace of a wave lapping at the sandy edge of a beach. Languid. Sensuous. The motion or his arms and legs pumping smoothly, the whispery sound created by sneakered feet pitter-pattering across the pool deck, the gentle bounce of wispy hair—a blond breeze...

The boy was an ocean in motion. Nicole thought she could hear pulses of soft salt-water swell, crest, and slip away.

Swish. Splash. Swoosh. Swish. Splash. Swoosh. Swish. Splash. Swoosh.

With the soothing sound to accompany her, Nicole followed silently behind, over the grass, to the sidewalk, up the stairs, down the hall, and through his apartment door.

Swish. Splash. Swoosh. Swish. Splash. Swoosh.

He moved to the center of the room, turned, and motioned her closer.

Nicole obliged, and her feet sank deep in the sea-green carpet. Sodden, it felt like moss under her sandals. Fine dew licked her toes.

She closed the door. It shut quietly with a soggy smack.

The room was barren. The shades were drawn and the air was humid. Too warm. The walls dripped water and droplets clung to the ceiling, looking like gems. Nicole felt as if she'd stepped into a tropical rainforest or an overgrown terrarium. Her skin was immediately damp. Without thought, she licked her lips. Sweet.

She stared at Loni and he bobbed his head down at a lump on the carpet.

Nicole followed the nod and found her sister.

Teresa lay on the carpet, arms out to her sides. Her head was turned straight up, her mouth slightly open. A lone drop of water broke free from the ceiling and splashed on her open eye.

Teresa didn't flinch. She was as still as a stagnant pond. Not a current of breath to move her.

"Teresa?"

She didn't answer. She wouldn't—couldn't.

"Teresa? Jeeze, get up off the floor."

Nicole stared, incredulous. There was no urgency. Because the situation was unreal, immediate action wasn't required. Nicole's mind took her to a safe place where denial reigned supreme.

She'd been a witness to the marvel of blind disbelief several years ago, when she'd worked in the emergency room of a small hospital. One evening, the ambulance crew had cruised through the electric doors with an old man dressed in bib overalls and flannel shirt strapped to the gurney. His brown eyes were wide open as was his mouth, which was held that way being stuffed with macaroni and cheese. The old man had been dead for twenty-four hours. He had suffered a fatal heart attack while seated at the dinner table the night before. At the time, his wife had failed to see the urgency of the situation—unreal. She'd left the man sitting in his chair. After a new day had dawned and he'd remained fast in his seat, she'd felt the need to feed him. That explained the macaroni and cheese. The old man's daughter had stopped by to find her mother, fork in hand, and her father...full.

The wife had been sedated and taken to observation. The old man had bypassed the ER and gone directly to the cooler.

"It's time to go home, Teresa. I picked up a pizza. And a six-pack. And a movie."

Teresa stared up and said nothing. Nicole wanted her to speak, to explain herself. Teresa didn't look well. Her eyes—the pupils were milky white as if they'd burned in the sun. Rashy red skin, oddly blistered in wavy patches, pulled tight over her arms, belly, and legs. Her nose was a ruby knot. Cracked lips were an ugly shade of brown.

"Come on."

The skin on Teresa's body appeared brittle and shrunken as if there was no fluid to plump up the soft tissue underneath.

"Told you to get out of the sun. Now look. You're all dried out."

Teresa lay motionless.

Finally, Nicole found the courage to touch. With a stiff finger, she poked Teresa's shoulder. Her fingernail popped through crisp skin and touched down on bone. A crack started at the puncture site and splintered downward, so the skin split in two, then fell away. Bright white bone, an elbow joint, and a few twisted charcoal-colored knots—dehydrated tendons, muscles, and blood veins, were all that was left of the arm.

Nicole's mouth opened. She screamed—almost loud enough to wake the dead.

Almost, but not quite.

Teresa didn't stir.

A rain shower of liquid beads dripped from the ceiling, wet Nicole's hair, and spiraled down her cheeks like tears. Eventually, her scream grew weak, then frittered out. Shock held Nicole's feet fast. Wide eyes pulled up to find Loni.

He stood in the middle of the room, wearing a quivering smile. Eyes steamed, moist and ravenous.

"I thank you for Teresa. Sweet nectar. Warm from the sun. Warm and sweet. I bet you're a little sour. Potent. Strong and hot."

Nicole fell into his stare and paddled around. It was nice in there. Soft. Sympathetic. Secure.

Loni's smile widened, and as it did, he changed. The skin on his neck and shoulders rippled and the golden bronze color morphed to a marbled swirl of purple and green (lovely pastels), and slowly his outline mutated into a softly rounded form, his head and limbs sinking into the bubbly mass.

Green and purple strands oozed over the carpet like roots to support the bulbous body, then rippled forward toward Nicole, pulling the thing along. It was pretty to look at, the only think marring the perfect backdrop of luscious color being a dark hole in the upper portion. A rim of hydrous flesh curled up around the mouth and trembled expectantly.

Liquid lips moved and it spoke. "Sweet and sour. Sugar and salt."

Moving quickly, gracefully, it slithered to Nicole.

She thought about screaming, but didn't. The swirling colors and wavering outline were soothing, hypnotic.

"Time to liquidate your assets, Nicole." The thing laughed and it sounded like bathtub farts. Smelled like them, too. A contradictory odor, like candied sewage.

Nicole giggled as she was swallowed up with pillowy wetness. Its soggy mouth opened and a slippery tongue lapped a circle on her shoulder. It stung. She heard the thing slurp as if it was sucking through a straw.

Over the top of it, Nicole saw a pile of something stacked in the corner...colorful bathing suits, shorts, sneakers, and sandals. An assortment of bags and a mound of lotion bottles. Sunbathing supplies. And a pile of bones. Bones covered in dead flesh. A putrid, mildewing stack of debris.

Fear surfaced. After being stuck underwater, anchored down in the bottom of her conscious mind, it broke free and floated to the top.

Nicole pushed against the thing as its mouth moved down to her chest. She could feel her skin being sucked into the moist hole while its tongue worked over her flesh. Then the mouth slipped under her throat and over to her other shoulder. The creature's progress was slow, as if to savor the flavor of the treat, like a child licking an ice cream cone.

Nicole felt weak. Thirsty. It was suddenly more important to quench the thirst than to remove herself from the creature's grip.

Its mouth worked down her back. She was woozy. Her eyelids fluttered. Nicole wanted to drink. She licked her lips as the creature mouthed her flesh.

The creature sipped. Slurped. Sucked.

With a juicy slap, her left arm disappeared into the green and purple drop. She used her free arm to push at the creature. The pressure of her hand started a wave that bubbled from the top of the monster's body, to its bulbous bottom, and over the slippery streams of goo that held it erect. The suction held.

So thirsty! Her legs wobbled and her head pounded. Drink. Have to…

The creature drew in her arm with greater force. She could feel the lips pressure around her biceps as if to squeeze the fluid from the flesh by force.

Nicole ran her tongue over her lips. Dry. Stale. She inhaled a mouthful of moist air. It was delicious. It tempted her throat, but was not enough to satisfy her need.

Black dots danced before her eyes.

Drink. Nicole opened her mouth, bared her teeth, tilted her head forward, and bit down. At first, her teeth slid on the creature's slick filmy skin, then she heard a soft pop and her teeth sank deep. Nicole ground the monster's squishy hide until the click of hard enamel ticked in her ears.

The suction on her arm broke.

The monster bellowed and slunk away.

It's green and purple body flattened out, then sprung back upright. The mouth pulled open and globs of colored drool dribbled to the floor at Nicole's feet.

The creature howled. Fluid poured from the tiny hole made by Nicole's teeth. Then the creature's hide gave out and liquid gushed.

A purple and green shower soaked the floor.

Nicole dropped to her knees and splashed down in the puddle while the creature slithered on the carpet. Slippery strands spread on the floor and swirled in a sweeping motion as if to reclaim the seepage.

Nicole watched. Desperately thirsty. The sounds of liquid spattering, pouring from the bite, tantalized.

The creature flattened out and its mouth fell forward, sucking the carpet fibers. The sad slurping sound filled the room as the stain grew, wider and wider, until the recognizable outline of the creature's body shrank. Finally, it spread out flat and released a moist exhale. Gummy lips sucked at the air, gasped, then burbled away.

The carpet acted as a sponge and soaked up the final remains.

Nicole sat in the slop for a minute, dumbfounded. The unreal turned insane. But not as crazy as the wild thirst, the overwhelming urge to drink.

The smell in the room was refreshing.

She was so thirsty.

Cool colors dribbled on the floor.

She crawled into it. Then, she closed her eyes, stuck out her tongue, and licked.

* * *

"Hey Nicole? Wanna swim a few laps."

Nicole looked at the boy and laughed out loud. He was in the pool, doing his best to impress.

He was beautiful. Sweet nectar.

She stepped back from the heavily chlorinated splash. "I was just going up to get myself something to drink. You thirsty?"

"Yeah. I could use a drink." He swam over to the edge and stared up at her. "You know, for a groundskeeper, you sure don't work very hard. Your boss lets you get away with murder."

Nicole laughed again. "Follow me. I'll give you a little lesson on sucking up."

With a luscious smile on her face, she turned and walked away, stepping lightly around a puddle on the pool deck.

The boy lifted himself out of the water, retrieved his towel, and watched her walk away.

"She moves like a wave on the ocean." Dripping and grinning, he followed.

GRIM EXPECTATIONS

Although the sun had recently set, it had left behind an orange halo, a dabble of light to shine a path for children in pursuit of candy. Giggles and shouts sounded from the street. Doorbells rang. "Trick-or-treat!" There was laughter and the patter of sneakered feet.

Leo Grimes sat in his recliner, feet up, belly on his lap. Beside the chair was a TV table loaded with beer cans, all empty but one, and a bowl of tootsie rolls. He unwrapped a candy, popped it into his mouth, chugged some malt and chewed.

His attention traveled from *Wheel Of Fortune* to the window. Through the dirty glass, he glared at the little ones dressed as ghouls and princesses, monsters and cowboys, scurrying in a hurry to fill their bags with treats before the Halloween curfew forced them home.

Leo snorted. "Rugrats. Snot monsters."

A group of youngsters stopped in front of his house and one little boy (outfitted as an alien with glow-in-the-dark antennae, an orange pulsing belly, and a red ray gun) put his foot on the grass in Leo's yard. Immediately, an adult hand grabbed his shoulder and steered him back onto the sidewalk.

"That's right, little boy, follow your mama. Big bad Leo might eat you up." Leo laughed, drooled brown spit, wiped his chin, then refilled his mouth.

"What's that, Leo?"

He turned to Summer and grimaced. She'd dressed for the occasion. He'd invited her over, promising her a party and twenty dollars.

Summer worked with Leo at the factory on the assembly line, and at one time or another, she'd partied with every male there, married and single. All it took was twenty dollars. Leo had sweetened the pot with the offer of a party and, apparently, she had put two and two together and assumed "Halloween Party." Summer had come dressed as a cat.

When he'd opened the door and found her standing there, swinging a pinned-on tail in her hand, dressed in black stretch pants, black turtle neck sweater, and cardboard ears glued to a pink headband, he'd had to fight the desire to slam the door on her face. Or worse, punch her for being so sorry.

Leo needed Summer, however, so he'd swallowed his insults and allowed her inside. Without speaking, he'd motioned her to the couch and there she'd sat for an hour and a half while Leo drank beer and stuffed his mouth with candy. He hadn't offered her anything, not even a snippet of conversation.

She stared at him, awaiting an answer. Reluctantly, he obliged. "I'm talking about the stinking trick-or-treaters."

Her eyes lit and she smiled. "Oh yeah? Yeah. Ain't they sweet, Leo, all dressed up for Halloween?" Summer straightened her shirt. She was braless and her baggage was slightly inviting. The black whiskers she'd painted on her face were almost cute.

"No. They're not sweet. I hate them and their stupid costumes." He wriggled his rear in the seat, adjusted his crotch, and took his attention back to the television.

"Oh?" Summer fiddled with her headband and twiddled her thumbs. "Well, uh, I always liked Halloween. Good times, usually. Get to dress up and be something you're not."

"So what're you telling me? You're not really a cat?" Leo glared at her.

Surprise shone in her gray eyes. "Oh! What? Of course not. Now, Leo, ya know I'm wearing a costume. You're a tease."

"Uh huh. Can't say the same about you, now can we?"

"Huh?"

"Never mind." Leo stuffed his mouth and looked out the window. Two ghosts and a tall zombie wearing a blood-soaked mask, eyeballs hanging onto the cheeks, moved toward his door. "What?" Leo leaned forward.

Three eggs splattered on the window. Before he could rise from the chair, three more joined. Raw scramble dripped down the glass. "Little sons of—"

Leo yanked open the door and screamed profanities at the trio. Several adults yelled back and warned him that small children were within earshot. He told his neighbors to stuff their complaints in the soundproof vacuum located within the flaps of his furry rear. Before anyone could take him up on his offer, Leo slammed the door.

Summer giggled girlishly. It was a sad sound coming from a middle-aged woman. "Boys will be boys."

"You're profound, Summer. Anyone ever tell you that?"

Summer blushed. "No, Leo, you're the first."

"Bet it's been a while since you've said those words without lying."

"Huh?"

"Never mind." Leo walked directly to the recliner, plopped down, grabbed a fistful of tootsies, and swallowed some beer.

"Ya gonna clean your window?"

"You think it deters from the beauty of my home?"

"Oh, now, I think ya got a real nice place here, Leo. It's…it's very…utilization." Pride bloomed like roses on her cheeks.

"Yeah. And the word's 'utilitarian.'" He stuck his finger in his nose and twisted.

"Oh. You are? Well, good for you. I, for one, couldn't live without my hamburgers. I'm a real beefeater. It's real good for your heart not to eat meat. Good for you, Leo."

Leo wanted to laugh, but feared it would encourage more conversation. Instead, he wiped his finger on his pants and watched egg yolk dribble on the widow.

"Ya got some nice posters." Summer pointed out the collection of nude pin-up girls draped over toolboxes, pickup trucks, and motorcycles. Tanned skin, long hair, high-heels, and silicone. "And them's nice neon signs ya got. Kinda looks like a bar in here."

Leo didn't answer. He was busy fiddling with the remote control.

Summer fidgeted a moment, then cleared her throat. "Um, Leo, I was wondering…when's the party start? Ya told me there was gonna be a party. I dressed for a party. I mean, if it was just gonna to be us, that would'a been okay, but then I wouldn'ta dressed for a party. I mean, look at me. I'm dressed for a party."

"Shut up. My guest should be here soon."

Leo stuffed several tootsies in his mouth. Colorful wax papers littered the floor. They looked pretty against the stained, orange shag carpet. The last time his house had seen redecoration, Nixon had been in office. He swallowed the rest of his beer, dropped the can, reached into the blue and white cooler by his chair, and opened a fresh one.

"Guest. Did you say *guest*? Cuz that sounds like one other person…guest. Did you mean to say guests? Cuz a party should have guests. More than one, see what I mean?"

"Look around. How many do you see?"

Summer did as she was told. She turned her head in every direction, then faced Leo with a smile. "Two."

"That's right. And a guest makes three. More than one. More than two. Three makes a party."

Summer drew her lips tight, nodded, and stared at the television.

She amused him in the same fashion a mouse excites a cat on the hunt. Leo laughed and burped at the same time.

The procession of trick-or-treaters beyond the window continued for another hour. No one came to Leo's door for candy. The egg on the window dried. Sitcoms replaced game shows.

Leo ogled, ate, burped, and scratched. He pointed a dirty fingernail at the television. "You know what I'd do if that little hottie came at me, shaking those melons in my face?"

"What?" Summer waited for an answer.

Leo shook his head, grinned, and slugged more beer. He'd always looked forward to Halloween, but that evening was proving to be the greatest fun yet. "Summer, you're a real—"

The doorbell rang.

"It's about time." Leo laughed and sprang from his chair. "Thought you chickened out on me. Wussy. That's 'wussy' with a capital 'P'!"

"Wussy? No. I think that's spelled with a 'W.'"

Leo stopped in mid-stride. "Unbelievable. You really are as stupid as they say, aren't you?"

Summer looked confused, as if she wanted to respond, but couldn't find the answer.

Leo helped her out. It was the only help he'd offered to anyone in his life. "Let me answer for you. You look a little stuck. Yes, Summer, you are as dumb as they say. You are *way* more than twenty dollars worth of stupid." He turned his back to her and walked toward the door. "You just sit there and keep your mouth shut. Every time you open it, I'm taking a dollar off the top. You're right now at nineteen."

"Oh. Okay. Uh huh." She frowned. Her whiskers twitched.

Leo grabbed the knob and pulled open the door.

The streets were vacant. Streetlights glowed, casting buttery beams on black pavement. Porch lights all over had been doused and the glow from the houses had softened. Candy corn kisses had been given and grease-painted faces washed. Excited children had finally been tucked into their beds.

On Leo's front stoop stood a tall man dressed in a charcoal-gray hooded cape. His face was hidden. In his hand he held a scythe.

"Boo!" Leo shouted, then laughed.

The Grim Reaper didn't respond. Rather, he walked past Leo and into the house.

Leo smiled. "Come on in!" He slipped his hands into his pants, scratched his rear end, sniffed his fingers, then slammed the door. "Trick-or-Treat!"

Summer turned around on the couch and stared. "Now, that's a costume! Well, well, well, I'm glad I didn't dress up for nothing. Looky Leo, now you're the only one at the party who ain't dressed up. Maybe you oughta—"

"That's a lot of words, Summer. You're about down to a ten-spot."

"Oh. Okay. Uh huh." Summer smiled. A smudge of lipstick dotted her front teeth. It was a nice color.

The Reaper turned to Leo.

"Tootsie?" Leo pointed to the bowl.

The Reaper shook his head, No. The action seemed slow, almost sad.

Leo nodded to Summer, curling up his lips. "Can I get you something else?" Excited, he bounced in place. The exertion forced a fart.

The Reaper held out his arm, cloaked by the heavy robe, and motioned toward the door.

"I'm not going with you and I'm not in the mood to dance, Mr. Bone Man, so why don't we just make our deal now and be done with it."

The Reaper took a step toward Leo.

Leo flinched. "Are you nuts? Don't you want her?"

Summer watched with the eager anticipation of child awaiting a surprise.

"What's the problem? We've been trading out for years. You've taken my mother, my stinking wife, a crazy wino…the list goes on, pal." Leo shook his finger at Summer. "What's wrong with her?"

"Yeah, what's wrong with me?" Summer had a proud look on her face as if she'd just recited the Declaration of Independence in Latin.

Leo balled his fists. "Shut your stupid mouth."

With a pout, Summer fell into the couch, mumbled, and played with her fingers.

Concerned, Leo turned back to the Grim Reaper. The trades had begun twelve years ago. Death had come to his door on Halloween. Leo had put up a good fight and finally offered his mother in exchange. The Reaper had been appeased and had returned each subsequent year. Every visit, Leo had offered a substitute. It had always been a sure thing—

Until then.

Sweat rolled down the back of his neck. Leo scratched his underarms. The Reaper took another step forward.

"You know something, you stinking coward, I'm not going to make this easy for you. You stand there and think about what it'll take to seal this deal. I'm going to sit down in my favorite chair and finish my candy and beer."

Leo plopped into the recliner, passed gas, giggled, and stuffed a handful of tootsies into his mouth. He grunted as he chewed, breathing loudly through his nose, then guzzled warm beer. Brown foam bubbled from between his lips.

The Reaper stood watch.

Leo laughed. Summer joined the laughter as if she understood the joke.

"I'm really glad you came, Summer. Now as I look at the two of you together, you make a nice couple."

The Grim Reaper swung his scythe.

A wad of tootsie's lodged in Leo's throat. He punched his chest. The chocolate ball slid deeper and completely closed off his windpipe.

Summer pointed her finger at him and laughed. The Reaper took a long step closer.

Leo kicked his feet. Beer cans scattered to the floor.

Summer jumped up and clapped her hands. "Charades, Leo?"

He fell out of the chair, grabbed his throat, and crawled to her.

She scolded him. "Ya have to signal how many words first. What you're doing ain't in the rules."

He grabbed her feet and looked up. Fermented drool leaked from his lips. He couldn't speak.

"Looky, Leo, if you've never played before, that's okay. I'll tell ya the rules."

Leo fell onto his back.

Summer stared down at him, watching the color on his cheeks blur to blue and his lips purple.

"Leo?"

He glared up.

Summer turned to the Reaper and winked. "Well, I ain't gonna save him, so I guess he's yours."

The Reaper nodded.

Summer bent, bunched up her nose, stuck her hand in Leo's pocket, and pulled out his wallet. She looked up at the Reaper with a cute smile. "He owes me twenty dollars." Summer removed a ten and three fives and dropped the wallet to the floor. "I know he'da give me a tip." She stood, smoothed down her pants, and stepped over Leo, her stuffed cat's tail dragging across his face.

"Let me tell ya something..." She took the Grim Reaper by the arm. He allowed it, seemed to welcome it. "Ya did a real good job here. Good to see ya take a stand. Shows your backbone. Ya should've never let the likes of him push ya around. Made ya look bad."

The Reaper nodded.

"Ya know, we've met before. Recognized ya right away. Ya may remember me, Sol Santa's wife? Sol! He told me his name meant 'the sun.' Now that's a hoot. He was the sun, all right. Son-of-a-ya-know-what!" Summer patted the Reaper's arm. He returned the affectionate gesture by leaning close to her. "Anyhow, ya did me a huge favor taking him away. I wondered if I'd see ya again. And now looky, here ya are!"

The Reaper walked through the door, Summer on his arm.

"It feels real good being with ya. You're a good listener. I think Leo was right. We're good for each other."

They turned down the sidewalk.

"Anyhow, while we're in the neighborhood there's a coupl'a guys ya might be interested in. A few of the boys from the factory. What'a ya say we pay a little visit. I mean heck, after all, I *am* dressed for a party. It *is* Halloween. How about we do a little trick-or-treating? And after that...well, who knows Mr. Reaper...anything can happen now, can't it?"

BOOGER

Dee was exhausted, glad to see a bad day come to an end.

What a mess. Schedule all screwed up. Left work early to make her doctor's appointment, then waited in the office for two and a half hours. Apparently, Doctor Ransom had the privilege of flexible timing, something her patients did not enjoy.

The receptionist had told Dee that "Doctor" (always called Doctor Ransom, "Doctor," as if it were her name and not a title) had been called out on an emergency.

Liar. What kind of emergency could a shrink have? After all, isn't it all about pills? Pop a pill—pink, yellow, blue, a half of this combined with three of these and you'll be just fine. If you still feel like shooting your neighbor or jumping from the top of a building, call tomorrow and make an appointment.

Emergency. Bull crap.

Probably a big buffet down at Piggles Bar-B-Que. Doctor Ransom looked like the kind of woman who'd call off a few appointments so she could stuff her gizzard. Big all over, with a huge head that was oversized even for her wide shoulders. Tiny puckered mouth, looked like someone had used it to blow up her face then tied the lips in a knot to keep the air from leaking out. Dee often wondered if she poked Doctor Ransom's face with a pin if it might leap from her shoulder and blllllrrrrrpppppp its way around the office.

Kind of mean, thinking like that. After all, being big wasn't a bad thing. Dee was no small woman. Hefty. Stocky. That's what her daddy had called her. Big-boned. It's in the genes. Just another inherited curse to suffer.

Some people poked fun out loud. Once, Doctor Ransom had commented on Dee's size. Told her that because she had multiple personalities, she wasn't obligated to feed them all.

That had hurt and Dee had said so. Doctor Ransom simply laughed and said that being able to have fun with one's self showed confidence and high self-esteem.

But Doctor Ransom hadn't been funning about *herself*, had she? The joke had been aimed at Dee. No, Doctor Ransom had never said, "Geeze, look at me, big as a house and no one to blame but my one gluttonous personality. Ha Ha Ha!" Too good for that. Wore her size as if it were an accomplishment and deserved a reward.

Her refrigerator was probably stocked with all the best high-calorie foods.

Wonder if she eats all alone. Doctor Ransom looked like she might have cats as pets. The kind of animal that keeps its own routine without messing up its master's life. Or maybe fish. They're easy. And it would be great for them. They could push up against the glass and marvel at Doctor Ransom's little mouth, might even love her more because of it. While they were at it, the little fishes could see themselves multiplied in Doctor Ransom's glasses.

Dee hated those glasses. Like those big, bejeweled things that were popular in the eighties. Garish. And they were tinted so dark that the doctor's eyes were hidden.

What kind of person needs to keep their eyes hidden? Someone with horrible secrets.

Dee had no secrets. After being forced to report to Doctor Ransom three times a week for four years, what could be left to talk about? Sometimes Dee dreamed of being free, taking care of herself, but she was called a ward of the state. That meant she had to get her medication from the local health department, had to have regular blood tests and checkups, and *had* to keep her appointments with Doctor Ransom.

Life ain't fair.

The day had been a waste. "All that and I missed my Spongebob Squarepants. Stupid Doctor. Stupid." Dee told her sorrows to her reflection while inspecting her face.

Not a pretty sight. Warning signs. Brown eyes, small and pinched, outlined with blond lashes, drooped sleepily. The combination of humidity and tension had worked wonders on her hair. Mousy brown and dull, it looked like crayon scribbles on her neck and shoulders. A matching set of bracket-shaped wrinkles dug trenches around fat lips. The day had carved its story in bold letters.

Stress.

She'd been warned about stress. It's a killer. People such as she should adhere to a strict schedule. Impromptu decisions, overexertion, irregularity in routines were no-no's.

"A slow-paced life is a safe and happy life." Words of wisdom from her doctor. What a hoot! It was Doctor Ransom's fault that the schedule had been so screwed up. Because she'd had to wait so long in the office, Dee had missed her regular bus, had had to wait for twenty-six minutes for one that was going downtown. Then, because it had been so dark, she had been afraid to go in and get her usual Tuesday night meal at the Bell—three Tacos, refried beans with cheese, and a large lemonade. Worse than the pain of her stomach growling was the pain of missing her cartoon. One can live without dinner, but not without Spongebob.

"Hate you Doctor Ransom. Hate you."

Now it was eight-thirty. Time for one blue pill and one green and black stripe. Brush teeth, wash face, and off to bed. Half hour reading. Maybe tomorrow would be a better day.

Dee sighed and flicked at the faucet. Her finger slipped. She clucked her tongue, then pulled down her eyes, ready to try again.

"Oh!"

It sat in the sink. Booger. Dried onto chipped porcelain. A brownish-green wad, the size of a nickel. The edges curled up slightly as if it had tried to pull free.

Bile rose in her throat. Dee gagged, fell onto her knees, then hobbled to the commode. She vomited. The picture of what she'd seen flashed in her mind and her stomach emptied again. Finally, she pushed back her hair, wiped the sweat from her forehead, and crawled to the sink. Gripping the edge of the counter, she pulled up.

"W—who did this?" Anger washed her face crimson. Her lips trembled. "Which one of you did this?"

Dee forced back a gag as she swatted the faucet. It spun, and cold water splashed over the dried snot, but the wad remained stuck.

Dee pulled her eyes up to the mirror. The return image glared with an equal eyeful of hate.

"Who did this?"

The reflection, too, awaited a response.

"Answer me!"

Dee's eyes drew tight and her lips pursed in a snarl. "Tell me who did this."

The reflection challenged with an identical grimace.

"Coward."

"Big words from a nancy girl!"

Dee glared. "Paula."

"That there booger's mine, missy Dee. A little present from me to you. Don't you like it, Dee? Don't you like my present, you cry baby, nancy girl."

"You clean that thing up right now."

"I won't."

"Do it!"

"Make me."

"You clean that thing up or I'll…I'll…"

"What? Missy Pissy Dee? You can't do nothing to me and you know it. You got me and now you got my big old snot rocket. Both of us are on you like stink on a turd."

"Shut up!"

"Make me."

"I can, Paula. I can make you shut up."

"Uh huh. You ain't got the hohos to do that, Dee. Seen you try before and you always fail. You can't do nothing right, nonetheless kill yourself."

"I can."

"You bore me."

Dee stared at the mocking smile, the flaring nostrils, the challenge in the eyes. "I'll do it."

"Uh huh. Show me."

"I can. I've got a secret."

"The rope? Big secret, Dee."

Dee stared, calculating, then looked into the sink full of water. The repulsive morsel held fast. It was all she could do not to vomit again.

"Just covered one nostril with my finger and blew. Wham! Snot rocket! Sticky little sucker. When ya try to clean it off, I bet you get it on ya. It'll never come off. Forever an' ever you'll have that booger and no matter what you do…"

Dee ran. Charging through the kitchen, she stumbled over a chair and fell. "Damn it! Damn! Damn! Damn! Damn!" She stood, picked up the chair—"Damn! Damn! Damn!"—and smashed it over the table.

And she ran, she kicked the rocking chair in the living room so it skidded over the floor and smacked into the front door. A dent smiled back.

"Damn! Damn!"

She charged into the bedroom, then rammed her fist into the closet door. Four bloodstains shaped like red dimes glistened on the white painted wood. Dee kicked the door. A large hole stayed behind.

"No more. No more."

She'd been trying for so long to gain control. Hopeless. It was too much work. "I can't take it. Can't. Can't. Can't…"

Daddy would have said it's like pissing into the wind. A lot of effort just to get yourself peed on.

She was sick of being peed on. And sick of the rest of it. No one should have to live like that, never knowing what to expect next.

Whether it be Chenille and her whorish clothes and taste for whiskey. Men calling at odd hours asking for her, some stopping by the apartment, pawing Dee, asking her to take a tumble with them for old time's sake. There was the time Chenille had placed the personal ad. Foul thing. It'd taken months for the calls to stop. Miserable whore.

Or Diamond. Just her name was a joke. Ran up Dee's only credit card and sent her into collections. Bought a bucket full of shop-at-home zirconia. A tiara sat on the top shelf in the closet. Dee wanted to pawn it, but could never find the courage to go into the shop. So it sat. Five hundred dollar piece of junk.

And Dori. Stuffed her face with glazed donuts and ice cream. Loved to eat in bed and leave the mess for Dee to clean up when the feast was over.

Broke, overweight, afraid to talk to any man for fear she'd already been with him. That was Dee. What kind of life was that?

Bad. Made worse by Paula. Pig. Destructive. Fouled the floor whenever she could. Left messes in odd places. One day Dee had come home to find all her clothes stuffed in the toilet. Even after she'd washed them several times, Dee had never been able to get the thought out of her mind. Her things touching…it was inhuman!

Dee cried. What a mess. The past—ugly. The future—a question mark. The present—she was hungry, had missed her cartoon, and there was a booger stuck in the sink.

Too much.

She was justified.

Dee tore open the closet door and threw everything within reach out and onto the floor. The rope was on the bottom. Rolled up like a snake. Waiting for Dee. Saved for such an occasion.

Making the mess didn't bother her at all. Shoes, a stack of winter sweaters, a photo album, a wicker basket of yarn with a ski hat in progress. The pile grew and she knew she was getting closer. A box of old boots and underneath that...an army shovel.

Dee pulled it out, held it up to her face, turned it back and forth. Daddy's shovel. He'd given it to her for protection. Best utensil the army had ever invented. With that shovel one could dig a foxhole, fry an egg or gut a man. Pea green, heavy-duty metal, sharpened blade, and it folded up neatly for easy transport. Great protection for a single girl in the city. No ammunition needed. Just pop it open and—

Dee laughed. "Oh yeah."

Shovel in hand, she walked directly to the bathroom. The sink had filled with water and gurgled through the overflow. The offense was still there. Through the ripples it looked bigger, greener, viler. A hot lump jumped in her throat. Her tongue swam in a salty sea.

"Paula, I'll give you one more chance to clean that up."

"Oh yeah. Once more chance or what? What if I don't, Dee?"

Dee pulled up the shovel and rested it on her shoulder.

"What? Missy Pissy Dee? You'll smash me? Oh! What a mess that'd make. Glass all over. You'll have to sweep, then vacuum. The sink'll have glass all over it. Might even get it in the tub. Whole place'll be trashed. You'd never make such a mess. Never in a million years. And even if you did...there'd still be the booger." Paula laughed.

"It'll be worth it."

"Do it, then."

Dee held the shovel over her head. She looked at her mirror image prepared to swing. How she wanted to send that snarling face to oblivion in a thousand loose splinters. Could she?

"You can't do it, can you, Dee?"

She wasn't sure. What if she broke the mirror and Paula still...

There was always the rope.

"No more." Dee lowered the shovel behind her shoulder, grunted, then hefted the weapon up and forward.

It slammed into the mirror, sending a rainbow of shards through the air. Glass peppered the rug and settled in her hair like a sprinkling of diamond dust. Freckles of blood dotted her face. Another swing knocked out a slab of glass the size of a dinner plate. Paula fell to pieces.

"No more snot in the sink. No more colors mixed in with the whites. No more calls from bill collectors. No more food in my bed. No more stains in my underwear. No more. Go away. All of you. Go!"

With each command, Dee rammed the shovel into the mirror. When the glass had completely fallen free, the sharpened blade drove into plywood. Wood splinters joined glass slivers.

Finally, exhausted, Dee fell back against the wall and stared at the mess. And it was a mess. Wood and glass and bits of wallboard all over. She'd be in big trouble, too. Last time Dee had damaged the apartment, she'd had to spend a month in the hospital.

But maybe not this time. After all, she'd ruined the mirror and wall for a good reason.

Pushing her hair off her cheeks, Dee sucked in a deep breath, then walked to the sink and looked down. The offense had loosened and swam in the currents. She punched off the faucet and watched it swirl out of sight. With a final dry heave, she bid it farewell.

"All gone." Dee looked at the wall. It was a beautiful sight. No one sassed her back. How proud was she?

Dee had solved two huge problems at the same time.

She was efficient and brilliant.

Humming, she carried the shovel into the bedroom and was about to fold it up and put it away when something caught her attention. Movement in the periphery. Dee spun and faced the vanity mirror. The reflective lips parted, prepared to speak, and she charged. The shovel swung up and down in a perfect arc, shattering the mirror with one blow. Pieces of glass clinked into a basket of cosmetics and over the rug.

Peace. "That's it. That's all there is to it." Dee looked at her shovel. It was a magical thing. Medicine be damned. All these years she'd struggled with the others, and in one afternoon, she'd managed to silence them twice.

Dee held the shovel over her head and danced. Then she leapt onto the bed and bounced.

They didn't live in her. She was not crazy. No loony tunes lived in her house. They lived in the glass! Reflections!

All she had to do was keep away from the mirrors.

"I can do that! I can!"

Dee nodded and pictured herself sharing the good news with Doctor Ransom. In her mind's eye, Doctor Ransom laughed out loud and apologized for the crazy mix-up. Then she told Dee that she wouldn't need to be coming back to see her. And as Doctor Ransom came around the desk to give Dee a farewell hug, Dee saw the glasses.

Twin reflections of herself, sitting square on a puffy face.

They'd have to go.

EXCAVATION

"Hey Doc, this goes beyond any allergy headache I've had in the past. This is like…it feels like a construction crew's set up in my head and they're erecting a city." Mac Luger pulled his hands down his face, mauling his already grim expression. Bloodshot eyes; purple puffs below. Swollen lids. Pupils like pinpoints. "I can't take it."

Doctor Nora Pearle stepped close, rested Mac's head in the palm of her hand and peered into his eyes. "Does the light bother you, Mac?"

"It's killing me. If you weren't so pretty I'd kick you."

"Ever have a migraine?"

"No."

"Hmmm."

"You see something in there?"

"Yeah, Mac. A colony of miniature aliens. Not building a city, though. Looks more like an excavation."

Mac snorted, sounding like a puppy that had sniffed up a dust bunny and was trying to clear its nose. "You're a real comedian."

"I try." Doctor Pearle grinned, took a seat next to the exam table and thumbed through Mac's chart. "We gave you the allergy shot one month ago and you say you felt great until just last week?"

"Yeah. Everything was… Oh, wait! I forgot something. This…" Mac reached into his pocket and pulled out a neat white square. "This came out of my nose yesterday!" As if he held a trigger-activated bomb, he unfolded the tissue. "Disgusting. Can't begin to guess what it is. Yuck."

"Oh!" Doctor Pearl took the tissue and leaned in for a closer look. Stuck to the center of the square was a greenish-yellow wad of phlegm with a glittery silver object gutting from it like a tiny Eiffel tower. "What is this?"

"You tell me! If I knew, I'd be the one with the MD after my name!"

"Hmmm. Metallic. Have you been around metal flakes, a mill, a garage...anything like that?"

Mac grabbed his head, pinched his eyes shut and moaned. "No!"

Doctor Pearle scowled. "Better let me have a look up there."

"Is nothing sacred with you?"

"It's just your nose, Mac. I'm not asking you to undress."

She shone the light up his nose, then stepped back and frowned. "Hmmm."

"Well? What do you see? What's there?"

"Nothing, Mac"

"Can't you get me a CAT scan or something? I could be dying right now. I could have the mother of all brain tumors."

"I don't think it's a brain tumor."

"I'm not leaving this office until you help me. I can't go on like this."

Doctor Pearle patted his knee. Poor guy was suffering. She'd help him. Not only because it was her duty, but she liked the guy. Lumberjack build, southern manners and eyes like twin moons—soft swirls of dark and light. "I'm going to look at this sample under the microscope. I'll be back in just a minute."

Mac sighed and dropped his chin to his chest. He looked like a school kid who'd just learned summer vacation had been canceled.

"Mac? You want to lie down?"

He did, dropped back with a crinkly thump. A wrinkled halo of exam-table paper blossomed around his head. Sad little angel. "Can you dim the lights, too?"

With a smile, Doctor Pearle doused the light and went to her private office at the back of the clinic. It only took a second to focus in on the foreign object and make identification.

Incredible. Couldn't be, but was. Scaffolding. Brain tissue dried to the sides.

Nora shook her head, picked up the phone and dialed. As usual, Jamison, aka *Mr. Efficiency*, answered on the first ring. Nothing better to do but hatch a phone?

"Hey, Jamison. It's Nora."

She fingered the phone cord and listened to her superior's curt greeting.

"I'm doing great," she replied. "But I've got a slight problem. I need the go-ahead to abort a crew."

She scowled at Jamison's predictable and irritating tone—his *disappointed-dad* tenor.

"I know. Second one this year."

Blasted braggart gave it to her good; reminded Nora that none of his crews had ever needed to be aborted. Of course not. Easy task working with the mentally ill. No one listened to their complaints, took them seriously. Let *Mr. Efficiency* work with sane, healthy men and see how his research progresses.

Nora grit her teeth and rolled her eyes. "Uh, huh. They've been excavating in my subject for three weeks. I used the usual injection. Everything started out fine, but now it seems they're making a mess of things. Ophthalmoscopic exam showed all the inspection reflectors erected in the correct positions. They've built a nice frame up and around the frontal lobe. But the crew's probably gone too deep, too fast, and injured some nerves. My host is experiencing extreme headache. And more than that, they must have had some kind of accident. A piece of scaffolding came out of my subject's nose. Must have blown right through one of the sinus cavities!"

While she waited for Jamison to stop laughing, Nora twirled in her chair. Pompous, anal-retentive. How she wouldn't love to send a syringe full of radical miners into his system with the orders to rewire. Smiling, Nora pictured Jamison, his neural pathways crisscrossed so all he could do was drool and grin.

When the horse's ass finally quieted down, she pushed away the image and continued. "I've got to abort before they do more damage, or worse, my subject goes elsewhere for a second opinion."

That sucked the joy out of him. Nora thought she could hear his tight butt turning inside out. Another physician's "look-see" would mean disaster. Jamison flipped into managerial mode. Yes, do it. Right away. Beware of financial losses. There were time limits. Blah. Blah. Blah.

"You know, Jamison, maybe someone needs to reeducate these excavation crews. Slow them down. Offer incentives for a job well done. A bonus for accident-free days."

Jamison said he'd consider her suggestions. On a final note, he reminded her of the conference next month. He'd see her there and it would be nice if she had some better news to share.

Yuck. Nora stuck her tongue out at the phone, slammed it down and revisited Mac.

He was prone and breathing slowly. Asleep.

"Mac?"

"Huh?" His head wobbled side to side and his eyes opened wide.

"It's okay. It's just me."

He spun up and sat facing her, his face a big question mark.

What a cutie. All hassles aside, Nora enjoyed working with her assigned research group—men ages twenty-five to forty. Especially Mac. She thought he liked her, too.

She smiled at him, hoping he'd notice her dimples—one of her better features. "First of all, the thing in your nose was a sliver of metal. Steel's my guess. Who knows how it got up there. Anyway, as far as this headache goes, I'd like to treat you with a medication here in the office. An injection. After I administer it, I want you to lie still for an hour or so and I'll check on you every fifteen minutes to make sure you're all right. If all goes as expected, you should feel better by the time you leave today."

Mac's expression morphed to happy and he grimaced. Poor thing, even hurt to smile. "You're a lifesaver, Doctor Pearle."

"Well, let's see if this works before you give me any awards. Lay back, please."

Mac settled on the exam table and Nora administered the shot into a bulging vein on his inner arm, then taped a Band-Aid over the tiny wound.

"Does that feel all right so far?"

"Yeah. I mean…wait. My head feels kind of funny. Dizzy."

"It'll pass."

"Hey! You're right. It's already getting better." He grinned.

"Good." After she patted his shoulder, Nora picked up Mac's chart, sat down and waited. It'd take two or three minutes for the crew to expire.

Shameful.

Maybe she should ditch the human research and begin a study on extraterrestrial impatience. Save everybody time, energy, money and alien lives.

Nora looked at Mac. Nice guy. Trooper. He'd put up with so much and Nora had looked forward to working with him. Thanks to the little boogers running amuck in his head, however, she'd have to start again with a new subject.

"Hmmm."

"What's that, Doctor Pearle?"

"Oh, nothing. Just thinking, Mac."

The scaffolding—the outer frame of the project—was nicely built and in good position. Perhaps after Mac rested a bit and lost the headache, she could introduce a new crew. They'd already have a foundation, so there'd be no worry about them depleting his blood of minerals for raw materials needed to manufacture building supplies. And Mac was a regular allergy patient, used to getting shots. And he kept his appointments, never canceled or was late. And he was so cute.

It might work. Nora nodded. Completely against the rules. Subjects had never been twice excavated. Jamison would have her hide. Unless...unless she took the dig deeper than ever before. With the framework already established, the new crew could focus solely on the excavation. Maximal use of time. Who knew? Perhaps Dr. Nora Pearle would be the one to rewrite the excavation procedures. What a rush. It would surely mean recognition...respect...a promotion! What a hoot to rise above Jamison. The first thing she would do is reassign him to pediatrics. Let the little sissy work with the brats and their overbearing parents.

"Mac, can I take a peek in your eyes."

"If you have to."

"I do." She leaned over him, shone the light into his pupils and searched. Excellent. No activity. Everything was as it should be—except for the crew. It was all over for them.

"So Mac, how're you feeling? Any better?"

"Getting there. Yes."

"Great news. Those little aliens I was telling you about, the medicine killed them all. It's toes up for those naughty boys."

"Are you sure you're a doctor and not some mad scientist or something?"

Nora laughed and squeezed his arm. "Actually Mac, I'm both. I'm a physician and a member of The Forum, an elite group of doctors and scientists from all over the world working hand in hand with an alien race with the hope of completely mapping out the so-far-unknown functions of the human brain. There's a lot of uncharted territory there."

He laughed out loud, a frail moan trailing behind. "That's nice,

Doctor Pearle. As long as you take away this headache, I don't care what you do with your free time."

"I'm glad you feel that way, Mac," she said, squeezing his hand.

BABY DADDY

I want to place blame. Point a finger. Cast a curse. But where to start? Daddy Jack? Emily? Marcus? How about I turn that finger around and point it at yours truly?

Whoever said "you get what you deserve" was an idiot. Little Jack...Baby Daddy didn't ask for what he got, but he got it all the same.

Let me fill you in on the past so you know where I'm coming from.

I'll begin with Daddy Jack, Doctor Jack Gascon, founder and head honcho of Gascon Bioevolutionary Institute, aka GBI, aka cornerstone of life, aka turnstile to hell; all depends on who you're asking. The scientific community and a great number of the populace thought GBI held the secrets of the universe. Christians and lifers and others of that ilk thought the doors lead straight to the fiery pit.

I saw it as a dream come true.

After graduating from Yale and interning at GBI in genetic engineering, I caught Daddy Jack's eye. He took an interest in me and my natural ability to splice genes with first-shot accuracy. After two years, I became lead man in his research department and began to help him in his evolutionary studies, which included cloning—something he titled "replicating" (just so he'd have the honor of coining a phrase)—and species alterations. His goal was to take the creation theory and the simmering-in-the-muck theory and rise above it all with his This-is-how-it-was-and-this-is-where-we-are-going theory.

Anyhow, he was a genius and his words not only rang true, but mirrored my own thoughts. I, too, was a genius and loved life in the lab. I also had my eye on his daughter, Emily, and well, I signed my name on the dotted line, said goodbye to my doctor daddy and psychiatrist mommy and moved to Idaho.

Daddy Jack owned half of Idaho. Thanks to the soil virus six years ago, farming was out of the question and the land there was "dirt cheap" (a direct quote from Daddy Jack, each time followed by a slap on the shoulder and a round of laughter). He bought up all he could and built his empire. Seven thousand acres of property under his reign. Wow.

The complex sprawled like something out of a sci-fi movie—shimmering, mystifying, and so big it had a perimeter. Yes sirree, there were guards assigned to *watch* the perimeter.

Very cool.

Office buildings and labs sat in the middle of all, silver and white buildings reaching for the heavens like robotic fingers. It was a complete, self-functioning entity plopped in the middle of nowhere. GBI had it's *own* everything: peace officers, food services, shopping areas, movie theaters, laundromats, day care and elementary school facilities—anything to keep the people happy in Daddy Jack's World.

It was great, like living in Disneyland and getting a paycheck; a big, fat, choking wad of money.

Anyhow, after debunking scores of hoaxes and bowing down to the lack of proof, admitting that the missing link may never be found—might not even exist—the mind's of science drove a truck through the holes in Darwin's Theory of Evolution and deemed it a tad hallucinatory. Everyone from the educated professional to the average Joe began to question man's intelligence and his ability to prove his origins.

Many turned to God and the Christian Community exploded their numbers.

Before the whole world turned Christ-Friendly, however, Jack Gascon stepped in.

We joked that the day he unveiled his premise to thunderous applause at the *Collective Minds Of The Future* conference, the world stalled on its axis and, in a communal gasp, the people spoke, "Did you hear about Jack Gascon's Facts of Life? If we don't pay attention to the failures of the past, we are doomed to extinction! Uh huh. Can't believe I never thought about it like that before. Makes perfectly perfect sense."

What was Gascon's Facts of Life?

In a nutshell, it went something like this:

"In the beginning...Who Cares!

"Nothing good came from the beginning, People!

"Everything that *was* then is *gone* now! Do you see a dinosaur around anywhere? Can you walk up to a Neanderthal man and bum a smoke?

"No!

"And do you know why, People?

"Because they are extinct!!!

"Whatever came from primordial ooze was junk. It did not survive!

"We are here and if we don't take heed to the losers of the past we are doomed to repeat their fate.

"We can either force evolution on our own, or we can wait for the big catastrophe that wipes out mankind and see what the soil coughs up again in another zillion years.

"Look at Darwin! See the years wasted on that maniac's teachings. What Darwin had overlooked or failed to be able to prove was that missing link—that one piece of evidence that showed a gradual change.

"There was no gradual change, people! Junk lived and died because it was inferior—couldn't keep up with the ever-changing environment, couldn't outsmart disease—didn't have access to bioevolution.

"Do you want to die, People?

"No?

"Then quit worrying about where we came from!

"We're talking about the advancement of science here, People! Let's get busy and make ourselves better and save lives!

"God saw what he had made and said it was good. Jack Gascon sees what's out there and wants to make it perfect!"

Gascon. God. God. Gascon. It was in his voice, the way he said his own name, you knew that in his mind it was only a matter of time before Daddy Jack and God would be interchangeable—equals.

I didn't believe in God. Had no use for supernatural explanations. Daddy Jack was a flesh-and-blood man with a plan to preserve humanity and I would help him.

Cloning was not only illegal, but idiotic. Bioevolution was the intelligent man's answer to reproduction. It was cloning with a twist, taking an existing cell and making it perfect. Replicas without disease, without defect, with enhanced brain functions and motor skills. Orchestrated humans, each note hand-picked by the greatest scientific minds in the world. To hell with the morons who believed that choosing eye color was a touch of magic—we were advancing the species, bringing man out of the muck and into excellence.

How was this accomplished? By combining primitive sources—moist soil (that's right…goo), heat, and energy sources—light and low dose radiation. Put it all together in the lab and introduce complete cells (cells ready for cloning) and you have a scientifically produced breeding ground, an oddly simplistic environment for the "simmering of cells," encouraging genetic changes—Bioevolution!

I enjoyed describing the process to that of making pudding. In the old days women gathered ingredients—milk, sugar, cornstarch and flavorings—and stirred them together over low heat, simmering, until the ooze came to a boil and *was changed* from runny yuck to a creamy, sweet treat. We don't still hunch over obtrusive ranges, stirring things atop burners, do we? No. When we want pudding, we order it up nicely packaged in single-serving cups. Ready to eat and enjoy. Perfect every time. Now, if man can take food service to such an enlightened state, then perfecting reproduction should be a natural desire.

In the name of humanity, bioevolution was not only legal, but federally funded *and* open to donations from the private sector *and* charged a hefty fee for services. We were world-renowned. Hard not to be, considering GBI was one of kind. It was a win-win-*WIN* situation.

And I won again when I became Daddy Jack's son-in-law. Emily was a great addition to my life. Although not the prettiest, many of her features had come from her daddy, and well…let's just say she'd have made a really great looking man. And when it came to physical affections, she was submissive and uncreative. But I saw beyond the exterior to the person inside. Not only was she the most intelligent woman I had ever met, but she had a relationship with Daddy Jack that was tangible and powerful, the feelings so buoyant they could have kept the *Titanic* afloat. With Emily as my wife, I was guaranteed permanence. The limits seemed…

…Seemed like my first opinion about the whole world loving Daddy Jack's premise was a tad off. Right about the time Emily and I became one, the CAGERs (Christians Against Genetic Engineering and Reproduction) emerged with a quiet anger, sending a ripple of discontent over the airwaves. They had a strong voice for an upstart. And they had multiplied their numbers from a handful to millions in a short time. Apparently some people were ruffled by bioevolution. Appeared a significant portion of the world population did not fear catastrophic demise and was ready to gamble on natural reproduction.

Stone-age thinkers. I thought Daddy Jack had simplified it all to a bite-sized wad, simple enough for even a Christian to chew, but I was wrong. The creationists stood fast against forward movement—told us we were tempting God, called Daddy Jack the antichrist, said we'd be sorry.

Whoopty-doopty-doo! GBI emerged from the raucous-like cells from the primordial ooze and grew. All the CAGERs this side of the heavenly host couldn't stop us—or the baby.

Daddy Jack wanted a grandson. We broke the rules of replication, and fertilization took place without alteration. Clone. That's what we made. Plain old exact copy. Guess Daddy Jack didn't need to strive for perfection in himself—apparently he thought he was already there. So did Emily.

I wanted to have a *real* baby first. One of our own. It would have been nice to see what happened naturally and...

But this wasn't supposed to be about me or them. This was supposed to be about Jack...Little Jack...a boy called Baby Daddy; the beginning of the end, for us all.

*   *   *

August 28, 2020

It was a wet windy day at GBI when Jack Randall Gascon Palmer began his life under the amplified lenses of a microscope, at the skilled hands of yours truly. It was 3:33 PM.

We watched him grow for two weeks, then implanted him into Daddy Jack's daughter—my wife—Emily Gascon Palmer on September 10, 7:30 AM.

Thinking about something, making a plan and watching it become real, are completely different experiences.

I was distressed. I mean, for Pete's sake, we were trying to impregnate Emily with an egg that carried her father's genetic code. Nothing physical had transpired; it was all completely sterile—white coats and stainless steel—but I felt dirty, and when I saw the unholy glitter in Emily's eyes, I turned away and silently hoped that the incestuous implantation would not occur.

Six days later, we knew for sure that Jack Randall Gascon Palmer had attached and settled in for a thirty-seven-week growth period. When I watched the tiny quiver on the ultrasound—nothing more than a blip, an artery with a different pulse rate than the neighboring arteries—I saw Daddy Jack. Looking at that gray thing moving like a tiny river—formless and seemingly inhuman—I swear Daddy Jack's face glared out at me. Daddy Jack in Emily's womb.

I closed my eyes and wished him away.

Where was the joy of creation? Why the repulsion? Every day I created in the lab and was excited. The change in me was sad and disturbing.

And Emily changed. It was sick. She rubbed her belly and whispered to the baby, already calling him Baby Daddy. She prepared for his birth, not like I envisioned a mother to ready herself, choosing blankets and tiny outfits and booties with maternal love. Rather, she dove into the task with urgency and anxiety as if being tested, as if the baby might awaken in the nursery and rant about the color scheme, and in place of teddies and colored balloons, demand a humidor and an oil-on-canvas of ducks in flight.

Emily didn't ask me what I wanted or what I thought. She did, however, take Daddy Jack on several shopping trips. Surprisingly, the theme was blue and white and babyish. No mahogany desks and microscopes. Maybe later—for Toddler Daddy.

When Emily began to read books on breast-feeding my stomach fluttered, landed in my throat, and there it stayed, like an incestuous hairball.

*   *   *

February 5, 2021

Rumors spread that Daddy Jack was going to retire. Odd. Never pictured him for the sitting-in-a-rocking-chair-reading-the-golden-years-away kind of guy. I personally thought Daddy Jack would die of heart failure carrying his recorded earnings from boardroom to boardroom.

I wanted to ask him about the gossip, but he was getting harder and harder to track down. Our communications had become limited to memos.

In a blunt retort to my inquiry, Emily told me that her daddy deserved time to enjoy the fruits of his labor. Had I ever thought that maybe he wanted to relax or travel? I had, and said so, and agreed that he should enjoy himself. She told me to do my job and leave her alone, then walked her chubby self into the bedroom and closed the door. The tumbler clicked. Locked out. After a while, I thought I heard her crying.

Hormones? It was still the same Emily on the outside. Overlooking the swell of Little Jack (I refused to call him "Baby Daddy"—I had my limits) and the girth of her widening hips, she looked like the Emily I had married: tall, dark, ebony hair, eyes like little black planets. But on the inside, something was amiss. It was more than moods. Under the surface she seemed to be fighting a private battle and had grown increasingly edgy, distant, and I have to say, secretive.

As her body expanded, she withdrew from me, as if her love worked on a sliding scale.

Babies...blessing or curse? My answer disturbed me.

* * *

May 3, 2021

Jack Randal Gascon Palmer was born. In attendance, along with a score of doctors, vids mounted on all walls, and one dangling like a ailing alien from the ceiling, was myself and, of course, Daddy Jack.

After everyone had his or her turn with the baby, I got to hold him.

Relief. He didn't look like Daddy Jack. Wrinkled. Yes. Hair standing up straight in a black shock. Yes. Slight, arrogant snarl. Looked like it. But still not an exact replica. Not yet, anyway.

"Hi, Jack," I told him.

His eyes opened at the sound of my voice and, I swear on my life, he looked at me, turned down his lips, and in the black part of my subconscious, I heard him ask, "Don't you love me, Daddy? Don't you love me?"

I hoped he couldn't read my mind.

* * *

May 18, 2021

The media got wind of a rumor from an undisclosed source that the experiments at GBI did nothing to advance humanity. According to this secret advisor, Jack Gascon's private lab and his concealed products of bioevolution were something out of mad scientist's nightmare, complete with monstrous mutations and jars of indescribable creatures.

Daddy Jack had no comment, offered no personal interviews, but opened up parts of the lab for a media tour. Reporters oohed and aahed. Pictures flooded the airwaves, showing a sterile environment, smiling workers, and Mandy (my favorite gorilla) resting peaceably with her hands over the protrusion of a pregnant belly. Who could fault perfection? Not even the gutsiest reporter. The hubbub died down to nothing more than a discontented breeze.

Hopeful Christians let loose a dejected sigh. I felt it. The world swayed. I wondered if that was how this globe of ours got tipped on its axis eons ago. Had a depressed population exhaled their despair all at once, pushing the spinning ball on its side?

Why was the world cockeyed, anyway? I heard a story once that the great flood had knocked it off balance. Hmm. Some people will believe anything.

Christians! Gotta love 'em.

* * *

June 1, 2021

Daddy Jack took to his home and refused visitors, except Emily and Little Jack.

I was worried, and was about to demand an appearance, when he memoed me a raise and gave me access to a sizeable grant. Before he could change his mind or claim error, I expanded my research, immediately promoted Markus (my college chum and bestest buddy) to second in command, and gave him an equal raise. He bought a plane.

Emily was feeding the baby with a bottle and had given up trying to nurse. She said she wasn't producing milk. I knew she was lying, but couldn't have been happier.

I kept my distance from Little Jack. Oh, I changed him from time to time, fed him a bottle or two and held him when needed, but it made me uncomfortable. Still thinking about him as a mini Daddy Jack, I guess. Kept expecting his little eyes to pinch, lips to part, and him barking out a speech about succumbing to predestination and forcing human perfection.

So far, he'd only burped and coughed. Oh, and he did this little thing with his nose, kind of made a whistle sound with his nostrils. I had to laugh at that. Wondered what little part of his brain had figured out he could make music?

* * *

August 30, 2021

Mandy delivered a dead baby.

Mandy had been with us since she was a baby herself, a beautiful silver gorilla. She'd already given birth to a son via C-section, whom we'd taken away immediately. He wasn't quite what we'd expected. Since we had played around with brain mass, he had been oversized for his skull dimensions. Horrible mistake. Back to the simmer pot.

Thankfully, he didn't live long, and by the time Mandy came out of anesthesia, we'd preserved him on ice. But Mandy missed her baby. She watched us through the bars, fastened her stare on our hands, trying to see which might hold her infant. After a few days, I avoided looking her in the eye.

Anyhow, we'd planned on another C-section for her current pregnancy, but she'd fooled us all, having her baby early and without making a sound.

It was Markus who first noticed and he immediately called me over. If I live to be two hundred, I'll never forget the sight. Not just the misshapen little thing she'd birthed, but the look in her eyes. So deeply sad, and at the same time, issuing a warning. No one tried to take away her baby. Mandy clutched it to her and rocked and glared.

Everyone was affected. Some cried, others slunk to the break rooms, one tech tendered his resignation.

Markus prepared a sedative. He volunteered to put her out and take away the corpse. Out of respect for Mandy, we decided to burn the remains and forgo the usual dissection.

When I left for home, she was sleeping, her mouth curled down. Even powerful medication couldn't relieve her mourning.

I felt like…like…that night I rocked Little Jack in my arms and listened to his heartbeat and felt his breath on my shoulder and I cried. What I felt for my child seemed so minor, so inhuman.

Evolution? How could it be? I'd seen a primate naturally exhibit intense parental feeling, display a deep capacity for emotion that I…

…I had never cuddled Little Jack like I did that night. It had taken a silver-haired gorilla to show me my vacancies.

And I was glad she did. Little Jack responded to my affections. He nestled into my neck and cooed. Through my tears, I told him, "Daddy loves you, baby. Daddy loves you."

I swear, in that bright white part of my mind, the part reserved for fantasy and joy, I heard him say, "I know, Daddy. I know."

* * *

December 24, 2021

Lisa Ripple, my best and brightest engineer (next to Markus) quit. She told me she could no longer be a party to genetic mutations—killing more than creating—and that she'd been having doubts for a while. She said that the issues of generating life and altering genes for advancement of a species, mostly unsuspecting animals and superrich humans, bruised her spirit.

And I knew she was sincere. Behind her big blue eyes I saw purple and black.

When she left, she immediately took a key position as a CAGER.

My feelings for my job and life were slowly spinning in a downward spiral. I wanted to stand firm and hold fast my convictions, but I felt accused. My wife's eyes, my son's eyes, Mandy's eyes, Lisa Ripple's eyes.

Before Lisa left, I asked her if she could stay and do what she did and consider it a helping hand to God; like she was taking what He made and giving it a boost. She said if saying or doing something that, in her heart, she knew was wrong, then her life was a lie and she might as well jump on board the first truck to hell.

Hell? Lisa Ripple believed in hell? WOW!

I not only did not believe in hell, but knew for a fact that you couldn't drive around in something described as a fiery furnace.

Think, People! Think.

I missed her.

*   *   *

May 3, 2022

Jack Randall Gascon Palmer turned one. What a freaky day.

Daddy Jack sat in a chair most of the time, staring into space with a grin on his face, as if enjoying a private comedy routine. When he did find his feet, he'd come to me, ask how was work (as if I worked as a chef or a mechanic or in some field of which he knew nothing about) and I'd tell him what we were doing and what was coming up and he'd say good and return to his seat. He repeated this routine five times.

Annoying little money tree. Apparently he had so much on his mind he couldn't compute basic data. A vacation seemed like a great idea. I told Emily and received a look that stopped my heart for a second or two. Did I have to ruin everything for her? "No," I said, "I'm sorry."

For the remainder of the party I enjoyed Markus' company and that of my son. Seemed they had become my two favorite people.

While Little Jack and Markus and a gang of toddlers and myself tried to pop balloons by sitting on them, I saw Emily escort Daddy Jack out the front door.

He didn't say goodbye.

I never saw that man again.

* * *

July 30, 2022

CAGER's brought replication up in front of the House Senate Committee, claiming it nothing more than murder, and demanded a thorough investigation into the practices of GBI. The grapevine whispered Lisa Ripple's name and I pictured her on the podium, talking about hell-bound trucks and heart-felt lies, and dipped into sadness.

I overheard someone saying that the CAGER's didn't have a snowball's chance in hell of denting the image of GBI.

And he was right. GBI continued undaunted. We in the research department sustained animal testing for the betterment of the species and to avoid human accidents, while in the replication clinic, babies were made…not necessarily more deserving or gifted or good, but able to swing the GBI price tag. It was a running joke that we charged six million a head, the second head is free. (A sick reference to unforeseen birth defects. Forgive. We're scientists, not comedians)

Actually, they made babies for a buck twenty-five (125 K) and the rest of the money went directly back into the GBI.

GBI grew and we all got rich.

Emily and I grew further apart. Her fixation with Jack was abnormal and I worried. I had been forbidden to speak of Daddy Jack. His memos continued, however, and Emily took Little Jack for frequent visits, so I assumed the old fool had simply acquired a few eccentric quirks and let it go. I hoped I could be a good influence on Little Jack and save him from such personality peculiarities in his old age.

Our lives became a gray routine—the only bright spots being my time alone with my son.

Little Jack was learning in leaps and bounds. According to Emily, there had never been a smarter boy! I wanted to remind her that there had been an equally smart child some sixty odd years ago, but I held my tongue, avoided a confrontation, and simply played with my son.

We made funny noises with our mouths, stacked soft blocks and swatted them down, drove little cars over our bodies, and mooed and oinked and quacked and hooted and just had fun. Who needs a gym when there's a toddler around? I don't think I walked more than a few feet at a time without the little guy grabbing my leg or hanging from my back or perched atop my shoulders.

Fatherhood was great.

* * *

January 20, 2023

An unidentified woman on a suicide mission strapped a pound of plastique to her belly and, disguised as a lab courier, entered the clinic. Tough mission, considering the security at the GBI. I gave her credit for making it past the front gate and wondered who on the inside had helped.

She blew herself up along with a sizeable chunk of the replication clinic and six staff members.

My discomfort with my job increased. I wondered if Little Jack and I would be happy in a little house somewhere—me working a simple job and him able to run and play freely, without Emily demanding he repeat the alphabet or name objects or regurgitate quotes on cue.

My discomfort with my marriage increased. We had ceased to be intimate. As a matter of fact, the last time we had enjoyed each other's bodies (or she had allowed me to enjoy hers) had been several months before Jack's implantation. Emily had always been tight with her affection, but physical contact had dwindled to accidental bumps here and there, followed by her giving me an evil glare, as if even an unintentional touch was disgusting.

My confusion over our place in the universe, ethics, and the origins of life increased.

I found myself working in the lab, splicing and mapping, watching cells simmer and wondering about the original cells. Suddenly, instead of asking *how,* I rearranged the letters and asked myself *who*? *Who* had initiated life? The first little wiggle? The first heartbeat? The first breathe of air? Here we were geniuses, educated to the point of obnoxiousness, and we were failing over and over even with workable, time-proven originals at our disposal.

Who gave us the originals? And if they've been working so well, for so long, why was I eager to change them?

Was I freaking out?

Oh yeah!

If not for Little Jack, I might have chucked the whole business and run screaming. But because of Little Jack, I stayed. To deny my work in the lab would be to deny my son. I could not do that.

Little Jack, he was beautiful—dark hair, brown eyes, warm skin tones. I could imagine him mine. After all, he resembled me. I didn't realize how much I looked like Daddy Jack until I watched my son grow.

Emily, in her unnatural closeness to her daddy, had obviously chosen me *because* I looked so much like him. I was a tall, dark brainiac—just like Daddy. I'd been duped. Nothing more than a stand-in for the real thing.

But I had Little Jack and she had her neurosis and life went on. I'd never been one of those "looking back" kind of guys. My eyes were on the future.

* * *

March 8, 2023
The End
4:00 pm

"Come home now. I need you here. Baby Daddy's screaming…at…at that giggly doll again!"

"For Pete's sake, Em, calm down. Take the toy away from him. Put the blasted thing in the closet. Throw it out, for all I care. If it upsets him, then get rid of it." Maybe if I spun in my chair, she'd disappear. Maybe I'd be transported to another dimension. I twirled and did find a new world. Through the glass partition separating the inner office where Marcus and I punched computer keys, were the geometric patterns of cool white counters, silent sterile equipment and my rock, my assistant and best friend, Markus. As soon as my eyes set down on him, he looked up and nodded. Not merely a shake of the head, "Hi," but a token of sympathy. He always seemed to know what was going on without being told. Wonderful guy.

I gave him a pained smile and spun around. It was hard to do more with the thorn in my side gabbing in my ear. Wonder if I can type her away? I tried. Tapped letters on the keyboard—g-o-a-w-a-y-g-o-a-w-a-y-g-o-a-w-a-y.

It didn't work. "Randy! Are you even listening to me? I'm telling you something's wrong with him! Baby Daddy's sick."

There's work to do and she needs to get off the phone. "I'm listening and it's the same thing you tell me every day. And I'll say it again, he's three. It's probably a stage. Every time Jack has a moody day or throws a tantrum you can't run to the phone and call for help. Every time the boy acts in a way that you don't like, you can't complain about it and ask me to fix it. People can't be fixed. He's going to grow up with a complex."

"He's going to grow up perfect. Baby Daddy's…"

Baby Daddy! I hated that nickname more each time she spoke it! I don't think she'd ever called him by his real name. Kid's going to be cursed with it. I could see him walking across the stage to accept his diploma from Harvard. "And congratulations to Valedictorian, Baby Daddy Palmer." For an intelligent man, I'd allowed some insane things to continue.

"*Jack* is a baby. Babies go through stages. Is he teething? Did you check his mouth? Give him Motrin?"

"Well now, Randy, that's brilliant advice. If you think I can't think of the obvious, you're sadly mistaken. Baby Daddy's crying and it's got nothing…"

I stopped listening. "Baby Daddy." It was eerie and unsettling. So many things had become eerie and unsettling. I'd like to find the guy who coined the phrase "hindsight is 20-20" and stuff my glasses right up…

"…when I was little, Daddy always said…"

Please stop. Maybe the ESCAPE key? Poke. Poke. Poke. Nope. No matter how much I poke ESCAPE, I stay. She stays. We all stay locked in this life we made. "Emily, I want you to be quiet and listen for a minute. This is getting out of control. I told you…you know…you promised me…Jack is all right. Your panic is unwarranted."

"Liar. You're lying right now. I can tell by the tone of your voice you don't believe that for a minute. You know there's something wrong, too. You know it." She sniffled.

There was a knock on the glass partition. I snapped up my head to find Markus. He had his arm in the air, finger tapping the crystal face of his watch.

"Em. I've got to go. It's time to…"

"Some father you turned out to be." The phone slammed down in my ear, leaving me with mixed emotions. It was great to be rid of her voice, and annoying that she had the power to disconnect with such ease—a privilege I had yet to acquire.

The office door opened with a sterile swish—a gentle displacement of manufactured, filtered air. Constant temperature, regulated humidity. Inside the lab it was always a perfect seventy-two degrees with a relative humidity of seventy-five percent. As usual, Markus had strapped on his wool cap, complete with stiff brim and ear flaps so he looked like an African Elmer Fudd, only his weapon of choice was a microscope, his prey—perfect genetic combinations.

His voice was bigger than his size and always came as a surprise. "Emily?"

"You got it."

He moved inside the inner office, closed the door, then slipped off his latex gloves.

"Problem with Jack?" Markus rubbed his hands together and blew into his fingers. Poor guy, he was never warm enough. Should have been a chef working over bubbling soups and handling pastries warm from the oven. If I didn't need him so much I'd let him transfer to the simmer lab. It was plenty warm there.

"Yeah. She's all freaked out."

"What's wrong now?"

Genuine worry cut a furrow into Markus' forehead, smooth brown skin puffed into hills around coal eyes. I love that guy. "He's...he screams. He screams at things that he used to love, like he's scared. Last night he cried when I helped him with his prayers."

"Maybe he doesn't believe in God."

A year ago I would have spilt my gut laughing. Not today. The prayers were my idea, seemed like a nice way for a child to say goodnight, thinking there was someone bigger than Daddy looking over them.

I frowned.

Marcus curled up his eyebrows. "What do *you* think?"

"At first, I thought it was nothing. Stages. Three-year-old growing pains or something. Emily panics over every little thing so I usually just try to block her out. As if it's possible to block out Emily. I should be so lucky." I made the sound of little marching feet on the keyboard. Left...left...hila...left. Left...left...hila...left. "Now, I think she's right. It kills me, Markus, but I think she's right."

He approached the desk, set both hands on the edge, and leaned in close. "You think something's gone wrong?"

"No!" Wrong? When referring to my son, something going *wrong* sounded so trite. One picked up the *wrong* salad dressing, or put on the *wrong* tie. There couldn't be anything *wrong* with my son, right? "Yes! As far as 'wrong' goes, why not take it to the very beginning? The whole idea from the start was wrong. How stupid was I? Super stupid. And that old fart Daddy Jack and Emily, with the both of them hounding me and the thought of the money...stupid, all of us. Selfish."

"Randy, you're a great friend, brilliant scientist, usually funny, but when it comes to your research, you're a wet rag. You let those two rule you so you can do what you love."

Hmm. That kind of made me mad. "Are you trying to help, or push me to suicide?"

Markus laughed me off. "Stick around. I still...we *all* still need you." He nodded toward the lab. Several assistants dressed in white cloaks, hairnets, facemasks, and elastic slippers moved around. A few had on knit caps decorated with colorful pompoms. One was wearing a Winnie The Pooh hat and someone else had donned an old-fashioned beenie, complete with whirligig. That moment, their touches of individuality and humor in a repetitious and deadly serious job, irritated my mood.

"Why don't you draw some blood? I'll run a few tests and we can take at peek at his strings and make sure everything is in sync as far as the genetics are concerned."

I looked at Markus and was reminded why I needed him. "You're a simplistic son-of-a-gun. Check his strings. You don't think there's been a chromosomal mutation any more than I do."

"Nope. I bet his genie-weenies are perfect. But I always like to start with the basics and take it from there. If there's something obvious, we'll know what we're up against. If not, then we proceed from there. If you ask me, it's probably something else...at home...perhaps Emily is expecting too much...demanding too much."

Bingo! Sometimes I wondered if Markus wasn't my twin, my smarter, more rational missing half. "I'm hoping you're right. The way she looks at Little Jack, it's like she's expecting her daddy to materialize out of the boy. Shoot. I don't know anymore, Markus. Can't think straight."

"You're a daddy."

"You might want to tell Emily that."

"That's enough of Emily. I still have a bit o' breakfast trying to digest." Markus moved to the window, took his pen out of his pocket, and drummed on the glass while he looked over the city. It was his habit, to beat things with a pen or pencil while he thought. The beat was slow. A tap-tap-tappity-tap-tap-tap-tap. I wondered what he was thinking, if in his mind's eye he was picturing a world without Emily. I knew he often did. The two of them together created natural friction.

Through the glass, the sun turned Markus' chocolate skin ugly gray—like an old guy melting away to a terminal disease in hospice. Shoot. Everything looked that way. Smog cuddled the upper floors of the buildings like chubby dirty arms. The sun was nothing more than a buttery smear. Compared to the bright white and stainless steel of the lab, it looked like someone had puked on the windows.

The scenery matched the humor in the room. Markus' drumming picked up pace. Tappity-tappity-tappity-tap-tap-tappity-tappity. Oh yeah, he was thinking up a storm. His lips twitched to the beat and his eyes boiled into saucers.

I felt myself being carried into his unspoken squall. "I don't know what to do. I never thought that something could go wrong so late in the game. We've never seen it in the lab. None of the animal studies have shown any disruption in maturation. If anything..."

"Oh no!" Markus turned and shot up his hands. His pen sailed from his fingers like a missile and touched down on my keyboard.

I jumped up. "What?"

"I forgot...I came in here to tell you I've got that..."

"Missy?" Missy was Mandy's replacement. Mandy had been mercifully put to sleep. After the incident with the dead baby, she'd turned mean, biting at the staff and throwing feces out of her cage. Sobbing like an infant, Markus had had to put her to sleep.

"That's right. I've got the slide ready for your eyeball. Looks good to me. Ready to implant, I'd say."

"She ready?"

"Yeah."

"Bioevolution? Ever regret it, Markus? We could have been plastic surgeons. Stretching skin and tucking tummies."

Markus' eyes drained of emotion, went blank. "Don't ask, don't tell, my friend."

* * *

March 8
6:20 pm

I was not eager to face Emily, but was anxious to check on my son. The car ride home—usually a time to unwind and enjoy the quiet of Daddy Jack's self-made world—was unusually tense.

I called up the radio, hoping for some music.

"...his infant son, Leonardo, will be put to rest in the family burial plot..."

Sad. I made a note to remind Emily that there were bigger problems in the world. While she whined about stuffed toys and crying fits, some people were burying loved ones. That woman needed a reality check.

"...funeral services will be held for two-year-old Rosario Rueger, daughter of Texas Senator, William Rueger. The family asks that in lieu of flowers, donations be given..."

What? I poked the radio buttons and received an earful of static. All the advancements of the twenty-first century and we still lost radio transmissions. Rueger. Sounded so familiar. Rueger. Not just for being a senator. Rueger. Where had I heard that name?

"...her sudden death has shattered the senator and his wife. Rueger has already withdrawn his senate seat and..."

Gone again! Blasted smog!

"...Christians against Genetic Engineering and Reproduction have gathered in Washington for a protest prayer rally. What had started as a few hundred faithful has multiplied to nearly one million. The president will be..."

Could the news be any more depressing? I flipped off the radio, rolled down the car window, and took a deep breath of clogged air.

I choked all the way home.

* * *

March 8
6:45 pm

The door popped open forcefully, banged my forehead, and nearly knocked me down. Good thing I was fumbling with the lock-code or I might have lost my nose.

"Finally, you're home." Emily stumbled onto the step, Jack squirming in her arms.

I dropped my satchel and caught them in a hug. "Whoa! What?"

"Baby Daddy cried all day. Everything I do makes him cry."

Both wife and baby whined. Who to console first?

"It's like he's going backward, Randy. Fast! This day has been the worst. He was doing so great. He was so smart. And now...he won't even tell me colors."

Contempt twisted her face, anger at her son for a bad day. Had I ever really loved her?

"Look, Em. It could be a lot of things. Maybe something psychological. Maybe..."

"Psychological? Bull! You just can't admit that you may have made a mistake!"

Her voice was accusatory, piercing, and I suppressed the urge to strike. Instead, I shoved my forearm against her and held out my hands. "Give me the baby. You're scaring him."

Without hesitation, Emily released the child, so fast I almost dropped my son. Little Jack wriggled and squirmed, uncomfortable in my arms, but I managed to hold him. Quick, I dropped several kisses to the top of his head. His hair was sweat-soaked, but his scalp cool. No fever. Licking my lips, I tasted an odd sweetness to his sweat. Perhaps Emily had bribed him with chocolate and he'd fingered some through his hair. Even odder. Usually, I was the one who broke the nutritional rules, giving Little Jack secret treats. I couldn't imagine Emily breaking one of her own sacred laws of child upkeep. I imagined her frustrated, bribing him with candy, and felt a wave of delight at her misery. I was about to ask her about the sugary taste when she clucked her tongue in disgust.

I looked up to find her glaring, the look in her eyes like that of someone who has just caught a dog relieving himself on the floor. Apparently my affection toward Little Jack made her sick. She repeated the noise, turned away, and wobbled a crooked line through the living room and into the kitchen where she headed directly to the counter, grabbed up a glass full of something pink, and swallowed.

Like an obedient dog, I followed. As if his leg was caught in a bear trap, Little Jack howled.

Emily chugged the remainder of the drink, went to the refrigerator, pulled out a bottle of wine, and refilled the glass. She swallowed noisily and sputtered. Tears came to her eyes. "L—Look at him. Baby Daddy used to love me. Nothing makes him happy. He's in his own world."

Emily was ugly, her face puffy—not with mere tears, but swollen, I guessed, from an increased consumption of alcohol—and pinched with self-pity. The tears dripping off the end of her nose weren't for her son, but were egotistic.

Little Jack choked for a breath, then freed up another scream. I wanted to join him.

Glass in hand, Emily continued to talk, undaunted. "He pooped his pants today."

That explained the previous look. Apparently she was holding a grudge.

"Did you hear me?"

"Uh huh."

"I said he pooped in his pants. Fouled himself, then walked around as if everything was just fine. He sat in it. It was all over him. You remember how he used to scream if I didn't change him right away. Well, today he just sat in it."

Finally Little Jack stuffed his thumb in his mouth, bringing uncomfortable quiet. He hadn't sucked his thumb for more than a year. It was a habit he'd quit on his own. Now he sucked noisily and kicked against me until I finally let him down. Thumb secured in place, Little Jack half-crawled, half-walked across the floor and fitted his body into the corner. Big brown eyes, reminiscent of Emily's and Daddy Jack's and oddly mirroring mine, stared at us with caution.

"What went wrong, Randy? He should have been perfect. I know that Daddy—"

Blocking her words with my hands, I took a step forward. "No way! Don't you dare. Don't you pull that innocent, ignorant act with me. You were raised in this world and *you* of all people know that there are no guarantees. You and father wanted a clone! A carbon copy. You both thought Daddy Jack was the perfect specimen and now you've got what you wanted. If there's something wrong with Little Jack, then it's…it's…no wonder the kid acts weird. Look at you. You're drunk. From the looks of the bottle and your eyes I can't believe you're standing, nonetheless fit to take care of a three-year-old."

Emily straightened, indignant. "How dare you! You have no idea how I feel, how it is being at home all day with him. He was doing so—"

"Yeah. I heard you the first time. He was doing so great. Now he's not doing so great. He's not your perfect child. He sits in poop. He cries. I'm sorry for all that. Sorry for *you* that everything in this world doesn't fit into your cookie-cutter fantasies."

Spittle dribbled down her chin. Emily grossly licked at it, then lifted the wine bottle. "You can do better? Prove it. You feed him. Baby Daddy won't eat for me."

If my son had regressed, so had my wife. Where was the refinement and perfect manners? Shoot! She was acting like an animal. "Sober up, Em. Sober up and act like a mother."

Emily guzzled wine and turned her back.

I fetched Little Jack from the floor and carried him to the kitchen counter. "What do you want for dinner tonight?"

Jack didn't respond.

"Pizza puffs?"

Jack looked over my shoulder, around the room, then down at his hands, watching his fingers curl and uncurl with great fascination.

"Pizza puffs it is." I set him into a cushioned seat, pushed him up to the counter, and moved to the freezer.

"He's not going to eat. Baby Daddy doesn't like pizza anymore."

"Get out of here, Emily."

The pizza box instructed five minutes at med-high. I followed the orders, tossed the squares onto a plastic tray, and fingered the buttons. Had the little bleeps always been that annoying? I shivered. From behind me, I heard the clinking of glass on glass, then the sound of an empty bottle tipping over on the counter and wobbling from side to side. The unholy orchestration was topped off by the grating whisper of Emily's feet dragging over the floor. In my mind's eye I pictured her, slumped over, lips curled in pity, hauling her despair elsewhere.

I tried to sound cheerful. "Just a few minutes, Jack, and we'll be eating pizza! How about that? Sound good?" He didn't shout with delight, as I would have loved. "Jack?"

He rubbed his fingers on the smooth counter, drawing little circles. Dark brown hair curled around his ears, drawing lines toward purple circles under his eyes. He'd changed since breakfast. He looked older and, I had to admit, sick. Olive skin—slightly grayed, no longer dimpled at the knuckles, showed that the boy had lost weight or was dehydrated. Funny, without the baby fat, Little Jack looked much like he would when older. Was I looking into the eyes of Big Boy Jack? An evil voice crawled out of the dark part of my mind and told me "no," I was looking at the last of Jack.

"Jack?"

Nothing.

"Are you thirsty? You want some chocolate milk?"

The counter held his attention.

"Come on! You love chocolate milk." I lifted him up and searched his eyes. What was missing there—recognition of his daddy, love—made me cry. I held him to my shoulder like I should have when he was a newborn, but hadn't. Suddenly I regretted those lost moments and I was sorry I hadn't taken him away from that place long ago. Away from the men and women playing God. Away from the murderous clinics. Away from the simmer lab where we cooked cells to either perfection or damnable mutation. Away from dead gorillas and their babies. Away from the library of accidents—shelves holding the preserved remains of those who had failed to evolve properly. Away from Emily, who was incapable of loving two at a time.

Jack offered neither resistance nor affection.

"Please don't be sick, Jack. Please don't be sick."

My son opened his mouth and bit down, his teeth puncturing the soft flesh on my bicep.

*   *   *

March 8
7:30 pm

"What do you mean you won't go? I told you we need to do something and this is what I think is best. Of course you'll go. If you won't, then I will."

Emily tipped her head, then quickly brought it up and reached for her glass of pink. Her knuckles knocked the side of a fresh bottle of wine and it nearly toppled. Her movements reminded me one of those antique dolls held together with elastic bands—jerky and inhuman. "You won't go anywhere near my father. I told you *no*, and that's the end of it."

Confusion and a splash of contempt burned my cheeks. I tethered both anger and voice. Jack was freshly diapered and asleep in his old crib, curled up like a newborn and I did not want to wake him. "Our son is sick. I want to consult with your father about his grandson—his freaking carbon-copy grandson. I need help. I want us all to go to the clinic. Markus is already there, running out some slides. I need Daddy Jack. *You* will ask him, or *I* will. *That*, Emily, is the end of it."

"No."

I punched a dent into the mattress beside her and she didn't flinch. "Are you too drunk to understand the urgency of this? Your son is sick."

"He's ruined."

The choice of words left me speechless. I stared at her and suddenly pictured her with a set of spiked horns and a barbed tail.

"He's ruined." Her hand slipped down the side of the damp glass, and brought it to her lips. She sipped noisily. "We can try again. There has to be something wrong with what we did the first time. We can make a new Baby Daddy. This one…"

"What?!" Red and black swirled before my eyes. For the first time in my life I imagined murder, and was exhilarated. "Stop! Stop talking!" Control? I had none. That particular conversation was undeserving of control. My body responded in kind, arms and legs twitching. "You're talking about our son! Our son is sick!"

"He's not your son." Her voice was quiet.

"He *is* my son." My teeth grated. "He is sick and I will do everything I can to help him."

"He can't be fixed."

Emotional overload. I put a period to Emily. Her problems would have to wait. Little Jack came first. I popped open my satchel, fished around, found my phone, and snapped it open. Sharp bleeps sounded. What the...it was so loud it hurt my ears. So did the obnoxious burble on the other end of the line.

Ring. Like a bomb blast. And Emily murmuring, "Can't be fixed." Ring. Like a gunshot in my ear. "Daddy. Baby Daddy. Broke." Ring. Had someone thrust a poker through my eardrum? "Can't be fixed." Ring? Dear God, make it stop! Emily slurped and it sounded like she was trying to suck up a lake though a monster-sized mouth.

The noise! It was driving me—

Finally, someone picked up and I concentrated on the sleepy female voice, which was way too loud for someone who had apparently been awakened.

"Yeah. Hello? This is Randall Palmer. I want to speak to Jack, please."

She knew who I was and seemed to be relieved. Her sigh bounced with the quiet of a cannonball. After a moment she told me hello and asked how I was doing.

Made me more anxious. I bounced in place. "I said I want to talk to Daddy..."

With quick caution, precisely chosen words, she enlightened me.

My feet stilled. "What?"

She continued, detailing the situation.

"What the hell are you talking about?"

An apology, followed by another bellowing sigh of relief that someone had finally decided to help. Poor Miss Emily hasn't been acting herself lately.

"I don't..." My lips trembled. Poor Miss Emily? "I—"

The phone left my hand, jetted across the room, hit the wall, and shattered. Gray plastic pieces littered the eggshell carpet.

"Can't be fixed." Emily's voice was a whisper punching through the air.

"What have you done?" I turned to her, slowly, trying not to tip over, my head whirling, emotions out of control.

"Can't be fixed."

And I ran, grabbed her by the shoulders and pushed her into the mattress. "What is going on?"

"I want Daddy." She sniveled the pleasure of a pig guzzling slop.

"Emily!"

Little Jack cried from his room, his voice weak and scared.

"Baby Daddy's broke again."

Was she smiling? "Talk to me now. I swear I'll take your neck in my hands—"

"Trying to fix what was broke." Tears formed in the corners of Emily's red and brown eyes. "Daddy was broke. Trying to fix him."

"Talk to me."

"All I wanted was for Daddy to be fixed."

"Talk to me."

Emily squirmed against my hands. Jack bawled.

"Let me up."

"Talk to me." I pinched her flesh, wanted to tear through her skin.

"I…he was…I went there, to see Daddy." Her eyes went someplace else, to a faraway world, and she told her story in a dreamlike voice. "So long ago. When you came to GBI. Right about when I met you." She grinned for a moment, then pouted. "I went to see Daddy. He didn't answer the door, so I went around back, through the kitchen. The place was a mess. Food and dishes and clothes. The water was on, just running and running. The refrigerator was open, everything in it warm. It smelled like…like garbage. I thought something bad had happened to Daddy. I ran through the house, called his name. Daddy! Daddy!" Emily closed her eyes. Tears flowed.

Her breath came at me sour and sweet. Made me nauseous. "Talk to me." I tightened my grip.

"He was in his den. Naked. Completely naked. The computer was off and he was poking at the keyboard and humming. Humming a song or something. When he heard me, he turned around. He looked at me and smiled. He smelled like a toilet. He had used the floor as a toilet." She cried.

"Talk to me."

"I called his doctor. He told me Daddy was…had been slipping for some time. He'd been on medicine, but must have gone off it, or forgotten to take it. He…we put him back on. It didn't really help." Emily blinked and her tears stopped.

"What's wrong with him?"

"Let me up."

"What's wrong with him?"

"He's broke. He can't be fixed."

"What was wrong with him?"

Emily turned up her face and looked directly into my eyes, defiant.

"He...we thought it might be Alzheimer's."

"Alzheimer's? We can cure that. Why didn't his doctor—"

And I knew why. It was rare. But it was. I felt like someone had set off dynamite in my bowels.

"He tried gene therapy and it didn't work. Oh God! Little Jack! If I'd have known, I would never have—" For a moment my tears stopped my tongue. Finally, I found my way clear to accuse. "You wanted a new Daddy."

She blinked. I pictured one of those Disney characters—wild animals, softened with fluff and given human emotions. A bear that would naturally chew off a man's arm, suddenly pastelled into a cuddly, little, friend-to-all. I hate Disney.

"Your Daddy was broke and you wanted a new one?"

I squeezed until the wounded-animal look was replaced with a very real grimace. "Yes. Yes. A new Daddy." Her face lit with expectation. "I love my Daddy."

"You're a murderer."

"I wanted to fix Daddy."

"No! You wanted a perfect Daddy. When yours got sick, you made a new one. You as good as killed our baby."

"I thought maybe even if Baby Daddy did get the disease it wouldn't come until later and surely by then they'd have come across a cure. You said yourself within the next decade disease will be obliterated. You said that."

"You damned our son to a vicious deadly disease with the hope that there would be a cure in time to save him?"

"I thought—"

"You thought about yourself."

"Don't you fault me. You're not so different. Look in the mirror, Randy. For Pete's sake, open your eyes. We're one in the same."

Jack cried.

I turned my back to Emily and asked her over my shoulder, "Who's been sending all the memos from Daddy Jack these past two years?"

She sniffled, a sound like water chugging down a clogged drain, but didn't tell what I already knew.

"It was you. You kept things running, as if everything was just perfect. You're crazy, Emily. Absolutely whacko."

She slipped back into a haze. "Baby Daddy's broke. Daddy's broke. I'm broke. You're broke."

Calmly, I left the room, walked down the hall, and picked up my son. He had wet through his clothes. I stripped him and diapered him and dressed him in his once-favorite *Bug-a-Boo* sweat suit. Little Jack loved *Bug-a-Boos*—an animated spider and firefly and inchworm and ant and talkative grasshopper just trying to get along in a silly world of miscommunications, learning each other's personalities and cultures all the while teaching little ones a sweet life lesson—Love one another.

Too bad people couldn't be more like the *Bug-a-Boos*. Miss Spider loved Mr. Glow Bug even if he did sometimes keep her awake at night with his flickering fanny. Once, she wove him a little muff to cover his light but found him the next morning stuck to a blackberry bush, tired and frustrated. After a good laugh they'd decided not to try and change each other again.

I sat in the rocking chair, holding Little Jack, thought of my life and Emily's life and Daddy Jack, and I cried. Cry and rock. Cry and rock. Gently until...

* * *

March 9
6:20 am

Someone was knocking on the front door.

"Shhhh," I told Little Jack as I carried him down the stairs. He was very quiet.

The knock wasn't. My ears throbbed at the sound. Who would be making such a noise? The amplification made it hard for me to walk. I stumbled ahead, cussed under my breath, and opened the door to Markus. He looked like he'd crawled out of a war. Shirt ripped, hair mashed down with sweat, dotted with droplets of blood. He was crying and his eyes...scared me.

"Randy! I'm so sorry. Randy...I..." He hobbled to the overstuffed chair, plopped down and sunk deep, the sigh of air like a storm. Would that noise wake the baby?

The baby? I looked down at Little Jack. His chest shuddered and he coughed. I'd heard that sound before. Some people called it a death rattle.

"It's all right, baby. Sleep. Daddy's got you. Sleep." And I swear, in that beautiful part of mind, the piece of me that hadn't turned black heard him say, "Hold me, Daddy. Don't let me go."

I did and I wouldn't. I rocked him from side to side in my arms until he settled, then I trailed my stare from my little boy to my friend.

Markus was sitting like a stain in Emily's big flowered chair, the chair she'd purchased so she'd have a nice big soft place to sit and nurse the baby. He was still struggling to catch his breath. I'd let him regain his composure while I told him what I knew.

"It's all over, Markus. Little Jack's sick and I'm...I'm...there's no...seems Emily wanted a replacement for her daddy. Daddy Jack's got Alzheimer's. Incurable. Won't respond to therapy. Pretty sure Emily's lost her mind. I'm glad. I hope it hurts. And now, Little Jack...he's dying."

Tears popped from Markus' eyes as if under great pressure. Never had I seen a man so desperately sad. "It's not Alzheimer's. It's... Oh! How do I start?"

"Start what? Markus, didn't you hear what I said? Little Jack—"

"Is yours. Was supposed to be yours, Randy! I couldn't stand Emily and the old man having their way and—I mean, look at you. You and Daddy Jack look alike and I figured we could pull it off for a long time, until Little Jack grew up and then, well... I swapped cells, Randy. I used one of yours, so Little Jack would be yours. It was supposed to be my gift to you. One friend to the other."

With my mouth open, I stared at him and wished myself dead. It had to be a dream or a joke or a trick. Whatever it was, I was unable to comprehend. My mind was a blur and I was so tried and my body ached and I was overwhelmingly thirsty. It was as if all at once everything was wrong. I took a breath, heard a gurgle deep in my throat, coughed loose a phlegm ball, and licked my lips. So dry and sweet, like sugar. "What the—"

Marcus cut me short. "Let me finish. It gets worse, Randy. I was at the lab and I pulled up the files we have on you and Little Jack. I ran a question through the computer, trying to find anything, anyone, with a problem that resembled the boy's. You know, a tracer, and it came up with...insane genetic matches. You and Daddy Jack are matches, as are thirty-three children produced at GBI in the replication center."

It was if something punched me in the head, as if an invisible fist had come out of nowhere and clobbered me. Stars blinked in front of my eyes and my brain slapped into the sides of my skull. Whatever Markus was saying, I didn't want to hear.

"Yes, my friend." Markus' voice cracked, reminding me of the radio coming in and out of range. "Seems Daddy Jack has been replicating himself for a long, long time."

"No."

"I cracked into his personal files, Randy. It's all there. He thought he was…do you know what his password was? God! As I was trying to break in, it just popped into my head. What *would* he use? And I thought, *God*! And I was right! Bang! I was in. And in those files it's all black and white. He's been using his own cells, first in the fertility clinic, then for replication. According to the fertility clinic numbers, there are sixty-six perfect clones of Daddy Jack ranging in age from nine to forty-two, you being one of them."

"God," I said.

"Yes. God." Markus wiped his face and nose with his hands. "And it gets worse and worse and worse."

I was one of the unreal, a lab experiment. I was a chip off Daddy Jack? My parents were not my parents. My son was not my son. My wife was…closer to a daughter. Incest? What could you call us?

"Something bad is happening, my friend. Something wicked…evil. You can call it what you want. They stormed that facility. GBI is like a war zone. CAGER's are tearing the place apart." He broke down again. "And they're all dying, Randy. All the little babies made there in the clinics…all dying."

It had to be a dream or a joke or a trick.

"They're calling it the Wrath of God Virus. It hits and kills pretty quick. Most of the parents haven't even had the chance to take their kids to the doctor before it's too late. I don't even know how it works. It just kills."

I looked down. Little Jack had his thumb in his mouth and appeared to be sleeping. His cheeks were blue under the brush of his black lashes. He was gone and I knew it. Baby Daddy would never cry again.

"Randy?"

Tears slipped down my face and filled the crack of my lips, tasting like sugar. Hours earlier I'd kissed my son's head and tasted the same. Sweet Little Jack. I could die for the pain. How was it possible that I could hurt so much yet remain on my feet? I tucked my son against my shoulder and rubbed his back. So small. So freaking innocent! And I loved that little boy!

"Is Little Jack…"

It was in Markus' eyes. He knew the answer to the question he could not ask.

"They're *all* dying, Markus. What do you mean by *all*?"

He talked through his pain, and I knew then that Markus was the strongest man I'd ever met. I had been blessed to have him for a friend, and I was glad to have him with me. "From what I can see, it's every clone and replicated human in the world. Not just Daddy Jack's, not just the ones from our replication labs, but every person who—" Markus moved to the wall unit and punched a button. "I'll show you, my friend."

Stories poured from the speakers like hellfire as he scanned through the broadcasts.

ABC—"...twenty-four children, from newborns to some as old as twelve, have been pronounced dead in the past twelve hours. The mayor of New York has declared..."

CBS—"...the death toll is rising at a rate that cannot be calculated..."

WBC—"It seems that the virus is not selective to age. In Colorado, twins, age twenty-two, have been diagnosed with The Wrath of God..."

INW—"...there have been reports from China, Japan, Spain, Greenland, and Germany and the numbers and locations are expected to mount. Two cases are human clones from early experiments who, until yesterday, had been living..."

CND—"...one major link has been followed to GBI in Idaho. Doctor Jack Gascon, Founder and CEO, has yet to offer comment..."

NBC—"...CAGER's continue their prayer vigil over the ruins of GBI, while newly formed groups have begun attacks on offshoot labs studying bioevolution in Mexico, Germany and..."

Once again, with my mouth open, I stared at Markus and wished myself dead; a request I imagined would soon be answered. It was not a dream or a trick or a joke. I remembered the look in Lisa Ripple's eyes. If anyone could be, she was the snowball that would survive this hell on earth and bring the flames to simmer. And there was the lone woman and her suicide mission—dying for her convictions. I recalled all the voices caught together in prayer, the warnings and more, the subtle internal feelings of knowing something was wrong.

It was real.

There I was, holding a little boy who never should have been. He'd suffered to appease the fears of a madman.

I should never have been. And I guessed I wouldn't be much longer. My head was pounding, and even the minutest sounds were painful. I was sick. Was that how it began? Painful sensations, the noises of the giggly doll blasting like rockets in a child's ears? Poor Baby Daddy. He hadn't deserved that.

"Pudding. When did it become so bad to make pudding, Markus? To do it the way it had always been done, before the world got fast and perfect?"

He stared at me with what I believed was the same expression I'd offered to him several times in the past few minutes—mouth gawking, eyes incredulous.

"Never mind, Markus." I carried Little Jack to the flowered chair and set him on the cushion. So small, he lay on it, looking like a toy. "I love you, Jack. Always did. Always will."

In the fresh and wonderful part of my mind, Little Jack said, "I love you too, Daddy. I love you, too. See ya soon."

"Yeah. You will."

Then, while I was still able, Markus by my side, we drove to the news station and I took over the microphone. With every ounce of power I had in me, I told the world what had happened at the GBI—everything I knew—and I warned them.

My end speech went like this: "There was a madman who claimed a seat above God. He told us not to look back, People! He told us to command our futures.

"And we believed him, People. We believed him. You did. I did. We believed a lie!

"A little boy died in my arms today. A boy without origins in the natural processes of life—a boy who was created in a lab to fulfill monstrous desires.

"I, another cursed creation, will die soon, and I pray my soul will find a place beside that little boy's, that we may love each other in heaven.

"That's right! Heaven, People! I'm talking about heaven and hell and…and a man who claimed he did not believe in God, but at the same time, spent his life trying to outsmart Him.

"Who can claim to outsmart God, but one who truly believes? The man who told us not to look back believed in God with such fear that he refused to die, made copies of himself and sent those human copies all over the earth, thinking he would therefore always be a part of this world. He feared God to such a degree that he lied and murdered, killing his own to survive!

"Why? What would drive a man to such extremes? Did he fear Hell? Oh yeah, People, Jack Gascon feared Hell.

"How do I know? Because I *am* that man, People! He is me. I am him. We are one in the same, except…I…I will not deny what I know. I will face the truth and am thankful for the chance to do so.

"And so should you, People. So should you.

"Look back! We haven't moved forward into an age of perfection and enlightenment. We've disevolved, People. *See* what we've become and stop it. *See* what we've done to ourselves and our children? Lust for perfection engenders a deadly cost. We have become programmed to love with such prejudice that we are repulsed by natural differences. The wonderful, unique qualities that make us human we call flaws.

"The flaw is in our hearts, People!

"The big catastrophe is here! In trying to evolve to perfection, we have damned ourselves!

"But there remains hope. Change.

"We can seek the truth, learn to love again, put our faith in One who is higher than us, smarter than us, selfless and loving—One who will not be mocked by human pride.

"When you think about life, about where we came from, remember it's all about *Who* put us here, People.

"It's all about *Who*.

"The babies and children and men and women dying all over the world today should not be dying. They should never have been at all.

"It is a sad lesson, People.

"It hurts.

"Even now I feel the sickness, the Wrath of God, killing me, and I'm ready.

"Please, People, think…think and learn and know that it's all about Who made us, Who created life.

"It's all about Who, People.

"It's all about Who.

"He is showing His anger, making us face our mistakes, but He loves. He is doing what has to be done, telling us, 'No. No more.'

"It's too late for me. Too late for my son, Baby Daddy. For all the Baby Daddy's.

"But it's not too late for you, People. Be thankful for life! Go home, hug your children, hug each other, turn on the *Bug-a-Boos* and make pudding…the old-fashioned way.

"It's not too late for you, People.

"It's not too late for you."

FREAK OF NATURE

"Lucas! Lordy son, what's happened?" His mama's big, warm arms wrapped tightly around him and lifted him from the rowboat. She was crying. "Lucas? Where's Michael? Where's your brother?"

Lucas snuggled, smelled her—lilac mixed with brown sugar and flour. "I love you, Mama."

She trembled and his little arms held her.

"Lucas, where's Michael?"

"The fish came, Mama. They came and took him away."

And she screamed.

* * *

The boat drifted atop the surface, looking like a toy. Black Bottom was an expansive body of water, its banks lining the sides of three counties. Kids thought it a hoot to hang out on the shoreline near the boundaries at night, beer cans in hand, ready to jump over the invisible lines when the cops threatened them with a ride into town. Bo, Lucas, and Robby had been those kids nearly twenty years ago, high school boys funning it up in a slow, southern town.

Time brought changes. A few. The boys, now men, still hung around the lake, drinking beer, but preferred to do it from the cushioned seats of the boat, with a cooler stuffed with iced six-packs, and fishing poles at the ready.

"Hey! Bo, what did you go and do that for?" Robby's voice rattled the soothing sounds of the lake, sounding alien as it bounced through the heavy sigh of misted breezes and the eager cries of hungry gulls.

"Can it, Robby. Ain't nothing more useless than a Strawberry Bass. Blasted nasty fishies eat every minnow they can till there's no good bass to catch."

Another round of bickering had begun. Lucas listened to Bo and Robby whine at each other and kept his eye on his line. He wondered if fish were deaf. He'd always enjoyed fishing and the peace that came with it, and had assumed fish were pretty good listeners. The way his friends were fussing it up in the back of the boat, he figured the fish of Black Bottom had gotten an earful and he might as well pull up anchor and head to shore. Somehow, hooking a deaf fish just didn't seem like good sportsmanship.

Robby continued to nag Bo. "What you did was just plain cruel. Don't do that no more. Dang it! This is why I don't like fishing with you. You don't care nothing about catching the fish, you're just looking for a way to be mean."

And Bo kept giving it back. "Dang, you're a lame one, ain't ya. For a grown man you talk like a baby."

"Shut up!"

Bo tuned his voice up an octave, loaded it with sarcasm, and squealed, "Shut up!"

Lucas took the cue to interject. "What's going on guys?" He reeled in the line, craned his neck toward his friends, and prepared to cast, holding the pole in front of him like the Olympic Torch.

Robby pointed at Bo, his lips dipped into a pout. "He's mutilatin' the Strawberries." With a big head on delicate shoulders, nescient green eyes, couldn't grow a beard if offered a million bucks and a supermodel bride, Robby looked like a little boy trying to wear a man's body.

Bo slipped a pair of needle-nosed pliers into his jeans' pocket and glared at Robby. "Now that's a big word there—mutilatin'. Can you spell that for me?"

Robby scowled, and Lucas knew he was putting letters together in his head, ready to accept Bo's challenge. He couldn't let him do it. "Never mind, Robby. He's just teasing. He probably can't even spell it himself." He turned to Bo. "Is what he said about the Strawberry true?"

"What?" Bo asked.

Lucas felt a wave break in his belly, an odd burning creep down into his groin. Bo's face—false ignorance married to a bully's sneer—stirred up a fire deep inside. As Bo blinked at him, waiting for an answer, a little boy's voice—an audible memory—sounded in Lucas' ear. *You're hurting him, Michael. Stop it!*

Lucas quivered, tried to tune it out, and addressed his friend. "Don't play me for stupid, Bo. Did you mutilate, m-u-t-i-l-a-t-e, a Strawberry?" Hot energy coursed down his legs and he felt the pulses of anger. Usually a tame man, Lucas could spark a temper when provoked.

Once he had kicked in Old Man Mueller's car door so it had to be pried opened with a crowbar and the hinges torched in order to finally remove it. Lucas had watched Mueller pull into the driveway, run over his dog, Lucy—who was known to sunbathe on the gravel—then stumble drunk into his house without a glance back. The dog had been put down the next day, the vet bill to fix two broken legs and a shattered hip too steep a climb for Mueller. And there was the time when Lucas was about ten or eleven and his grandfather had returned from a hunting trip with a doe strapped to the trunk of his car. The sight of her face, tongue lolling, eyes wide and glazed, her white belly ripped and bloody, nipples sagging and leaking milk, had flipped a switch. He'd pictured the doe's fawn starving and had literally seen red, and attacked his PawPaw's weapons, smashing his bow, quiver, and arrows to pieces.

His mama was proud of him, told him he was more sensitive than most and not to be ashamed. But his brother...Michael wasn't so kind. *Lucas Pucas, the crybaby. Ya little nancy boy, you're gonna grow up to be a big, fat sissy!*

Now, Bo manipulated the handle of the pliers, looking like a leathered skeleton fondling the keys to the gates of hell. He suffered from small man's disease—five-foot-two, weighing in at a buck twenty-five when soaking wet, full to the gills on Old Milwaukee before taking his daily constitutional. Bo had a wife four times his size, with a mouth as big as her fist as big as a grapefruit. She loved to use the first two and wouldn't be caught dead eating the third. Bo spent his time away from her blowing off pent-up steam. He and Robby were well suited. Robby sucked up the attention, negative and all, and Bo got to be the big guy. "You bet I did," Bo said. "I crushed the little car-nee-vores mouth and he won't be eating no more minnows. Every baby he eats is one more Big Mouth I get to catch."

Lucas shook his head. "Ya know, Bo, I don't think old Black Bottom needs you to be playing God with her life cycles. There's a reason for every fish in there and there's plenty for us to catch and eat without you deciding who gets to live and die."

"Well, thank you for that informative lesson on nature, but I ain't caught me a ding-dang thing today and I bet that Strawberry's got a belly full of Big Mouth minnows." Bo's lips curled up into a dare.

"Geeze, Louise." Robby sighed, slipped the plastic lid over the top of the bait bucket, sat down, and lifted his beer. "I wish I'd of stayed home. Ain't caught nothing and now I gots to watch evil Bo mash fish mouths. It ain't how I wanted to spend my one day off."

Bo snapped his pliers at Robby. Defensive, Robby dropped the beer can and flapped his hands in front of his face. "Uhh ii ouuw." Amber foam dribbled from his lips.

Bo was on a roll. "What's that? You trying to tell me something? You think them little fishies at the diner like being dipped in bread crumbs and pitched into a vat of boiling oil?" He grabbed Robby's baseball cap with the pliers and lifted it off his head.

Robby wiped his chin with one hand and grabbed for the hat with the other. "That ain't the same thing, and you know it. That's my job and them fish is dead. You're a jerk."

"And you're a kitty." Bo toyed with the hat. "Here kitty kitty kitty. Come and get your hat, kitty."

Take me home. I wanna go home. Please, Michael. I don't wanna fish with you. Take me home. Lucas grimaced at the voice in his head—Michael's voice, still stinging him as it had decades ago.

He rubbed his burning gut and glowered at his friends. "Give him the hat and sit down and both of ya shut up. If I wanted to be in the middle of a raucous, I'd go on into ShoeBooties, punch up The Dixie Chicks on the jukebox, and ask someone to dance."

Immediately Robby and Bo grinned, obviously picturing the trouble that would cause. ShoeBooties wasn't a dance club. Laborers from town—carpenters, electricians, field hands, and mechanics—went to the ramshackle bar to swill Busch on tap and eye up the twins, Misty and Kristy. Fresh out of high school, soft as kittens and sassy as badgers, the girls carried their trays over their heads, balanced on cotton-candy pink fingertips. Their denim shorts rode high on their thighs, and their T-shirts were tied into knots in the back, so when they sashayed up to tables, the offers to refill a pitcher or mug seemed to come from their pretty bellybuttons. ShoeBooties was a man's hangout, where married and single alike gathered in artificial dark to ogle twin bellies, swap bull, and exchange never-to-be fantasies of lives they could have had.

Lucas was single, and a man, and therefore should have been a natural fit into a ShoeBootie stool. However, being thirty-five, never having had a girlfriend, and not making an effort to amend his bachelor situation, he wasn't one of the guys. He rarely went there. It was kinder on his soul to stay home where he didn't have to play deaf to the grumbled comments, "Ya think he's one of them fag-boys? Ya think that thing when he was a kid turned him queer? Ain't natural living like he does...he's...he's a freak of nature."

Lucas turned back to the lake, sighed away the rumors, and was momentarily comforted by the beauty before him. Nothing was as magnificent, serene, or mystifying as Black Bottom, and he loved it. A natural formation, it was fed by an underground spring, therefore maintaining a constant frigid temperature. It was a hungry body of water, and over the years it had chewed away shoreline, steadily increasing its girth. There were no sandy beaches or grassy flats. The lake was an inky swell wrapped up in a band of muck and drowning timber. Anyone crazy enough to wade into the water would either sink in black goo or be swallowed up in one of the countless, undetectable drop-offs.

Perhaps Bo and Robby were trying too hard to be comical. Possible. The lake affected everyone differently. Spooked some. Excited others.

And then there was the mystery of Michael.

Thirty years earlier, Lucas and his big brother had rowed onto the lake to fish. Days later, Lucas had drifted to shore alone, his misted recollection of fish taking Michael away marked down as a five-year-old's need to cloak what had probably been a horrifying, tragic drowning.

Over the years, Black Bottom had made many claims. Fishermen, drunken swimmers, kids on dares, boaters, and cars and their drivers. Divers recovered what they could, but most of the victims of Black Bottom remained her hostage. Aggressive rescue was costly and dangerous. The locals didn't complain. It was accepted. Some things were better left alone.

And some things were better left at home.

Lucas peeked over his shoulder. Bo and Robby were air-punching each other. Grown men locked in childhood, they were more suited to spend the afternoon in the Burger Hut indoor playground. Lucas hadn't invited them; they had begged to come. Every time he hitched up his boat it seemed like someone invited themselves, as if it was some unspoken law that he couldn't be allowed on the lake alone. How he longed to do just that.

Bo cuffed Robby's ear. "You dickhead."

Robby curled up his nose. "You...you wish you had a dick."

"You wouldn't know what to do with your dick if it crawled out of your pants and whispered instructions in your ear."

"Screw you, Bo!"

"See! Now I'm really hoping you didn't mean that, Robby. 'Cuz if you meant that, why, I'd have to kick your butt. You ain't one of them girly men, are you?"

An embarrassed quiet settled. Lucas knew that if the conversation had taken place outside of his earshot, sooner or later the term "girly man" would have been applied to him.

You're gonna grow up to be a sissy, Lucas. The voice of twelve-year-old Michael blurred with the snickers of his friends.

Lucas pinched his teeth together and forced his words through them. "Shut up! And if you can't shut up, then get out! Just get out!"

Bo winked at Robby. "Get out? Be quiet or get out? Now that's a hoot, Lucas. Do you think we can walk on water?"

Robby joined in. "Yeah, Lucas. Get out? Who do you think I am, Moses or something?"

Poor Robby, dumb as dirt and just as common. Bo wouldn't let the opportunity pass. "That's Jesus, you idiot. Jesus walked on water."

Lucas kneaded his pole.

"I knew that," Robby said.

"You wouldn't know your name if you didn't have it pinned to your shirt."

You quit your crying or I'll toss you to the fishes. Lucas Pucas. Crybaby of all crybabies.

Lucas forced a deep breath, cast out and reeled in the line, wishing himself calm. Let them bicker. Next time, he'd come alone, if it meant sneaking out in the middle of the night. The day would close with or without the three of them getting into a senseless brawl, so Lucas was determined to enjoy what time he had left.

Already the sun had slipped over the horizon, afternoon having bowed to evening. With a muted glow, the water looked surreal, something an artist would covet, yearning to be able to capture in manmade oils what nature so easily created. A soft breeze came from the south, carrying the scent of pine. A pair of gray gulls circled nearby, knowing that the end of the day brought treats, fishermen dumping bait buckets overboard.

Lucas smiled. He loved being out here adrift, catching his dinner and throwing back what he didn't need, knowing that Black Bottom was there for him—their relationship one of mutual respect.

Wistful, he pictured his dinner plate later that evening—side of potatoes, greens, and a roll. No fish. His friends and their slapstick comedy had ruined a good day. Lucas was about to tell them so and reel in his line a final time when a sterling flash caught his eye. He leaned over and there it was again. A metallic ripple in the dark current. Slowly, the silvery slash took form, wobbled to surface, then skittered sideways.

"Strawberry." Lucas shook his head. "Damn it, Bo. You're Strawberry Bass is over here doing the death dance."

Sad thing, the death dance. Wounded, unable to swim properly, therefore not allowing a proper flow of water through the gills, the fish was destined to die. He'd either suffocate or be made a snack by a larger fish.

Robby and Bo joined in a laugh.

"Not funny." Lucas reeled in his line and set down the pole. The Strawberry zigged a crooked line.

"Look, Lucas, all I did was give his lips a squeeze. It wasn't enough to kill him. He shouldn't be doing no death dance. What a wussy fishy."

"Liar! I saw what you did. You crushed its mouth. Hurt it real good."

Michael! No. It hurts him. Please! Please stop!

Tension rode up over Lucas' back and down his arms. He felt dew tickle his lips, perspiration scratch his underarms. "Well, Bo, from the looks of it, you did more than you say. He's suffering."

"Too bad evil Bo caught him. If I'd of caught him, I'd of killed him right off. I'm not cruel." The little boy in Robby came out in his voice. Lucas thought that if he turned to look, he'd see a five-year-old boy swimming in a man's T-shirt and jeans.

Bo giggled.

Lucas stiffened and his mind rewound to a fishing trip thirty years ago...

You ain't no brother of mine, Lucas Pucas. Little sissy. No brother with my blood would be crying and sniffling like a big baby over a busted up fishy.

And Michael continued to torture the fish. He dug its eyes out of the sockets, laid the slippery balls on the bottom of the boat, and mashed them with his thumbs. The fish flopped crazily—tail slapping, mouth

working.
Lucas screamed. Cried. Grabbed for the fish.
Michael laughed and cut off the fish's tail.
Why did the poor thing live? Dear God, make Michael stop. Lordy! Lordy! It hurts him. Please! Stop!
And the boat shook. There were thumps on the sides. Michael dropped his blade and grabbed for a hold.
Lucas snatched the fish and...

Lucas clenched his fingers. It hurt. His nails were short but still dug into the flesh of his palms. The Strawberry did several circles near the edge of the boat. Lucas was about to grab the net when his stare landed on the fish's eye.

Man and fish united. Lucas felt a change, as if he'd stepped through a door into a new world. He became the Strawberry, seeing and feeling as the fish.

And he hovered in the throbbing current. Through the wavering light he saw shapes above him—the outlines of monsters, their forms coming in and out of focus. Afraid, he wanted to escape, submerge to the cool, dark deep, away from the harsh light. He longed to cuddle in muck, camouflaged and safe, free to lunch on minnows and greens.

But he would not. Could not. His mouth...the agony.

The vision blurred, turned gray, then cleared, and he was Strawberry deep in the lake. Through the murk he watched seaweed dance—graceful bands of grass. Slick, black logs made puzzles atop a mat of black leaves and moss-coated rocks. Then a fish—huge, a monster, the biggest Brown Bass he'd ever seen, its mouth open, gaping like a cave, rows of needle teeth—moved forward and bit down. It was torture. His side...the pinching and tugging...an explosion of pain. Loosened scales dotted the water and a slimy slip of radiant skin caught in the current and wriggled by. The water fogged with blood, innards, and mauled flesh.

He tried to swim away, but the bigger fish kept chewing, eating the Strawberry—Lucas!—alive...

Frigid water splashed on his face and Lucas shook his head. The image scattered and he returned to reality. The terror of what he'd seen, however, remained. Salted bile tickled his tongue, and he gagged down a mouthful of vomit, an acidic path scorching his throat.

He held Strawberry cupped in his hand, fractured mouth opening and closing, gills rippling useless, sucking fresh air. Had the fish jumped? Had Lucas scooped him from the water? The Strawberry's black eyes shone like beacons and Lucas recalled Michael's eyes, shocked wide. It was the last thing Lucas remembered before the riot of fish...

"Lucas?"

Gently, Lucas set the Strawberry in the water and turned his head. Bo stood over him, fishing pole in hand, metal lure fitted with a tri-barbed hook flashing in the sun. In his jeans' pocket were the pliers.

"Lucas? You all right? You—"

Lucas leapt, wrenched the fishing pole from Bo's hand, and threw it into the lake. Before Bo could react, Lucas pushed him, grabbed the pliers, and flung them overboard.

"Holy crap. What the—" Robby took a step backward and dropped his pole.

The boat wobbled. Soft knocks underwater. Thumps—little drumbeats against the metal bottom.

Robby stared down. "What is that?" He flapped his arms and hopped, as if to step over the noise. The frantic wallop of his boots mixed with the pitters and patters from below and sounded like a tap dancer acting out a murder scene.

"What the—" Bo's question cut off.

All eyes turned up to see what had caused him to stop short. From the edge of the horizon the water lifted up in a beautiful curl—a wave decorated with writhing, vibrant colors, like gemstones catching the sun's rays.

"Oh, holy hell!" Robby toppled backward and fell headfirst into the water.

The swell rose up, moved forward, crested over him, and the lake came alive with a thick mass of fish. The water festered with bubbles. A dense wave of iridescent colors rippled on the surface. The boat rocked side to side and the noise grew loud—splashing, thudding.

Robby bobbed to the surface and screamed for help.

Bo extended his hand, but a knot of fish threw their bodies against him, thwarting the rescue.

"Help!" Robby choked on water. "Help me! They're—" His head sunk, then snapped back. "They're pulling me under. Help—I'm drown—"

Large Mouth Bass, Perch, Sunfish, Bluegills, and Strawberries swam together as a unit, churning around the boat—around Robby.

"Holy crap, Lucas! Help him!"

Lucas stared.

A hand popped through the fish, grabbing at air. Then Robby emerged, flopped on his side, and kicked.

"Death dance." Bo's voice was soft with wonder.

For a moment it appeared that Robby would be delivered back to the boat. Atop the fish, he waved his arms, kicked his legs, and opened his mouth. He didn't get a chance to make a final plea. Shimmering scales and fins blanketed Robby, and sucked him out of sight. The water calmed. Ripples fanned out in concentric circles. Robby and the battalion of fish vanished.

"Lucas? W—What happened." Bo sniveled, wiping his nose with the back of his hand. "What just happened? Lucas?"

Lucas glared.

"Lucas?" Bo scooted on his fanny toward the front of the boat. Without Robby, he was the dumb one, the little guy, the whipping post. Lucas wondered if his wife saw the same feeble expression just before she planted her fist up the side of his head. He guessed so as he spun and kicked Robby's pole into the water.

"Lucas. Stop man. You're...you're scaring me. You really are."

Lucas cleared out the boat. Cushions. Bait buckets. The cooler. He grabbed his tackle box, opened it, and turned it upside down over the water. Lures, line, swivels, sinkers, leads, and tools scattered and sunk. A few red and white bobbers drifted away. He chuckled and dropped the empty box.

"Lucas?"

The boat rocked from side to side. Muffled thumps came from underneath. The lake morphed from a crystalline gray sheet to a wriggling mat of fish, the renewed attack more vicious than the one that had taken Robby. Large fish thumped against the sides of the boat, denting the metal. Several sleek fish leapt from the water, sailed over the boat, and landed atop the living weave on the other side. Fish jumped into the boat. First one. Then two and two more. Then three. Slowly, the boat filled.

Bo screamed, tried to bat them out of the air, managed to catch one, and threw it back. His efforts were wasted. For every fish he averted, several landed at his feet. Within minutes, the silver-bottomed boat was covered.

"Lucas?" Bo looked up in question, his eyes begging.

Lucas answered with a smile, his body swaying side to side, his hair tugging in the wind as the boat cut a path to the middle of the lake, carried atop the thick of fish. The mossy bank and slick timber outline grew smaller and smaller until it looked surreal—like a child's watercolor painting.

Still, the lake churned around them. Fish piled on top of each other in the boat, rising up to Bo's belly.

He pulled up onto his knees.

The boat rocked back and forth.

Fish knocked the bottom and sides and filled it.

Bo howled, his eyes bulging.

Lucas stood calm, knee-deep in fish.

The boat tipped. A steady flow of fish slipped over the side. Even as the boat sunk, Bo pushed at the thick, slippery wave.

Lucas remained standing atop a platform of fish. He watched Bo struggle, momentarily awed by the man's physical strength—as powerful as he was cruel. Coughing and spitting, Bo rolled. Face up. Face down. Face up. Face down. Each revolution quicker, his time to gather air shorter.

His death dance was beautiful. Bo fluttered over the surface, lingered, then disappeared.

Carrying Lucas, the fish submerged, spinning in slow circles. Around and around they turned, and he immersed to his waist, then his chest and chin. From over the top of the colorful, squirming bodies, Lucas was pleased to see Strawberry wriggle to him. Lucas laughed and water filled his mouth, nose, covered his eyes.

Deeper and deeper.

Curious, fish swam around him like old friends come to assess the changes that had occurred with the passing of time. They told stories that burned Lucas' soul and he knew he'd never leave them. He smiled his promise and winked at Strawberry, who hovered in front of him, black eyes fixed on his, injured mouth set to the left as if he held a smoldering cigar. Lucas put out his hand and Strawberry swam into it, wriggling back and forth like a puppy begging for pets.

Beyond the Strawberry, Lucas saw Bo. Arms overhead, body limp like a marionette. Fish twirling around him like harem dancers' scarves.

Down Lucas sunk, Strawberry secure by his side until he settled on the bottom.

A pile of boats littered the floor like an underwater port. Dim light illuminated water grasses and flickered off shiny lures and catgut line. There were skeletons sunk in the muck, reaching upward, swaying gently as if ballroom dancing. Weeds sprouted from gaping jawbones, while minnows darted in and out of empty eye sockets.

Robby was there, sitting beside a rock, his body nestled in the curl of his legs. There was air trapped under his T-shirt, so it swelled around him as if he'd grown a man's body on the way down.

Lucas imagined Bo and the boat would get their placement soon, and he wondered which bone man was Michael. Perhaps Strawberry would know.

Several Large Mouth Bass swam to inspect and nosed against Strawberry as if they'd enjoy him for dinner. Lucas waved them away. As they scattered, he felt pride swell. He was above them all, in this world below.

Lucas giggled a burst of bubbles, wondering who'd come to him first.

And he knew they'd come. Sooner or later, they'd seek him out.

Oh yeah! There'd be talk at ShoeBooties. Twin bellybuttons gasping in horror as grizzled men with stale beer souring in the beards told tales of Black Bottom and the creature living there. Damned Old Black Bottom, once a wonderful fishing hole turned into a deadly body of water.

It'd only be a matter of time before they came to Lucas. And that Freak of Nature, he'd give them all he had. He'd start with a tap on the bottom of the boat. Then he'd give it a little wiggle just for fun. And when they were good and scared, Lucas would pull up, drag his arm out of the water, slip it over the edge and...

SLAB GAB

"Hi."
"Who said that?"
"You can call me Doc."
"Where are you?"
"I'm right beside you. I—"
"Help! I can't see!"
"No, you can't…"
"Sweet mother-of-pearl, I'm blind. Help!"
"Please! Stop screaming and listen to me."
"Who are you? What happened? Why I am blind?"
"Like I said, I'm Doc. And what may I call you?"
"Me?"
"Your name?"
"Oh my! My name. M—Margaret. Maggy, if you like."
"Maggy it shall be."
"I can't see you. I'm blind. W—Where am I?"
"Maggy, listen close. We…you and I are in the morgue."
"Did you say morgue? Like…morgue, for dead bodies, morgue?"
"Yes. That kind of morgue."
"Oh my! Help! Help me! Someone help me!"
"Maggy! Please!"
"Sweet mother-of-pearl, I've lost my mind! Help me! Help!"
"No! You have not lost your mind. Please!"
"Dreaming? I'm dreaming. Help! Someone wake me up! Sweet

mother-of-pearl..."

"Maggy, stop!"

"Morgue's are for the dead! I can hear you! I am not dead!"

"Well, you are both right and wrong. The hearing is more of a mental communication. We will call it 'hearing' to simplify the matter. And as far as being dead—correct, you are not dead. It seems the scientific community may have made a tiny mistake when determining the moment of death. It was presumed that the absence of a heartbeat was the point of measure. That was the time we put on the death certificate, anyhow. But now I'd have to say, it goes beyond that."

"No."

"It appears that the brain continues to function independently of the heart, at least for several days. I've been here for three days and am quite alert and thinking clearer than I ever have."

"This can't be. I won't believe it."

"Well, believe it, Maggy. Being a doctor for more than thirty years, it came as quite a shock to me, too. To think that I've declared people dead who in fact were not...well, not dead. Took me more than a minute to swallow that bitter pill. Albeit fascinating, it is a rather disquieting fact. You...we are presumed dead, but are not dead."

"No. No, Doc. It isn't true."

"I understand your distress. Quite normal, I'd say. But there will come a point of truth for you. Depending on how long ago you...uh...your memory will revive and you will see things much more clearly. It happened to me and I have talked to someone else who came in and out of here and the same thing happened for her. You'll see."

"Memory? I know who I am. There's nothing wrong with my memory. I have a husband and two children. My son, Max, is at FSU, third year psych major. My daughter, Brenna, has just passed the BAR and is looking for a job in Orlando. My husband and I are planning a cruise to Alaska this fall. Nothing wrong with my memory, Doc."

"Maggy, it will come. The rest. Believe me. All of—"

"Oh my! Oh, Doc! Oh my!"

"Slow, Maggy. Take it slow."

"Sweet mother-of-pearl, I—I see myself in my car and then...an accident. Oh my! Now there's people all over. They're pulling at me and trying to get me...oh my!"

"Slow. Slow, Maggy."

"I'm a mess! It's horrible! Sweet mother-of-pearl, save me!"

"Maggy! No. No. It's okay. It's a memory. It's past. Over."

"Oh my!"

"Maggy! Listen! It's all over. What you're seeing can't hurt you. Do you feel anything right now? Any pain? Anything at all?"

"What? Pain? Oh my. No, Doc. Not a thing."

"Are you understanding now?"

"Car accident. I had an accident and now I'm dead?"

"Dead as far as the heartbeat goes, but in some fashion, alive."

"Doc? I don't know what to say…to think. This is all so weird. I mean, one minute everything was great and now I'm here and you're telling me I'm dead, but not dead. And there are more like this?"

"Yes, Maggy. I've conversed with a woman named Gert who went to great lengths to explain her circumstances. She'd been on life support for several months after suffering a stroke. Her doctor had declared her brain dead and finally convinced the husband to let her go. Well, all the while she was in the hospital, she heard…heard the thoughts of everyone who came into her room. Poor woman. So many of them wished her dead. Thought she'd be better off. Made her sad. But she kept a good spirit in spite of it all. It was great talking to her. She was a fountain of information."

"Where is she now?"

"She…uh…she was moved. Funeral. It was time for her funeral."

"No. Buried alive? No, Doc! No!"

"Well, I can't be certain if that will happen. Like I said, I don't know how long this lasts. But Gert was not at all upset by the idea. She was quite looking forward to listening in on the thoughts of friends and family who came to say goodbye. Really."

"Too incredible. It's too macabre, Doc. How can it be? How can this be happening?"

"Well, from what I can guess, the brain functions after the cessation of the heart, probably through the use of electrical impulses, waves on a frequency that cannot be detected by our most modern medical equipment. I have to assume there will come a time when the impulses fade—organic matter being perishable—and we will all cease to be. But for now, we are in some dimension, alive."

"I applaud your wording, Doc."

"Well, I've boned up on my bedside manner. I'm afraid all my previous talk of decay and such gave Gert the willies."

"Fancy that. She's in the morgue talking to a not-so-dead man, eagerly awaiting her funeral, and she gets upset about decay! That is…oh my! Doc! Something's happening!"

"What is it?"

"I'm remembering more. More than the accident. I remember being a baby. It seems like my mind just came alive and it's playing out memories in front of me, like a movie. I can see my whole life all at once."

"Ah, yes. That's good, I hope. I had a wonderful childhood and there were so many things that I had never been able to remember. Now, it all seems like only yesterday."

"Oh my! Yes! It is wonderful. I see my mom. Oh my! She's so young and she's making funny faces at me, calling me her sweet little baby. I'm a baby! And I can feel the emotions, the love. What power! What a rush! And now I'm a little girl and there's my sister. We're swinging. Now we're at school. Oh my! I'm at the movies. Now on the beach. There I'm cooking breakfast, egg and cheese burritos. And I'm in college. Now I see my wedding. Oh my! I'm getting married. Oh, Doc, it's all so clear. So real. What a wonderful, beautiful thing this is!"

"I have to agree. The memory expansion is one of the best parts of being...dead."

"Oh my, yes!"

"And it helped me to think about the whole situation. If you can see beyond the fact of the obvious, that we have been declaring people dead who aren't, and we have been sending people to the morgue, to funeral homes, to the grave, who are still able to think—if you can get past all the ethical ramifications, then you can see this life-after-life as a great gift. With this extra time and the wonderful capacity to remember, we all have the chance to take heed of our lives, to come to terms with our past."

"You think everyone has this chance?"

"Well, I can't prove it, but Gert came in loud and clear, and now you."

"I know you're a man of science and I respect everything you've told me so far, Doc, but I wonder if maybe you aren't considering the size of this morgue. This is a big city. Shouldn't there be more than two of us here? I mean, I would assume with a population this size—"

"Not so fast, Maggy. I have thought of that. And there certainly should be more than two of us. This place can hold up to thirty. The fact that only you and I are communicating tells me that not everyone wakes up at the same time. Only a short time passed for me. I recalled choking, seeing the room spin, then I awoke in here with Gert. Combining her memory with mine of what had happened, I concluded several hours. But it could be different for each person. Just another question I am dying to answer."

"Cute, Doc."

"Excuse me?"

"You made a joke."

"A joke?"

"Never mind. So you think everyone will have this experience, but the timing varies?"

"Has to be, Maggy. Everyone has a brain, so it has to be true."

"I wonder. I read somewhere that people only access a fraction of their brain. What if people like us are using a bit more?"

"It could be just that. But lying here, separated from everyone who could help us, we'll never know. Oh the torture of not being able to tell someone, someone alive."

"Be a good time to have a personal connection with a psychic, huh?"

"Psychic? Psychic! Brilliant thought, Maggy."

"Well, thank you."

"No, thank you."

"For what, Doc?"

"Psychics claim to be able to talk to the dead. Well, what if they can? What if they are talking to people like us? What if they can tune in to the thoughts of the undead? And if they can do that, maybe one of us can do it back. Initiate communication."

"You think it could be possible?"

"Perhaps. Gert heard everyone's thoughts around her and when I was out having my autopsy—"

"What!?"

"Autopsy. When I was out there, I heard everything they were—"

"Sweet mother-of-pearl. Autopsy? I never thought. How awful!"

"Maggy, calm down. Really, it was quite painless and even pleasant. I eavesdropped on some interesting conversation. It was a nice break from being in here."

"And they kept on...doing it...with you awake and listening? Torture!"

"Maggy! It doesn't hurt at all. I promise!"

"Did you try to get their attention? Tell them you were alive? Did you try?"

"Of course. And as I had expected, they were unresponsive. Listening to them is not as easy as it is between you and I. In here, we are alone and the conversation is clear. Out there, I was busy trying to sort through a number of voices from different people. At first, all the thoughts kind of ran together. It wasn't until I focused on just one voice that I was able to listen with ease. Even so, no one heard me. And chatter, I did."

"No one heard you. How awful! If only you could have let someone know what was going on."

"Perhaps if I had been around someone more receptive. Or maybe my voice was lost in the jumble. I don't know."

"Too bad we couldn't...couldn't...couldn't combine brain waves and give them a good shout."

"Yes! Combine brain waves! Maggy! You're nothing short of genius! If we combined our thoughts, focused a simple message on a single person, maybe we could break through."

"I'm game, Doc. Let's do it!"

"It might be wise to wait until they come for you...for your...uh...you know, and then we will..."

"No way! We can't wait, Doc. Sweet mother-of-pearl. No autopsy!"

"Maggy! Calm down. It would be better for us, I think. There is usually just one person out there shifting the bodies and we can really give him all we've got."

"No, Doc! I won't...can't! No!"

"I think it's our best shot."

"I can't wait. Why can't we start now?"

"Now?"

"Please, Doc. I can't bear the thought of an autopsy. It's too much."

"We could be screaming for a long time. I don't know if that's a good idea."

"I'll do it alone if I have to."

"Maggy, wait. If you insist on starting now, I'll do it, too. We'll do this together. How about we start by hollering, 'We are alive'—'We are alive'?"

"That's great, Doc. We'll go on three. One. Two. Th—"

"You two start screaming and I swear I'll get up off this slab and kick your asses."

"Ahhh! Sweet mother—"

"Who's there?"

"Name's Curt and I'm sick of the two of you blabbering. You're ruining my freaking death. I didn't stuff a .45 in my mouth expecting to wake up in the morgue listening to Stupid Is and Stupid Does puking out crazy theories about life and death. For your info, Doc, I can't have much brain left. A .45 leaves a big hole. So your brain theory might be crap. Second of all—memories suck. Reliving my life is just as hellish as it was living it and just a little less hellish than having to listen to you two. That said, both of ya, shut the hell up!"

"Curt? You've been here listening all this time? I didn't hear you?"

"Yep, Doc. You didn't hear me 'cuz I wasn't talking. Unlike you other freaks, I keep my thoughts to myself. Between you and that old fart, Gert, and now this crazy bag of wind, Maggy—Margaret—mother-of-pearl, you're driving me loco. I can't wait till they get me out of here and throw my fat ass into the furnace. If there's a God, that oven'll put an end to this and I'll finally be able to rest in peace."

"Curt! You can help us! I can't bear the thought of an autopsy. If you join us in Doc's plan, the three—"

"Holy crap! You're one stupid lady. And Doc, you're no better. Couple'a dim bulbs. Did ya even stop to think what would happen if your dumb-ass plan worked and someone out there heard ya? Think about it? They'd pull our happy asses out of here and the next thing we'd all be freaking experiments. Autopsy? That ain't nothing to what the scientists would do with a tele...tele...tele-freaking-pathetic corpse. I ain't spending eternity in a jar of formaldehyde."

"Doc, if he doesn't want to help, it's okay with me. I'm going to try. I'm going to start screaming. You in?"

"Well, I was willing before when I thought it was just you and I, so I'm still with you, Maggy."

"Freaking idiots."

"On three, Doc. One. Two. Three."

"We are alive! We are alive! We are alive! We are alive! We are alive!"

"No. No. I'm cursed. All I wanted was to be dead. I wish I was dead! You two freaking screaming Mimi's, shut up!"

"We are alive! We are alive! We are alive! We are alive! We are alive!"

"I told you to shut up!"

"We are alive! We are..."

"I can't stand it no more. Ricky! Rick! Can ya hear me, buddy?"

Yeah, man. Hey you buncha noisemakers! Like my friend Curt said, shut up!

"Oh my! Doc? Who said that?"

"I don't know. Curt? Who are you calling to? Who's Ricky?"

"Seems pretty simple to me, Doc. Ricky's my buddy. He works out there slinging bodies. I think he told you to shut up."

"Sweet mother-of-pearl!"

"Ricky? You work out there? You can hear us? You've spoken to Curt?"

Yes and yes. And you're singing an old song. We are alive. I heard it all before. Now all of you, shut up! You're giving me a headache. Sheesh. No matter how long I work here, it still gives me chills listening to the slab gab.

"You must tell someone about us. Please, Ricky. We are alive in here. You must help us. You…"

I don't gotta do squat. I need this job and I ain't gonna tell no one that I hear a buncha stiffs gabbing in the drawers. Sheesh. Could have been a garbage man, but no—wife says work in the hospital. We need the insurance. The morgue'll be quiet and you'll have some extra time to read. Who can read with all your talking? I need a break. Coffee and donut? Yeah, that sounds nice. Take me a little break. I'm outta here. See you later, Curt.

"Yeah, later, Ricky. Eat a cream-filled for me."

Cream-filled, huh? Yeah! I think I will, Curt. I think I will.

"Wait? You, out there? Ricky! Don't go! Please!"

"Doc? Stop him!"

"He's gone, Maggy. I don't believe it. He carried on a conversation. He knows we're alive and doesn't care. I never imagined…some idiot carrying bodies from table to drawer…he could help…won't…I can't…Curt, how could you?"

"I saved you from being sliced up and put under a microscope, Doc. You owe me a big, fat thank you."

"…of all…so many…"

"Doc? Are you all right? You sound funny."

"…Maggy…sorry…"

"Doc? Doc! Answer me! Sweet mother-of-pearl, Doc!"

"Holy crap, lady! He ain't gonna answer ya! Sounds like your wussy Doc got fried by his own thinking. Lesson learned? Quit thinking! Shut up and enjoy your death!"

"Curt? You knew all along?"

"Someone save me from this woman and her questions!"

"You've got to help me. If that worker heard us, there could be more, someone who cares. Help me, Curt, please."

"No."

"We have to try!"

"No."

"Please, Curt!"

"Curt? W—who's Curt? Who's there? Where are you? I can't see you."

"Oh my! Oh! Someone else…you must be new."

"Who said that? I can't see you?"

"No. No you can't. First things first. My name is Maggy. What's your name, please?"

"I'm M—Mona. What happened? Where are you? Why can't I see you? Am I blind? Where am I?"

"Mona. Listen to me. I've got so much to tell you and not a lot of time. I need your help!"

BODO

It was dinnertime. I fired up the gas grill, then threw on a couple of marinated chicken breasts and a hot dog. Chenise popped open a cold bottle of Chardonnay, filled two glasses, and I lifted one to her.

"Congratulations to my wife! Or should I say, Doctor Wife?"

"I'll go by wife for now." She blushed.

I had picked a beautiful woman to marry. Her smile reminded me of this. Some men would have called me lucky. Wrong. "Luck" implies a gamble, a chance that one might not come out a winner. Not so with me. Everything I did, all decisions were calculated, and my possessions were proof of that.

I wasn't lucky to have Chenise, I deserved her. The fact that she was beautiful and smart, had made me a remarkable daughter, was *why* we were together—not an accident.

"You want to frame that letter of acceptance, put it up on the wall?" I put an intentional sparkle in my eye, hoping she'd want to celebrate her acceptance to medical school in a physical way.

Again, she blushed, her cheeks glowing like a virgin's. "I don't think so, Tony. Why don't we wait until I actually graduate and earn the title 'doctor' before we start boasting."

"Oh now, it's never too soon to brag, baby…or celebrate."

"Tony, you're embarrassing me."

"If I was you, I'd be shouting from the mountaintops. Look at me! I'm going to be a doctor! Saving lives! Curing disease! See me!" I raised my arms up high to accept silent applause and spilled a bit of wine on my head.

"You do it for me. You're the show-off."

"You know it. Who better to blow your horn than yourself? I'm going to Manny's tomorrow and brag, brag, brag about my new computer and my new contract."

"Like I said, show-off."

"That's me! A shining star. Just like my new unit. It'll make Manny's computer look like a dinosaur, not fit for a dog to use! I'll be able to outrun, out-speed, out-fax everyone on the block!"

"Don't count your chickens."

She couldn't knock down my enthusiasm. I was high on pride. "I don't want to hear it. Admit it, Chenise, we're on an upward spiral. Marissa's soaring through accelerated day care. Kid's going to be the next Einstein. She'll be reading the dictionary by the time she's four! You're going to be a doctor and I'm going to be rich while I sit at home and surf the net. Up. Up. Up. We're all moving up."

"I don't know if there's enough room in this neighborhood for the three of us and your ego."

"You know you love it."

"I know I love you, Tony."

Man, she was great. I kissed her to let her know it, then whispered in her ear. "Maybe later, after we tuck in the little genius rugrat, we can take this further."

"You know we will."

Man, she was awesome.

"It's a date."

We clinked glasses to seal the deal.

"Bodo."

The little voice startled me. Almost forgot my daughter was so close. But there she was, sitting on the deck by the picnic table, holding onto a purple pony, pulling a little silver comb through its mane.

"Bodo," she said.

Thought it might be the name of her toy, but when I looked back to Chenise, she wore a scowl. "What's wrong?"

"That Bodo. She's been talking about Bodo all week. I don't know what it is, but for some reason, it gives me the chills."

Silly woman. I wouldn't let a kid's vocabulary douse my thrill.

Marissa giggled. "Bodo's coming."

How cute was she? But there was the date with Chenise later, and the word disturbed her; I'd settle the issue. "Marissa, what's Bodo? Is that your pony's name, Sweetie?" I poured myself another glass of wine. The first one only wet my whistle. Whistling was weak. I wanted to sing!

"No, Daddy." She clucked her tongue and held up the pony, giving me a look that said, "For a Daddy, you sure are dumb." Marissa could make me feel mighty stupid at times. Funny. "This is Pony Pop. Bodo's coming, Daddy. Coming here."

"That right?" I didn't want some Bodo spoiling my night. "I don't recall inviting any—"

"Bodo!" Marissa jumped to her feet, dropping the tiny comb. It fell through the cracks in the wooden deck flooring. Darn it! I'd be down there later, digging it out.

"Bodo!" Smiling, she jumped up and down. "Bodo!"

While she screamed, Manny's dog let loose a howl. The hair on the back of my neck nibbled my skin. I drained my glass in one swallow.

Again, the dog howled and I felt sorry for him. I'm not up on dog talk, but the little beagle sounded scared.

"Marissa stop it! You're upsetting the dog."

"Bodo! Bodo!"

Clouds rolled across the sky. Gray and black splattered shapes, like a paint spill, completely blocked the sun. Instantly, any lasting patches of powder blue, the beautiful remnants of a remarkably wonderful day, were gone. Suddenly it was dark, and cold.

Oddly, I was reminded of a girl I'd dated in college. She'd designed sets for the drama society, her attention to detail, wildly effective. Gifted, she'd been able to see things like no other. With a paintbrush and a couple of lights she'd been able to instantly change mood. Everything she did placed the players up against the perfect backdrop. The sets had added an exclamation point to the performance. Although I had never been able to pick out which particular detail had made the change so compelling, I appreciated the work behind it, the powerful insight that had made the transformation possible. The overall variance had been bold and obvious due to small pieces that had come together as one.

As I stood there, the delicious smell of grilled chicken spoiled at the sound of fat and blood sizzling on lava rock. The taste of sweet wine turned sour on my tongue. The anticipation of a rich life roiled into a knot in my stomach, and the sensuous light of impending sunset mutated to ugly. My mood evolved as effectively as if my old girlfriend had designed a new set and transported me into it, unawares.

The anomaly was too much. I wanted the old set back.

"Bodo!" Marissa screeched.

I was concerned the neighbors might hear. If I couldn't understand her, what would others think?

Chenise set down her wine. "Calm down, Sweetie. Mommy's right here. I've got you." She grabbed up Marissa in her arms, but the child didn't want comfort.

"Bodo. Bodo." She wrestled her way down and pattered her tiny sandaled feet over the wooden slats until she stood on the edge of the deck. "Bodo!"

My anxiety turned to anger. I wanted her to stop. Mad. For the first time, I felt like taking that little girl over my knee and giving it to her. I don't why I felt that way. I simply did.

"What is it, Marissa? What is Bodo?" I hated the sound of my voice.

"Bodo." Marissa shook her finger at the clouds. Little neck bent at an angle, black eyes wide, she stared straight up.

"What's wrong?" Chenise asked me.

My anger grew. What was I, a child psychologist? She was supposed to be the brainiac, up-and-coming doctor, not me. For crying out loud, I didn't know what the kid was doing. If I did, I'd have stopped it.

The dog yelped and howled. Finally, Manny yelled out to him. "Shut up, Bogey!"

Marissa screeched. "Bodo. Bodo. Bodo."

"Bogey! You stupid mutt. I said, knock it off!"

"Bodo. Bodo. Bodo."

In my mind, I said, "Marissa shut up! Knock it off or I'll come over there and make you stop!"

"Bodo. Bodo. Bodo."

She didn't stop.

Neither did the dog. He yelped and howled, "Bodo, Bodo, Bodo," mimicking my daughter. I don't know how I knew that was true. It simply was.

"Tony? What's happening?" Chenise's question hit me like a fist.

I opened my mouth, ready to make my anger known, when a booming sound punched my ears. It was like the noise of a can opener puncturing an airtight seal. Only amplified, like a sonic boom.

And the sky split in two.

"Bodo!" Marissa cried.

"Tony!" Chenise cried.

"Bodo, Bodo, Bodo," Bogey yelped.

"Shut up! Shut up!" I shouted. It was all I could do.

"Bodo. Bodo. Bodo."

The clouds separated. It was like watching a huge knife slice through dirty whipped frosting. The split opened and a shiny, wet, black beam jetted out and slapped the ground in Manny's yard.

The dog stopped howling.

"Oh my God! Bogey? Hey! Give me back my dog!" Manny's voice was a fright. I wish I hadn't heard it.

Marissa laughed. "Bodo took Bogey."

The black stream slipped back into the crack like a tongue curling into a mouth. The sound of the vacuum repeated, and again, the watery beam emerged, touched down in Manny's yard, then rolled away.

"Bodo took Manny."

Before I could register the meaning of the words, the noise sounded again.

"Bodo." Marissa pointed her tiny finger. On it was a slim gold band, a gift from her Grandma past Christmas. Such a pretty little hand. Lovely ring.

"No!" Chenise opened her arms and rushed toward Marissa. So did the wave. It slapped down from the clouds, stuck to our daughter, twirled around her and was gone.

"No!" The voice was mine—or Chenise's. I don't know whose, or if we both screamed.

There was so much noise.

The wave shot out again and again. Screams filled the neighborhood. Several neighbors disappeared. Everything the thing touched instantly vanished. Dogs and cats. A kid on a bike. A lady with a shopping bag. Two little girls on a swing. A pregnant woman with her hands wrapped around her stomach as if to protect her unborn child. An old man sitting on his front step, a smoldering pipe in his mouth. Even after he was taken away, a white curl of smoke remained, proof that the man had been there.

Most of the people I knew. Some I didn't.

The screams were broken up by the sound of the vacuum and the wet smack of the beam. Black and slithery, it sprang, gathered up a victim, then curled out of sight.

How long this lasted, I don't know. Forever. For a minute.

The next thing I remembered, I had Chenise in my arms. We were inside the house, on the floor, huddled in front of the glass doors that lead to the deck in the backyard. Together, we watched Bodo, its movements quick and precise. Soon, the streets were clear.

All at once, it was quiet.

"Marissa." Chenise's voice was eerie. Sounded like she was talking from underwater. I guessed she was in shock. "My baby. My baby girl. Where's my baby?"

I listened to her for a moment, dumbfounded, until I finally remembered my legs and went to the phone. Out of order. Dead. Like the air. Like the power. No lights. No refrigerator hum. No television drone. Gone was the soothing, friendly whine of the computer hard drive. The ceiling fans were still. Never in my life had I experienced such quiet.

All was silent, inside and out.

Except for Chenise. She cried and rubbed the windowglass. "Marissa. Where's my baby? Marissa. Baby?"

I tried to block her out, to keep my hope alive.

Time passed. I don't know how much. My watch had stopped. Nothing worked. Not even me. Useless, powerless, I remained still. Everything else was, why not me?

I waited.

No one came.

Little girl gone, wife in a ball on the floor, and I simply stood there…waiting…watching my manhood spill over the floor into a lengthening shadow. I couldn't take it anymore. Where was help? The big rescue? Where were the heroes?

I decided to go for help. I grabbed my keys and had my hand on the doorknob, ready to make a dash for the car, when Chenise found a new word. "Stop."

"What?" I was relieved. I didn't want to go.

"Mr. Casper's in his garage. He's going to his car."

I ran to the door just as Casper jumped into his Lexus. A knight in a shiny green sedan. His gray head dipped down and his shoulder worked back and forth.

Brave man, Casper. I offered some inspiration. "Come on. Turn over. Turn over."

His head bobbed, his bald spot looking like a little frisbee, then he beat at the steering wheel. The car wasn't going anywhere. I imagined a hot blast of foul language filled the soundproof cabin space when Casper realized his leased luxury—like time, like the air, like everything but a handful of people and a wicked black wave—was dead.

Chenise gasped. "Stay. Stay. Don't get out. Don't." Mr. Casper defied her warning, opened the car door, and ran for the house.

The sound of a vacuum, followed by a black shadow under a charcoal puff of clouds, slapped at his feet, rolled up, and he was gone.

"Should've stayed in the car, old man."

"What?" Chenise looked at me as if I was an alien, like I had three noses and one eye. I couldn't believe I'd said it either. Maybe I was an alien. I felt like someone else.

"What do we do, Tony?"

She was so needy.

"What about Marissa?"

So helpless, I said nothing. Did nothing.

The light faded until it was completely dark. No moon. No stars. The cloud cover cloaked any trace of light. I'd never known such complete blackness. It was repulsive.

We slept on the floor in front of the sliding glass doors. In case Marissa fell from the clouds, we wanted to be right there to run out and catch her. I can't believe I slept at all. But I did. It was an occurrence that should have been a blessing, but was not.

It was a horrible sleep. I wish I hadn't done it. It was a dreamless sleep that left an aftertaste of terror in my mouth, as if I'd screamed all night.

Wednesday morning dragged by. Still no help and no sign of Marissa. We watched two more of our neighbors get swallowed up. Rene and Willy Franklin ran like madmen from their house on the corner. Once they reached the street, they split up. She ran to the left and he to the right. The strategy didn't work. Bodo got both of them. I made a mental note.

Wednesday afternoon I ate food that tasted like cardboard and Chenise stood watch. It was all I could do. All she could do. What else could we do?

Wednesday night a helicopter tried to pass by the cloud. It was destroyed. Not by the black wave. Rather, it disintegrated. One second it was there, the next, gone. Looked like rescue via air was out of the question. It gave me hope, however. Even as it evaporated, the sight of the helicopter told me that the cloud did not cover eternity. Beyond Bodo was life, and *they knew* we needed help. I sighed relief. Chenise cried.

SHIVERS

Thursday morning a rocket of some kind came from the west. It sailed over Manny's rooftop and headed in a direct line for the center of the cloud. Before the missile could hit its target, it was erased. Like those pads I had when I was a kid, a sheet of plastic over a black sticky thing. When done doodling, just pull up the plastic and the drawing goes away. Poof. That rocket poofed.

Friday came and went. Saturday followed the same.

Sunday was too much for some.

Chenise was still camped by the door when I heard her tell our friends, the Jared's, goodbye. "Goodbye, Lana. Bye-bye, Benton. Tell Marissa I love her."

I ran to the door to see Benton and Lana walk slowly to the middle of their yard. It struck me odd that the grass hadn't grown at all. Trimmed short and neat. On the perfectly groomed lawn, Benton stood with Lana's hand in his. They wore matching glazed expressions, both grinning.

I pounded my fists on the door. "No! Get inside! Benton!"

Chenise chanted at my feet. "Bodo. Bodo. Bodo."

"Stop!" It sounded frail. The circumstances magnified my weakness. I'm positive that if I'd looked in a mirror, I wouldn't have seen a reflection.

"Bodo. Bodo. Bodo. Bodo"

"Stop it!"

"Bye-bye."

"Benton, don't go!" Smeared with fingerprints and tears, the glass showed a bleary picture of the outside world. The sound of a vacuum was followed by a perfect horizontal split in the dingy clouds. From the incision came Bodo. Greasy, black, and slick, it slurped over Lana and Benton, wrapped them up, then spun back into the clouds.

"Bodo. Bodo. Bodo."

"What is Bodo?" I fell to my knees, grabbed Chenise's arm, and forced myself not to punch her.

"Who."

To just slam my fist into her face, close her mouth, her eyes looking to me so helpless...

"Chenise, *who* is Bodo?"

"He's Marissa's."

I hated the answer, so I left her there and went to the study. My room. It was full of boxes of new computer components. What a sad sight. I might never have the chance to hook them up and relish the technology behind it all. How I'd looked forward to the new business, riding my cool machines into the future. Now, it was just so much clutter.

The rest of the day was bad. Time and terror broke down several more of the neighbors.

I heard Chenise say goodbye to Wendy Falco and her sons, Jordan and Scotty. She also said goodbye to Wanda Williams, Mr. Bevins, the Frieze's with their baby, and Mr. Copper and his three kids.

All the while, she chanted. "Bodo. Bodo. Bodo. Bodo."

Let her. There was something I could do. In the kitchen. I emptied the cupboards and took inventory of edibles. The refrigerator had warmed up and everything in it that I hadn't already eaten was ruined. To this point, Chenise hadn't eaten anything, but I rationed the food for two.

There was an assortment of canned foods—vegetables, baked beans, tomato sauce, and several fruit cocktails. Marissa loved fruit cocktail. The cans pleased me. The juice would sustain us. The water didn't work, so it was all the fluid available.

After I'd sorted everything, I imagined we could probably stretch it out for several weeks. Surely, by then, someone would have this thing figured out.

Next, I took my mission to the bathroom, where I'd already set up a wash bucket for waste collection. Beside the sink, I set out a large measuring cup. I'd read somewhere that in extreme situations a human could survive by drinking urine. I didn't think it would come to that, but there's nothing wrong with being prepared.

I was in the bathroom when the sliding glass doors opened, a soft swish that sounded like a rocket blast.

"Chenise!"

"Goodbye, Tony."

"Chenise!" By the time I'd made it the door, she was on the deck. "Chenise! Come back inside. Please don't do this! It won't help! It won't bring—"

She stared at me and her mouth worked. "Bodo. Bodo. Bodo." She'd gathered up some of Marissa's favorite toys—a bear, an alphabet book, and a plastic hammer. Marissa loved that hammer. It was one of those things that left a parent with a big question mark. Of all the expensive toys she'd had, Marissa would spend forever banging on anything and everything with that hammer. Go figure.

"Please don't do this, Chenise. Don't be crazy!"

"Bodo. Bodo. Bodo."

I looked deep into her eyes. Crazy? She was already there.

"Bodo. Bodo!" Toys in hand, Chenise ran in crazy circles.

There was the sound of a vacuum. I closed my eyes. Coward, I couldn't watch the sky split to make itself ready for my wife.

Above the slap, there was a cry. Not Chenise. It was a sorrowful bawl. It reminded me of old women in some third world country, dressed in dusty black and wailing for the dead. It was that kind of cry. Powerful. Even though it had come from a distance up the street, it was loud, intense, and filled with emotion. "Bye-bye, Chenise!"

I listened hard. The voice was familiar, but I couldn't put a face to it. It made me angry. Someone had watched my wife go, had bid her farewell, and I didn't know who it was.

Odd that such a thing would bother me. But it did. I thought about the voice and its owner for the rest of the day and most of Monday.

I didn't watch by the door. On and off over the next week, I heard the sound of the vacuum and the slap of Bodo.

Much of the time I spent in the study with my computer. I unpacked it, carefully arranged it on the workstation, and plugged everything in. Then I sat and stared. Countless hours were wasted, lost in thought. It would have been nice to use the equipment. I missed it. The touch of the keys. The global connection. Power with the push of a button. But all I could do was sit and imagine. There wasn't anything else I could do. After a while, that bothered me. I should be able to do something.

No help came. I imagined men and women on the perimeter of Bodo, standing behind police barricades, gawking, full of "Oooohs" and "Ahhhhs." Had some of them witnessed the kidnappings? The thought made me sick. A group of strangers intermingled with sorrowful family members grabbing at their moment in the sun, riding the wave of my monstrous tragedy. Repulsive. I hated them.

Days passed in a gray and black blur. I lost weight. Funny thing is, my hair stopped growing. I'd expected to sprout a beard, to look like some kind of caveman when I was finally rescued, but nothing.

After some mental coercion, I convinced myself to go to Marissa's room, as if I might find her there asleep, the whole thing a dream. I went. She was gone. No dream. I found Rolly-The-Hamster dead. We'd gotten Marissa the little rodent to teach her responsibility. It'd been her job to care for him. She'd been good about it. I, however, had forgotten about him. His food was gone. I pulled out the water bottle, uncapped it, and stuck in my tongue. It came out dry. I left him in his cage.

That was when the tears began. At first, I tried to stop them. They were a waste. I licked as many as was possible, for the fluid.

My rations had dwindled to a cup of potato flakes and some flour. If I was careful, it would last another week.

Did I want to *be* another week?

Guess so. Against my inner voice screaming in disgust, I tried the urine. Enough said.

Who was left out there, on my street?

No one. I knew that life in my neighborhood had been whittled down to one.

I'd never been a religious man, but I took a moment to wonder about the Old Testament story of Jonah and the whale. How had he felt, trapped under the eyes of the omniscient? Was I nothing more than a reluctant Jonah?

Bodo waited for me. I don't why or how. It simply was.

Accepting this realization, I went to the study, packed up the computer, then stacked it neatly in the corner. Useless hunk of plastic. It could do nothing. Junk.

Much like myself.

Somewhere along the way I'd become dependent on the wiring. Without the bleeps and blips, I didn't have purpose. Through the recent loss, I'd mourned for what I'd never be, for myself. It had taken all this time for me to understand that I was already gone.

I had become a piece of the thing, the buzzing whining system that ran for its own sake. Neither husband nor father, I was barely a man.

Bodo showed me this. He'd taught me more than I could ever have learned in a million years with a billion circuits.

"Bodo. Bodo. Bodo." I chanted and looked at the study a final time. Boxes. Empty desk. Briefcase, a gift from Chenise, finest hand-stitched leather stuffed with worthless contracts and—

"Marissa!"

I ran, unsnapped the briefcase, and threw papers around the room. Where? Excitement boiled in my belly. I'd never felt so alive. It was there! I threw aside proposals, memos, an appointment book, until I found Bodo.

How could I have been so thoughtless? I held the picture in trembling hands. My heart ached. Marissa's artwork. A gift to me. I hadn't taken time to look at it before. Tears flowed so I could barely focus.

Bodo. I laughed out loud. Probably sounded like a madman. It was a crayon sketch of a stick figure. He was seated on a cloud, feet dangling, his hands huge rolled coils. He smiled a crooked crescent. On his pillowed seat were tiny figures, arms in the air, waving. Miniature houses spread out on both sides of the odd monster.

Marissa knew Bodo. She'd drawn him, wanted him. And he'd come.

Beyond the smeared glass doors, he...they wait for me.

"Bodo. Bodo. Bodo."

With the blind faith of a child, I opened the door and stepped outside, to be with my wife and my daughter, be the husband and father I'd never been before.

I don't know why this was true. It just was.

EVERYTHING BILLY

The smells in the garage were suffocating. Oil, gas, stale exhaust. Arabella pulled the laundry out of the dryer, sniffed, and winced. Never clean enough. There was a lingering stench connected to everything Billy Poteete touched.

She threw the load of whites into the laundry basket, turned her head, and glared at Billy's feet wiggling from under the "Antique, Vintage, Classic, 1965 Convertible Ford Mustang." The long title was Billy's creation, one he liked to spout whenever possible, as if it added a M. D. to his name. "Hi, I'm Billy Poteete, owner of an 'Antique, Vintage, Classic, 1965 Convertible Ford Mustang'"—insert "Ooohs," "Ahhhs," bows and curtsies here.

"Come on, baby. Come to Daddy." Billy's grunts mixed with the dull tap of metal on metal so it sounded like a caveman striking gold. "Gotcha." He giggled and a bolt rolled across the concrete floor, a band of oil drooling behind it.

Arabella took her stare from Billy's feet, to the bolt, to the car, to Billy's feet, back to the car, and sighed.

What a divergent tribute to the passing of time. The Mustang was as beautiful now as Billy had been a decade past. Through the years, and thanks to Billy's loving touch, the machine had improved with age. Not so with Billy—King of the Prom, Varsity Letterman, All American Boy-Wonder. Immediately upon high school graduation, void of accolades, pep rallies and "Atta boy" pats on the back, Billy had changed. The "thirty-something" Billy Poteete found happiness in beer cans and transmission fluid, was humored by his body odors, and had secured a permanent position on a horizontal plane, working as a brakeman from eight to five, playing in and under the Mustang after hours.

"Hey! You still out there?"

Arrabella packed the washer with a load of filthy work uniforms. "Yeah."

"I dropped a bolt. Can you get it?"

She walked to the car, leaned down to pick up the bolt, and cringed. Billy's feet were a few inches from her face. Huge and flat. Gnarled toes. Brown and yellow corns. A smell that never went away. Even after a shower, Billy smelled like bad feet. Fungus and sweat.

He wiggled his toes. "Trick-or-treat, smell my feet."

"You're disgusting."

"You think that's bad. I had tacos for lunch. Wait'll you get a whiff of that?"

Again, Arabella clucked her tongue.

"You know, baby, if I was to take offense at your dirty looks and all your little sniffles and pooh-poohs, I'd have me a complex."

Arabella stood and was about to turn away when she changed her mind, grinned, and knelt back down. "I told Kirby I'd be able to work some extra hours. I'm gonna start working on Friday nights and Sundays on and off."

Silence. Billy didn't move, twist a wrench, breathe. Nerve hit! Without having to look, Arrabella knew he was red in the face. He hated Kirby. She talked about him as often as possible.

"Did you hear me, Billy?"

"I heard. And the answer is no. Over my dead body."

"I wasn't asking. Kirby needs some extra help on the weekends and the store inventory is coming up after the holidays."

Silence.

"Besides, since when do I need your permission to make personal decisions?"

"You know something, Arabella, when we got married you used to ask me to make up your mind for you all the time. You never even took a pee without asking me if it was all right. You used to treat me like I was somebody special."

"When we got married you didn't—"

"Didn't what? Didn't work as a grease monkey? Didn't stink up a uniform every day? Didn't have nasty feet? You didn't used to have so many prissy hang-ups. You used to screw me no matter what I smelt like. You used to rub my feet. And I remember times when you let me put my toes right in your—"

"Shut up!"

Billy laughed. "What's the hang-up you all of a sudden got for my feet? Must be your boss man Kirby's got small feet, huh? Little girly-man feet. And he wears his little pressed shirt and tie. Probably polishes his little fingernails, too. Fag boy. Geeze, Arabella, I didn't know you was attracted to girls." Billy farted. "Whew! Juic-ey-y-y!" He kicked his feet and waved his hand back and forth.

"You're a pig."

"And Kirby's a girl. You ain't turning lesbo on me, are you, Arabella? I hate to be the one to tell you, but I bet old Kirby'd be more interested in me."

"You're an ass. You think any man who don't have dirty fingernails is gay. You're jealous."

"Should I be jealous?"

"Maybe you should."

"You going to leave me and run away with little Kirby—the assistant manager of the Piggly Wiggly?"

"I've thought about it."

Billy laughed. "You ain't going nowhere."

"You think it's funny, Billy? You think he hasn't come on to me? Well, you're wrong. All I have to do is say the word and he'd be—"

"What word is that, Arabella?"

"What?"

"What word you gonna say to turn Kirby the fag boy straight?" Billy giggled and rubbed his toes over her forearm.

"Don't touch me."

"You know what I think? I think you're long overdue for a big slab of Billy Poteete. I'm just about finished here. Why don't you run inside, get yourself naked, and I'll make you forget all about your little girlfriend Kirby." Billy rubbed his crotch and wiggled his toes.

Working on the Mustang had kick-started his libido. It sometimes did. Arabella looked at his feet and shuddered, picturing him on top of her, stinking, grunting like a pig. She envisioned the aftermath—him recanting the speed of his performance in minutes and seconds. After touting his prowess, he'd fall back on the bed, scratch his underarms, give a sniff, laugh, fart, give a sniff, laugh, paw her with his feet, laugh, then ask her to be a "good girl" and fix him a sandwich.

Arabella wondered what Kirby would be like. He'd be a sweet thing. Surely he'd smell good. He always did at work. And Kirby would be complimentary during sex. At the store, he always had kind words. After the loving, they'd cuddle and he'd offer to fix her something nice. Not a sandwich—maybe an iced tea with lemon. Something fancy.

"The sooner you hand me that bolt, the quicker we can get to business."

She stared.

"Arabella, I'm loosing my mood."

Her eyes traveled the length of the car. The jack was fitted under the front bumper, hydraulic fluid leaking from cracked seals. A puddle of ooze had pooled on the concrete.

Billy kicked his foot at her. "Hey? You gonna give my that bolt, or what?"

Scratchy, knobby toes scraped her arm.

Still kneeling, Arabella walked on her knees to the jack.

* * *

"I appreciate the call, Kirby. How considerate you are." Arabella Poteete held the phone with her chin. Hands free, she pressed her index finger against the middle point of an embossed card and flicked the corner, spinning it in circles on the kitchen counter. Around and around twirled Billy Poteete's funeral announcement, complete with The Lord's Prayer and a photo—the only picture of Billy taken post high school with him wearing a button-down shirt and tie.

Kirby spoke softly. "I...I just wanted to call and talk a bit...to make sure you was all right. I didn't get a chance to speak to you earlier."

Billy's face spun. Arabella nestled her ear against the phone and blushed. "Oh, I'm doing as good as can be expected. Never imagined I'd be a widow before I turned thirty. Makes me feel all old."

"Shoot. I won't hear you talk like that. You're a beautiful young woman with her whole life ahead of her. Maybe you should think of this as a new beginning."

The paper card spun. Dates of birth and death complete. Three-by-five life story. "Oh now, that's the best advice I've got yet. You always know the right words." Arabella's cheeks burned. Heat tickled her belly.

"Well, I'm glad. I'm glad I could help." Kirby paused and Arabella wondered if he, too, wore a set of cherry-colored cheeks. She guessed he did. "Anyhow, I...I want you to know I'll keep you off the schedule for as long as you want. A month. Maybe two?"

She flicked the announcement; it skirted over the counter, then slipped into the crack between the oven and cupboard. Grinning, she walked to the refrigerator, opened it, and scanned the shelves. "Oh, I'd planned on coming back to work much sooner than that. After a week or so I'll be more than ready to get back to my job. Anything longer and I'd probably just go crazy." She grabbed a bottle of white wine, stepped sideways, and kicked the door closed.

There was a thump upstairs.

"Oh!" Arabella snapped her head to the noise and the phone slipped off her shoulder. She juggled it back to her ear. "Kirby?"

Another thump.

"Yes. Arabella? You there?"

"Oh...excuse me. I...uh...I dropped the phone. I got...my cat's upstairs making a fuss about something. Scared me, is all. I'm sorry for dropping you like that."

"It's all right. I'd be honored to be dropped by someone as pretty as you."

Arabella laughed. "Oh, you. As if." She wrestled the cork free, filled a juice glass, then winked a toast at the bottle.

After a pause, Kirby finally spoke. "You let me know if you need anything. You just give a call. You hear?"

"Yes. I will. Thanks for calling, Kirby. You gave me back my smile with your sweet words. I'll talk to you soon. Bye, now."

Arabella sipped the wine and took a deep breath. "Billy's gone. He's really, really gone." She smiled, giggled, and brought the glass to her lips. Golden droplets splashed to the floor, spilled onto her chin. "I'm free!" She danced in wine. "I'm free! Arabella Poteete is free!"

Grabbing the bottle around the neck, she carried it up the stairs to the bedroom.

"Woohoo!"

The room was a jumble of clothes, piles of dresses and blouses and sweaters. It'd taken hours to find a funeral outfit—one that exhibited bereavement and femininity. Not an easy task. Finally, she'd chosen a straight black skirt and fitted gray sweater. Good choice. Kirby had smiled a compliment.

Arabella dodged the scattered clothes, set the wine bottle and glass on the dresser, and shook her finger at the cat.

"Don't play sleepy-face with me. If you was sleeping, I'm a horse's bee-hind. I heard you kicking it up in here. I see what you've been up to. These clothes was sorted. You made my mess…a mess!"

Jessie rolled onto her back and stretched until her feet pulled her plump belly skinny. Upside down, the cat looked at Arabella and blinked magnificent green eyes.

"No matter. I'll be buying me some new clothes now. And with that thought in mind, I'll be making me some room. Time to get rid of everything Billy."

She yanked open the closet doors and threw shirts and work uniforms onto the bed. "Stinking man. What a vile thing he turned out to be, huh? Who'd of thought? Old Billy Poteete—the envy of every teen girl's eye. And I thought I hit pay dirt! Shoot! When we got married, I thought our whole lives would be one big prom night! Ha! Be careful what you wish for. He never did grow up. He didn't grow at all. Except his belly! What a pig! And those feet. Smelly. Dirty. And these…"

Arabella kicked a pair of heavy-duty, tie-up work boots. They thudded over the floor.

"I'd burn those things Jessie, but the stench would pollute the air and probably kill most of the wildlife in the area. That man had the rottenest feet ever!"

Jessie's tail snapped back and forth and she sunk her claws into the quilt.

"Feet like a monster. Toes all curled into each other. Calloused. All yellow and hard. And toenails like an animal." Arabella shuddered. "Make's me wanna puke. Just nasty." She turned a sly eye to Jessie. "I bet Kirby's got nice feet. Slender and soft and sweet."

Jessie blinked and sneezed while Arabella kicked a pair of slippers and two battered, moccasin-style slip-ons into the shoe pile.

"Humph." She searched the room, then rushed the cat. "Watch out. I need that." Arabella didn't wait for Jessie to move, but snatched the pillow out from under her, stripped off the case, and stuffed it with Billy Poteete's clothes. After it was full, she grabbed another pillow and repeated the process. "No more sleeping with his bear claws and stink."

As she worked, her memory played out Billy's nightly ritual. He'd come home from work, flop down on the bottom stair, and take off his boots. Then he'd search out Arabella, singing, "Trick-or-treat, smell my feet, give me something good to eat." Every night, without fail, smelly feet and stupid song.

"Trick-or-treat this." She twisted the pillowcases into knots, grabbed them, and ran to the banister. "Bye-bye, Billy." She threw the sacks downstairs.

"Woohoo!"

Arabella drained her glass, refilled it, then went to work in the bathroom. Everything Billy went into the garbage can.

* * *

"Mmmmmmm." Annoyed, Arabella kicked her legs. "Get off me." She pulled her hand from under the pillow and punched at Billy's side of the bed. "Get! Get off me!" She pounded up and down, expecting to feel a connection with flesh, but found only mattress and goose down.

Finally, she rolled up on her elbow and smacked a circle in Billy's pillow. "I said, get off me. You—"

Arabella stared at the bed and blinked. "Billy?"

Jessie was curled up on the foot of the bed.

"Dreaming. It was just a dream."

Jessie nodded and closed her eyes. Arabella smiled and did the same.

She snuggled her head into the pillow and felt something sharp scrape her thigh. The quilt wiggled, tugged, and slipped off her shoulders. The mattress quivered, dented under her back as if someone had settled down beside her. Another scratch on her leg. Cold and hard, rubbing up and down. She felt her skin tug, could hear the whispery sound of skin on skin.

Arabella held her breath, tried to remain still, but couldn't restrain a shiver. It began in her chest and rippled down her belly and legs. Goosebumps erupted and the thing in the bed grated against her. She wanted to jump and scream. She wanted to pull off the quilt and look, but to move, to open her eyes, to search the dark would be an admission that what she felt was real.

Whatever was clawing her leg was becoming more powerful, digging deeper. And it hurt. Arabella felt skin tear free, screamed, threw off the covers, and kicked her legs up and down. Finally, she leapt from bed, fumbled with the lamp, and snapped on the light.

Nothing. No little monster come to nibble in the dark. No red-eyed, razor-toothed demon. Nothing but the imprint of her body, a dent in her pillow. No Billy. His side of the bed remained unruffled.

She glared at her leg. Scratches. Three parallel lines ran from mid thigh to below her knee. Tiny rivulets of blood dribbled from the wound.

"Dang it, Jessie! Go stretch your claws on someone else." Arabella threw an air punch at the cat. "You scared me to death…and look!" She pointed to the cut. "You drew blood. Bad cat!"

She picked up the pillow and swung.

Jessie leapt free and hid under the bed.

"And stay there. Naughty thing."

* * *

Morning came as a surprise. Arabella awoke, bolted upright. She blinked at the sunlight—harsh, burning. When had she finally fallen back to sleep? She remembered watching the bedside clock blink from 1:12 to 3:05 before she'd slapped it onto the floor. Regretful action. Without the glowing numbers, the bedroom had been incredibly dark.

She blinked and rubbed her eyes. Morning. Late. She had somehow slept. Panic washed through her belly, the remnants of the late-night scare. She shuddered, rubbed her arms, and spotted Jessie on Billy's side of the bed.

"Get up lazy. We've got things to do."

She pushed the cat, who rolled away in a furry ball with no intentions of rising.

"Thanks to you, I got no sleep. If you think you're gonna lay around up here and snooze now, you're sadly mistaken." Arabella slapped the mattress, startled Jessie into a gallop, then walked into the bathroom to shower. "You better run."

She stripped off her nightie, pulled aside the curtain, and bent to turn on the water. "What the—" She stumbled backward. "What?"

Two footprints in the middle of the tub. Big feet. Knotted toes.

"Dang it. Dang him and his gross feet." Grabbing the nightie and holding it over her breast, Arabella turned on the water and waited for the prints to dissolve.

They remained.

She sniffed. Sweat. Must. The air carried the flavor of Billy's feet, fresh from his work boots.

Her mind rewound and she tried to remember when she'd last used the shower. Yesterday morning, right before the funeral. Arabella didn't recall seeing them, but they had to have been there. The thought that she'd stood on his dirty footprints and somehow overlooked their presence was not only repulsive, but disturbing.

She walked backward out of the bathroom and into the bedroom. Two steps onto the carpet, she knocked her heel into wood. "Ouch! Dang! Dang it!" She spun and stared at the bed. Billy's bed. The first bed they'd ever had sex in.

"Everything needs to go. Everything Billy."

Enraged, Arabella dressed, attacked the bed, stripped off the covers and sheets, grabbed the top mattress in a fireman's hug, and shoved it to the staircase. With a grunt and a push, the mattress slid down the stairs. Along the way, it knocked against a framed picture of the Poteete farm. The mattress hit bottom, slid, and fell sideways. The picture hit bottom and the glass shattered.

"Damn man is dead and still causing me work. Damn him. Damn him to hell and back."

Next came the box springs. Not as easy. Arabella cursed under her breath, found extra strength in her anger, wrestled it sideways, and snorted satisfaction as it slid down the stairs. She followed behind, grabbed it before it could fall, and pushed. Glass crunched under her boot heels. She heard material shred, shards biting wood. Arabella knew she was digging groves in the floors, but did not stop.

Later. She'd clean it all up later. Footprints in the tub. Broken glass. First things first. Everything Billy had to go.

Hunkering behind, she shoved the box springs in a crooked line to the garage door, then shimmied to the front, opened the door, and pushed. The box spring landed beside the Mustang and toppled. Within minutes, the mattress joined the pile.

The headboard and frame were cumbersome, but weighed much less than the mattress and box spring. Arabella was pleased with the speed with which she was able to disassemble the bed and add it to the stack beside the Mustang.

Billy's personal effects had grown into a mountain. Pillowcases full of clothes and shoes. A box of CDs—country classics and old rock and roll. High school memorabilia—yearbooks, photos, trophies. Comic books. Old action figures. It looked like the life savings of a teenage boy and summed up Billy Poteete. The evolution from boy to man had ended upon high school graduation.

Arabella looked at her husband's belongings and felt her first touch of postmortem sadness. She had loved that Billy—the one stacked in the garage. They'd had good times as teens. "Billy Poteete, you was a good kid." She patted a tear. "But you was a rotten man."

She turned, walked into the house, and slammed the door behind her.

"Too late for tears now." Arabella brewed a pot of coffee, filled a bowl with cereal and milk, and leaned against the counter to eat. "I got no regrets. None."

She was poised to shove a spoonful of cereal into her mouth, when a noise upstairs startled her. She gasped. Milk dribbled to her chin.

There were two soft thumps. Then two more. It sounded like Jessie chasing her tail in the tub. Stupid cat loved water.

"Jessie!"

She heard a cat's purr and something warm and soft rubbed her shin.

Arabella dropped the bowl. Milk and wheat squares spread in a checkerboard smear.

Jessie leapt, skidded in the spill, then kicked her legs in the air while she stared at Arabella with angry eyes. Drops of milk spattered from her paws.

*   *   *

"Arabella?"

Sprawled on top of the couch, she heard her name through a misted sleep. She opened her eyes, cringed at the grit, and covered them with her hands. What time—

"Arabella?" A knock on the door.

Had she been dozing? Having been without sleep for several nights, she had begun to spend an incredible amount of time on the couch. Her stomach rumbled. Slept through lunch...or dinner?

Another knock.

Arabella pressed her T-shirt with her hands, went to the door, opened it a crack, and peered out at Billy's brother.

"These keys is yours. I kept the car key 'case I need to move it later on. But you might want the rest." Wayne held up Billy's key ring.

Arabella reached her hand through the crack and snatched the keys.

"I...uh, I got the car at Ma's and uh...the you know...the bed..." A flush blossomed on Wayne's cheeks, as if in mentioning the bed he'd overstepped his bounds. Arabella was reminded of Billy. Wind-tossed hair. Sparkling eyes. Cockeyed smile.

"Arabella?"

"Huh?" She blinked. "Oh, thanks, Wayne. I appreciate the favor."

"Welcome. Ma says thanks for the things. And she wonders...you know...you been with Billy for so long and she knows you're mourning and all, but if you change your mind later, when you recover a bit, all you gotta do is ask and I'll bring you anything you want...of Billy's."

Arabella stared.

"Well, that's all, really. I can see you was sleeping. I just wanted to give you these keys and tell you what Ma—"

A screeching howl rang from upstairs. Arabella spun in time to see Jessie airborne, soaring over the banister. The cat twisted in the air, fell to the floor on her side, and clawed a path to the front door.

"Jessie!" Arabella ran several feet after the cat, but Jessie had already disappeared into the cornfields surrounding the house.

She turned and found Wayne staring at her, his eyes asking a question she couldn't answer. Instead, she forced a smile. "She's always been a bit high strung."

"I can see that. Don't think I ever saw a cat jump like that. Something musta spooked her real bad."

Arabella stepped back inside the house and looked up the stairs. "Probably just shadow boxing and knocked herself out."

"You want me to go try and find her?"

She turned to Wayne and pulled the door, making a barrier between them. "No. Uh uh. She'll be back when she's hungry."

Wayne stared.

"Thanks for the keys. I am pretty tired. I think I'll lay down a bit."

"I'll go on and go, then. Remember, if you want anything back, you just call."

"Thanks, Wayne. I'll do that."

Arabella closed the door, glared at the keys in her hand, and held her breath. Her heart raced. Sweat tickled the bottoms of her feet. Finally, she heard the rev of Wayne's truck engine, followed by gravel popping under tires. When she'd counted to ten, certain Wayne was on the road, she exhaled, opened the door, tossed the keys into the yard. She slammed the door and locked it.

Gone. Everything Billy was gone.

To assure herself, she ran to the garage—the place where Billy Poteete had taken his final breath. Arabella stepped barefoot onto the cold concrete and stared. Antique, Vintage, Classic, 1965 Convertible Mustang—gone. Leaking hydraulic jack—gone. Tool boxes—gone. Crates of car parts—gone. And Wayne had done a good job cleaning up. He'd swept and even poured a pile of kitty litter over the stain in the middle of the floor.

Yes, he'd cleaned up very well. There was nothing—

Except the stain.

Arabella stared at the litter pile and her thoughts traveled back in time. In her mind's eye she saw her hand on the jack handle. One twist and the car had dropped. Billy groaning. Feet kicking. Fists beating the underbody. Arabella had watched and waited for the noise to stop, for Billy to still, before she ran inside and place a frenzied 911 call.

Arabella snapped to the present and swallowed bile. The picture of what she'd done seemed crueler in retrospect. She'd kill her husband with the same emotional backing as one slapping a blood-sucking mosquito.

Blood? She stared. What was under the pile of litter? Remnants of Billy's final moments?

Billy's blood. For two hours she knelt on the garage floor bleaching and scrubbing the spot until she'd scoured a bald circle on the concrete. Worn, aching, she stood and stared.

Gone. Everything Billy was gone.

* * *

Footsteps descended the stairs.

Arabella sat on the couch, an old army blanket wrapped around her shoulders, eye's wide, neck and shoulders tense. The television remote control lay on her lap, her fingers stroking it as if it were alive. "It's all gone, Billy. All your stuff is gone and you should be gone, too. Go away, Billy. Go."

Loud thumps bounded through the living room.

She wished Jessie were there. How she missed her. She'd been gone…three days? Four?

Footsteps raced in the garage. Bare feet on concrete. Around and around. Slapping. Running.

Arabella kept her eyes forward and shouted, "The car's gone, Billy. Jack's gone. Tools is gone. Junk is gone."

Anxiety chewed her belly. Her gritty eyes blurred from lack of sleep. A sharp pain throbbed in her temple. Every muscle tense, nerves on edge, she waited for him to complete his inspection. How many times would Billy have to check the house before he realized it was all gone—just as he should be?

Loud footsteps stomped into the living room. The couch jounced to the left as if it'd been kicked. The carpet indented under the pressure of phantom feet. Huge. Flat. Toes like claws. The dents showed a path around the couch, to the fireplace.

"Your pictures is gone. Your trophies is gone."

Sweaty footprints dotted the wallboard up to and over the ceiling. The noise escalated. Footsteps louder and louder, like thunder breaking inside. Then they were upstairs, chasing around the bedroom. Muffled on the carpet, pattering through the bathroom, in and out of the tub.

Tears slipped down her cheeks. "Your bed is gone. Your clothes is gone. Your razor is gone. Your—"

The phone rang.

Startled, Arabella dropped the blanket over her knees and stared around the room.

The footsteps stopped; the phone rang again.

Arabella turned her ear, listening for the third ring. It came from beside her. She slipped her hand between the couch cushions and found the phone. She couldn't remember the last time she'd used it, the last time she'd had a conversation with someone besides Billy. "H—Hello."

"Arabella?"

She wiped her nose with the back of her hand. "Yes."

"Hey, I called to check on you, to see if you're all right."

"Kirby?" She straightened and smiled crookedly. "Kirby. Oh, it's so nice to hear your—"

The phone shot from her hand, landed on the carpet, then shattered under an invisible blow.

Feet—cold, sticky, and hard, toenails like razors—rubbed against hers as if to generate heat. Over her toes, up and down her shins. The blanket rippled over her legs in waves. Two lumps moving back and forth, up and down.

"Billy?"

The air filled with the smell of fungus and must.

"I was only gonna talk to him a minute."

They moved up, over her knees. Knotted toes kneaded the warm flesh of her thighs.

"Billy?"

A coarse sole rested on her thigh. The toes of the foot kneaded her flesh, then worked under the elastic leg of her panties.

"No, Billy. No."

The foot pressured her down. Toes dug between her legs, and slipped inside.

*   *   *

Arabella Poteete emptied clean clothes into the laundry basket and was carrying it toward the door when she noticed a dainty coat of dust on the "Antique, Vintage, Classic, 1965 Convertible Mustang."

Quickly, she dropped the basket and grabbed for something soft. With a pair of her panties, she wiped until the car shone.

"Better." She exhaled contentedly, shot an inspecting glance around the garage, found nothing out of place, then smiled and went inside.

She'd been a widow more than a year and things had finally fallen into place. The peace had come when she'd called for the return of Billy's things. Immediately she'd decorated the house, proudly displaying Billy's trophies and their prom picture on the fireplace mantel. She'd reassembled the bed and situated it into the dented imprint in the upstairs bedroom carpet. Billy's favorite shaving cream and a brand new razor sat beside the bathroom sink. A new toothbrush held a place beside Arabella's. And of course, the garage was full of tools, crates, and the car.

Even Jessie had returned, straggled and hungry and eager to reclaim her rightful place.

It was as if Billy had never left.

She took the laundry basket to the kitchen and laid her work uniforms over the back of a chair. Her name was sewn in red letters over the pocket—"Arabella Poteete."

She had never returned to her job at Piggly Wiggly. She'd lost her desire to be near the effeminate Kirby. Instead, she'd secured a position at the egg farm. Half the time she peeled eggs in a cold warehouse, standing for hours, filling 50-gallon drums with eggshells. The remainder of her time was spent on the loading dock. It was hard work and oddly rewarding. She found she enjoyed physical labor. Nothing felt better than returning home after a long day, shucking her work boots, stripping out of her uniform, and relaxing.

Laundry done, Arabella carried two beers, a sandwich, and a bag of cheese curls to the living room. She settled into the couch and swung up her legs. Her feet ached. She stared at them. Ugly things. Corns. Cracked skin. And smell. No matter what she did, her feet stunk.

"Dang work boots."

She laughed and fiddled with the remote control.

"Tuesday night. Movie of the week. Looks like one of those cop things. Guns. Hookers. Fast cars. Good stuff, huh?"

Jessie looked at Arabella from the rocking chair and snapped her tail.

"You know you love it." Arabella set the volume, farted, sniffed. "PeeeUuuu! Eggs again for lunch! Stin-keeee!" She laughed, scratched her underarms, and bit into the sandwich.

She'd become...her life was...everything Billy.

ITTY-BITTY

The courtroom fell silent. It was the first time in three days that there hadn't been someone whispering, crying, or falling to the floor in a faint. Allison Greer had been loved by many.

From the first row of spectator seating, Mr. Rudolph Greer stared straight ahead, his focus on the defendant.

Gary Dalton stood with confidence, freshly washed, his curly blond hair trimmed short. He had removed his earrings, but telltale scars and tan lines remained to show that previously he'd worn three studs. Two white splotches on his right earlobe presented a set of pentagrams, while his left ear showed the outline of an upside-down cross. A neat gray suit, slightly large for his wiry build, presented false civility. Under the fabric, Mr. Greer guessed, the man was tensed like a big cat in a zoo cage, cued to survival instinct, nervous under staring eyes, panting, pacing, never resting, ever poised to attack. With a dry smile, a thin line barely etched in his smooth, tanned face, Gary shifted his shoulders and cracked his knuckles. Thick eyeglass lenses couldn't hide the animal hunger in his eyes.

"As to the count of murder in the first degree..." The foreman peeked up at the defendant, shivered, then quickly looked down. "We f—find the defendant g—guilty."

The room exploded with screams. Women shouted. Men howled and shook their fists. Rows of spectators stood up, sat down, rose again, then fell back into their seats. Mr. Greer was hugged, patted, congratulated, and cried upon.

The atmosphere in the courtroom swelled with the intensity of a mushroom cloud. People were moved with the energy. Mr. Greer saw the action in the periphery, felt it under his feet, but did not respond. He remained still, holding fast his stare on the man who had murdered his wife.

What is it that men fear most, Mr. Greer? Bits of a day-old conversation played in his mind, comforting Mr. Greer as he watched.

The defense attorney, an overweight, balding man dressed in a damp suit, wearing a thick mustache of beaded sweat, tapped his client on the shoulder. Gary shrugged off the touch and the attorney obliged, immediately wiping his beefy hands on his slacks.

Mr. Greer watched. *You want revenge, Mr. Greer? You want an animal to suffer? Eat him slowly. Disable him. Manacle him. Then savor the destruction.*

Gary turned. He casually shifted position. Not with the dejected slump of a man destined to spend the remainder of his life behind bars; rather, he moved with grace and self-assurance, chin upright, eyes wide and shining. Without speaking, he screamed defiance.

Mr. Greer watched, emotions and actions controlled, mind focused on a private plan. It was the only thing that kept him from jumping over the rail and ripping the murderer's head from his shoulders.

Gary Dalton swept the room with his stare and joined in the celebration of his conviction. He laughed, nodded, then shook his shackled fists in the air and shouted, "He got what he deserved! Damn straight!" His bright, white smile mocked the crowd.

Mr. Greer watched.

Finally, Gary's visual rounds brought him full circle and he locked gazes with Mr. Greer.

Gary grinned. Mr. Greer spoke. "You will see me again."

"Oh, yeah?" Eyes dancing, Gary laughed. It was a wild sound, like the cry of a jackal. "In hell!"

"Yes, Gary, that is correct. I'll see you in hell. Itty-Bitty Hell."

Gary hooted and slapped his hands on his legs. The defense attorney gripped a handful of his client's jacket, nudged him toward the side door, then threw a sad look at Mr. Greer, who offered nothing for the moot compassion. Armed guards approached.

Before they could secure him, Gary drew close to Mr. Greer. "She was the best of 'em, old man. Two of 'em called out to Jesus as if he'd put in a special appearance. One just lay there like a dead dog. But your little lady, she fought and screamed. She screamed for you, old man.

Even as I crushed her throat in my hands, she called your name." Gary stuck out his tongue, bulged his eyes, and gagged an imitation. "Rudolph! Rudolph!"

Guards fell upon the convict. His attorney stepped away.

Mr. Greer was not finished. "When you're screaming for mercy, you, too, will call out my name. But unlike my wife, death will not come for you." He stood, turned, and pushed through the crowd.

"Rudolph! Save me!"

Mr. Greer blocked the shouts and continued, his main concern to be free of the courtroom and frenzied people.

Sympathetic voices beat at him. A young woman he'd met last week worked his shoulder. "Congratulations, Mr. Greer. We can all rest easy now that that murderer is off the streets."

An old man smelling of smoked meat scurried to his side. "Too bad this state don't have the death penalty. Fryin's the only thing good enough for that SOB."

"You'll be in our prayers, Mr. Greer. Allison was a great woman. A wonderful woman." He recognized Pearl Winston from the bank.

Still, Gary's falsetto voice sounded over the roar of the crowd. "Rudolph! Help me! Oh! Help!"

You want revenge, Mr. Greer? You want an animal to suffer?

Finally, he made it out of the room, the walk through heavy swinging doors taking him from insurrection to amity. Mr. Greer knew the reprieve would be brief, however. The crowd would follow. They had to. Terror brought cohesion. The small-town locals had never been exposed to such a horror. Four women dead. Raped and murdered. One man to stand accountable. It was unthinkable.

Mr. Greer searched the outer corridor for an exit and was ready to run when it began. A shiver shook his fingers, worked throughout his body, then crested in his knees. He wobbled, grabbed the wall, and steadied.

"Mr. Greer!" A concerned voice came from over his shoulder.

"I'm okay," he mumbled. How Mr. Greer longed to be home. He walked carefully, one hand pressed to the wall for support while all around him comforting words began anew. Voices from nameless faces.

"Why don't you sit down and relax awhile. No need to rush off."

"Now, now, Mr. Greer. You don't look well. Would you like some water?"

"Poor man. It's just been too much for him."

"It's all over, Mr. Greer. Be thankful for that. It's all over."

Mr. Greer quivered. It wasn't over. It had only just begun. He swallowed hard, fought tears, and continued.

As Mr. Greer had been forewarned, the process of changing was painful.

People swarmed. Merciful eyes gawked. Hands reached out to him.

Mr. Greer moaned. Already his sensations had altered. Fluorescent lighting came in and out of focus and he blinked through a quivering haze. His skin itched and he wanted to scratch, but couldn't afford the effort. All concentration was focused on getting home. Muscles fought against him. It hurt to breathe. More warnings came to fruition. Nothing that was happening to him was a surprise. The shock was the timing. Mr. Greer had hoped to be alone and safely locked behind closed doors.

"Why don't you let me drive you?"

Mr. Greer turned his head and focused in the direction of the voice. The vision of a balding man turned to water, spilled, then reformed.

Mr. Greer gagged. "No." He ground his teeth. "Thank you." He pushed by the man. "Leave me…"

Each step down the corridor was performed with the concentration of a gymnast on a balance beam.

Once outside, fresh air hit him like a fist. He nearly fell. Pressuring his lips closed, stride accelerated to match his heartbeat, he moved forward.

"Itty-Bitty." Mr. Greer freed up a pained growl like the mewl of an animal caught in a snare, wire slicing through furred skin and muscle. As he stumbled toward his car, he relived the conversation that had carried him to that agonizing point—stage two in the metamorphosis of Itty-Bitty.

*　　*　　*

"What is it that men fear most, Mr. Greer?"

"Death. The death of a loved one."

"No, sir. You put too much thought into the answer. As a solitary man facing death, what would you fear?"

Mr. Greer shook his head. It was a bizarre conversation, the raw emotion of it seeming out of place in Imel's baby blue and beige living room. Talking of revenge and man's secret fears, the two men would have been better scripted huddled in a dank, gloomy cellar, eyes wide under sweat-soaked brows, focused on each other in the extinguishing light of a waning candle nub.

The Martha Stewart décor agitated Rudolph Greer's strained mood.

But he would stay. There were reasons he'd come to see Imel, one being simply to socialize with someone he loved, if only to prove good feelings still lived inside him. Foremost, however, he needed a favor.

Mr. Greer searched Imel's coal eyes for a hint that help would come, but found nothing. Imel wasn't giving signs one way or the other. He still had a point to make. Mr. Greer would have to be patient, give his friend room. After a long, slow exhale, he cautioned a guess. "Looking death in the eye…I guess, I'd fear the afterlife."

Imel clucked his tongue and tensed, his spine stern against the chair back. "I am not playing philosopher, Mr. Greer. This is not a game show. I am talking of basic fears. Pretend yourself a child."

A child? What did he know of children? He and Allison never had any. Never cared to. Blast Imel and his eccentricities! Mr. Greer felt idiotic. His eyes scoured the room, going everywhere and nowhere, anywhere but on Imel.

He sighed, hating himself for being unable to answer a simple question. Fear. Pretend himself a child. He would have to. Mr. Greer's thoughts left the present and drifted back in time. What had he feared? Being a boy's boy, he had feared nothing. Rudolph Greer had always been the kid on the block everyone came to for help. He'd handled problems with big-mouth new kids, or out-of-line older kids, or just stupid kids who thought they could take him and crown themselves "king" of the neighborhood. No one, nothing, had scared him.

Further back, then, to the little Rudolph. There had to be something. What had frightened him…what?

Finally, he blinked, nodded, and exhaled one word—"Monsters."

"Ah! Monsters?" Imel's face brightened.

Relieved, Mr. Greer beefed it up. "I was afraid that a monster lived under my bed and, if I put my feet over the edge, he'd crawl out and eat me."

"You fear being eaten by a monster?"

"You said 'be a child.' When I was—"

"Yes. Primitive fear. Now take it a step further, Mr. Greer. What could be worse than being eaten by a monster?"

"Is there anything?"

"Oh, yes! Being eaten by *many* monsters. So many monsters that they could not be counted. Monsters so vicious that they did not consume, rather, they feasted on the pain. Itty-Bitty monsters. Millions of—"

"I don't get it."

"A big monster can finish the job, Mr. Greer. A tiny monster cannot eat an entire being at once. Small bites. Chewing. Eating to satisfaction, then later, eating some more. When will it begin again? When will the monster's hunger return? And the torture?"

The gleam in Imel's eyes added a punch to his soft voice. Energy seemed to pour from him, as if the man was plugged in, emitting a low electric whine. Mr. Greer shuddered.

"You quake, my friend. Itty-Bitty scares you."

"It's creepy."

"You want revenge, Mr. Greer? You want an animal to suffer? Eat him slowly. Disable him. Manacle him. Then savor the destruction."

"Eat him slowly?" Mr. Greer had no desire to eat a man, let alone take his time with it. He forced a chuckle.

There had been a time when he and Imel had laughed together. They'd been friends since college—Rudolph Greer, the rebel, and Imel, simply an oddball. With a heritage that included East Indian, Egyptian, Hungarian, and a touch of Irish, Imel's bloodline alone set him on a crooked road. Because his background afforded such a spiritual melting pot, he fancied himself an eclectic guru and had adopted a pattern of speech that swung between the clichéd kung-fu teacher and simply goofy. His trademark was using formal addresses like "mister" and "miss" in lieu of a first name. Odd?—certainly. Irritating—sometimes. But as big a part of Imel as his heart.

"You laugh, Mr. Greer."

"You're not serious."

"Yes, Mr. Greer. Serious. It is called Itty-Bitty. It is one that is millions."

"What is it?"

"It is in you. Your emotions brought to life."

"Emotions?"

"Your anger, hate, pain...guilt."

Mr. Greer cringed. The guilt was real. Allison. He should have been able to protect her. Had she died thinking of him? Wishing—no!—expecting him to rescue her from the hands of a murderer? And where had he been? On the golf course, wooing an investor, trying to seal a deal for a half a million dollars, all for the proposed betterment of some blasted medical supplies. Freaking I. V. bags and tubing. He'd gotten the contract signed and the phone call about Allison in the same hour.

Oh, yeah, the guilt was real. And the hate. And the pain.

"Itty-Bitty lives in you. He is eating you up right now."

Mr. Greer dropped his chin, knowing he couldn't hide from Imel, but having to try.

"This beast who murdered Allison…Itty-Bitty can get under his skin, eat away at him slowly for the rest of his life."

"How do we do it?"

"You do it."

"How, Imel? Tell me!"

"Mr. Greer, revenge is a draining process. Understand this, you cannot, if you decide to—" Imel stopped, gathered his composure, then continued. "In setting free Itty-Bitty, you will cease to be as you are now. You will…"

"Die?"

"No, not die. Itty-Bitty needs you alive."

"Then what?"

Imel stared with serious eyes. "You are…Mr. Greer, if I had imagined that someday we would be breaching such a topic, if I had known that my gifts would assist you in such a horrific manner, I would not have been your friend. I…I love you. If you do this, if you set free Itty-Bitty, not only will I never see you again, but I will be helping you damn your soul. I do not know if I can."

Mr. Greer tightened his jaw. "I can't live while he breathes, while he has the opportunity to smile, to enjoy a single second of his life. I am already damned! Help me, Imel. *Because* you are my friend, help me."

Imel closed his eyes and breathed deeply, his chest rising and falling gently under his white T-shirt. "I've seen it work. When Itty-Bitty comes out, it is not pleasant."

"Every breath I take is hell. *Living* is hell. What could be worse?"

"Itty-Bitty bonds antagonist and protagonist. It is unbreakable."

"Will it get me what I want?" Mr. Greer gripped his pants' legs, wadding the cloth.

"Yes, Mr. Greer. Itty-Bitty is brilliant revenge. But it is not without…"

"I'll do it. Let's go. Now."

Imel paused. His black eyes teared. "I will say goodbye, then, old friend. I, too, loved Allison. You both will always be in my heart."

"Thank you, Imel. I have been blessed to have been close to you."

Imel reached out. "This will start it."

Mr. Greer palmed a small, soft knob. It looked like a dried prune.

Oddly, he knew before he put it in his mouth that it would be foul, and was not disappointed.

"Faster is better, Mr. Greer."

The taste was indescribable, spoiled and dirty. But worse than that was the feel of the thing. It moved over his tongue and against his teeth as if it had come alive and was squirming against his bite, trying to crawl out of his mouth. Mr. Greer gagged, but continued to chew. His eyes watered and saltwater stung his nose.

"All of it, Mr. Greer. There is no second chance for Itty-Bitty. If you cannot swallow, then spit now and we will forget about it."

Cheeks burning, snot running from his nose, Mr. Greer shook his head, *No.*

"Mr. Greer?"

The sorrow behind Imel's eyes was obvious. Human emotion inspiring him, Mr. Greer swallowed, then dropped forward out of the chair, landing on his knees, his face pressed into the carpet. He forced his head to the side so he could breathe and cough. The knob was gone; the taste, however, remained. A minute passed. He remained hunched, peering over the beige fibers that looked like a monochrome forest, tiny tan trunks swaying back and forth to the vile air chugging from his nostrils.

And it was uncomfortable, as if his musculature had been forced into another man's skin. It was like trying on suit jackets, picking up the wrong size, pulling it on, and finding the cuffs riding tight on the wrists, range of motion limited, armpits taut and unyielding. Mr. Greer fought the invisible restriction, tried to pull his arms out from under his body, but remained stuck.

He trailed his eyes up and found Imel staring down, hands gripping the seat of his chair, poised to help if necessary. "The first fades quickly, Mr. Greer."

It was true. Soon Mr. Greer was able to take a deep breath. A minute later, he pushed off the floor with his hands and pulled up to his knees. "How…" His voice crackled like an announcer's at a ballpark, screaming out plays over a poor P. A. system. Mr. Greer cleared his throat, swallowed a mouthful of sour spit and tried again. "How will I know?"

"You ask this with the naiveté of an adolescent questioning love, Mr. Greer. Itty-Bitty comes when it comes, without instructions. You will know. Just like you knew when it was love."

Yes. Rudolph Greer knew love. He hadn't been looking for it, didn't think he wanted it, but when he'd met Alison, he'd found it. Love. The first time he'd looked into her sea-green eyes, he'd known it.

* * *

He slammed the front door closed, ran to the bedroom, and flopped onto the bed. The ten-minute drive home from the courthouse had been a carnival ride of terror and agony, and he was amazed that he'd made it without an accident.

"Itty-Bitty."

Mr. Greer grimaced, ground his teeth, and kicked. He imagined himself on fire, every nerve ablaze.

"Stupid name."

His flesh roiled in knots over his body. Mr. Greer wanted to scream, let the world know his suffering, but did not. Neighbors. Intervention. No. He'd find control.

He rolled, buried his face into the pillow, and howled. A bolt of pain zigzagged a path through his skeleton, giving a bite to every joint along the way. And Mr. Greer thought of Allison, her death, the pain of being raped and beaten and strangled, and more, the terror she must have felt.

He should have been there…should have been able to help her…and her murderer had confirmed it, yes, she'd called—

Rudolph! Rudolph, help me! Help!

When Mr. Greer reached a point where the agony seemed unbearable and he thought he might die before tasting revenge, it stopped. From torture to sweet nothing in a heartbeat.

Immediately afterward came weightlessness, and Mr. Greer separated from the physical mass of his body. He felt skin, bones, muscles and tendons slip away as if they were nothing more than a T-shirt being sloughed off at the end of the day. Then he levitated, felt himself being lifted higher, and stared at his body on the bed, stretched out and relaxed as if napping. Currents shifted him over and around, and as he gently rolled, Mr. Greer saw movement—a muddied swirl—reflected in the vanity mirror. The blur wavered, then disintegrated, so all that remained was a rippling suspended midair, the faintest essence of movement.

Mr. Greer was Itty-Bitty—

And he knew exactly what to do next.

An airborne wave of nearly imperceptible specs, he moved across the room, then slipped through the window screen. It was effortless, even pleasant. A cool night breeze carried him north.

* * *

"You see something you like, Caruthers?" Gary Dalton rested his upper body against cold steel bars. He was wearing a state-issued blue jumpsuit and a smart smile.

Caruthers continued to mop the floor, speaking to Gary while keeping his eyes on his work. "When you address me, you will use the word 'mister.'"

"Fancy yourself someone important, do you? Well, let me try again. You see something you like, *Mister* Caruthers?"

"I haven't seen anything I like in this pit for six years. It was then that I found Jason Kirby in the shower. Dead. Someone'd got a hold of him and stuffed a plunger handle up his..." Caruthers peeked around at Gary, shivered, and rubbed the worn arms of his prison blues. "Can't stand the look in your eye. And I ain't gonna finish the story. I ain't gonna do or say nothing that gives an animal like you pleasure." Caruthers pushed the wheeled bucket with the tip of his black boot.

"Aw, don't you like me, Mr. Caruthers?"

"I hate you and wish you were dead. Murderer and rapist. You make me sick."

"Now, don't be that way." Gary giggled, pressed his face into the bars, and kissed at the air.

Caruthers huddled into his shoulders and pushed the mop over a seemingly clean floor.

"Say, when're you getting out of here, Caruthers?"

"*Mister.*"

"When're you getting out of here, *Mister* Caruthers."

"I got eleven months left." Caruthers soaked his mop, rung it out, and swirled blond ropes over the floor. Water rippled in foamy patterns. "Eleven months. That's three-hundred and thirty-six days. I'm on the downhill slide."

"I'll miss you."

"You ain't gonna miss anything. You know you ain't gonna be here for more than a week or two. Soon they'll be packing you up and shipping you upstate. Pervert. Where you're going, they'll eat you for dinner. It makes me smile to picture it. You think you're so smart. Up there you'll be just another nobody. You'll be spending the rest of life with *men* who's killed other *men*."

Gary laughed out loud. "Aw, you'll miss me. I can see the cheer in your eyes, old man. You're loving talking to me. You can go back to your dorm room and tell all the other lightweights that you had a face-to-face conversation with a *real* criminal. A lifer. A serial killer. Makes you feel like a big shot."

Caruthers stopped mopping, turning around. "Should be a death penalty. You are evil."

"I'm blessed. I'm looking forward to three squares, television, and air-conditioning. I'll get me a little job and all the baby boys I can handle."

"You're sick."

"Sick? No, sir. Honest. Can't tell me you never dipped your wick into the pucker-pot. A piece is a piece, Caruthers. As long as it's face down, who's the wiser?"

Caruthers scurried away. Mop water slopped onto the floor. "Sick man. Evil."

"I saw you looking at me! I saw you!" Gary watched the old man until he faded from sight, then settled back on his cot.

The cell was small, but he didn't mind. He'd been in and out of temporary lockdown for months. Gary enjoyed the transportation sequence from courtroom to holding area and the stay in-between. It was easy time, relaxing.

Gary.

Gary bolted upright. "Caruthers? You change your mind. You come back to tell me you're sorry?" With a giggle, he stood and moved to the bars. "Caruthers?" Gary's voice bounced down the empty hallway. "You're nothing but a tease, old man." He walked back to the bunk and jumped onto it, butt first.

We meet again.

"Huh?" Gary pulled up his head, perked his ears. The voice was familiar and ignited a flicker of tension. The small hairs on his arms stood upright. Gooseflesh tickled his chest. Gary scratched through his shirt.

I'm here.

Grabbing his shirt's coarse material in a tight fist, Gary spun around.

He was alone. The one-man cell was now uncomfortable. Seemed smaller, constrictive. "Guard!"

I'm here.

The voice was directly beside him. Gary whipped his head to the side, swishing his face through haze. "What the…" He swung his fist through it.

Forever and ever, together we will be.

Gary stumbled backward, fell onto the cot, and scanned the cell. Nothing. No one.

He lowered his smart-alec grin to half-mast and was about to call out again, when he felt stinging pinpricks all over his body, like standing naked in a firestorm. Holding up his hands in a defensive block, Gary saw a translucent wave ripple over his skin, then soak into his pores. Blinking, he looked at the corridor ceiling. It glowed in a continuous ray. Had it flashed? Had a power surge tricked him?

The pain told him it was not a mere power flux. He was hurt.

"Help! Guard! Help me!"

He slapped his arms and chest and tore the jumpsuit, trying to strip. The touch of fabric was excruciating and knocked him into the past.

Gary saw his mother, her face sweaty—always sweaty, regardless the weather. There were purple semi-circles under her eye. Gary's fault. According to her, the forty hours of hard labor she'd endured birthing him had left her permanently bruised, spoiling her natural good looks. His mother's voice was raspy and masculine, like Oscar the Grouch from the T. V. show, and came at him from between yellowed teeth, carrying the sour smell of damp tobacco. She yelled a lot. It was welcome, compared to her favorite punishment. While sprawled on the couch, television tuned to her stories, she'd bark at Gary to keep quiet. Didn't she deserve some rest? Didn't he know how hard she worked to keep him in shoes? If Gary failed to be quiet enough she'd pull off the cushion, puff the cigarette until the coal burned cherry red, then extinguish it on him. Usually his arms. Sometimes, if she was really mad, his chest or belly. If he cried, she'd fetch a cold stick of butter from the fridge and rub it into the wounds. If he resisted, she'd suck the cigarette back to life and put down more burns and apply more butter. Only when Gary swallowed his tears and screams would she let him loose, tell him to get lost and keep down the noise.

Years later, when he'd started dealing blow—she being first in line for a freebie—his mother had apologized for how she'd treated him, begged forgiveness, and he'd told her it was nothing, already forgotten.

Lie.

His skin burned then as it had when he was a little boy, but now Gary could not withhold his cries. "Help!"

I want to tell you about my wife, Allison. It's a long story, Gary. I'm afraid it'll take forever.

"What?" Blanks filled in. Images of his childhood washed away and Gary remembered Mr. Greer. "Holy…help!"

When you took her away from me, you left me with nothing but memories and now I'd like to share those memories with you. It's all I've got to give.

Mr. Greer spoke in his ear. Itty-Bitty spread. Gary screamed and flopped to the floor.

How about our wedding? That sound like a good starting point? Kind of suits the situation. It was the beginning of a lifelong commitment. Kind of like today, Gary. Between you and me.

"Help me!" Gary writhed.

Itty-Bitty nibbled.

Anyway, my Allison was beautiful that day. Her hair was pulled up into a bun. Not an old lady's bun. A soft bun with a few fine hairs hanging loose on her cheeks. Never had I seen a woman so beautiful.

A wound opened on the back of Gary's hand. Invisible fire spread throughout his body. "Help! Someone!"

Metal slapped metal. The cell door wiggled.

It wasn't a formal wedding. Just a simple Justice-Of-The-Peace affair. She wore a yellow dress. Really looked good with her green eyes. I'm sure you didn't notice, but Allison had beautiful eyes. She couldn't hide anything behind those eyes. And that day was no different. Every time I looked at her, I saw love. She was beautiful.

Tears sizzled on Gary's cheeks. "Someone help me! It hurts! Mr. Greeeeeer!"

Guards arrived. They grabbed Gary, aggravating the pain. He shrieked.

After we said our vows, we went for a drive up the coast. We stopped at a little Italian place. I know we stood out in the crowd. Two kids grinning and kissing, planning a future. We glowed. Love will do that.

"Get him…get…Mr. Greeeeer!" A sore erupted on Gary's cheek. He howled, punched, and kicked.

Prison guards returned the violence with blows of their own, then secured his hands behind his back with plastic cinch-ties.

Gary fought against the painful restraints.

Mr. Greer talked.

Itty-Bitty chewed.

*   *   *

So there we were in the boat and Allison was screaming and yanking on her fishing rod. You'd think that she'd hooked Moby Dick himself. Well, I ran to help her, but slipped and fell overboard. Don't you know, right at that exact moment, whatever she had on her line threw the hook and she stuck me right in my behind. Boy, did that sting. But not as bad as when Allison gave a great big tug, thinking that the fish was still on the line! That was a funny moment. The pain didn't matter at all. You should have seen the look on her face. It was priceless!

"Medicine, Gary."

Gary sniveled, looked up, and saw a familiar face. The ward nurse. She was a foul-looking woman. Worn-out skin, thick glasses, and gray teeth. Gary loved her. He lived to see her and take what she could give him. Momentary peace.

Two pills every eight hours. Sixteen minutes for the pain to ease. Another nine before Mr. Greer's voice faded. The entire anesthetization would last two hours. For three years Gary had sat in the mental hospital timing the pill.

That cut took seven stitches and I had to sit on a donut for a week. Still have the scar. It looks like a smile. Allison thought I'd be mad. I could never be mad at her.

"It chews and chews and he talks and talks."

The nurse held a cup to his mouth. "Take this." She tipped it and wiggled, trying to empty two pink pills onto his tongue.

Gary was denied freedom of movement. Unpredictably violent, he'd tried to beat himself to death on several occasions. Restraints kept him from harm. The pills landed. Gary swallowed before the nurse could bring up a paper cup of water.

"Calm down now, Gary. Can't have you choking to death. Not on my shift." She laughed at her joke.

That's my story about the "one-that-didn't-get-away!"

The nurse touched Gary on the forehead. "You've got another lesion brewing here. Poor Gary. One sore heals and another breaks out. Darndest thing I've ever seen."

Her touch was gentle, but it felt like fire. Gary cried out. Fingers clenched; he tugged against the restraints. "I want to die."

The nurse blinked down at him, dull eyes, amplified behind heavy lenses. Without another word, she walked back to the nurse's station to continue her medication rounds.

Gary yelled after her. "I said, I want to die!"

"Now, now, now, Gary, that ain't no way to talk."

Gary turned his head to the voice.

Maxwell, a minimum-wage ward attendant with a terminal smile.

"You don't want to go back in for shock treatments, do you?"

"I want to die. I'm in pain."

"Yep. I see you got another mark on your face." Maxwell extended his finger, but didn't touch.

Gary flinched, regardless.

"Mr. Greer still chewing your ear off, Gary?" Maxwell laughed like Santa.

"It's not funny!"

"What's he telling you about today?"

"Fishing stories."

"I love to fish. When I retire, I'm gonna take my pension, get me a little dinghy, and go fishing."

"It hurts."

Maxwell trailed his stare over Gary's tattered restraints. A small smile lingered. "You're a murderer, Gary. You hurt people and now, well, you're hurting."

"I'm sorry. I told him I'm sorry."

"Well, that's good. I'm sure Mr. Greer was glad to hear that. But being sorry don't bring back the dead, now, does it?"

"I said, I'm sorry."

Maxwell turned away from Gary, then came back around, lowering his head and his voice. "Sorry don't get you much in Itty-Bitty Hell."

Hey! Now that guy is smart, Gary. Itty-Bitty Hell! I like him. You go ahead and tell him that for me! He's one bright cookie! Now Allison, that girl was smart...

Gary moaned and looked at the clock.

OUT OF THE BLUE

It was finally starting to look like a carnival. Colored lights boogying on the rides. Strings of blinkers dancing over the game booths. The smell of cotton candy—diabetic perfume to the air. Candy apples shining like Christmas ornaments behind clear plastic windows. The Italian guy on the corner, Vinnie Bag-O-Donuts he called himself, had turned on his fans, sending a drift of onions, peppers, and Italian spice drooling overhead. Later sweat and beer and teenage pheromones would add to the aromas. For now it was the carnival at its finest. Clown's favorite part of the night. Before the drunkards and rowdy teens and after the mommies and daddies pushing strollers of squalling, puking babies. Jeeze.

Clown wished they'd start the carnival after dark. More magical. Cooler, too. Already he itched, with sweat tickling a trail down his spine under his pink ruffled shirt. Beneath the baggy hound's-tooth slacks, he wore briefs that were soaked and holding his buttocks like warm, dead hands.

Blasted summer tours. Clown hated heat, loved cool. But there he was in the middle of summer, coming off a blistering afternoon in blasted Florida, of all places. Mosh pit of northern uptights and southern bumpkins and lazy locals. Never knew what to expect. Made for a rough ride. Clown felt like one of those rubber blow-ups, taking it from all sides. And Clown could take a punch. Had been taking them all his life and would until he fathered a son and retired. Not for a while, though. He was looking forty straight in the eye but figured he had another couple of years before he had to worry about such things. Keep saving money for now. Work and stash.

Clown looked at the upside-down top hat he kept by his feet, scooped up a handful of bills and stuffed them deep into his rear pants' pocket, then chased a rowdy bead of sweat down his ribcage. He missed and it trickled to the edge of his briefs. Itched. But there it would stay, annoying him. Couldn't be playing with his underwear in front of the kids now, could he?

Maybe just a little tug. Clown was ready to slip his hands into his pants when a kid ran at him, screaming, "Me! Do me next!"

The little boy jumped up and down that weird way kids can; knees bent, both feet planted—the kangaroo hop! Made Clown envious; he couldn't move like that. Had been able to years ago, but thanks to time and a touch of arthritis, his days of jumping were over.

"Me! Please! Do me next!"

Hop. Hop. Hop. The boy's black hair flapped around his face like a velvet cloth, as if the individual strands were connected, moving as one. Swish. Back and forth. Swish. Swish. Beautiful? Yeah, he was, with his smooth skin, heart-shaped mouth, crimson cheeks, and Asian eyes. Animated Kewpie.

Ah, what Clown wouldn't give for that kind of energy. He couldn't help but give the kid a nod and grin.

The little boy stopped in mid-jump, clapped his hands, and squealed, "I want you to make me a—"

Quickly, Clown put a finger to his lips, tipped his head, and shook it, "No." Just as fast, the boy quieted and their stares locked. Perfect. Clown went inside and found a mind full of sweet stuff. Smiling thoughts bouncing about like those happy faces glued to T-shirts or gummed to car bumpers: plain yellow circles, black dot eyes, sideways "C" for a mouth. Clown wandered through the little boy's park of feelings and memories—mellow dreams speckled with energetic gusts of play and frequent peals of laughter all floating beneath calm, cool blue.

He'd had a blissful life—pure Norman Rockwell. Birthday parties, mother's lullabies, father throwing a ball, friends in school trading cards, multicolored heads riding a circle-go-round in the park. Mmmm. Clown liked it in there. Would've been a nice place to stay a spell, but he couldn't. Not his job to loiter in the minds of the children. Back to work.

He had to find that one thing...the special little secret...beyond the dreams and fantasies...skirting imagination to...there! It sprang up at Clown with a playful growl. Little dragon perched against the battered slats of a crib. Orphanage in China. Infant hands gripping the crib as if it were alive. Sadness linked to the stuffed toy. When they'd taken the boy away—adopted to a couple from America—they'd left his stuffed friend behind.

With a wink, clown slipped his hand into his pocket, pulled out a yellow balloon, then blew it up into a long tube and began to manipulate the rubber into the shape of a dragon. Always amazed him how it happened. Alone at night, home in his trailer, Clown could never make anything more interesting than a snake or a pretzel. Only when he was with the children did it work, could he transform balloons to gratify their needs.

It'd been like that in his family for centuries. Stories went back to his great grandfather's grandfather, who used to whittle for the children, gave them what they needed from timber. Gifted, and damned they were. It was wonderful to be able to share the minds of the young and bring them joy, but a curse that the trips into the subconscious weren't always pleasant and weren't limited to youth.

With a final snap of rubber, the dragon's tail curled up to a blunt point. Fine looking creature. Serpentine neck. Angled head perched atop a muscled body. Good job. Clown was pleased.

The little boy squealed glee.

But the father looked at Clown with a question in his eyes, one his mouth brought to life. "I had a picture of my son when he was a baby in his crib, asleep...a toy just like what you made here...it was clutched in his hand. How would you know that?"

"It's great, Daddy. See it? See?" Hop. Hop. Hop. Black hair. Swish. Swish. Swish. Smile like a lightening strike.

The father looked down at his son and his question faded away. "Do you like it, son?"

"I love it. It's just what I wanted." The little boy kissed the dragon on the top of the head, leaving behind a sugared lip print.

After he dropped a ten spot into the upside-down top hat at Clown's feet, the father grabbed up the boy, kissed his head, then carried both dragon and son away in the cradle of his arms. There was a bounce in his step. Good. Clown had pleased them both.

Made him feel special, blessed. And he was. Clown could slip into a mind with the ease of pushing aside a curtained door. That's all. Nothing fantastic. Not an out of body experience with flashing lights and symbolic visions. Just entering and walking around like one wanders through a park, marveling at the scenery and sky. Skies told a lot. Secrets lay in the open like rocks marring a path. Truth couldn't hide, didn't try. People he knew, mostly carnies and wanderers, didn't get too close. Liked their privacy. Didn't want to share the color of the sky. Pushed him away. No matter. His life was the children.

They needed Clown.

The little ones were the best. Sky's in their parks were usually pretty blue, pastel and pure, sometimes swirled with soft yellow and orange or lime green and pink. Made his sweet tooth sing, longing for one of the old-fashioned all-day suckers. The older the kids got, the deeper their colors, soiled with experiences and many times blistered to midnight blue, red, and purple, and the worst, gray or black.

People seemed compelled to take what's pure and good and blot it with sorry until it was truly hard to look at. Sometimes he wished he could…

"…me? Can you do me next?"

Startled, Clown looked down. There was a new child at his feet. Not the cutest thing he'd ever seen. Freckled on the nose only. Eyes like dirty blue balls. A smile that showed crooked teeth all knocking up against each other. There'd be an orthodontist in her future. Big bucks to fix that smile. Worth it. Her grin was powerful, seemed to open a hole in the universe. And her park was a flurry. Blue and yellow and pink with a marbled twist of red gashing a path straight through it all like an angry snowplow.

Clown popped his eyes wide, blinked several times quickly, and fashioned his mouth in a big "O."

"Did I scare you?" She'd lowered her voice, but her park remained a color burst.

Shaking his head, Clown reached into his pocket and pulled out a pink balloon.

She gawked, breathless. "Are you gonna make me—"

"Are you *going* to? 'Gonna' is not a word, Francine." Her mother's voice chopped the girl's sentence as if the woman had swung an axe through the air.

Clown spat out the balloon, licked his lips, took a step back, and tried again.

Without hesitation, Francine fixed the grammar and persisted. "Are you going to make me a—"

He hated to interrupt the kid twice, but he had to. He put up his hand and waggled his finger back and forth, "No."

"I think he wants to surprise you, honey." A set of perfectly manicured hands reached over the child's shoulder and gripped, blood-red nails curling into the soft cotton T.

Clown looked at her, and even though he didn't want to, there he was, standing in the woman's park. Red sky. Fussy and angry. Divorced with a grudge against humanity. He could see why she was alone. Jeeze. Her park was a storm and she made up for the mess in her mind by taking control of her life and the kid's. Immaculate at home and work. Power junky. Neat freak. Didn't allow the kid outside without her. Couldn't get dirty. Neighbors and friends might interpret a soiled child as flawed parenting. Coming fall, Mommy was shipping the kid off to private school, abroad. Couldn't wait. Finally get her life back to herself.

With a shiver, he jumped out of the mother's vicious park and enjoyed the kid. She was watching him with a dopey smile, her eyes fixed on his fingers as they twisted and snapped rubber. Her controlled panic was soon rewarded with a kitten.

She broke out a smile that looked as if it might shuck her jaw from her face and screamed, "Kitty! A kitty! Oh, thank you. Thank you. Thank you. Mommy won't let me get a kitty."

"I'm allergic." The mother tried to smile an apology. Crinkly lips. Moved with all the grace of a cellophane wrapper on a pack of cigarettes.

Clown was thrilled by the allergy. Too bad. So sad. He worked for the kids.

"It's just what I was thinking about. Oh, thank you. Thank you so much." Francine rubbed her cheeks over the balloon and purred at the little pink kitten. "I love her."

The mother sneezed and swept Francine away, leaving a smiling Clown behind, already searching the grounds for the next.

The wait was short. The kid wasn't. Tall and fat. Big all over. Jeeze.

"Where's your face paint?"

The kid's eyes were pinched under a swell of white cheeks that looked like a baby's butt seated square on his face. If not for the matching set of black eyes, Clown might have given those luscious cheeks a quick pinch. But he wouldn't. Probably send the kid screaming. What a set of shiners.

Clown answered the question by slipping his fingers over his ruby lips shaped like a plump, upturned hot dog, then patting the red heart on his left cheek and the twin black diamonds on his right. When he'd finished touching his decorated face, Clown spread his fingers wide and turned out his hands, palms forward for the kid to inspect.

The boy drew in close. "Hey! What about the paint?"

Clown shook his head, then emptied his side pocket to show empty.

"No way."

Clown nodded, "Yes."

"That a wig?" He pointed a sausage-shaped finger at Clown's flashy red hair.

Clown dipped his head and allowed the kid to tug it.

"No freakin' way."

Clown stood up and nodded. Hard to stifle a laugh. He loved it when the kids realized he was for real.

"How?"

Clown reached behind his back and pulled out a sign, a painted piece of plywood with the words, "I was born to Clown around" printed sloppily in the center.

"Born a clown?"

Clown nodded.

"For real?"

Clown tipped his head and stared back without answering.

After a moment, the big kid grinned and flinched. Smile hurt. "For real. A real clown. That's cool."

Clown bowed.

"Can you make me something?"

Clown was already on it. The kid's park was clouded with gray. Bullies at school. Black eyes had come from a guy named Todd. Go figure. Todd? Anyhow, the bully had kicked the kid off his bike and he'd landed face down on a curb. Broke his nose. Jeeze.

While the kid watched, Clown blew up a long red tube, then twisted it and coiled it and flicked rubber into place until he had what the kid needed. Guard dog. Head high. Ears perked. Thick legs at his side, ready to spring.

The kid grinned kind of sadly, took the dog, and brought it close to inspect it. "Cool. Looks like he could jump up and take someone down. Just like that. Too bad he ain't real."

"Hey double stuff! Fatty fatty four by four, can't fit through the outhouse door."

Todd? Had to be. Skinny thing, he sauntered up to the big kid, wearing oversized jeans riding low on his hip, a sideways cap and smile. "Hey, double stuff. Whatcha got there? Old clown man whip you up a pizza?"

The big kid looked down at the balloon, up to Clown, back at the balloon, then slowly walked toward Todd. A noise like a ghost on fire came from the rubber dog and Todd's smile slipped off his kisser like it had melted. He took a few steps backward, tripped, and fell onto his fanny, his jeans showing the crack of a flat, alabaster butt. Laughter all over. Kids and adults alike. Todd jumped to his feet and ran. By that time, his lower cheeks were dressed in a girlish, pink blush.

The big kid turned to Clown and grinned in spite of the shiners. "Thanks! I...he...thanks!" And he walked away. Seemed taller somehow. Not quite as thick around the middle.

The hole the big kid left was filled with a handful of youngsters. All shapes and sizes. Needs just as varied.

Clown whipped up an orange train for a little boy with a pale blue sky. Not a care in the world. Just liked saying "Choo Choo."

After that he made a set of matching teddy bears for some twins, one pink, one purple. They loved bears.

He fashioned a red rose for a young girl who thought she was the ugliest thing God had ever made. Little thing grabbed the rose, stared at it, and walked away with a sparkle in her smile.

Then Clown put together two white hearts, one interlocked with the other, for an older boy whose mother had died in a car accident. He slipped it under his shirt and whispered, "Mama" before walking away.

Clown blew up balloons and transformed them into yellow giraffes, green hippos, pink pigs, many little dogs in yellow, red, orange, green, and white—a special yellow and orange mix for a little boy whose puppy had had to be put to sleep—a handful of pink and white hearts, and an orange sun for a little girl who was afraid of the dark.

Time passed like magic and the crowd changed. Less kids. Time for Clown to retreat. And he was glad. Tired. Stinking. Ready for a shower and a cold one. Clown had his hat in hand and was on his way to the trailers when he saw her moving toward him from a break in the masses. Something told him to wait.

She was a tall girl. Slender. Long, chocolate hair. Dark eyes, older than her years, locked onto Clown through a break in the bodies. He beckoned her, extending his hand and curling one finger out and in.

She moved forward, and behind her came a man. Kept himself close to her. Too close.

When they stood before Clown, the man knelt beside the girl, brought his face to hers, and lifted her chin so it sat in the cup of his hand. "You want something special, Sweetie? Don't be shy. Tell Mr. Clown what you want."

Her chin quivered.

"Now, don't be that way. Tell Daddy, then, and I'll tell Mr. Clown for you."

Clown stepped forward, set his hand on the girl's shoulder, and drew her out of the father's grip and closer to him. At first she tried to pull away, but Clown kept a gentle hold and urged her forward. She moved slowly. Cautiously. When she was near, he took her hand and set it on his cheek. The girl gasped, drew her fingers over the heart and diamonds, then circled the outline of Clown's mouth.

Her eyes brightened and opened wide. "No makeup?"

Clown shook his head.

"Does that mean you're a real clown?"

Clown pulled out his sign.

The girl read it out loud in a soft voice, "I was born to clown around," then giggled and pulled up on her toes to rub his head.

Clown purred and she laughed.

The father did not. He tensed. Jealous monster.

"And your hair? That red can't be real." The girl stepped closer still, inspecting his hairline, and Clown took a walk in her park.

It hurt. Her sky was a bruise, purple and black. Everywhere was the father. A greasy shadow blotting the colors. Lingering stares through the shower door. Slipping into her bed at night. Called it "cuddling." She was dying inside.

"You were born to clown around? You're a real live clown? Born with your face and hair just like that?" The girl's voice was light and amazed.

Clown flashed his biggest smile.

She returned it. Added a flicker of light to her park. Not enough, though. Still a deadly place. Sad, Clown reached into a small slit sewn within the inner creases of his pocket. He didn't go in there often. Last resort. Only way to help the girl. In an instant, he had the balloon tucked between his lips and was blowing up a long, blue tube.

Daddy stepped closer, his chest puffed like a baboon throwing out a territorial warning. "Oh, he's going to make you something wonderful, Sweetie. Something special out of the blue."

Her eyes sparkled, seeing only Clown. With a twirl, snap, and flick, he fashioned the balloon and held it tightly for a moment before setting it into the girl's waiting hands.

Inhaling sharply, she caressed the balloon in long, soft strokes. "A lion. So strong." Then with her eyes turned up to Clown, she said, "I'll keep him on my bed. On my pillow. He can sleep with me."

Clown nodded.

"I think he's hungry. I can feel his tummy rumbling."

Clown nodded again. She understood. She knew.

"What did he make you, Sweetie? Are you going to show Daddy?"

She turned away and walked toward the parking lot, the lion clutched to her chest. "Later, Daddy. Can we go now?"

"Well, sure. You going to save your little secret until we get home, huh?"

Clown only wished he could be there to see the look on Daddy's face when he got the surprise of his life, a balloon animal with teeth like razors, tearing him to pieces.

That would be sweet.

Jeeze.

RIVER OF WOLVES

She sat on the wooden seat, fingers gripped into narrow grooves—physical memories left behind by thousands before her.

It was a rough ride. Her teeth clacked and her hips bounced and she thought if she could hear over the din she'd hear her ribs snapping together. In her mind's eye she pictured the carriage—large wheels with cylindrical spokes—beating over an old route through furrowed red clay.

But that was not so. The small square window beside her showed that there was no road, no dusty weathered trail; the carriage crashed along on a river of running wolves.

A rippling wave of fangs and fur.

The clamor of beating paws, echo of labored breathing, thump of the burden on muscled shoulders was deafening. She wanted to cover her ears, but held fast the seat.

A thunderous voice rose above the noise. "Who are you?"

She turned to the passenger beside her; stickman dressed in black, eyes like cracked marbles gullied in mud—the shadowed lines on his face seeming to draw a roadmap to hell. A knob in his throat hitched up and down and he raised his voice and boomed, "Who are you?"

I am..." How could she speak with his glare upon her? It was as if his emotions were alive, wriggling under his skin. "I am a citizen...a woman...a..."

"Liar!"

"I am..."

"Damned!"

The floorboards of the carriage clattered, then split. Furry tufts angled through the crack. Visceral spittle speckled the floor like a glittering disease. One eye, chocolate brown with a pupil large and black as a movie screen, sought her, found her.

She stared into it...and saw flowers and rain. Warm colors and cool air. Rainbows slipping into the moon. Green and white stretching out forever toward blue.

A longing to be...

"You can't go there!"

"I was only..."

* * *

He was a thing of beauty.

His stomach was a masterpiece of hard muscles beneath soft skin. Tracing lazy circles on his flesh, her head resting in the pillow of his shoulder, she breathed over him. Gooseflesh rippled over his chest. He laughed.

"Your body is like another world and I am the explorer." She walked her fingertips over the swells of muscles and into the valley where his bellybutton looked like a kiss forever set in flesh.

Dark hair curled down the back of his neck. His lips were...Mona Lisa. Black paintbrush lashes drew lacy shadows on his cheeks.

"You have me, my love. No need to pursue the quest."

"I will never be through."

Smiling, she dreamed of a future as beautiful as they. She rolled up to kiss his lips and stopped. "Why are your eyes closed?"

"I hide."

"From me."

"I don't want you to see what will be."

"Oh! I know what—"

"Will you follow me, always and forever?"

"Yes."

"Words from the heart do not fulfill the soul." He sighed, turned away his head and softly cried.

* * *

Floorboards split. Gaps widened. Dripping fangs gnawed the wooden wound, wetting the edges so it looked like swollen brown lips.

"Who are you?"

She pulled away from her passenger's accusatory eyes. "I am a citizen. I am a woman. I am..."

"You are a liar!"

"I am…"

The carriage rocked and shuddered. A split crawled up the bench seat, pulling it apart beneath her fingertips.

* * *

Ugly paint peeled, exposing a slab of weathered blond wood.

She picked with her finger, trying to loosen the flake.

Once soft white, the paint had dirtied with time, grime so long stuck to the surface to have become married.

She grasped a chip, squeezed it, felt it, rubbed it between her fingers. Dust sloughed off, coloring her skin. Yet, even after the cleansing, the paint remained soiled, sad.

Like her spirit.

He'd left to chase the dream that lived in his eyes. And she'd remained behind.

She stared at the house. Peeling paint falling free—or being pushed; wood shucking an ugly coat?

* * *

Balls of shed fur drifted into the carriage, clogging the air. The howling, growling increased. Paired paws, engaged with ready claws, clung to the ragged floor. Through the gape came head, shoulders, then body of a wolf.

His jaw spread. He bared his fangs. A red tongue lapped the air and he snapped at her.

Soon, he'd be inside.

Holding fast to the seat, she screamed.

"Who are you!?"

She whipped her head toward the passenger to answer, but he was gone.

* * *

Snowman died on the hill beside the house.

At first he simply shrunk—poor thing suffering to time as an old man. Once tall and proud, then bent—leaning.

Where was his hat? Bare head so small without it.

And he melted, droplets swirling down his body—tears, each one stealing his substance.

One eye sunk into his face before it slowly disappeared.

Mercy, as he would not witness his decay.

Shriveled mouth slouched and drooped.

No matter. Who would he talk to?

When his arm fell, the dead twig landing in a browned puddle, he was no longer real, simply a mound of spoil.

No one to hold, nothing to reach for.

"Don't go," she told him. "Stay. Stay with me. Don't leave me alone."

* * *

She huddled against the back of the carriage and peered out the window.

A river of running wolves. White-tipped tails, currents of gray, black and white. Ears perked, pointing ahead. Damp noses leading the way.

Claws tapped on hard wood.

Inside, the lone wolf stood before her. Poised, his body swayed.

Their eyes locked with a silent click that spoke of familiarity—a key slipping into a well-worn lock, the motion perfect.

Tears wet her cheeks, fell from her chin. "Who am I?"

His stare burned a hole through her defiance, scorched away the seasons of her life and showed her all.

Then he turned and looked at her over his muscled shoulders…and waited.

Mate for life.

With an ethereal howl, the bawl of decades of blinders falling free, she ran to him, fell into him, became as him.

And they leapt, running away free in a river of wolves.

PASSING ON

With her hands cupped around her face like parenthesis, nose pressed to the glass, she watched him get into his mini pickup. He moved slowly, settling his cooler behind the seat before turning his body so he could enter fanny first. It he didn't hurry, the rain would soak him through. Getting old.

As was she.

Mommy? Help me, Mommy!

It seemed to take him forever to center on the seat and fasten the belt before reaching to pull the door closed. With his hand on the latch, he turned up his eyes. They sparkled in the moonlight and Rafaela Luca wondered if it was raindrops she saw dotting his cheeks. Hopefully so.

She waved.

He waved back, then pulled the door closed.

Mommy? Help!

"It's okay, baby. I'm right here."

The taillights flickered, then burned red as he drove away, his tires drawing lacy, silver trails on the blacktop.

Already, she missed him. Odd. Rafaela spent most nights alone in the lab and had never before felt the bite of loneliness. Now, without Jack, it was there, nibbling away, sad and annoying, like their last conversation...

"Dr. Luca, will you be leaving on time tonight?" he had asked.

"Oh, I'll be late, Jack. I've got...um...I've got a few things that I'm working on...timing and all. I'll be late."

A hopeful expression had slipped into the deep wrinkles of his face. "Oh. Uh huh."

"Why, Jack? Is there something you need?"

"I was just wondering if you might want to grab a cup of coffee with me or something. Or maybe a sandwich. That's all."

Had she blushed? Oh, yeah. And her belly had knotted up tight. The last time a man had asked to share time with her outside of work, Rafaela had been thirty years younger, fifty pounds lighter, and a hundred percent less gray.

Surely, his blush had matched hers in both hue and heat. "I've been meaning to ask for a while. Just now got up the nerve."

"Oh. Well, it's a nice offer." She should have gone. Locked up the place and left with Jack. Never returned. "But I really can't. I've got something critical in the works."

Their eyes had locked and she'd seen her lie reflecting back. Jack nodded. "Well, all right then. Perhaps some other night."

"Sure, Jack. Some other time."

Another lie, and it, too, had bounced back, hitting Rafaela like a punch. There would be no other time. And Jack had known it. The evidence had been on his face, in the downward curl of his lips, the slack of his jaw.

With his head lowered, he'd turned to leave, his shadow falling over the desk in her compact office, covering Rafaela like a storm cloud. But before he reached the door, he'd stopped, and looked toward the ceiling, his eyes seeming to draw a grid in the air as if dissecting the atmosphere. "Quiet tonight."

She'd shivered. Quiet? "No more than usual, Jack."

Jack hooked her eyes a final time. "Seems quieter. Yes, it does." He moved through the door and down the short hallway, taking his shadow with him. It was as if the billowy gray thing had left against its will, as if that little part of Jack had wanted to stay behind. "Goodbye, Dr. Luca."

Like his shadow, Jack's voice had lingered...

"Goodbye, Jack," she now whispered to the empty parking lot. The glistening imprints of his tires filled in, and once again, the pavement shone like an ebony sea.

Mommy?

Rafaela wiped tears off her cheeks, then rubbed her arms. Looked cold out there. Weather turning sour fast. The wind had picked up and was throwing rain hard against the glass, like a scold. It would have been nice to sit and watch the burgeoning squall, listen to the sounds of nature at war.

Mommy. Help!

But that was not to be.

Mommyyyyyy... The lone voice whispered away, inhaled into the cries of the others.

"I'm here, baby. Just a few more minutes."

With a sigh, Doctor Rafaela Luca turned around. The only light in the lab came from a green banker's lamp that sat hunkered over a heavy brass stand. How out of place it looked against stainless steel and beige. A gift from her interns a decade ago; the card attached had read something about she being light in a world of dark, giving couples a chance at parenthood when God had told them, "no."

God probably didn't need a lamp. Holy shining, and all. What was that her mother had called it? The *something* glory. Mama couldn't wait to get to heaven and bask in the *something* glory. What was it called? Rafaela pinched her brow in a scowl and pictured her mother talking, watched her lips move but couldn't get that one word to come through. Figured. After listening to her mother talk for years about everything God and Jesus, Rafaela had finally stopped listening and apparently had stopped remembering as well.

Frustrating to loose a memory. Scary. "What is it? Shaka...Shanana...Shaqu..."

The crying became louder, the agony of ethereal voices overpowering the word search for God's glory.

"Shhhhh. Don't cry, babies. Shhh. Mommy's right h—"

The phone rang. Rafaela gasped and grabbed her throat. Another ring. Who would be calling so late?

She followed the noise down the rows of small office doors and found a white light blinking on Polly Newsome's desk. Four more rings were followed by a click as the call was routed to Polly's cell phone. The light went out. Rafaela shook her head and sighed. That Polly was a wild one. Brilliant young woman with cover-girl looks and the sex drive of a marine battalion. Just listening to her after-hour stories was exhausting.

Oh, to be young.

Mommy? Mommy?

"I'm right here."

When Rafaela Luca had graduated medical school, the now-Doctor Polly Newsome had probably been trying to master the fork and spoon and playing with baby dolls.

At one time, Rafaela, too, had played with dolls. Lots of them. Mama had raised her a real girl's girl. Tea parties, pigtails and bows, ruffled dresses and patent leather shoes. Church, confirmation, singing in the choir. Prepped from birth to be the perfect wife, mother, Catholic.

But Rafaela had taken a different road. She'd won a scholarship to college, then medical school, and after training with the top fertility doctor in Chicago, had opened a clinic of her own, giving babies to couples who would otherwise be childless.

Her mother had never understood, or forgiven. For a tiny woman, Mama had had an enormous voice. It'd matched her opinions. She'd accused Rafaela of being insane. After all, what normal woman forgoes marriage and motherhood and chooses instead laboratories, late hours, and loneliness? What about grandchildren?

Not from Rafaela. No time. Busy building a reputation. Busy making babies for other people. Busy growing old.

And now Mama was so old. Admitted to a nursing home after a paralyzing stroke, all she could do was lay in bed, hands curled in toward her skeletal chest, quivering clawed fingers entwined in the strands of garnet rosary beads—blood drops on ashes. Didn't recognize her daughter. Couldn't talk, just hummed. Stared with gray eyes, drool pooling in the thick wrinkles around her lips, humming, rubbing beads, humming, rubbing beads.

Rafaela saw herself when she looked at Mama and worried that someday—

Mommy?

"Yes, baby. I hear you."

So many times, Rafaela had tried to break through to her mother. "Mama, what do I have to do to make you happy, to make you love me?"

As if cued by her daughter's pain, Mama had been equipped with an ever-ready reply. "You need God, Rafaela! Now. Seek Him. Call on His name! You'll burn in hell for all eternity for what it is you do. Doing His job!...mocking Him! You will burn!"

Needle skipping on a scratched record, playing out for decades.

Mommy! Where are you, Mommy? Help!

Sighing, Rafaela answered. "I'm here, baby. Finishing up some things. It won't be long. I promise." That one voice sounded like a little girl. Made Rafaela sad.

What's a promise?

"It's something mommies tell their babies, something that they will do for them that no one or anything can stop. When I make a promise, you know I will do it."

Crying and crying. It's so noisy, Mommy. And so cold.

Rafaela moved down the corridor to her office, reached under her desk, and pulled out a small black bag. "I know, baby. It'll be better soon."

Cuz you promised?

"Yes."

I love you, Mommy.

"I love you, too."

And me too, Mommy?

"Yes, baby. And you, too. All of you. Every one of you. I love you. You're my babies."

Parents loved their children. That's how it's supposed to be. Had been the case for the young man in Rafaela's office one year ago.

The only thing Rafaela had wanted was to keep the crazy from shooting her.

He'd had desires of his own, and had made them clear while pointing a fat black gun at her heart. "I want my babies."

He and his wife had come to the clinic for implantation. Success! Twin boys. Shortly after, the couple had split. The husband wanted his babies from the freezer.

"I can't just give you those...those..."

"Babies. *My* babies. I want them. Now."

The gun quivered, his trigger finger slipping on and off the shining black "C."

"Please, put down the gun and we can talk about this."

"Go out there and get me my babies right now or I'll blow you out of that chair."

A mental picture of her body falling in little pieces over her office swivel chair played out in her mind, while his slick finger continued to rub the curled slip of metal. "If I do what you want...if I get the...they'll...they won't survive. Do you understand what I'm saying? It's not that simple."

"My babies would die?"

"Well...it's complicated. I can't just go and get—"

His head lifted from his shoulders, then fell back. Red, white, and gray splinters of what had been his skull and brain splattered Rafaela, her desk, and a portion of the wall behind her—some kind of sick outline. A bass boom bounced from wall to wall before dwindling to bells ringing in her ears.

His body remained standing for a second that felt like an hour and Rafaela waited for him to say something. No mouth, but she'd expected it anyway.

Ghostly quiet, the young man fell to the floor.

Now, fresh tears dribbled down her cheeks and she cuddled the black sack to her bosom. Soon there'd be an end to the sorrow—and the voices.

The first had called out to her after the suicide.

Rafaela had been hunched over the counter, her eyes pressed to the microscope, working miracles, making new life in a dish, when it'd happened. The cry. High-pitched and strong. Not a voice in her head calling out from some dark recess of the brain, rather a howl—like that of an angry newborn.

The microscope and prep tray and lab files had fallen to the floor with a crash that was bested by Rafaela's screams.

Suddenly she'd been the center of attention. Staff had huddled around her like little chicks, peeping questions, big eyes blinking, heads bobbing.

"Dr. Luca? My God, are you all right?"

"What happened?"

"Dr. Luca?"

Mother hen, she'd reassured her brood. "I'm fine. I...uh...I pinched my finger, is all. Let's not make something out of nothing."

Big smiles all around. One of them had cleaned up the mess. Sealed it up in a red bag, then shot it down to the incinerator.

After that, the voices had come more and more frequently. Little cries from here and there. In the lab. In the office. The babies. Some simply whimpered. Others cried, angry and loud. A few talked. And Rafaela talked back.

Doctor Silverman would not have approved. According to him, it was never acceptable for a person to hear voices.

"What about stress, Dr. Silverman? Could job pressures or personal problems make a person hear...voices?"

He'd practically giggled through his answer. "Stress does not cause auditory hallucinations."

"Guilt, then? What about that?"

Doctor Silverman's eyes had narrowed and he'd dropped his smile.

"The guilt would have to be extreme, the patient psychotic. There is no *normal* voice in the head." After a pause, he had whispered. "Have you been hearing voices, Rafaela?"

"Me? No! I was just curious."

Mommy. Where are you?

"I'm very, very close."

Nice.

And by me, too.

"And by you, too."

Rafaela started up the single Bunsen burner (a barely used relic that simply added to the feel of the lab, an antique in a modern world of machines and artificial memories) and set a small vile of yellow fluid on to heat. It would produce gas like the old chambers they had used to terminate unwanted animals and death row convicts before the civility of the needle.

Want you, Mommy.

Mommy. Mommy. Mommy.

The windows were coated in fog, the rain making tiny pinprick speckles on the glass like vaporous measles. Sweat tickled Rafaela's underarms. Getting hot. She'd emptied the freezers and turned up the heat hours earlier. Soon the embryos would reach a point in the thaw where they would—

Mommy! Mommy! Help!

A few little cries and sighs.

"It won't be long now. Shhhh."

Rafaela Luca had promised her babies freedom, and they would have it. So would she. Finally.

Too bad Jack hadn't asked her for coffee years ago. Things might have been different.

But at that time, when Rafaela had still felt the pang of womanly desires, Jack had been a happily married man. Last Christmas, breast cancer had ended his wedding vows. For several months afterward, his conversations had circled around his wife, the suffering of disease, her final moments and the peace she'd received when she'd passed on.

Strange phrase, passed on. Time and youth passed...away. Gone, without recourse. But passing on suggested a new existence, going from here to there, a continuation.

Help me, Mommy!

"Shhh." Rafaela winced. "Shhhh."

Mommy! Help! Help!

What if it hurt? The thawing?
Mommy!
"You'll feel so much better...soon. I promise."
The rain increased as if God were out there grabbing up handfuls of droplets and pitching them at the glass. If He was trying to get her attention, she was past listening.

So tired. Old. Worn.

Rafaela sneezed. The air in the lab smelled like Rosalinda Juarez's backyard. New to the neighborhood from over the border, she'd refused to pay men to carry away what she could burn. After all, that was how they did it back home. When the cops had come with citations, she'd yelled, "It's just garbage!" Rosalinda had never stopped burning and the cops had never ceased with the citations.

Burning trash. Sweet. Stale. Disquieting.

Rafaela coughed. Sounded like her father. Coughed to death. Pneumonia. Actually drank himself to death, but no one would admit it. Chased his antibiotics with alcohol, ignored his doctor, laughed at Rafaela's warnings, and finally hacked up blood until he'd died.

Papa had loved his beer and Mama had loved him—a man who beat her, peed his pants, and wore the musk of another woman's bed like a badge.

Perhaps Mama would have loved her more if Rafaela had been a drunk.

Mommy, I don't feel good.
"I'm sorry, baby. Soon, you will."
Sick. Help. Help me, Mommy.
"Me, too. And I really am sorry. But—" She coughed again, bringing up a mouthful of phlegm. Tasted sour. Rafaela hoped she wouldn't vomit. Messy. Humiliating. Papa had died like a pig, wallowing in his own waste. "It'll all be over soon."

She longed for the end. The voices—the babies begging for help, calling her "Mommy," she who'd put them together, the woman who had, over the years, worked with thousands of them, some now healthy little boys and girls, some destroyed, the rest frozen in limbo.

Rafaela laid down her head. Smoky, stinking air filled her nose. Her eyes watered.

Mommy? Can you hear me?
"Yes."
Mommy?
"I'm right here. I won't leave you."

Promise?
"Yes."
Mommy?

The little voice was muffled, sounding as if it'd come carried on a gentle breeze—like a child on the beach playing in the waves, her cries of joy melding with the splashes of water and gushes of sea air.

"Yes, ba—" Rafaela fell from her chair. "—by." The buffed tile floor spread out before her like a checkerboard—the players, plastic roller wheels and stainless-steel table legs. The flicker from the Bunsen burner threw down shadows that crept closer and closer. Silent and black and long. Cartoon scribbles on black and white.

Mommy. What's happening?
"We're passing on."
What?
"We're all going someplace beautiful."

In a sudden rush, all the little voices joined in a chorus of giggles and laughter. Closing her eyes, Rafaela pictured them alive, boys and girls of all shapes, sizes, and colors at play on a circle-go-round in the park, swooshing down slides and chasing each other in games of tag.

Bye-bye, Mommy.
Bye-bye.
Bye, Mommy.
Bye.

Their voices were moving away. Rafaela smiled. "I'll be right behind you."

No, Mommy.
"What?"
No, Mommy. You can't come.
"Yes! I'm coming with you."
Can't, Mommy. He says you can't come.
"W-W-What?"
He's beautiful, Mommy. Dressed in the Shekinah Glory.
"Who?"
Father.
"No! Wait! For me!"
We'll miss you, Mommy.
"Stop!"
Bye-bye.

"No. He can't have you. Mine. You're mine." She spat and gathered a mouthful of vile air. "You can't have them. They're mine!"

Her cry ricocheted through the lab and came back to her as an echo. "Mine. Mine. Mine."

She was supposed to have—

Alone. The babies had gone on without her, left her behind. Everything she had done, her entire life had been for them, and now they were...

Gone. He'd taken everything from her. If not for Him, her mother might have loved her, and Rafaela wouldn't have had to push so hard to succeed to impress her parents, the world, herself. He had ruined her.

Rafaela wanted to get up, stand in defiance, prove her strength, but could not. Her lungs were stuck in an exhale, and although she wished herself to breathe, it was futile. The poison had done its job. And it hurt. Every cell in her body begged for air. Muscles contracted. Her heart felt like it was an open wound, as if it was wrapped up in twine, coarse fibers ripping into soft muscle, prickling, rubbing it raw with each beat. It pounded in her chest as if it was trying to escape and seek out oxygen on its own.

Air!

Rafaela clawed at the floor, tried to drag her body to the door, but moved only a few inches before she lost control of her muscles and laid stiff, face down, wet cheek pressed to warm tile. A pain like she imagined she would have felt a year ago, had the crazy young man pulled the trigger and pierced her chest, now rippled throughout her body. Her bowels and bladder released. Rafaela was alive long enough to regret the indignity.

Then she passed on, her mind plunging into the dark, where flashes of her life came one after the other like full-fisted blows. And with the memories came a hideous noise, as if a pack of wolves had fallen into an abyss. Howls of fear and pain, teeth gnashing at air, the animals trying to save themselves from rushing down and down and down and...

Rafaela splashed into a seething lake.

And she opened her eyes to fire.

And she was fire.

And burning, she cried—"Mama!"

KATHERINE IRVING

Having been born in a small upstate New York town in the early sixties, Katherine Irving's first memories are of cows, demonstrations on the television, cows, moms with weird hair, cows, the smell of manure in the spring, and cows.

With nothing to occupy her free time besides pulling weeds from the family garden and riding the neighbor's cows, she spent countless hours exploring the rural countryside on her bicycle and scribbling stories and poems to satiate her imagination.

For nineteen years she survived the small-town boredom and never-ending bawl of livestock until she shucked country living and moved south, to the beaches of Florida.

The next fifteen years were a blur of sun, fun, crazy jobs and wacko roommates. She liked to ride her Harley, attend motorcycle races—drag or track—drink frozen libations or cold beer and dream up stories. Whether lying on the beach scorching her skin, or watching blacktop reel away beneath her wheels, her imagination thrived.

At times, unable to satisfy her inner voices with writing, she turned to pranks and has been known to—suffice it to say, a wild imagination without restrictions can be dangerous.

Luckily, at the age of thirty-four, the sworn single married, and within the next five years had three children, sold the Harley and moved to a lazy town in Northeast Georgia. The new lifestyle came with restrictions and she was forced to learn self-discipline.

Surrounded by mountains, trees and chicken farms (Thankfully, cows are not equipped to be mountain climbers, to which she say's 'Moo!') she home schools her children, spoils her husband, tends to a wild bunch of pets—hound dogs, cats, a cranky rabbit, two tarantulas and one fat black widow spider and writes.

To learn more about this author, please visit her website at: http://www.katherineirving.com.

AMBER QUILL PRESS, LLC
THE GOLD STANDARD IN PUBLISHING

QUALITY BOOKS
IN BOTH PRINT AND ELECTRONIC FORMATS

ACTION/ADVENTURE	SUSPENSE/THRILLER
SCIENCE FICTION	ROMANCE
MAINSTREAM	MYSTERY
PARANORMAL	FANTASY
HISTORICAL	HORROR
YOUNG ADULT	WESTERN

AMBER QUILL PRESS, LLC
http://www.amberquill.com